Secret Pleasures

Secret Pleasures

THEA DEVINE

BRAVA

KENSINGTON PUBLISHING CORP.

http://www.kensingtonbooks.com

BRAVA BOOKS are published by

Kensington Publishing Corp.
850 Third Avenue
New York, NY 10022

ISBN 0-7582-0299-7

First Zebra Books Paperback Printing: July, 1995
First Kensington Trade Paperback Printing: July, 2000
10 9 8 7 6 5 4 3 2

Printed in the United States of America

For my guys—John, Tom, Mike—
I owe you for this one . . .

Prologue

London, 1895

She had become addicted to the small pleasures—the look in a man's eyes, the brush of his fingers against her flushed skin, the feeling of his arm around her as he swung her into a waltz, the world of meaning expressed in the intensity of his gaze.

The hot lush wetness of a forbidden kiss. . . . She loved the kisses, and it had taken her so long to love anything at all.

And now she was on the brink of the next step; she felt dizzy with desire and longing and the anticipation of pleasures she had yet to experience.

This time she had been the pursuer, relentless in her desire for this one man who sat beside her now in the speeding carriage that could not deposit them soon enough at her house on Green Street.

This time it had been her decision, her needs, her fantasies superseding her marriage vows, her treacherous loyalty, her pride.

This time . . . *her* act of defiance out of an innocence that would not be denied.

She had chosen him; he would be the one.

"I want you—*now*," he whispered against the delicate shell of her ear. "Let me . . ."

He had given voice to her need in the most primal way and she suddenly understood the reality of what she was unleashing.

Oh God . . . did she really dare?

"Not here," she murmured, lifting her mouth for his kiss to prolong the moment.

"Let me . . ."

"Soon . . ."

"Now—"

"Not yet, please—I can't . . . just kiss me, kiss me . . ."

He knew how to kiss her—he knew . . . just the right pressure, the right tease, the moment to persist, and especially when to turn away.

He was so skilled, she was already his slave.

"More . . ."

"No . . . no—it makes me too crazy; can you feel how crazy I am? I could explode—and then there would be nothing . . ."

Explode—explode for me—

He was the only one who had ever made her yearn for his kisses.

And more . . .

He was the first man she had ever wanted.

"I need . . . I need . . ." she whispered in a frenzy because she was too inexperienced to know how to make the demand.

"And you know what I need," he said harshly.

His hands were everywhere, easing his way; she felt boneless, afraid to move, wanting to do nothing to obstruct the opulent sensations he aroused in her.

"I want . . ." She couldn't tell him.

"Let me then . . ."

"Soon . . . soon—" *Not yet, not yet.*

She wasn't ready.

Yes she was . . .

It felt like hours; it felt like eternity.

His mouth crushed hers; his hands crushed and tore at everything that confined her.

Everything.

Every rule, restriction, moral, every commandment . . .

Thou shalt not . . .

But someone else had not kept that commandment either . . .

His kisses made her forget everything.

The carriage suddenly shuddered to a stop and she slowly pulled away from him and slipped from the carriage before he could stop her, her cloak concealing the upper half of her dress that now draped around her hips.

She had the key ready in her shaking hands.

She had brazenly planned it all: servants' night out, her husband gone, and she didn't care where; and the long dreamed of, never hoped for seduction of the man she had pursued for months, the man she had chosen to make her a woman . . .

He was coming; it was real. She was shivering with fear, desire, anticipation—she didn't know which—but he was coming, and the moment she had longed for was almost at hand.

Up the stairs she ran, discarding what she could, tearing at buttons, hooks, and whalebone stays . . . slipping out of her corset, her dress, her bustle, her petticoats.

She could hear him below, following her at a leisurely pace. He was coming, he was coming, his footsteps slow and measured on the staircase.

She stopped in her tracks and waited, waited, and waited until he was almost there, almost there . . .

He had discarded every trapping of a civilized man, and he came to her naked and in all his glory.

She felt her heart stop, and then, suppressing all her doubts about her inexperience, she reached out her hand and took him, sinking to the floor exactly where she was, and in the first moment of ecstasy, reveling in the feeling of him sinking into her and claiming her virginal soul.

Like a flower, she felt drenched with dew, open to the light, bending to the breeze, fragrant with the scent of sex.

He played with her like a flower, with sleek long strokes down her body, dipping into her honey, feeling the fragile petals of her womanhood, making her moist with longing.

And he feasted on her nipples, making them bud into hot hard points of pleasure.

He was the sun, heating her body, melting all resistance and liquefying her desire.

He blinded her with his potency; she wanted nothing more than to ride the tide with him.

When he mounted her again, she felt as if she had caught the wind.

But she knew she could never tame him.

She fell out of the sky into a maelstrom of sensation and release into oblivion.

This was eternity, lying in her lover's arms, listening to the silence and luxuriating in the aftermath of the pleasure.

They had forever; there were no boundaries at all, not time, not words, not conscience; not the nameless emotions that surged up which she ruthlessly quelled.

She wanted this moment, all the moments, to be photographed in her consciousness just as they were: perfect entities that would live on forever in her mind, where she could sift through them later and savor each and every detail.

She felt molded to him, her body inseparable from his, as she relished each new sensation.

She never wanted to move again.

She felt him tense suddenly and make a sudden forward motion.

"Oh . . . don't . . . ."

"I thought I heard something—"

"You couldn't . . . no one is here, I made sure of it. And he is never here. He disappears for weeks at a time. I promise you. I promise you."

She drew him back, reaching up to cup his face and draw him down to her.

He pulled back. "I heard something . . . ."

She bit her lip and slid up onto her elbows. "The servants. Maybe someone has returned early."

"Maybe not," he said, as he sat up and swung his legs over the edge of the bed.

She felt him slipping away from her. "I suppose you're going to look then?" she asked, her voice tinged with a faint resentment.

"We can't take chances, you know that . . ."

"I tell you, he's away on one of his everlasting trips."

He propelled himself out of bed, sleek as a cat. "Men have been known to lie to their wives."

Oh they do, oh yes, they damned do, she thought angrily, as she watched him walk naked out the guest bedroom door, as confident as if he were on the way to Parliament.

"I'll pick up my clothes on the way down," he said mockingly as he closed the door behind him.

And maybe you won't ever come back, she thought in anguish, wrapping the covers more tightly around herself.

But what did she expect after a night of debauchery? A declaration of undying love? Abject commitment?

Him?

She resolutely pushed every thought out of her mind. He would find it had just been the cook's cat or someone outside rummaging through the trash. He'd be back in a trice . . . how could he not?

The minutes ticked away, agonizingly slowly, while she concocted every outrageous scenario she could think of to avoid accepting the inevitable: he had lived up to his reputation.

He had used her and now he would abuse her.

She felt like a fool.

She scrambled across the bed to get to the armoire on the opposite wall.

At least I had the decency not to defile my husband's bed, she thought as she rummaged through the closet to find one of the many dressing gowns they kept on hand for the convenience of unexpected guests.

The rich *were* different . . .

She slipped into a paisley silk robe and wrapped it around her slender waist.

It was time to face the unpalatable truth.

But she had done that before too.

She crept into the hallway and paused at the head of the stairs, puzzled.

There was a light down below where there had not been any light before.

And a shadow.

Slowly, she walked down the stairs, her heart pounding, her nerves jangling with fear.

The stairway wound down, a graceful architectural conceit, until she could see the whole of the substantial reception hallway.

And her heart leapt: he was there, dressed now in his breeches and boots, his chest bare, kneeling on the floor.

His muscles flexed as he slowly got to his feet and looked up, almost as if he had sensed her coming down the steps.

His face was impassive, his eyes inscrutable, and his hands were covered with blood.

And then he moved aside and she saw—her husband lying sprawled at an awkward angle at her lover's feet, his lifeblood spurting from a wound in his chest, painting the marble floor red.

Chapter 1

Her mother had been the ambitious one.

"You must marry well, there is no other course."

She had been the practical one.

"You are dreaming, mother. We have no money, no status, no one to sponsor us, not even the wherewithal to hire a marginally fashionable house for the Season."

"Well—now I will know better than to leave any kind of planning in your hands. You will see, my dear; an eligible party will present himself, you will see . . ."

". . . Lady Tisne? Lady Tisne, ma'am?"

The speaker was a young investigator from Scotland Yard, timid and properly respectful.

". . . you will see . . ."

Yes, mother, now I see—

"Can I help you?" She was swathed in a white lace and satin robe that was embroidered with knots of flowers and strung through with ribbon, and she huddled in a woolen throw by the fire in the library as her husband's body was examined, lifted—with all proper respect of course—and finally taken away.

"Inspector Stiles would like to have a word with you, ma'am, begging your pardon, and he knows how upset you must be."

"Of course," she murmured, waving him away, as she furiously turned over in her mind the story that she and Tony had concocted.

There was only one *must:* Tony *must* be kept out of it. They had agreed. The servants had been out, Sir Arthur had gone away; she had been alone upstairs, returned home alone from the ball, gone upstairs, and sometime during the night, she had heard a noise. When she had gone to investigate, she had found her husband awash in blood on the marble floor.

It was thin—too thin. Too many variables and ifs and whys to present themselves for which she had no time to parse out the answers.

She had to admire the way the Yard worked—they left you no time to predicate a lie.

"Ma'am—?"

Stiles's voice behind her, slightly hesitant, but—still respectful.

"Inspector—" She waved him in and toward a seat opposite the small sofa on which she was curled up.

"Yes ma'am." He sat, and from his overcoat he removed a small pad and pencil. "I'm sorry to have to . . ."

"It's quite all right," she said softly. "It just doesn't feel quite real yet."

"You said Sir Arthur had been away this weekend. And you had stayed in town."

"That's correct. I—" *How much to tell him? How much would simple words reveal? And was he smart enough to weigh the hesitations and the evasions—and did he make allowances for the marital vagaries of the aristocracy?*

"—I had an engagement—the Landower Ball, as you already know. Sir Arthur had no . . . desire to . . ." *Oh God, she was tripping over her words already, trying to find the right combination which would not arouse suspicion.* ". . . interest in—didn't wish to attend with me. I believe he was with friends at Fanhurst."

"I see."

And he was writing things down furiously, and she felt desperate to know *what* he was making of *two* simple facts: that she had been one place and Sir Arthur another.

As usual.

As always.

"And so . . . ?" he prompted.

"And so—since he was to be away, and I was to be engaged for most of the night, I gave the servants the evening off. Frankly, I didn't expect to return until daybreak. You know how long the Landower Ball goes on . . ."

She faltered then. Maybe he didn't. Neither had she five short years ago. She had known nothing, and her mother had known everything.

She mentally shook herself and went on. "In any event, Sir

Arthur left for Cheswickshire early Thursday, and the Ball, of course, was last night. I hadn't heard from him—I didn't expect to hear from him . . ."

She paused again and he murmured that damning, "I see . . ." and waited for her to go on.

"There isn't much more to tell, Inspector. I came home long before I had planned to, I did not feel well—and frankly, I think it was the mayonnaise of salmon. I believe one or two others had some reaction to it as well. In any event, Lord Lethbridge was kind enough to escort me home and I went directly to bed—"

Yes, directly—Tony was so direct, in all ways . . .

"Yes . . . ?"

"I went directly to bed," she repeated resolutely, "and sometime during the night, I heard a noise . . ."

"What kind of noise?"

Ah yes, what kind . . . indeed . . . what kind could she have heard a long winding flight above the reception hallway. What kind of noise would carry up the stairs, down the long hallway, and beyond the thick mahogany wall of her bedroom door?

How smart of him—and how damning for her if she did not concoct the right answer.

"I heard—I heard . . . I can't describe it exactly—"

Or at all . . .

"Take your time, Lady Tisne."

"Thank you.

What could Tony have heard, beyond the door and below the stairs? She couldn't even put herself in his place; she couldn't conceive of the scenario—she had no imagination whatsoever . . .

Or she was so unnerved she couldn't think straight . . .

"You heard a noise—" Stiles prompted again, gently, respectfully.

"I—yes, a noise . . ." *In for a penny . . .* "Scuffling, thumping . . ."

"Nothing fell over?"

Nothing? "Why, I don't know. I didn't think to look."

"I see." More notes.

She bit her lip. "I didn't . . . I didn't go down immediately. I was frightened and I was still feeling ill . . ."

"Of course."

"And you know what I found."

Stiles nodded his head, still scribbling furiously, and then finally he looked up at her.

"Well, that will be all for now, Lady Tisne. Just the bare bones, so to speak. Of course, I'll have more questions, but not tonight. Not tonight. Your servants are due back—when?"

Her eyes shot to the mantel clock. It was almost four in the morning. "Surely they are back by now," she said loftily, in a tone that brooked no argument.

Oh, she had learned that tone of voice very well.

"Very good then. Perhaps sometime tomorrow afternoon, after the body has been attended to and we have a probable cause of death."

There is a hole in the man's chest, Inspector.

She bit back a comment and watched him march through the double doors and out into the reception room where all that remained of her husband's body was a swath of red staining the marble floor.

It was not over—not by half. If she even let herself think about it . . . any of it.

She bit her lip, staring at the flames. One could not just go back to sleep—there were too many things, too many feelings, too many impressions, too many emotions, and she did not want to examine any of them too closely.

If one got too close to the fire, one got burned, and surely the death of her husband was but a spark to set off a conflagration.

She watched the time tick by.

At five o'clock, the servants began to stir. She watched curiously the ritual that had always gone on behind the scenes: the maids trooping in to lay the fires and dust and brush each and every room; the footman with the newspaper; the butler with her breakfast tray, frowning a little because his routine had been disrupted.

"The staff want to say—" he began, as a footman drew up a small table for her by the sofa and he set down the tray.

"I so appreciate . . ." she murmured.

He poured the tea. "Thank you, ma'am. I will convey that to the staff."

He left her to pick helplessly at orange sections, curried eggs, honey and toast, a side dish of sardines, and a basket of scones.

She wasn't hungry, and she didn't want to move.

She had mere hours before the stormburst of speculation and gossip erupted—and then . . . and then—

She closed her eyes and inhaled the steamy lemony fragrance of the tea.

And then who her husband was, and what he was, would be fair game for any tattletale in the whole of England.

"His name is Lord Arthur Tisne and he's looking for a wife, not a dowry. He wants a younger woman; he wants a son. Member of Parliament from Cheswickshire. My dear, don't frown at me like that. Just agree to meet him."

She agreed to meet him; she disliked him on sight and she didn't know why. Perhaps he was too courtly, too precious, too anxious to please. He was smitten so fast—or maybe, she thought in hindsight, he was just in a tearing hurry to get the thing over with.

"My dear, he adores you."

"How can he, in the space of a visit?" Ever practical, she was. And her mother hated that. All her mother saw was the color of money, and Lord Tisne had plenty of that, and he wasn't averse to flashing it now and again where he knew it would do the most good: right before her mother's eyes.

"I don't like him."

Her mother snorted. "Nevertheless, my dear . . . we will consider any offers he wishes to put on the table."

"Why? So you can put meat on your table?"

There it was—the prime disobedience: not remembering how much her mother had suffered.

Her mother slapped her. "You ungrateful little bitch. The only thing your beloved father left behind was a string of bastards all over London who had first claim on his money. I'll never forget— never—and you, young missy—you're the only one who can make it right. You owe it to me, so I expect you to do your duty, no matter what it costs you.

"Look at it this way: the older he is, the sooner he'll die, and the faster we'll get his money."

And he was old—not so old but surely in his late forties. His hair was thinning, his body was slack, his clothes were expensive, and his determination was unswerving.

"She is just what I want," he murmured in a private conversation with her mother on which she intentionally eavesdropped. "Just. Beautiful . . . graceful . . . from a good family; she'll make a beautiful baby. That's all I ask—one child, one heir. Her duties won't be onerous. But the wife of an M.P. reflects a certain status. We'll dress her befitting her station. She will live in the lap of luxury. She will command an allowance, and as long as she is good to me, and understanding of my little ways, why—you too will command an allowance so you too may live out your days in comfort."

"She is the most biddable girl," her mother said.

"Yes. And I will mold her. She will be mine; you may trust me with her innocence. I will not defile her."

"A gentleman to the nines," her mother pronounced when he left them.

"I hate him."

"But you will marry him."

She had shown one fragile thread of defiance. "You cannot make me."

"Can I not?" her mother murmured "Oh, but I can, my dear. I have only to declare insolvency, and send you to the workhouse. Believe me, I can do it, and I will if you do not obey. Surely a mansion in Cheswickshire and a townhouse in London are preferable to the drudgery and dirt of the workhouse—hmmm?"

She seized the one last faint hope. "Perhaps there will be someone else . . . ?"

"My dear, you haven't grasped the situation: our creditors are hounding us. The poorhouse is just around the corner if we do not do something immediately. You see—once we are perceived to be in dire straits, we will never ever, ever be able to pull ourselves up to the point where someone like Lord Tisne would even give us the time of day. But I have only to announce your betrothal to Lord Arthur and all will be well. So therefore, my dear, you are going to say yes when his Lordship offers for you, and we are going to get married and have all the money we could ever want.

"That's what's important, isn't it? Lots of money and freedom

from creditors. Do you see, my willful daughter? It's a matter of weighing the inconvenience of being poor, and the overwhelming good fortune of marrying rich. How can there be a choice?"

She felt hemmed in, trapped; her mother had promulgated this scene for so long now, it had always seemed as if it were merely her mother's delusion and not something that could ever happen.

The creditors were always at the door, and she had used the poorhouse as a threat for so long that Genelle thought it was merely a figment of her mother's imagination.

But a declaration of insolvency—that was something different, and she saw by the expression on her mother's face that if she did not agree, her mother would indeed sacrifice her because she wouldn't make the ultimate sacrifice for her mother.

One hand washing the other.

And if he were the only light on the horizon, who was she, young and naive as she was, to naysay her good luck in attracting him?

There were no prince charmings for those who hung on by their teeth to the fringes of society.

"If someone else gets him"—her mother whispered in her ear at one public function where he was paying rapt attention to some other young thing—"if someone else gets him—I will kill you—and then I will die . . ."

And so, someone had died. But not her mother. Her mother lived to see her daughter's splendiferous marriage to Lord Arthur in the chapel at Fanhurst, with his mother and dozens of his London associates in attendance.

Genelle had felt like a Christian being led into a den of lions.

What had she known about sacrifice then? That Lord Arthur had settled a suitably large sum on her mother so she would stay on in London and not interfere with their lives? Not a sacrifice—for him.

That his own mother occupied the dowager house at Fanhurst and poked her nose into all of their affairs? Not a sacrifice, not for him who welcomed her daily visit with open arms, almost as if he were seeking respite from the company of the child-bride he had so precipitously married.

That he was fumbling and inept as a lover and sought only to relieve himself quickly, so as not to offend her sensibilities, and to get a child as quickly as possible? Not a sacrifice for him who had not relinquished his pursuit of other pleasures.

And surely not a sacrifice for her since she was living in the lap of sanctimonious luxury at Fanhurst, immured like Rapunzel in her tower.

Except that she could not spin straw into gold.

And she was wholly dependent on *him* and he was never anywhere around.

The trips—the everlasting trips. And her mother-in-law with full access to the house and servants—it was a tyranny. She had never pleased her mother until she had married Arthur, and she could not please her mother-in-law after she had.

"A child, a child, there must be a child . . ." It was both mothers' endless refrain.

"How can there be a child if I am here and he is not?" she would ask reasonably.

"And why is he gone?" his mother would retort. "Whose fault is it he is not in his own home?"

Such a dirty little burden: he couldn't bring himself to touch her; he had been every bit as repelled as she, so whose fault? Whose fault?

When she could stand it no longer, she feigned illness, and then sneaked off to his house in London in the family carriage by bribing the driver and a footman with some of her wedding jewels.

It took no time at all for the butler to answer the door, still less time for him to dismiss her: "The Master's wife would never lower herself to appear where she wasn't wanted . . ."

Where she had found the courage to push him aside and take possession of the house, she would never know.

But the end was swift and sweet; she burst into his bedroom to find the root of the truth: not only did he not want *her*—he did not want any *her*. He wanted *him*—the sweet gawky innocence of his special male friend who lay intimately beside him.

"Here are the terms."

When had she become so cold-blooded?

"Anything you want," he muttered, seating himself behind his desk and picking up a pen so that she could dictate what it would take to keep his repugnant secrets safe.

She had thought long and hard; she felt like blinders had been removed from her eyes. It accounted for all of her feelings, all the reasons why things were not the way they were supposed to be.

She felt stupid, gauche. Naive in the ways of men and women. But all that, now she had discovered his propensities, was about to change. Innocent no more—no wonder he had sought a child such as she was: she would not weigh him down with demands and she would be grateful for everything he gave her.

As if a toy or a trinket could buy off her malaise, her discontent.

He was more naive than she, and he had probably married her just to get his mother off of his back about getting an heir.

Which was the first thing. She would never have a child when she knew his father to be a pedophile.

"No children."

Her voice was like ice. He looked up.

"That is the sole reason I married you."

"Oh, I think not. I think not, Arthur, so I think you will agree to that condition. You need me—more now than I need you."

"That remains to be seen."

"Secondly—" *Secondly—yes, she had considered exactly what she wanted in great detail, and one of her desires was the sight and sound of people and events and things to do—and no mother-in-law to interfere with her life. So* . . . "Secondly, we will move to London together, full-time, and you may then go off and do as you like when you like. However, that is provided that I may do as I like. In return, I will hold you to nothing, except that the marriage remains in force for the sake of appearances—which, I believe, is the real reason you married me."

"Never. *Never.* Lady Tisne must be above reproach."

"Of course she is," she agreed coolly. "Just as you are, my dear."

She held his blazing eyes for a minute, two, three. "Surely, if you have learned how to be circumspect, anyone can, even someone as unsophisticated as I," she added maliciously. "I think you have no other choice."

It was blackmail, pure and simple. And she still hadn't delivered the *coup de grace.*

"Very well. Surely that is all."

"My dear, my dear. There is still one last thing."

"Isn't there always?"

She had never disliked him so intensely. He acted as though he was the victim . . . it was unconscionable, and it made her final demand easy.

"Money. Pots and pots of money for my own use in my own name with no restrictions whatsoever."

He froze. "How much money?"

"Whatever you think will keep me quiet, my dear."

"Nothing short of murder—*my dear.*"

"Too civilized, Arthur. A hundred thousand pounds."

He looked as if he might attack her right there.

"Ten thousand a year."

"Twenty-five."

"*Never.*"

She shrugged. "I'm counting on your generosity in all matters, Arthur. Just as you are counting on mine."

"Twelve."

She held his gaze. The silence lengthened. His mouth worked. His piggy little mouth that she could never stand having kiss her. That mean pursing little mouth that pursued other willing prey.

He knew exactly what she was thinking.

"Fifteen," he muttered finally.

She wanted to squeeze him then, just take his slender ascetic body and squeeze it dry of all its juices.

What juices? She was already squeezing him tightly to the wall.

"That is satisfactory. Now would you please write down the agreement between us . . ."

He wrote, slowly and painstakingly, almost as if he wanted to annoy her by dragging out the process.

"I trust this will suffice," he said grudgingly as he handed over the paper.

In accord between Lord Arthur Tisne and his wife, Lady Genelle Alcarr Tisne, the following is agreed:
    Lord Tisne relinquishes all rights relevant to his wife; there will be no children; she will conduct her affairs as she sees fit with no interference or advice from him.

Lady Tisne will occupy the townhouse in London as her main abode.

Lord Tisne undertakes to support his wife on an allowance of £15,000 a year from this month forward until such time as a new agreement is reached, and no accounting is required of Lady Tisne.

Lord Tisne agrees to provide to Lady Tisne an income in the amount heretofore agreed upon should he predecease Lady Tisne and this will be incorporated into his will. It is also agreed that Lady Tisne will have the use of the house on Green Street during her lifetime in the same event.

Lady Tisne relinquishes all other rights relevant to her status as Lord Tisne's wife except that she will remain married to him and they will present an appearance of unity whenever circumstances may warrant.

Signed this day,
Lord Arthur Tisne

"Satisfactory?"

"Entirely." She added her signature. "I won't be going back to Fanhurst again except to collect my belongings. Perhaps you could inform your staff? Or perhaps you wish to install them at Fanhurst?"

"We will work out the details later," he said stiffly as he watched her tuck the agreement into a dress pocket.

"Not too much later, Arthur."

And then—freedom.

She had loved it; he had not.

She found it was quite one thing for him to indulge in his proclivities, and it was quite another for Lady Genelle Tisne.

He didn't like it. *He* was still respected. No one knew about *him* and he didn't like *her* flaunting and flirting.

Not that it stopped her. She liked flaunting and flirting just fine. She had no conscience about it whatsoever. It had been *his* betrayal, but it had been a mistake she was not prepared to live with for the rest of her life.

Especially after she discovered the power of her sex.

Chapter 2

The silence of the house was deadly. She felt as if she were a character in a book as she walked aimlessly through the curtain-shadowed rooms, knowing that the servants had waltzed through hours before, sweeping and dusting, and making sure that all the mourning rituals were observed.

She need do nothing; it was one of the perquisites of the rich. And yet she wished she could do something to still her trembling hands and divert her overactive imagination, which still could not comprehend how her husband had turned up dead in the downstairs hallway.

She wondered when she would feel the grief.

She wondered how soon the gossip would spread.

It was still too early; she never expected callers before noon and it was barely eight o'clock now, and she did not know what to do with herself.

It was too early, even, to get dressed.

She felt a sudden, urgent desire to flee from the house and never come back.

But you love the house and now Arthur is gone and will never come back.

It felt the same, his not being here in death; nothing had changed.

No, something has changed—she wrestled with the idea for a moment; something definitely was different . . .

You are free . . .

The insubordinate thought blasted into her consciousness like a gunshot—

. . . you are free . . .

But she couldn't fully comprehend what that meant—not yet,

not until she was told that it was some kind of grisly accident and no one had actually taken a weapon to her husband and violently assaulted him.

Then—then, she would be free.

At nine o'clock she went upstairs to bathe and dress for want of something to do.

Tony will come; surely Tony will come by later to see how I am holding up . . .

But her first visitor was Inspector Stiles.

"If we could, ma'am?"

So respectful he was, as he followed her into the small parlor, the one where he had questioned her the night before—or had it only been in the early hours of the morning?

She felt as if a week had passed.

"Inspector."

She rang for tea, which he waved off. She, however, needed it, needed something hot around which to wrap her nerveless fingers; needed something to hold onto now that everything was falling apart.

"Yes ma'am." He consulted some notes. "I have some preliminary information on Lord Tisne's death. He died of a knife wound straight to the heart. There looks to have been some fresh bruises which might mean he tried to fend off his murderer or that the murderer might have tried to attack him before resorting to the knife. Which might account for the noises you said you heard, ma'am . . ."

"Yes?" She was going to drop the cup, she was.

"The knife—which is missing—is from your own kitchen, ma'am, one of a set of carving knives with a long wide blade. Nicely balanced, I might add, and not impossible for a woman to wield."

He let that statement sit in the thick air for a moment, watching her reaction, making a note.

She had all she could do to maintain her composure. "Surely you're not suggesting . . . ?" she said faintly, and then she thought how impossibly ridiculous that sounded in response to exactly what he *was* suggesting.

"Ma'am?" He looked up again. "Perhaps you'll tell me—"

She made a conscious effort not to fall apart. "Whatever I can, of course, Inspector."

"I'll need a list of his friends, acquaintances, and business associates."

"I'm not sure I know them all."

"Of course—however many names you can provide. The servants—whether any of them could have held a grudge, or any of his friends . . ."

Or any of those with whom he toyed . . . oh my God—what if—what if . . . ?

"Lord Tisne's mother is at Fanhurst; she has no taste for the city," she answered in response to a question she only half-heard.

"And you say Lord Tisne spent a great deal of time at Fanhurst."

Do not volunteer too much information . . . "He did."

"And yourself, ma'am?"

"I live here."

"All the time?" The Inspector's eyebrows inched up.

"Not at first, of course. But Arthur understood—" *What had Arthur understood—really? Scandal? Loss of reputation and standing and the wherewithal to do as he pleased, which he had not foreseen would be hampered by one such as herself?* "Arthur understood," she went on, "that I was still young and needed the excitement of London."

"So—he lived at Fanhurst and you lived in London . . . ?"

The rich were different and had license to do as they wished, until someone murdered one of them . . .

She could see that Stiles could not comprehend such an arrangement so early in a marriage.

"He lived at Fanhurst and came up to London quite often so we could fulfill *all* his many obligations," she said carefully.

"I see . . ."

Oh God, she hated that horrible all-encompassing phrase. What did he see? What could he see?

She felt a moment of pure panic. Nothing made sense: not the marriage or the original story she had told Stiles or the fact that it was mandatory that she protect Tony, who had not even sent word this morning to ease her distress.

She was going to bear the burden of this all alone . . .

Her stomach lurched.

You are all alone . . .

She stared at the Inspector, and she knew he saw a suspect trapped in the perfidy of her own lies—she *knew* it—and as vulnerable as a young animal cornered by a predator.

She felt wounded, open, and she knew she had to pull herself together immediately and not stumble over her story or tell the seemingly courteous and avuncular Inspector Stiles *anything* more than she already had.

And Tony be damned. She would get out of this herself, even if it meant she had to play detective and explore the entire length and breadth of her husband's prurient life.

. . . interesting thought . . .

She shook it off, pushing that little frisson of sexual excitement as far from her consciousness as she could. She was a grieving widow, *not* a prowling cat.

It was time to take the attack.

"My dear Inspector," she said.

He looked up from the book in which he was punctiliously noting down everything she said. Every *damning* thing . . .

"There is nothing so unusual about a town and country marriage, I assure you. When I met Arthur, I was very, very young. Naturally a man of some sensibility would not wish to . . ."

"Naturally," Stiles murmured, making another note.

"It *is* a common arrangement." *She was talking too much . . .*

"I'm sure, my lady. Now if I may—"

So polite, so deferential; he didn't believe a word, not a word. . . . She felt as if the ground beneath her was shifting too fast and she could not find a toehold anywhere.

"Certainly, Inspector." *The cool aristocrat's voice now, leavened with cold fear that had already rendered her as still as stone.*

He consulted his notes. "It is true you were at the Landower Ball. And true that you left early—"

She made a sound, startled by the speed with which he had corroborated this part of her story.

He looked up at her and she thought for a moment that something flickered in his eyes, and then he went on. "And, although my Lady Landower was loath to admit it, there were several who had reactions to the mayonnaise of salmon and left early along with yourself—"

He paused, flipped the page, and continued, "and Lord Lethbridge was heard to volunteer to take you home. You had indeed given the servants the night off and so . . ."

He looked at her again. "And so we come to the part of the story for which there is no witness, no shred of proof that it happened the way you described it."

She remained still and silent. She could not have opened her mouth if her life depended on it, and for the moment she couldn't remember one thing she had told him the night before.

"There was a noise—" he prompted.

She pushed a response out from beyond her clogged throat. "I—yes—a noise—after I had retired for the night." *What had she said happened after that? Her brain was numb, and she couldn't sift through a single thought without feeling as if she were already condemned.*

"I—" *Surely she could find some temerity somewhere; this man was not here to listen to fairy tales, and if she didn't stop cowering, he would arrest her with no compunction whatsoever— because she was the perfect suspect with the perfect motive and not one witness to what had happened behind the doors at Green Street . . .*

. . . except Tony . . .

. . . who would throw her to the wolves as soon as make love to her—and perhaps liked courting the danger inherent in both—

She pulled herself together at the thought of Tony. He was a predator if ever there was one; she had known that from the first. But now she was the one who was fabricating the lies to save him from—

—what?—

She took a deep breath. It was time to take the offensive. "There was a noise, indeed, Inspector; try to envision it: the servants are out, I am alone in the house, ill to my stomach and feeling vulnerable. There are very few lights, shadows everywhere, any of which could be an intruder—and the noise—the . . . thumping noise . . . do you truly think under those circumstances I would have rushed downstairs and . . . and done *what?*"

"I can think of one thing, my Lady."

Her heart bounded downward in terror; he was waiting for her to fall into his trap—she saw the hole yawning before her, waiting to swallow her up forever.

"You might have gone to the kitchen, taken up a knife, gone forward to investigate the noise and—"

"And, Inspector?" *Oh, she congratulated herself for the icy tone in her voice when it was all she could do to keep from bolting from the room.*

"And—attacked the intruder . . ."

There was something wrong there . . . something . . . if she had come after any intruder, she would never have confronted him . . .

"But from behind, surely, Inspector?"

She had jolted him, she could see it. It was the one flaw—yes—and she pressed it. "I would have seen that it was my husband otherwise . . ."

"Indeed," the Inspector said drily, bending to his notes again. "He was not a massive man."

That was sheer understatement. Arthur had been jaded, effeminate, brittle and frail. She could have overcome him with one hard meaningful shove; she could have knelt over his prone body and pushed that knife into him without using any force whatsoever.

"And I a woman without massive means as you must know by now, Inspector. I would have no reason whatsoever to want my husband dead. He had given me everything I could possibly want."

"There are no children."

"We were five years married, Inspector. Arthur respected the niceties and my youthful sensibilities. But I assure you we were planning to set up a nursery in due time. Perhaps you might talk with his mother to confirm this."

"I certainly will, my lady." He made another note.

Damn . . .

"Now—Lord Lethbridge . . ."

How annoying—how utterly, maddeningly annoying that this man was so thorough in his research . . .

She waited for the inevitable question.

"He brought you home?"

"Yes." *Careful now, careful . . . don't volunteer anything . . .*

"You attended the Ball with him?"

"No I did not. Lord Lethbridge kindly came to my assistance when he saw my distress."

"You danced with him?"

"Everyone danced," she said icily.

"You engaged in conversation with him?"

"And with others," she snapped.

"You sat at dinner with him."

"I did," she said tightly, holding a rein on her temper. *Don't let him make you lose it—don't be stupid, don't give anything away* . . . "But I need not explain the rules of etiquette to you, Inspector."

A guileless statement, tempered only by the anger in her voice and in her eyes. She could feel herself blazing with resentment at the questions, at the intimations.

And once he dug up the circumstances of her past—then what?

"No, my lady," the Inspector murmured, closing his notebook. "I think that will be all for today."

She reached for the bellpull. "The butler will show you out."

"I can let myself out, my lady."

"As you wish."

"And of course you will remain in town."

"I would not dream of leaving."

He touched his hat. "My lady." And then he was gone.

She was alone.

All that day as the news filtered here and there throughout the city, she had not one single visitor to offer condolences or collect gossip.

She had never for an instant thought that all of Arthur's friends would cut her off so completely.

It was as if she did not exist; it was a slight of the first water and she could not do one thing about it.

All day long she wandered from room to room, waiting for the doorbell to ring, waiting for Tony—at least Tony, who had been a long-time acquaintance of Arthur's—to call.

She sent a footman to find a copy of the afternoon paper, knowing full well that all the gory details would be spread throughout, seasoned with gossip and speculation about Arthur, and about her.

They were all fishmongers, all of them; they loved the stench of ripe gossip, couldn't get enough of it . . . wanted to just wrap themselves in it . . .

It was all in the paper—the whole bloody story about the little nobody who had been lifted above her station by the aristocratic Sir Arthur and then had shown her gratitude by banishing him to Fanhurst while she danced her way through balls, card parties, theatricals, fashion fittings and nights at the opera.

But the only thing that the writer could find to discredit her was the fact that she was a notorious flirt; no one had ever witnessed her going home with another man.

Her heart pounded wildly as she scanned the tabloid from front to back. *Nothing about the Landower Ball—nothing . . .*

Yet.

Someone had to have noticed. Someone would put it together. And that someone would tell.

But she had had a reprieve.

She didn't know if she were relieved or disappointed.

And still no one came.

She changed for dinner into funereal black and rolled her hair into a tight chignon at the base of her neck.

She had to *look* the part, even if no one saw.

She ate dinner alone, early, pushing pieces of meat and vegetables around her plate aimlessly, feeling all the while as if she wanted to cry.

Cry for what? For Arthur? The fact that she was a widow? That she had ever married him in the first place? Or that the moment he ceased to exist, she had become a nonentity as well?

"My lady . . ." The butler's respectful voice undercut her thoughts—or her self-pity.

"Yes, Tolliver?"

"The Bishop to see you—and Lord Lethbridge and his mother."

Oh God—Tony—and his mother! How—why . . . ?

"Show them to the small salon, please."

Again, the voice was right: the steeliness that betrayed nothing.

and her hands were steady as she dipped them in the finger bowl and then wiped them dry and blotted her lips.

Tolliver would observe the proper form: cook had already prepared the small cakes, and sherry had been laid into the pantry for quick service.

So all she had to do was allow the Bishop to comfort her in her hour of grief (and why *had* he taken so long to come?), and let Tony utter inanities and not ever question why he had taken all day to pay this call.

"My dear." The Bishop now, holding out both hands and engulfing hers in them.

She listened to his kind and concerned murmurs, nodded as he quoted scripture, all the while her eyes were raking Tony up and down and he was ignoring her and admiring the breastplate on the fireplace.

Lady Lethbridge had tears in her eyes. "Arthur was my dear friend for twenty-five years."

"We've all suffered a great loss," the Bishop said.

"Tolliver will serve the sherry," Genelle murmured as she saw him by the door.

He carried in the tray as if he were bringing in a trophy and set it down on the table.

"Thank you, Tolliver." She turned to the Bishop.

"Just a spot, my dear."

"The same," Lady Lethbridge said, and watched with an eagle eye as she poured. "Perhaps a little too much," she added censoriously as she took the goblet.

"Tony?"

He turned abruptly at the sound of her voice and looked her straight in the eyes.

God, he was so handsome, so fickle. So unwilling to take this sort of risk—playing Lancelot to the wife of his deceased friend.

Even his expression—

You can't play with fire if you don't want to get burned . . .

Yes, that was the way of it.

She had played—and had gotten singed within an inch of her life, and all he cared about was his reputation until her name was cleared.

Would he come back to her then?

Did he remember anything of the night, even a moment of the long sinuous moonbeam slide to ecstasy?

She could have been a lady on a street corner for all the emotion she saw in his eyes.

What she saw was a man on his guard, and trying to look as if he were only making a duty call at his mother's behest, and she felt an angry flare of resentment . . .

What would he say when he finally made his way over to the sofa to accept the goblet she offered him?

She handed it to him silently, and he sat down warily beside her.

She knew what she could not say. She took a small cake from the plate which had accompanied the sherry and filled her mouth with it before she committed an unforgivable *faux pas*.

And he waited until the Bishop had taken his mother aside for a moment of consolation, and only then did he speak.

"What did you tell them?" His voice was rough with the emotion he held in check.

"You took me home—there were witnesses to that; I found him. They think I did it."

His mouth twisted, that beautiful mouth that had so recently sent her to heaven.

"What are you going to do?"

"I won't throw myself into the ground after Arthur," she retorted acidly.

"Then what are you going to do?"

She jerked around to stare at him; surely that tone of voice didn't mean he thought she would be better off dead . . .

"I will find a way to prove I had nothing to do with it," she said stiffly.

"And bring me down in the bargain."

"Oh, I think not. Why would I want anyone to know I lowered myself to sleep with you?"

That stung him; an angry flush stained his cheekbones.

"You'll never do it alone."

Was he hoping? Or was it advice?

"I can do anything." But she wasn't sure; the point here was only to convince him of her certainty.

The Bishop turned away from the window, his gentle hand at Lady Lethbridge's elbow.

"Tony . . ." Her peremptory voice said it all: they had stayed the proper amount of time.

He rose to his feet and set aside his glass. "You had better find a very skilled investigator. Someone discreet and clever who knows the mind of a murderer. A word of advice, my dear. You can afford it now."

And then he turned, offered his arm to his mother, and without a qualm, left her.

Chapter 3

You cannot do it alone . . . a skilled investigator . . .

Men like Tony knew about things like that, and women like herself were left to burn in the hellhole of their own making . . .

"So you killed him," her mother-in-law accused her flatly when she finally arrived.

"Perhaps his vices killed him," Genelle retorted.

"But you were supposed to have been his virtue."

"You mean his brood mare."

They stared at each other in mutual enmity.

"Did you think he provided for you in his will?" the old woman asked cuttingly.

"Oh, I made sure he did," Genelle said insinuatingly. "After all, he had so much more to lose."

"Oh, my dear," the Dowager Duchess said pityingly. "I think you will find with his death that you have lost this roll of the dice. I will stay the weekend. We will observe the proprieties. And then—we will see who has been dining on pie in the sky."

Others came; finally and slowly as word got around that Arthur's mother had arrived, Arthur's friends came forward, reluctantly at first, and then, just before and after the funeral, in a steady stream.

The services were well attended. Genelle sat in the family pew, her mother on one side and her viperous mother-in-law on the other.

"How smart you were," her mother whispered as she entered the church and lightly embraced her. "Killed him off fast, and now all that lovely money is *ours.*"

She sat, chilled to the bone, hardly hearing the Bishop's homily on the nature of love and the burdens of death.

. . . money is ours . . .
Ah, mother—the money, the money, always the money . . .
Without money . . .
. . . you can afford it . . .

In the rear of the church, she caught sight of Inspector Stiles and she froze. He had come for her; there was no other reason for him to be here.

The Bishop droned on.

Her mother plucked at her sleeve now and again as he uttered some banality that seemed particularly apt, and she brushed away the grasping hand impatiently.

Her mother had never come near her during her years of freedom in London, had never asked how she was doing, what she was doing—but her mother had not yet run out of money.

But now things were going to change; there was no one to pay her mother's quarterly allowance.

. . . our money . . .

Her husband was to be buried at Fanhurst. Directly after the funeral service the coffin was loaded onto a hearse draped in black crepe and silk ribbons, and she, her mother-in-law, the Bishop, and several of her husband's friends, made the three-hour drive out to the estate.

It was wearing; she had nothing to say to any of them. None of them had been her friends, and neither the Bishop nor her mother-in-law had a word to spare for her besides.

It was better to keep the silence. The curate of the Fanhurst church conducted the services, a man who had baptized her husband, given him his first communion, and married them.

Afterward, there were refreshments at the house before the carriages lined up to take them back to London.

"I will see you at the lawyer's office," her mother-in-law said to her coolly after she bid the mourners good-bye. "And after that, I hope never to see you again."

The Bishop, who had remained with her after the others had left, looked shocked.

"Everyone is embittered by your husband's untimely death," he murmured, as he helped her into the carriage.

None more so than I . . .

"Time will heal everything," he went on as the carriage lurched back down the long drive from Fanhurst.

She watched the stately turreted house recede in the distance.

"Silence is golden," he intoned as they passed the ornate gates. "It is well to keep one's counsel in the face of such hostility; your mother-in-law will come around when she has come to terms with your husband's death."

"Thank you, Father."

And now, dear Bishop, would you happen to know a skilled investigator who is versed in the ways of a criminal's mind? Surely you belong to that club of men who has knowledge of such things.

She longed to speak.

She said nothing on the entire three-hour journey back to London.

And then, invitations did not come. She was a wife in mourning, prostrate with grief, her penance taken to the extreme—a year at least in seclusion, whereas if she had died, Arthur could have ended mourning within three months.

It was so bloody unfair.

The house was like a tomb.

Her only visitor was Inspector Stiles.

"It is true my lady that Lord Tony Lethbridge escorted you home. By his own account, he took you to the door, made sure you were safely inside, and went on home—"

Dear Tony, how kind of him to confess he had seen her to the door, but they had agreed on that—he had not gone into the house. He had seen her safely home, suggested a tincture for her stomach and left her to her own devices.

"None of the servants were in the house at the time you found Lord Tisne. No one was home except you . . ."

She felt the noose tightening around her neck.

"But surely—"

"Not one servant," Stiles said firmly, "and now I have it on good authority that your income was to continue in the event of Lord Tisne's death, and in addition, you inherit the London townhouse. Men have been murdered for less than that."

But how did he know the terms of the will? How could he have found out?

She felt as if she were walking a tightrope.

She swallowed hard. "He was so much older than I, of course he would make some provision in his will for me."

"And his lady mother of course," Stiles interpolated.

"He would naturally want to cede Fanhurst and the dower house to her. And the remainder of his estate. I was perfectly comfortable with my allowance."

Talking too much—far, far too much—

"Fifteen thousand a year—I should think so, my lady. And thank you for confirming that."

Talking incessantly—would she never learn? This man was out to prove her guilt, not track her innocence. Soon enough, he too would twist the knife and arrest her for murder—and then what would she do?

"I have nothing to hide, Inspector."

"Indeed, my lady." He made another note and she felt like snatching the notebook from his hands.

. . . a skilled investigator . . .

"I think that is all for today. I understand the reading of the will takes place—when? Tomorrow?"

"I believe that is correct. And there are no surprises, Inspector. I have known all along how Arthur has provided for me."

"As you say."

. . . damn . . .

"I believe you remember the way out."

And he did; not even that curt dismissal discommoded him— he was on the trail of a murderer . . . but then, so was she.

". . . there is no way to overturn it?"

Her mother-in-law, deeply dissatisfied, and itching to make trouble, leaned over the lawyer's shoulder and perused the terms of the last testament of her son, which had just been read out loud.

"Fifteen thousand a year! Impertinent! The townhouse . . . ! Utterly outrageous! Oh, my dear—you're as good as off to the Tower of London—what could you possibly want with a townhouse and all that money?"

"I'm sorry, ma'am; my understanding from the reading of the will is that *you* got all that money." Even she had been shocked by the size of Arthur's estate. Hundreds of thousands of pounds invested on the Exchange, in property, in the East India Company, and a dozen other commodities that brought in a healthy income to support his lifestyle, his mother, and his young and fickle wife.

It was perfectly clear to Mr. Morfit, who had handled Lord Tisne's affairs for years: Arthur had made the most equitable arrangement and his mother ought to be pleased instead of trying to overset the terms of the will.

"My dear Lady Tisne, all you need do is move back into Fanhurst and collect the interest from all these investments for the rest of your life. What more could you possibly need?"

"I need *her* provincial hands out of my son's pocket."

"But Arthur was very specific about this, my lady. I read you the very clause: 'in perpetuity or until she remarries, for favors granted, I hereby devise and bequeath the sum of fifteen thousand pounds a year to my wife, Genelle Alcarr Tisne, and in addition, she shall have full and total use of the townhouse at Green Street for the rest of her life, the mortgages of which shall be paid in full upon my death and title to revert to her.'

"You cannot be clearer than that, my lady."

"Oh, no, unless she is taken to trial for his murder."

"My lady!"

"What happens then, Mr. Morfit? What happens then?"

The lawyer's mouth pursed in disapproval. "The money remains invested until such time as she claims it—or dies—in which case, it reverts to the estate."

"Ahhh . . ."

Genelle felt the full brunt of her mother-in-law's obvious satisfaction. There was a way around it, and her husband's mother would be on her knees in prayer until she was convicted of murder and hung from the gallows.

And how did you circumvent that? How?

"But the house is mine?" she asked. "To pass on to whom I will?"

"I believe so, my lady; you retain title once the mortgages are settled, and I have already begun the process."

"Thank you, Mr. Morfit."

So her mother would at least have a home. When her mother's income dried up, which it would in the next month, and if she were brought to trial, her mother at least would have a roof over her head and a way to earn some money.

Maybe that was enough.

She rose to leave the lawyer's office.

"I hope they arrest you," her mother-in-law spat.

"And how may I collect my income?" she asked deliberately, sweetly, defying her mother-in-law with every ounce of fortitude she could summon in the face of such virulent hatred.

"It will be deposited wherever you direct, my lady."

"Excellent."

"In quarterly or monthly payments—whichever suits."

"Monthly please."

"Dear God—the interest . . ." her mother-in-law moaned.

"This is my account number."

"Very good, my lady. And I will execute the title as soon as I can."

Mr. Morfit stood up to take her hand.

"I wish you well, my lady. Feel free to call on me if there is anything you need."

She looked into his pale blue eyes. *Oh yes, there is something I need—a skilled investigator—one who knows the minds of murderers; I can afford it now you know . . .*

"Thank you, Mr. Morfit."

"My pleasure, my lady."

As she closed the door behind her, she heard her mother-in-law's strident voice: "I will not require your services any more, Morfit."

And the lawyer: "As you wish, Lady Tisne, but your son was most particular in naming me the executor of his will. I believe, no matter what you wish, you have no other choice."

Back to the townhouse and back to solitude.

Back to too much thinking about her untenable situation. The facts were inescapable. No one else had been at home. The weapon came from her very kitchen. She claimed to have heard a sound.

What woman would not have sought out a weapon before confronting what might have been a murderer?

A knife was a woman's weapon. Stiles hadn't said that, but he had just as nearly implied it—that, and the fact that her story was weak and that the only thing he couldn't reconcile was the attack to the intruder's face.

Such a slim little thing to keep her out of prison.

Where did one find a *skilled investigator?*

The house was eerily still. Even the presence of the servants did not mitigate that resounding silence.

I will be paying the servants from now on.

So many things to think about . . . so many things she didn't know and hadn't cared to learn.

And so many things to leave behind if Stiles took her away to prison.

She felt everything pressing in on her.

She had been living some little golden dream for the past year, manufacturing loves and a kind of life to take the place of the one Arthur had stolen from her.

Other women knew how to play this game better than she. Other women would have known how to handle Tony and how to get from him what they wanted.

And if their husbands had been found dead, and his hands had been covered in blood, they would have had no compunction at all about smearing it and him all over the morning tabloids.

How senseless to let him cajole her out of having him bear witness to the fact that she had not killed Arthur, and that *he* had found him dead.

But he had only wanted to protect *her* reputation . . .

And not his own?

What if all else failed and she had to drag his name into it?

"Yes, yes, Tony took me home, yes, he came into the house, into my bed and took me to ecstasy . . ."

. . . skilled—so skilled . . .

He would deny everything.

And no one could prove he had ever been there.

No one.

. . . a skilled investigator . . .

He had given her that much at least . . .

But why did men know these things and women didn't?

She felt real terror then, as if a net were dragging at her feet, pulling her into the undertow.

The note came the following morning, delivered by the maid,

who didn't know where it had come from; Albert the bike boy had given it to her and she didn't know where he got it except he got a gold piece to take it to Green Street.

It was a folded piece of paper in an envelope with a botched seal, one that was so smeared and stamped over she couldn't tell from whom it might have come.

But it was clear a moment later when she opened it and read the four words printed on the thin paper sheet inside.

Roak is your man

He had a conscience at least, but with this sop to it, Tony was serving notice that he had abandoned her completely.

And now she had no one else to depend on but herself.

On the heels of this, her mother arrived, waving a legal document in front of her face.

"Bald-faced liar, your husband: he said he would provide for me, and a gentleman would have even if he was dead. There's no more money, Genelle, and no more house—but what do I find when I question the lawyer? Why, that my loving daughter made sure she was set up for life and somehow forgot to tell her mum."

"Yes—well, those little details don't tend to come out at a funeral," Genelle said drily. "And if I'm arrested for his murder, at least you will have a roof over your head, but you'll have to take in boarders."

"I find no humor in the situation," her mother said sharply, motioning to Tolliver to take her baggage. "Which room am I to have?"

I hadn't given it a thought, mother dear . . .

"The guest room will be fine, Tolliver. Thank you," as she instructed the footman to take her mother's trunk. "Come, we will have some tea."

"Tea—blasted tea—who cares about tea when one's allowance has been dispensed with. What am I going to do?"

"You've already done it, Mother. You've thrown yourself on my mercy."

"Ungrateful baggage. You would have had nothing if it weren't for me."

"I may still have nothing, Mother. The Yard is this close to arresting me for Arthur's murder, and I don't yet see a way out."

"You will have to find one. That beastly lawyer will not pay your allowance to me."

"I should hope not," Genelle murmured, settling herself down at the little table in the morning room and ringing for tea. "There is plenty of food; Arthur's friends left me high and dry before his mother came to sanctify me. However, now she desires to bury me. But I will outwit her, I swear I will."

Talking too much once again—particularly to your mother, who is a vulture if ever there was one; did she not sell you to Arthur for the requisite pieces of eight? Is she not smacking her lips over the thought of having the house, if not the money, when they take you away?

"You have no choice," her mother said, snapping a cloth napkin onto her lap and taking a healthy helping from a plate of thin sandwiches that was offered by the serving maid. "We need the money."

"How nice of you, Mother, to be thinking of us both."

"I always have," her mother said complacently as she took a cup of tea. "Lovely cups. So thin and exquisite. Wedding gift, was it? You may have to get rid of some of the servants, my dear. There's no help for it. Wages are shocking, as I found to my dismay when I tried to hire the merest skeleton staff for my house. And the rents—I do hope this house isn't rented?"

"The house will be mine in due course," Genelle said carefully.

"Very smart of you, my dear; I should have asked for the same myself. One lives and learns."

Doesn't one . . .

. . . Roak is your man . . .

". . . the papers haven't been kind; I hope half of what I have read is not true . . ."

She barely heard her mother.

. . . Roak is your man . . .

". . . you read about the murder that was just solved by that independent investigator? Clever man, that. I think there's been a lot in the paper about him recently. Solves the case by evaluating the clues—things you would never think of unless someone pointed them out to you . . ."

She blinked.

Had her mother said *independent investigator?*

"What was that?"

"What was what?"

"The investigator you were talking about . . ."

"Oh that—some fiercely intelligent hermit who likes to pit his wit and brain against the muscle of the Yard. What's his name— oh yes, Roak—Rulan Roak. They say he is extraordinary—*when* he decides take on a case—"

"He . . . lives in London?"

"My dear, where have you been? He lives in the heart of the city—I forget just where . . ."

"I'll find him," she whispered, unaware of her mother's piercing look. "As soon as I can, I'll find him."

He was the one—

Roak is your man . . .

Chapter 4

Sometimes a man did not want to be found.

Sometimes shouldering the burdens of others became just a little too much.

And he was tired now; he hadn't thought this latest *contretemps* would take so much out of him.

He felt drained, as if all his juices had been sucked dry by the participants in this one circus of a murder case.

He needed time—time to reflect and to physically move away from the sights and sounds of London and the stench of this case.

He had tracked the killer—but he did not approve of the results, and sometimes, only sometimes, he wondered if the whole were worth the cost of the part.

But it was too late to back out now; he had spent five years making his reputation, slowly at first, circumstance by circumstance, inference by inference, deduction by deduction, until this final blast of a problem that had been detailed extensively by the tabloids and had raised him to a new level of notoriety.

He was so tired.

He didn't need such questionable fame. He was well known already through the mysterious underground of the rich, where he had become a commodity to be bartered for, safety for a sack of gold.

And it was clear why: he had made it a point to ensure that he was reliable and discreet. And that he could deal with any situation with the impassive sang-froid for which he was now so-well known.

And more than that, he believed in them. He believed in the worst of them, and he tried his utmost to save all of them, and with some he even succeeded, in spite of the cost.

It was so easy for him and so difficult for them; and yet he was fully aware that each success only embroidered the legend of Rulan Roak, and that there would always be a never-ending line of needy souls seeking his help.

They believed in miracles—and they believed he could conjure them up.

But this time—this time, because of the stale taste of the outcome of this last noxious affair, he wanted to retire his magic wand.

He felt tainted by it, unclean. He felt as if he were starting out all over again, pursuing the mission that had inadvertently begun his career, and he wanted to distance himself from it as much and as quickly as possible.

He needed a respite—and some time to regenerate his enthusiasm for the chase until this case faded into the background among innumerable others that he could barely remember.

He understood that with each new problem he was fast in danger of losing sight of that which had been his prime focus for the past five years.

And over and above that, he had suddenly come to an unexpected dead end in his personal quest, and that, coupled with the distasteful outcome of this last case, had left him feeling sapped and unsure how he was going to proceed.

Still, he needed to make no decisions now. Surely London was safe for the time being now that he had proved his latest client innocent of murder.

For the first time in months, he had the luxury of time—

. . . God, he had missed time alone, with nothing but his own needs to consider.

He stood by the window of his flat watching the parade of humanity loitering along Piccadilly Circus.

It was early evening, the light was just lowering behind the central fountain and the buildings beyond, and already the street was full of the swells headed for the Criterion Bar, carriages, drays and sundry workers on their way home.

It was a slightly unreal moment, when the light merged with the urgency of the movement below, and for an instant it felt to him like time out of context, as if he were doomed never to be a participant in the random moments of life.

And then the scene shifted, and out of the crowd he saw a woman walking briskly toward the line of rowhouses in which he was watching from one of the third-floor windows.

He felt a faint foreboding. She was walking too fast, and she was too well-dressed. Young. Sure of herself, but slightly distracted because she was probably used to travelling in a well-sprung carriage along the brick pavement of Piccadilly Circus, where no young woman would walk alone. Certain, nonetheless, of where she was going.

She stopped directly in front of the stoop of his rowhouse, paused a moment, and then determinedly made her way up the steps and under the columned circular stone canopy that shielded the entrance.

He waited, almost as if it were inescapable that in moments she would be knocking at his reception room door.

He counted the seconds, and then the sound of her footsteps, and then the rap of her imperious fist—once, twice, three times.

She needed something badly.

He opened the door and faced the inevitable.

She needed *him*.

He was nothing like she imagined. He was tall, graying, dressed in severe black, which made him seem even more formidable.

His face was long, impassive, chiseled out of stone and flesh, and his snappy dark eyes missed nothing. Just nothing.

For one instant she stared into those eyes, mesmerized. In them she read all the challenges that he would not issue. And impatience. And weariness.

What was she but one more wealthy chit in some kind of foolish trouble—and he a man whose loyalty could be bought for a sufficient sum of money.

She had it in her purse, but suddenly, inexplicably, she hated herself for having to beg and buy his mind.

. . . a skilled investigator . . .

"Mr. Roak." Yes, that sounded businesslike and not as if she were importuning him.

He stepped back from the door so that she could enter.

And she stopped, astonished at the sheer luxury of the room

when she had imagined him in sackcloth and ashes in the spartan cell of a monk.

The walls were papered in blue silk moire down to a white wainscoting that circled the room, and on the floor there was a wall-to-wall Turkish rug.

At the far end was a marble fireplace classically ornamented with pilasters and pediments and an over-mantel mirror. Just by the fireplace was a large tufted sofa covered in a rich red brocade, and two matching chairs.

And one whole wall on the opposite side of the room was covered, floor to ceiling, in books.

There was a table set in front of this and two chairs drawn up on opposite sides. He motioned her to seat herself in one of them and he took the other.

"Now . . ."

His voice was deep and rich like full-bodied burgundy wine, and his dark gaze never left her face, and again she felt that frisson of uncertainty.

She lifted her chin. "I need your help."

He nodded as if that were obvious—which it was—and again left the burden of explanations up to her.

"My husband—was found dead a week ago—murdered. I was alone in the house. There are no suspects, and I believe that the Yard is imminently about to arrest me."

That was about as succinct as she could make it. He didn't move a muscle.

"And you are?" he asked finally in that deep expressionless voice.

"I am the widow of Sir Arthur Tisne."

Oh . . . did she detect just the faintest pricking up of his interest?

He sat there for one long moment without moving, and she had the distinct impression he was weighing something, that there was something about *who* she was that was meaningful to him.

And yet there was also that weariness and a kind of reluctance, as if he had grappled with enough folly and imprudence and just did not have the energy to cope with anything more.

But then he leaned forward and with every evidence of interest, he commanded, "Tell me the whole."

* * *

And then he questioned her so exhaustively, she began to actively dislike him.

He knows you're lying.

How could he know? She had gone over and over the story so intensively in preparation for this meeting. There were no flaws: she told it to him as she had told it to Inspector Stiles, and in the retelling, she could not see one thing that could prevent Stiles from hauling her off to prison the very next day.

"We have a lot of work to do," Roak said suddenly, just when she expected him to pronounce that the thing was hopeless and there was nothing he could do.

"What do you mean?"

"I mean there is a lot of work to do, Lady Tisne. Your husband was a well-known man with a certain reputation."

She felt shocked that he seemed to know, and she knew he saw it, but he was unmoved by her distress.

"There are many avenues to explore: constituents who might have bought favors, former lovers, disappointed potential wives, political enemies, jealous friends . . ."

"I didn't know . . ." she whispered, agonized that this was no small secret and it was possible everyone who knew her husband had known.

He stared at her long and hard. "No, I don't think you did. But any or all of these possible suspects could have gained entrance to your house—servants or no servants—and confronted your husband. Perhaps even by appointment, if he thought the place were empty and you were not due home from the Ball until dawn. He might well have secretly come to town for an assignation. He had the keys? He might have left open a back door, or a servant's entrance.

"Yes—an open door," he murmured almost to himself. "Some-times one finds one's way via the most unexpected paths." His eyes snapped as he turned his attention back to her. "Take heart, Lady Tisne, for even though you have not told me the whole truth . . ."

You see, you see—he knew—instantly he knew . . .

She tried to hide her dismay, but he noted it and continued as if she had not reacted. "There are many jumping off points to the solution of your husband's murder. Consider—consider that he did not protest any of your demands once you had discovered the reality of his nature."

"But how could he? If I had abandoned the marriage, it would have become common knowledge."

"But he gave you everything you wanted, Lady Tisne. Why do you suppose?"

She looked at him, puzzled, actively disliking the fact that he was acting as if he knew.

"So I wouldn't tell—what everyone apparently already knew," she said bitterly.

He ignored that. She was so young, so innocent, so uncorrupted—even her years of marriage had not touched her.

He wondered about her, about the depths of the hungers within her.

She had certainly learned to be a lady: Lord Arthur's money had bought that for her too, and she was dressed expensively and exquisitely in a blue silk suit, the skirt and bodice layered with ivory lace and totally inappropriate for mourning.

And there was something in her beautiful jade green eyes—a defiance, perhaps, or a defensiveness—he couldn't quite decide— that had to have come from her exposure to the unexpectedly unpalatable side of her marriage.

"Exactly—so you wouldn't tell," he said finally. "You will search the house. He gave you the house because he didn't want someone else dismantling it in the event of his death . . ." He watched, amused, as she was struck by this deduction. "Therefore, there are secrets to be unearthed somewhere in that house."

"But would he not have taken everything with him to Fanhurst?"

"Perhaps—perhaps not. Begin your search, Lady Tisne, and I will call on you in two days to see what you have found."

"You might find me in some holding room at Scotland Yard."

He didn't smile. "I think not, Lady Tisne. I think you will be just where I expect to find you. Until then—"

He ushered her out so fast, she barely had time to comprehend that she was now in the hands of a *skilled investigator* who had very cleverly placed the onus of the initial research squarely on her shoulders.

* * *

She was not reassured.

His list of possibilities had given her a moment's high hopes, but once she was back in Green Street and confronted once again with the reality of the situation—and her mother—she began to feel as if it were all a palliative to keep her calm and—oh, how adroit he was—busy; she felt used and patronized, and not a little resentful.

That man was probably off somewhere this very moment hunting down the clues that would save her life while she went on a wild-goose chase through the house to find some elusive something she would only know if she saw it.

And then he would come to her in two days' time, present his proofs, as he had done in a hundred other cases, save her soul, demand his money, and notch up his already exaggerated reputation.

She felt such a consuming fury that she had been taken by him. Why hadn't she been instantly warned by the fact he had been recommended by Tony . . . Tony, who had the most to gain by steering her to someone who could allay her fears and devise some kind of workable solution with which she could stall Inspector Stiles.

Clever, clever men, both of them.

She felt so disquieted she could hardly eat, but the other end of it was her mother, who was sitting right there and watching her with an eagle eye as she condemned her wasting *their* money on such nonessentials as someone who might save her life.

"Fifteen thousand now must support *two*," her mother said stridently. "Just how far do you think it will go if half of it will line some nob's pocket who you don't even know can help you? And what if you don't even need his help, then what? How many thousands gone, my dear? And how helpless will you feel after that?"

"I believe you have exhausted the subject, Mother," she interrupted coldly.

"Not by half," her mother retorted. "You are still Genelle Alcarr, raised up from the trash heap by the wit and wiles of your mum; you didn't do it alone, fancy lady, and you owe me now. We almost had a good thing going until your nob popped off.

And I was certain you was smart enough to get cozy enough to inherit the lot—but I guess you weren't. All that lovely money in the hands of that awful shrew—and fifteen thousand and a house for you. Don't you think the *Gazetteer* will chew that over for months, my dear? Do you even *think* at all—?"

Genelle stood up abruptly, violently. How much she did not know—about men, life, her mother—

"It is an ungrateful guest who keeps gnawing at her host and still expects to be asked back to the table. Take heed, Mother. I feel very little daughterly affection for you right now; you are here on sufferance because I know you have no place to go. So I would beware of biting the hand that feeds you. In other circumstances, in other times, I would have let you go to the poorhouse and not blinked an eye.

"You threatened *me* with that once, remember? I have not forgotten. And I am no longer the biddable child you sold to that aging invert. So take care, Mother, just how you treat me and what you say to me. I've grown up in these last five years, and I've done very well without you."

But it was as if she hadn't said a word; nothing struck and nothing stuck. Her mother pushed her chair and stood with all the dignity of a queen and sneered, "Well, well, well—ain't you the fancy nancy. Well, let me tell you, you wouldn't've done nothing without me, my lady, and I will make sure you never forget it." And with that threat, she swept from the room, leaving Genelle feeling as limp and ragged out as the napkin beside her plate, and feeling as if she would never get control—of her mother or her life.

But that night, as she lay tossing and turning in bed and reliving those now almost fantasylike moments with Tony, and his subsequent discovery of her husband's body, she felt as if the whole thing had taken on the quality of a nightmare.

All the heady excitement of exploring those new realms of sensuality with a *skilled* lover . . . all that had dissipated; she couldn't remember what it had felt like with Tony . . . all she could reconstruct was the heart-stopping fear she had felt seeing him covered with blood beside Arthur's body.

And it hadn't stopped—the terror—she felt it now as she bolted upright in her bed at the sound of her mother's slippers shuffling down the hallway . . . past her door, thank God, and down the steps, perhaps for a midnight foray to the kitchen or to go to the loo.

Perhaps it was well that someone else was in the house; she didn't think she could stand to be alone, and now, she did not have sufficient funds to repair to a hotel until this thing was settled.

Settled—when she felt so unsettled, she felt like fleeing for her life. There had to be a way she could do something—anything—to at least seem to have the appearance of some power over what was happening to her.

Oh certainly—search the house.

Do what the skilled investigator suggested . . .

Well—why not? Perhaps he was worth his weight in gold just because he was able to present alternate solutions to be explored.

Obviously he was a man who dealt in optimism, in hope. What criminal wouldn't pay a fortune for that?

Including her . . .

She swung herself out of her bed, and turned up the lamplight. Immediately eerie shadows played across the room like subhuman beings stalking her.

Fantastic—her mind was playing tricks even when she was determined to get some hold of the situation.

It couldn't hurt to search the house, after all. Arthur had owned it forever, and while he had been most thorough in clearing out his belongings, there might have been something he missed in a crack or a cranny.

It wasn't really likely though . . .

Yes, but it was something to do—

And it wasn't the only thing she could do—she could search her memory, too, for any mention of places he had gone, things he had said or done that might provide her with a plausible starting place to begin her own hunt for the truth. One way or another, with or without the help of Tony Lethbridge or the fabled Rulan Roak, she was going to save herself.

* * *

She began the next morning at dawn in the most likely place—Arthur's bedroom, but it was obvious that he had been meticulous about removing everything; there wasn't even any dust.

He had taken all the furniture, his ornate bedstead, the armoire, his dressers and dressing table. The closet was empty and the woodwork was seamless so that there was nowhere for some telltale clue to lodge—she felt like a gothic heroine as she ran her fingers along the walls and floorboards . . . and she felt it was ludicrous as well that she thought she could outwit Lord Arthur Tisne, who had had years of experience outwitting any possible enemy.

Nevertheless, she sifted through the fireplace ashes and tried to find a secret hidey-hole in the bricks and above the damper.

She came away with her morning dress all smudged in spite of her having donned an apron as a precaution, blackened hands, sore knees, and a dark scowl that Arthur had been so fastidious about leaving.

She tackled the library next, which was on the second floor in the rear of the house overlooking the garden.

It was a bright sunny room with the walls lined with shelves, a floor-to-ceiling window in front of which had been Arthur's desk—but he had taken that as well, and the carpet. He had left her with several volumes of popular fiction that tilted forlornly on the middle shelves near the window, and a *recamier* sofa that was in sore need of reupholstering.

She sank into its formless cushion and surveyed the room.

It was hopeless—Arthur had taken everything valuable, everything reasonable, and left her with her escapist *ladyprose*—

. . . *the library down at Durning*—

She could just hear him saying that. What about it? *What?*

. . . *down at Durning*—

. . . *you can sample all the delights of the love for which writers have no words* . . .

Yes . . .

Durning—owned by an Honorable, she seemed to remember, a younger son whose family had a shire and a seat to spare . . .

The Honorable . . .

. . . Honorable—

She racked her memory. *Why* had she not listened to Arthur's prattling?

Was he in Parliament—was that how Arthur had come to know him? It seemed to her that he had spent many weekends down at Durning . . .

. . . *down at Durning . . . down at Durning—*

. . . *"My dear, you won't have a qualm about being left alone in this drafty old place?"*

"Why should I? It is warmer than you are toward me . . ."

. . . *no no—no no . . . that was after she had gotten so strong— after she understood . . . he had become more forthright with her, couching his little weekend forays in a kind of cryptography that could not be misinterpreted.*

And he thought, once he had paid the piper, that she had accepted it with the same equanimity most wives accepted a mistress.

But he reckoned without her shock and her shame and ultimately her bitterness that the conspiracy between him and her mother had robbed her of a life with a husband and children.

So she could afford to be just that little bit sarcastic with him.

"I'm going down to Durning, my dear, to sample the delights of the season. I so look forward to the feasting twice a year . . ."

She shook her head violently. *The feast . . .* She hadn't wanted to think it meant what she inferred it did; it was so easy to blank out those parts except when your life was at stake and you couldn't remember it all.

But she would—she would . . .

She could see already that a physical search was useless—but combing through her memory had already provided a name, an event, the season—fall and spring, wasn't it?

Perhaps summer, when everything burst forth, had been too fecund, too feminine for the likes of them . . .

And so he would go down to Durning—and do what?

She tiptoed down the stairs and into the morning room and sat down at her desk.

Her mother was still asleep; the day was young, a new sun now streaming through the window.

Here she could think.

She took a piece of paper and dipped her pen in ink and began writing.

Really she expected he might have forgotten all about it, but two days later, she responded to the pealing ring of the doorbell, and there he stood, filling her doorway, her entrance hall, pushing out the memory of what had happened there, taking over her small parlor, her house, her life.

She felt crowded by his presence and the sheer force of his self-control; there was an intensity to him, a discipline, as if always he held himself severely in check.

He dressed the part too—once again he was in black, with just the touch of his white shirt showing—and he seemed taller, leaner, and reined in even more tightly.

The small parlor was not the place to take him: his energy, intelligence, and ferocity were almost too much to contain in one small room.

He couldn't even sit.

And he didn't believe in preliminaries.

"What have you found?"

"I found that Arthur was exceedingly meticulous in removing his personal belongings and hiding his excesses," she said drily.

"So like the man . . ." he murmured.

"Did you know him?" she demanded, astonished by the comment and annoyed with herself that she had not even thought to ask him during the first interview.

"In a passing way," he said dismissively. "So there is nothing of a physical nature to be found here. Which doesn't discount secret hiding places—but of course that will require extensive searching—when you have the time, Lady Tisne. Meanwhile, you have a list of names for me . . . ?"

She blinked, but of course it was obvious that he had constructed this clever exercise in order to force her to remember details that she could not have pulled out of her memory otherwise.

No wonder they all go to him. No wonder. He makes it look like sheer wizardry when all he uses is sheer common sense.

She handed him the list she had compiled and over which she had pored for the past two days.

"Ah . . ." he murmured as he scanned it quickly, "Durning. Infamous—interesting . . ."

"Yes . . . ?" She waited for explanations and explications.

He gave none; he merely folded up her notes and tucked them into his frock coat pocket.

"And now what?" she asked just a little caustically, because it seemed as if he were about to leave and he had told her absolutely nothing, including what *he* had been doing during these two days.

"And now you let me continue the work of the investigation, Lady Tisne." His eyes raked over her as if he were seeing something other than her exquisite mourning dress and her angry expression. "I will report to you within the week."

"But—"

"You are to do nothing, Lady Tisne. You are in mourning. Whether you like it or not. You will not do anything foolish."

She stiffened. He was too perceptive by half. And he thought she was stupid. She hadn't expected he wouldn't explain the mysterious names and places she had summoned from memory.

But she would have bet he didn't expect her to have made a copy of the list of names so that when he told her what they were, she could make some plans as well.

Well, he had scotched that, but there were other ways . . . and she was not going to be some biddable fainting Flora who would stay still and let him do the sleuthing while she was paying his exorbitant fee and Inspector Stiles was camped on her doorstep.

Arthur's death was obviously going to be a nine days' wonder: the papers were still full of it and how Scotland Yard was making no progress, and how the prostrate widow was in seclusion at this time, but the scurrilous *Gazetteer* was making hay out of all kinds of wild speculations and accusations at the Yard's incompetence at not having arrested her already.

So it was time to act, and it would be a two-pronged attack. She would have the *skilled investigator* on the one hand, ferreting out the secrets of Arthur's hidden life, and on the other, she would . . . well, she didn't quite know *what* she would do, but she would have the whole day to think about it and study her list, and find all the obscure places to which Arthur had referred.

"My dear Mr. Roak," she said conciliatingly. "I am scared to death; the papers want to hang me. The kindly Inspector is waiting for me to trip over my tongue. My mother can't wait to get her hands on what there is of my money. Why would I ever want do anything *foolish?*"

He looked her sharply. "You are not a fool, Lady Tisne. And I warn you, you do not want to know any more about your husband's affairs than you already do. Let me handle it."

"But I intend to, Mr. Roak. Why would I be paying you to do otherwise?"

He pinned her with those dark eyes. "One wonders."

Oh damn him, he knows—he knows!

It took every ounce of will for her not to turn away from his penetrating gaze.

And finally, he said, "I will see myself out," and she watched his ramrod body disappear through the parlor door with such relief, she felt as if she might deflate like a hot air balloon.

She heard the door slam belowstairs, and she raced to the window just in time to see him emerge from the house, pause, and then continue on.

He doesn't trust me . . .

He shouldn't trust me . . .

But he was on her side, and she felt safe for the first time in days, and confident that she could finally exercise some control over her situation.

Chapter 5

The names made no sense to her in and of themselves.

Durning of course was the country house of—whoever. But there were city names as well.

Dominoes, Cleveland Street, the Cloister, the Holiest of Holies, the House of Correction . . .

All those names, drawn from foggy memories of her husband paying her the courtesy of telling her where he was going for an evening—at least at the beginning of their marriage, when she had been a naive and trusting little fool.

"My dear, I'm going to take a plunge with a mushed up fellow I met at the Casino last week—nothing too late—just a drink and a roll . . ."

A roll of the dice, she had thought; he had gambled endlessly and consistently during the term of their marriage, and she never could understand the seduction of it.

"I do play the ponies, dear child, you'll have to come to terms with it. There's nothing like a poke through the rails with friends on a Saturday afternoon . . ."

Now she understood—*now.*

"An evening in the Holiest of Holies—*strictly for men, my dear—that we may meditate on our sins . . ."*

But the church never sanctioned such prurient prayer books. Later, she discovered that he and his friends met in a particular bookstore to peruse obscene literature.

What else—what else? A bookstore that catered to those tastes should be easy to find. But surely there wasn't a murderer skulking behind the counter.

She had written on the list, *Fox and Hole, The Barracks* and

Newbury Arcade, Wolf's Den. And the *Salon of the Seven Pleasures*—yes—what had he said about that?

It was well before her awful discovery when they were still fumbling around with each other.

He tried once to educate her: *"If only you would play, Genelle, life would be so much more interesting. You don't need to take lovers or special friends. There are places . . . palaces of pleasure . . ."*

But he never got any further than that with her, and when she abruptly turned away, not wanting to hear it, he let the subject drop and never broached it again.

. . . there are places . . .

Things she had never thought of even after he left . . . the rich would have their secret pleasures . . .

And their abandoned wives . . .

She bit her lip.

The Salon of the Seven Pleasures . . .

The name appealed to her, as if it were something that was meant to lure the widest spectrum of tastes.

Who would know about such things?

"And why are you not doing something about this awful situation?"

She looked up to see her mother hovering at the small parlor door, looking rather rumpled and disgruntled.

"Which awful situation, Mother?"

"That stupid 'tween maid forgot to bring me my chocolate and now I must forage for myself."

. . . mother . . .

"Come sit down; I will ring for her and you can stay nice and comfortable here and answer some questions for me."

"I don't want to answer anything; I want my chocolate and I want to go back to sleep."

"Mother—"

"Oh, very well." Her mother plopped onto the small sofa like an overweight swan diving for a fish. "What is it?"

"I need to know about . . . certain establishments . . ."

A maid appeared at the door. "A pot of chocolate and two cups. To be brought here, if you please. Thank you."

The maid vanished and her mother said, "You cannot treat them so nicely."

"Well, when this is *your* establishment, Mother, you may treat your servants as you please. This is *my* way. Now—I need to know about certain other establishments—"

"Just what kind of establishments?" her mother asked suspiciously.

"The kind the men of infinite resources patronize—you understand exactly the ones I mean: the houses of infinite pleasures . . . I'm sure you know all about them . . ."

Her mother choked just as the maid knocked and entered with a tray containing a fat steaming pot of chocolate and two delicate cups.

"Just there," Genelle directed, "pull the table up close to us, please. Thank you. I will pour, Mother—you catch your breath . . ."

"I never—" her mother sputtered as the fragrant scent of chocolate permeated the air.

"I just want to know—as plainly as you can tell me."

"I know nothing," her mother said sullenly, greedily reaching for the cup as Genelle handed it to her.

"Mother—where else could you have met Lord Arthur?"

Her mother looked shocked.

"I finally figured it out," Genelle said complacently from over the rim of her cup. She wasn't going to tell her mother *when*—it had only struck her not a half hour ago, but her mother didn't have to know that.

"What do you want to know?"

"I remembered some things that might be useful to Inspector Stiles in his investigation of Arthur's death. Some places that he once mentioned. Maybe someone could be helpful. Maybe there was someone in his past who was out for vengeance. In any event, Mother—"

"You and your peculiar ideas," her mother grumbled and gulped a mouthful of chocolate. "I bet that fancy detective put 'em in your head."

"He did offer an amazing number of alternate possibilities to my having killed my husband. I was extremely grateful for that. Now, Mother—just tell me what *kind* of establishment it is."

"I don't like this."

"I don't care—I need this information. Now—I know about the *Holiest of the Holies*. But . . . the *Salon of the Seven Pleasures* . . . ?"

For one moment, her mother looked as if she would balk. "Arrrr—you're going to do something stupid; I just know it. Well, everyone knows it—everyone goes there who doesn't have particular tastes, if you know what I mean. Men and women both. You get to look or you can just pick and choose. Or both."

"Excellent. Now you will tell me where that is."

"Cromwell Road. I don't like this—just at the corner of the Brompton Turnpike. Is that all?"

"Oh no . . . *Newbury Arcade?*"

"Down New Street—lookers only . . . *tableaux vivants*—"

"*Fox and Hole?*"

"They're all laid out there—men and women—you take your choice and do one or do them all. It's on the Embankment. Are we finished?"

"The *House of Correction*—"

"You don't want to go near there, my girl. They play rough, they are violent; the girls service the prisoners, the prisoners are available to whoever can pay; and the girls discipline the customers. You understand? You don't go there, *ever*."

"*Wolf's Den*—" Genelle said inexorably.

"M.P.s go there. It's a house of introduction. It's discreet; you have to have a card, but you can get whatever you want as long as your tastes aren't too off the norm."

"*The Barracks.*"

"Soldiers. Wantin' you-know-what. It's on Troy Street."

"*Dominoes.*"

"You take off your clothes, you put on masks, and then you do whatever you want."

"Excellent. And where is this place?"

"You'd never think. Near Regent's Park. Are you done now?"

"For the moment."

"No," her mother said shrewdly, eyeing Genelle's flushed face and the glitter in her eyes. "I don't think you're done. I think you're only just beginning."

* * *

She didn't know *what* she was beginning; she only knew these were places that Arthur had in all likelihood patronized, which meant he had acquaintances there, perhaps even friends . . . and others—

. . . did she dare . . . ?

. . . Seven Pleasures—

It was enough to even try to imagine it . . . seven . . . pleasures—men and women both, her mother had said. Release for the rich and depraved—no, the rich and deprived . . .

Places to engorge the senses—

Palaces of purgation . . . expel the demons, experience heaven . . .

Men and women both, and probably every friend of Arthur's she had ever met had indulged himself or herself in just this way.

Why not?

Why not?

. . . if she had known . . . ?

Not then—

Maybe never if Arthur had not been killed.

Or perhaps he might have eventually convinced her . . . ?

To do what?

Just what she was planning to do.

"Don't do it," her mother said, standing at the doorway as Genelle primped in front of a mirror that night.

"I don't know what you're talking about."

"Let the man do it. The men always do it anyway, didn't you learn that?"

"Then it's time a woman had some pleasure too, Mother."

"Yes well—I tried that—and it doesn't work, not for women it doesn't."

"Perhaps not for you," Genelle said, turning her head this way and that in the mirror.

"They don't care how you look; they only care about the color of your money. Don't waste our money, my girl. You won't get any value in return."

"I might find Arthur's murderer."

"Innocent! Let *him* do it. There's no telling what you might find."

"Mother . . ."

"Girl—I'm warning you . . ."

"Chin up Mother—I can take care of myself."

"Just like you've been doing all along—without me . . ."

"Good-*night*, Mother."

She watched her mother shuffle off and then she reached for her cloak and swirled it around her bare shoulders.

She was the lady in red, with black pheasant feathers placed strategically across her bodice and in her hair and a masque to hide her eyes.

She had bought it in her first weeks of marriage at Arthur's behest on the theory that something a little racy might arouse his passion.

And what aroused mine?

She had yet to find out, but she clamped down on *that* thought.

She rang for Tolliver. "Summon a cab."

"Madam?"

"A cab, Tolliver, if you please."

"Madam."

She allowed him to help her in.

"Where to, Madam?" He was so polite—so curious.

"I will instruct the driver." Surely they all knew the prurient places in town. "Thank you, Tolliver."

He closed the door and backed slowly and uncertainly up the steps to the front door.

She knocked imperiously on the roof and the cabman's face appeared—a brutish face that almost scared her out of her determination to do this thing.

Her voice could not waver; she had to be in full control or he would never do what she wanted.

"Take me to . . ." How should she phrase it so that she sounded knowledgeable—and *sure? ". . . The Seven Pleasures,"* she commanded, her voice firm and authoritative.

"Mum?"

And he dared question her! "Do as I say."

"Yes mum."

He strapped the horses and the cab lurched forward.

She sank back against the seat, her heart pounding at her audacity.

But it was all of a piece: men knew everything, down to the meanest cab driver—and women knew nothing.

Some women knew nothing.

But she would never be one of *them* again because she already knew *something:* she would never be in that position again.

She didn't know what she expected, but it wasn't this: a line of respectable townhouses lining Cromwell Road and edging into the turnpike.

"The corner house, mum," the cab driver said with a faint leer as he opened the door and lowered the step for her.

She handed him some bills. "Come back at midnight."

"Mum."

She turned on her heel, imperious to the last, scared to her teeth, and walked up those shallow steps to a small columned portico which enveloped her in a concealing shadow.

She heard the clip of the horses' hooves as her cab drove away and she wheeled around, almost ready to run after him.

I'm crazy; this is stupid. Roak should be doing this; how do I know he's not doing this. Maybe he's at Dominoes or the House of Correction—or anywhere—

How clever—a number seven. A subtle clue . . . what am I doing here?

Her hand was shaking as she lifted the door knocker.

A very proper butler answered.

"My lady?"

She was totally taken aback. *Now what? What on earth do I say?*

"I've come . . ."

"I'm afraid . . ."

Think fast . . . think fast—was there a code, or . . . or a card . . . or was it by recommendation . . . ?

She drew herself up. "Tony Lethbridge . . ."

"Of course, my lady . . ."

She was astonished when the butler stepped back deferentially and swung open the door.

Tony—of course—voluptuary that he was; how many other doors will his name open? And how many others had he invited here?

"This way . . ."

The hallway through which he led her was opulent to the extreme, with glittery chandeliers overhead, gilt molding on the walls and ceilings, and a jewel-toned carpet on the floor.

They stopped at a door that was recessed into a small archway.

"May I take your cloak?"

She pulled it off and handed it to him.

"Would you like a masque?"

She pulled hers out.

"Very good, my lady. Lord Lethbridge has explained the procedure to you?"

Damn. What would he have said? "Not in so many words, I'm afraid."

"It is ever so with the gentleman," the butler said, with just the faintest degree of censure edging his tone. "Very well. You may subscribe on a visit by visit basis, or by a yearly contribution. Here is the card with the particulars. You may place everything on the silver salver and then enter through the door."

He withdrew then, leaving her to scan the printed card.

She was in shocked at the exorbitant expense: five thousand per year, five hundred per visit, neatly printed—just those two numbers—on a rich vellum finished card rimmed in gold.

Pleasure does not come cheaply, she thought as she put the requisite bills and the card on the table. *Neither does discretion.*

She was in for more than a penny now and she was shaking to her very toes. *Five hundred for a night of seven pleasures . . . and Arthur used to routinely spend that kind of money . . .*

. . . but Arthur had had that kind of money . . .

She bit her lip, straightened her shoulders, and pushed open the door.

She walked into lights, warm soft glowing lights and down a long carpeted staircase that made her feel like she was walking on a cloud.

She could hear the low murmur of voices, and music, faint, lush, so hushed it was almost as if she were hearing it in her mind.

Lulling music, and as she got further down, the sound of water splashing, a bird call—the Garden of Eden?

Down she went, her hand sliding down a cool brass banister

that seemed endless. And then suddenly she came to a landing where the staircase took a double turn—to the left and to the right.

The left side was in darkness, the right lit by a dim blue glow; she chose the right, stepped down another five steps and came to an octagonal anteroom which was as expensively furnished as everything else.

Illusion is everything . . .

A man appeared, dressed in a suit of white drill and a turban. He bowed respectfully before her.

"My lady. What is your pleasure?"

His clothes were so thin, she could see through them, down to the shape of his legs, the dark hair of his groin, and the press of maleness against the fragile cloth. He was barefoot as well, and silent as a shadow.

She searched wildly for an answer and unable to keep her eyes off of him—*all* of him.

I have to keep cool; I have to show him I am in control—and the less I talk the better . . .

"I have not decided," she said in her haughtiest voice.

He nodded. "My lady would like to see the menu then."

What did that mean? "Exactly."

"It is my lady's first visit." It wasn't a question.

"Yes."

"My lady will find that her friends come to us with very specific things in mind. But perhaps my lady is superior in that she does not set limits—and she is willing to try . . . everything."

He turned then and parted the curtain behind him, and stood aside so that she could enter.

She walked into darkness and he was suddenly beside her. "Does my lady wish my help in exploring the pleasures that await her?" His voice was hypnotic, low.

"How do you mean?"

"I can guide my lady, I can show her the salons and we can view together the pleasures; and if she does not wish to participate, I can be the instrument of her fulfillment in whichever way she desires. I am here to serve. You have only to command."

His husky voice was titillating in the darkness. "Or if my lady wishes, there can be yet another guide, another fulfillment. I serve as but one of the many fantasies my lady may command."

She swallowed hard, her body quivering at his words.

"Perhaps my lady wishes a gentleman guide; or a servant guide . . . or . . ."

He left the question delicately hanging.

She had to say something. "What is your name?"

"Call me . . . Sinbar."

She made her decision. "You may guide me."

He took her hand. His was warm, dry to the touch, the only eroticism about it the nature of who he was and who she was.

She was faintly aroused by the thought.

The blackness dissipated as still another set of curtains parted to reveal a hallway lit by flickering candles.

She moved forward at the pressure of his hand and they started down the hallway. Almost immediately it branched off to the right and into darkness once again.

But straight ahead of her, there was a room with a large window with lights behind.

"The first of the pleasures," Sinbar murmured. "Kissing. My lady may watch, my lady may choose to join, or my lady may use my services to explore any of the pleasures."

She felt her body constricting with excitement as she watched the tableau. She had never been kissed like that—never; never had she been held like that or touched like that, and she felt a sweeping anger that she had never even experienced an arousing sensation the likes of which she felt now.

"If my lady likes the gentleman, he would like very much to kiss my lady."

She felt like she would die. Sweet, long, melting kisses in the arms of that handsome gentleman who probably serviced a dozen women a night.

And yet, men had no problem with it. Why should she?

She could barely get the words past the lump in her throat. "And then what?"

"It is up to my lady's discretion where she wishes to stop and when she wishes to go on."

She couldn't bear any more of it. "Let us go on."

They passed into darkness once again. And then another lighted scene.

"The pleasures of undressing," Sinbar whispered, watching her face as she stared raptly at the couple who were slowly removing each other's clothes and feeling and exploring every inch of each other's body.

Never . . . in her life with Arthur had they done anything the likes of this . . .

"The gentleman would love to strip off my lady's clothes if she so desires."

She felt a gush of pure wet unfamiliar emotion at Sinbar's soft insinuating words. The gentleman would take her and slowly unhook her dress and slide it off of her shoulders and down around her waist, and down and down until there was nothing but her underclothing, and her secret underlying lust.

Oh God—he was removing his partner's camisole and corset to expose her breasts—feeling them, nuzzling them . . . his hands— where?

She felt faint. "Let us go on."

"The next pleasure is the pleasure of the body—you will see for yourself."

She saw. The gentleman and the lady were naked, and the gentleman was fondling the lady's breasts, and, as she watched, playing with her nipples, both with his fingers and his mouth while his partner squirmed and writhed in pleasure against his thrusting male member.

"The gentleman would like the pleasure of sucking your nipples, my lady."

"I—" *I want that, I want that so badly . . . but she could not get out the words.* "Let us go on."

Into the darkness and then the glow of the next delineation of pleasure. The woman was naked, reclining in a chair with low arms over which her legs were spread, and the gentleman was kneeling before her, worshipping at her mound of venus, taking her to breathless heights of ecstasy as she bucked against the feeling of his mouth and tongue exploring her there.

Oh my God . . . how could she? How could she? Could I?

"The gentleman desires the pleasure of bringing my lady to such succulent rapture."

She felt like she was going to explode. The very moment her counterpart in the tableau capitulated, she knew she would explode.

She couldn't let go—she just couldn't.

"Let us move on."

She was quivering with emotion as they came to the next scene: the gentleman was now prone and the lady was using her large knowledgeable hands to stroke his protuberant manhood while he moaned and pushed against them.

"She does well to pleasure her lover. The gentleman invites you to take off your clothes and use him this way."

He was huge—huge . . . Arthur had never been . . . never . . . what must it feel like in her hands, in her body . . . ?

Her breath caught as she imagined it.

"Let us go on."

Her heart was pounding wildly as they came to the next: a bedroom with the bed tilted forward toward the window so that every detail of what was happening could be clearly seen by the viewer.

The naked couple lay on sheets of black satin, opposite to each other so that their mouths were aligned with each other's sex. Her legs were spread to give him the utmost access to her; his male member was already in her mouth and she was sucking away greedily.

"The oral pleasures," Sinbar murmured. "To give mutually is an art in itself. The gentleman offers my lady a taste of his hard fertile manhood if she so desires."

She made a sound at the back of her throat as she watched them caress and stroke and suck at each other.

"Let us continue," she said hoarsely.

The darkness enveloped them and then they came into the light: a opulent bedroom, draped in the lushest silks and satins, dark defining colors against which the naked white bodies of the gentleman and the lady stood out like a painting against the dark blue silk sheets on the bed.

"The ultimate act," Sinbar whispered just as the man on the bed reared back to show off his massive erection to his voyeur, and then forcefully coupled with the woman who awaited him with every evidence of desire.

"The gentleman would like very much to prove his carnal skill with my lady."

She could not tear eyes from the copulating couple. The weight of him! The resilience of her! She wanted nothing more than to be the naked writhing receptacle of his seething sex.

Never like this—never . . . ! She never could have imagined—and this had been here all along for women to explore and enjoy without guilt and with every pleasure.

And he—the gentleman, he was so skilled, with so much stamina . . . she wanted to rip off her clothes and throw the other woman out of the tableau and take her place . . .

. . . oh yes, oh yes—

Arthur had been a fly—a flea . . . buzzing around her body trying to find the right opening, the right place . . . and all that time there were men—there were places . . . seven places . . .

This was what he had meant . . . this—he would have seen her in any of these scenes and watched with pleasure as someone else brought her to culmination.

She should have asked—she should have known.

"My lady wishes to undress?"

"I—"

"I will help my lady . . ."

"Ah . . . oh . . . she's . . ."

"Yes, she finds her pleasure, always—watch her, my lady—"

She couldn't help it: the woman was thrusting and bouncing against the gentleman's hips so vigorously; she could hear her groans and the sound of her hands slapping at the gentleman's buttocks and then suddenly her whole body stiffened and she moaned in rhythm with his thrusts—*yes, yes, yes, oh yes, yes, ahhh, ooohhh—yessssssss . . .*

And then she pulled away roughly, got up, and disappeared while the gentleman rolled over on his side to show off his male prowess, and made inviting gestures with his hand.

He was so big; she could never have imagined such length, such thickness. Arthur had had a toy. And she could have had *this,* if only she had kept an open mind.

"He is a strutting rooster that one," Sinbar murmured. "He will pleasure my lady well."

"I—"

"He won't wait; strip off your clothes now and go to him."

"I can't . . ."

"Too late, my lady. Another has claimed him."

And indeed, another woman, naked and willing, entered the room, climbed onto the bed, straddled him, and slid herself down his thick long length and began to ride him.

"I want him."

"My lady must wait. Or perhaps a substitute will do."

She felt him press himself against her.

"My lady can strip right here and experience all the pleasures to which she has been witness; she has but to say the word."

But Sinbar was not as tempting as the man in the tableau.

She felt a consuming envy of this new woman who now had him, that she could so easily strip her clothes off for a stranger and just take him like that.

She wanted to be able to do it.

Men could do it so easily—any whore on the corner, and they would drop their pants . . .

Anyway, who is to stop me? I can do anything here that I want—any and all of the pleasures. I ought to go back and start at the beginning—but I want every inch of that man's hardness— inside me . . . now—

"Ah, my lady—his lover comes to fruition already. See her head thrown back, see the grinding of her hips . . . she comes, she comes—"

"Help me . . ." She felt the urgency of it. She started tearing at her clothes. "Help me . . ."

His fingers were expert in unhooking and removing while she pulled and tore at everything until her dress and underthings were in shreds at her feet.

"My lady is beautiful . . ."

Her breasts were hot with longing, her body liquid with need.

"Get her out of there."

"She finishes, my lady."

Yes, the intruder was climbing off of him, and yes—he was still thick and huge and stiff as a poker and he glistened with the power of his sex.

"You may enter, my lady."

I want him forever . . .

She walked in the door, shuddering with anticipation.

"My lady . . ."

Yes, and his voice was just right too. It was a matter of taking control—commanding him to do her wishes: she had paid for it.

She climbed onto the bed. "I prefer you on top."

"As you wish."

No love, no preliminaries, none of the six other sinful pleasures—just the nudge of his engorged manhood seeking the ultimate possession—

And then the lifting of a weight, when she had expected to feel it engulfing her, the sound of a thump, and a voice—too well known already, rich and dark and disapproving, demanding, "What the hell do you think you're doing?"

She felt her heart plummet right to her feet.

Damn and damn and damn and damn . . .

Her body chilled, knowing those coal black eyes were looking right at her, right *through* her.

Take control, take control; you are paying for this, you are paying for him . . .

She opened her eyes. "Mr. Roak. Why am I not surprised?"

"Why am I?" he asked roughly. "Get your clothes. You are crazy, do you know it? This goes beyond foolish into stupidity."

She levered herself up onto one arm, aware, too aware of his scorching gaze. "Well, thank you. I now relieve you of all responsibility. I will handle the rest for myself."

"You could not handle a kitten, let alone what you almost got yourself into."

"And yet you are here," she pointed out acidly. "But—don't tell me—it's in the name of investigating the problem. What a coincidence. I am here for that very same purpose as well. Great minds, Mr. Roak, think alike."

She hated him just then, just hated him. The whole aura of sex had dissipated into something ugly and obscene. Sinbar had disappeared, as well as her would-be lover, and so had her explosive need.

She felt ridiculous now, too naked in all ways; there was no way to hide from those eyes and what he saw, what he knew and what he inferred.

He tossed what was left of her dress at her.

"I'm not going home," she said indignantly as she pushed the shreds of satin away from her face to cover her body. "I paid good money for this evening."

"I'm sure you did, my lady. I can even guess whose name you tendered to get you past the door."

That shocked her; he couldn't know about Tony—no one knew about Tony.

"Common sense; any of my husband's friends' names would have done," she snapped. "And I will continue. I will get my money's worth."

"Indeed, my lady—you want your money's worth, do you? You don't think I will give you your money's worth? Believe me, my lady, I am very much here to see that you get your money's worth. Get dressed."

Resentfully she swung to a sitting position.

"Forget your underclothes; they are ruined beyond using."

She slipped the dress over her head, thankful to be covered in some way against his fury. He had no right to be angry at her anyway; he could not know she was not a regular habitué unless he was one himself.

He thrust her kid boots at her. "Your stockings are shredded. My lady was indeed in a hurry."

"It's none of your business."

"Everything concerning you and your husband is now my business, Lady Tisne, including your rash decision to come here this night."

"But not yours," she shot back spitefully, as she slipped off the bed and stood. It was so much better to be dressed and on her feet where she felt more in control of herself and she could think clearly.

He did not bother to answer that; of course he would never do anything rash, it went without saying, and she knew it.

"You are too young, you have too much money and too little judgment, my lady. Witness the predicament you are in."

It was not a predicament; it was pure unadulterated lust-driven desire . . . and you spoiled it—you destroyed it . . .

She shot a covert and longing look at the bed. . . . *I will never forget that man . . . never—*

She felt him grab her neck roughly. "Is that it, my lady? Is that the whole—the momentary pleasure of the bed equates to your *money's worth?* I can give you that and more—much more."

His hand crept up against the nape of her neck and grasped her hair so that her head was pulled back and she felt discomfort and pain.

His eyes glittered as they speared into hers; his anger was palpable and something else she could not define. He was a man at war with himself and his baser nature was winning.

But that was ever the way with *men*. They always had a excuse.

His face was but an inch from hers, and his voice was as tight as his hand tight in her hair.

"My lady wishes to explore every nuance of a evening in the *Seven Pleasures*—? Very well, I will be your guide, Lady Tisne— from me you will learn, and I promise you, you *will* get your money's worth . . ."

Chapter 6

The rooms *en scene* were dark now, almost as if Sinbar had sounded an alarm and everyone had fled.

He had her arm in a firm commanding grip as he led her back down the hallway of the seven pleasures until they came to the anteroom.

Here it was as it had been before: the dim light, the flowing curtains. The sense of mystery and clandestine sex.

The curtains parted again, and there was the hallway. Or another hallway, she couldn't be certain.

"And now, my curious and wanton lady, now you will see the whole."

He propelled her forward into the hallway, and she wrenched her arm away.

"I am quite willing, Roak."

"Quite obviously."

"As are you," she said stonily.

"That remains to be seen, Lady Tisne."

"But one is not seen here unless . . ."

"It is the *Salon of Seven Pleasures*, my lady. Who is to define that what pleasures one, will pleasure yet another?"

She shivered. He knew so much; he knew too much—and her step slowed just a fraction. Perhaps she did not want to see much more than she had seen already.

That had pleasured her. Anything else would be a surfeit of the senses.

"You will come."

His voice was low, commanding, with just the faintest hint of aggression coloring his usual inexpressive tone.

She walked slowly toward him, feeling the slide of her dress against her bare body; that too was discomfiting in a place that was permeated with the scent of sex.

It made it impossible to ignore what she had felt for that naked man in the final scene of pleasure; it made her remember the feelings of need and greed and her urge to be possessed by his powerful throbbing member.

Wanton she was: the thought of him taking all those willing women one after the other, without any sapping of his endurance, made her weak with longing.

She would have wrung him to his very core, that proud naked piston of a man. She would have brought him to his knees.

She could have . . .

. . . who is to define . . . ?

She didn't want to look at the rooms . . .

But he was beside her in an instant as if he sensed her reluctance, grasping her hair, forcing her to face the orgy of pleasure beyond the first window.

Here they were bathing—many men and several women who offered themselves to the men, naked and slick with soap, inviting the men to wash them and play with them.

She watched, fascinated, aware of his strong hard hand entwined in her hair, aware of the fleeting little darts of pleasure attacking her vitals as the men began lathering up the naked bodies of the women, soaping every inch of them, in and out and all over, and the women twisting and bending to give them every opportunity to explore their wet and wanton bodies . . .

. . . the feeling of the soft slick soap on their breasts, over and over their nipples . . . so hard and ripe and ready . . .

"Perhaps you would like to join them . . ."

. . . and he was so experienced at this, he knew exactly what to say . . . perhaps he had even been a guide—the stoic who never revealed his emotions, but would willingly give his . . . his what?

She was being too fanciful by half; this man would give up nothing without a fight . . .

"I—" Nevertheless, emotion and need cramped her words in her throat. She *had* to get control. "A pretty scene," she said finally, snidely. "What else is there?"

There was everything—the imaginable and the unimaginable—arrayed as a menu of windows from which the participant could choose.

There were men with men, women with women; there were scenes of discipline and scenes with multiple partners of same and opposite gender.

There was a scene with the participants slogging in a clay-like mud, wallowing in it, slathering it all over each other's bodies, reveling in their nakedness and the feel of the thick wet muck soaking into their skin; there was a scene with three men and one naked woman who stood center stage while they smoothed and massaged oil all over her body until she was glistening with moisture and lust.

There was a scene with two men and one naked woman who was on her knees while one man serviced her from behind, and she attended to the other man with her hand and her mouth.

There was a scene with a woman lying naked on a bed, her arms bound to the posts, and three men servicing her, two at her breasts and one thrusting his way to heaven.

There was a coy little play in which a woman dressed as a maid entered her master's chamber and was willingly seduced into his bed as the voyeur watched and anticipated.

She loved this scene because the man within was the man she had almost had sex with, and this time, every little nuance was played out, every pleasure was explored; and at the last he serviced his maid once lying on top her, and once from behind as she held tightly to the bedposts and squealed her delight. And then he dismissed her and summoned the next willing maid, his erection as hard and thrusting and thick as it had been when the scene began.

She moaned at the sight of it, unaware of her reaction; her body felt weak, as if she had participated in the rigors of copulating with him. She wanted him to importune *her* the way he had pleaded and begged the coy little maid. She wanted his hands pulling at her clothes and sliding up into her secret places to explore *her* sex. She wanted to be naked beneath him, riding the lunge and plunge of that fantastic male root that seemed to have limitless energy and power.

She felt Roak's hand pushing her roughly.

"So my lady—" he whispered, "you've seen but half of the

pleasures of the *Salon*—and now it is time to participate in your own."

"I want that man," she moaned on a breath as she watched him take the next little maid onto his lap and begin his expert fondling of her.

And this time it was different: this time, she remained on his lap while he stripped off her clothes and caressed her naked body with such erotic precision that Genelle felt as if he were making love to her.

Finally he mounted the maid from behind, as she stood and bent over to ease his way, and then he sent them both spiraling to oblivion.

After, he slapped her buttocks and dismissed her, and lay back in bed for a moment's respite, angling himself so the onlooker could get the best view of his quiescent manhood and his magnificent male body.

And then, as if by magic, his member began to thicken and lengthen and harden until it was like a rock.

He lay sprawled there, waiting, and she felt the urgency of wanting all that male prowess centered in her.

And then he shifted, so that she could see all that throbbing maleness in profile, hard and hot and just waiting . . . waiting . . .

. . . *waiting for her* . . .

He was up on his knees now, still turned sideways so that his member was always thrusting outward and visible . . . and then he stroked its protuberant length with one experienced hand.

She made another sound, and pulled violently away from Roak.

"I want him."

He pulled her back roughly. "You *don't.* You want *this . . .*"

And he covered her mouth, pushing his way into her as forcefully as her fantasy man had possessed the woman in the first tableau.

And she let him. She let him. She wanted his kisses—she wanted . . .

Her body was liquid with wanting.

There was no beginning, no ending between her and him; the ferocity of her response was frightening. It was as if a dam had broken and all the water was pouring, pouring with furious intensity and centering deep deep down inside her—

Ahh God, his kisses—the first pleasure, the way she had never known . . . and then—and then . . .

Seven pleasures rolled into one—she was against the window, her skirt at her waist, and he was deep within her in all the ways she had imagined the man in the scene—

. . . *deep deep within her—pushing and thrusting, huge, thick, filling and slick with the wet of her longing, taking it, exploring it, waiting, wanting, slow, hard, lifting her, holding her so tightly, so deeply, and then slowly, slowly, oblivious to everything, possessing her, urging her with his kisses and his body and the scent of sex all around them . . . and then she remembered the man . . .*

. . . and she exploded . . .

. . . all over him she exploded, grinding her body so tautly against him that she was sure he could not breathe . . .

. . . and at that moment, he climaxed, pounding her body tightly against the window and expelling his lust in one long slow groan of pleasure.

And then it was over, and he moved his mouth from hers, and set her down, and in that long silence that followed, she thought she had imagined the whole thing.

"Your money's worth, my lady," he said sardonically, offering her his arm, and in the dim light, she could not read his opaque dark eyes. "This session is over."

And so Arthur had participated like that.

How seductive it was.

In the light of day, all she could think about was returning to *the Seven Pleasures*. Every scene played over and over in her mind as she lolled in her bed the following morning.

The end of the evening was blurred in her mind except for the pleasure and Roak returning her home to Green Street.

But the rest—oh the rest . . .

And that man . . . the vigor of that man—

And the power and sensuality of a man like Roak . . .

It had to have been all that visual stimulation; it would not have happened any other way—

She stretched languorously.

That man—what did one call that man who loved showing off his naked body?

She yearned to see him again . . . he had so loved to pose. *And she had loved watching him—watching him feel and fondle other women and wishing it was her—*

And then it was her, only it was Roak . . .

Ascetic, stoic Roak whose passion filled her body and dominated her lust. Made demands of her with the most commandingly male part of him—and possessed her every bit as forcefully as she had dreamt the naked man in the window would have done . . .

Roak—

And she had never even seen his body . . .

She had to go back, she *had* to.

What if that man had been there all the years she had been married to Arthur just waiting for her to come and participate in his scene.

But you did—only you did it with Roak . . .

. . . I want that *man . . .*

What if that *man can't pleasure you like Roak did?*

Then I'll take . . . Roak afterwards . . .

She was consumed with excitement at the thought.

Nothing seemed to matter; she walked around the house that day in a haze of sensuality, counting the hours until it was night, until she could escape to *the Seven Pleasures.*

"Oh and now my lady girl doesn't care about nothing but satisfying her lust," her mother said sagaciously as she watched her pick through her midday meal.

Nor could she let her mother get away with that. "Surely you once had some feelings yourself, Mother."

"Oh, I started with 'em—but it was too late by then. My mum hadn't gotten *me* a fancy husband and pots of money so I could indulge my fancy."

"It's cheap at the cost, Mother, considering what Arthur was really like."

Her mother rose up suddenly, looking like an avenging fury. "Oh yes? Well, my piss-smart lady daughter, I'll tell you what Arthur was like. He was like all men, no matter what his nature: he wanted a young wife, and an heir, and then he would have *given* you thousands to pursue your pleasure. He wouldn't be dead now, and you would have been the high priestess of *Seven Pleasures* with your life all your own.

"But no, my stupid lady has to go and push him off so that he gets murdered, and *now* she thinks she has discovered sex— when she is on the verge of being locked away from it forever.

"Well enjoy yourself, lady know-all. A woman's pleasure is fast and fleeting and any man will step right over her body in pursuit of his own."

And she pushed away from the table and stamped off to her room.

Blast her—she's like a damned Greek chorus. Cassandra of the mothers. Old woman. What does she know? What can she know?

I will see that man again.

. . . I will order him all to myself. Didn't Sinbar say . . . ?

. . . half of the pleasures, Roak had said—

. . . only half . . .

She understood, too, that part of the excitement and her arousal had been because she was naked under her dress: prim on the outside, seething on the inside.

She liked the contradiction. It made things easier. Roak had not had to tear through layers of impossible underclothes to get to her.

And neither would her lover tonight.

She wore her long, fashionable midnight blue satin dress over a pair of stockings and evening pumps, and nothing else.

Tolliver called the cab, and her mother, as she had the night before, secretly watched her go.

This time, she directed the cabman with firm surety. "The *Seven Pleasures*, driver."

"As you wish, mum."

She was shaking with excitement before they even arrived there, but her hand was sure on the knocker, and the butler remembered her from the night before, and bowed before he stepped back so she could enter.

"My lady was well pleased last night."

"Very." *Best to talk less.*

"Excellent. This way."

Again, he led her down the long entrance hall to the arched

doorway. "The card is there; make your selection. Do you have a preference for tonight?"

This part was different. She liked this part . . . the certainty that now that she had viewed the menu, she would want to make a selection.

"There was a gentleman last night—he was in the tableau with the maid . . ."

"Ah yes—"

"I want him to myself. And I want him waiting for me . . . naked."

"Does my lady wish to reserve a room?"

She didn't hesitate—it didn't matter what it might cost. "Yes."

"And your guide?"

"Sinbar was most satisfactory."

"Very good, my lady."

He withdrew then, leaving her with the card and the salver. She placed her money and opened the door and stood for a moment on the landing, inhaling the musky scent of forbidden sex.

She knew her way now, but that didn't stop her trembling. At the foot of the steps, as before, she waited, and in a moment, Sinbar appeared, attired has he had been the previous night.

"My lady. I am so happy you found pleasure." She could not help her eyes straying to his groin. He paused a moment, as if to give her time to examine his elongating member as it pushed out tightly against his thin trousers. "I am here to serve, my lady. Your master awaits."

The curtains parted, and they stepped into the hallway, stopping at a door midway down.

"Here is your private room, my lady, unless you wish for others to enjoy and participate in your pleasure."

"I will have this man alone—this time."

"I will draw the curtain."

She was shuddering with anticipation.

And Sinbar knew it: he pulled the curtain slowly, so slowly, so that she only caught glimpses of the wondrous naked animal within.

First his leg—he was lying on the bed, most excellent, and then his thigh, concealing that which she most wanted to see.

The curve of his buttocks, the arrogant placement of his narrow hip, his muscular arms.

She licked her lips in anticipation.

"I will strip my lady," Sinbar whispered.

She squirmed against the heat in his voice and the languorous heaviness of her body.

Let him turn—oh, let him turn, let me see him—

"A man like that—a woman wants to be naked for him . . ."

Oh yes, a woman does . . .

"Would my lady wish to see him perform first?"

She drew in a deep shuddering breath. "Yes . . . No! No one touch him—he is mine tonight."

"He is bursting for you, my lady—look . . ."

He had turned, finally he had turned, and he was there, the whole glorious length and beautiful nakedness of him.

She could hardly breathe. "Open the door."

Sinbar obeyed, and she stood framed in the opening, her senses filled with the sight and the smell of him.

He reeked of sex; hours of sex with anyone who would buy him.

She didn't care. She wanted to watch him. She wanted to strip for him. And then she wanted him to sink every inch of that thick long length of him into her.

And that was all.

That was *it.*

He lay back, propped up on his arms now, with his legs splayed in front of him so that his manhood jutted out and upward against the dark satin sheets.

She knew he could feel the heat of her gaze; she knew he loved showing himself off. She loved watching him preen.

All hers . . .

He canted his body toward her now, and slowly turned so that she was facing him head on, and then he spread his legs widely, and gave her a faintly lascivious smile.

She didn't move; she had the feeling this too was part of the game. He was posing, letting her see everything her money was buying.

She loved what she saw. She loved the faint sheen of sweat on his body as he shifted again, so that his massive manhood was in profile once again.

How many women had he serviced this night?

The thought was so arousing she began unhooking her dress.

They needed no words. He watched her, his eyes speculative slits; she reveled in his male nakedness.

He was the essence of virility, hard and taut, his vigor unabated by long nights of pumping and pounding whoever desired him . . .

Anyone could have him for the price of participation or exclusivity.

It seemed like a most excellent bargain to her.

No emotion. Pure pleasure, predicated by his skill and her receptiveness.

She unfastened the last hook and shrugged out of the sleeves of her dress, and it slid with just the faintest derisive whisper to the floor at her feet.

She kicked away and began walking toward the bed.

He shifted again, this time lying prone, so that she could mount his throbbing column of lust if she desired.

No one had to know. He was hers—for an hour, a night, for as long as she could contain him and he could pleasure her—he was a master at it—the way he looked at her, assessing her breasts, her narrow hips, the bush of hair between her legs, all the things about her that would incite a man . . . even a man like him—

But she had bought him, and he must submit to her fantasy.

She climbed onto him and stretched her body out over his, sliding her legs around his thrusting manhood and squeezing it between her thighs.

In this position, she could prop her elbows against the thick muscles of his shoulders and lower her mouth to his.

Kisses first, the first of the pleasures . . .

She felt her nipples grazing the rough hair on his chest. She felt his hands grasping her naked buttocks; and suddenly she was aware of his kisses, his frenzied, wet, *aggressive* kisses grinding against her mouth, making her ill with disgust at the taste of him.

She wrenched away, insanely disappointed. "No kisses."

"Whatever you want."

She hated his indifference. The flood of yearning in her abated like tide from a sandbar. She felt confused suddenly, and not at all certain that this was what she wanted to do.

Because of his kisses—

. . . insane; you didn't want his kisses, you wanted . . .

. . . you wanted—

"My lady—" Impatience in his tone now; he had a hundred other women to service who would want his kisses and his body.

Why could she not, when he had excited her so?

Or did she like being a voyeur and never participating in the dance?

"My lady—"

She disliked the brusqueness in his voice. It was time to show him who paid the piper.

She rolled off him and stood up. "You may go."

"My lady—"

Conciliating now, reaching a hand to touch her arm.

She pulled it away. "I am not in the mood."

"If there is anything—"

"I am not of a mood to participate tonight," she said firmly.

"It will be reported that there is one who was not pleasured tonight."

"I will take the blame. It is me. You are perfect."

Oh God, and he was. It was she who could not respond, could not perform.

And yet—and yet—the previous night, with the impervious Roak, she had become a creature of the senses . . .

"I know who you are, Lady Tisne."

She froze.

"Perhaps you are one like your husband . . ."

She felt the fear generating like a windstorm inside of her. Even the most debauched among them knew about her husband.

"I don't know what you mean."

"I can send one of the maids to you if that is your preference."

She started shaking. "I don't understand. What do you know about my husband?"

She saw the edge of uncertainty creep into his knowing gaze.

"I know he is dead, my lady."

That was as brutal as anyone could be. But she did not see condemnation in his eyes that she had chosen to mourn him less.

She saw something else there—a kind of patient wariness as if he . . . expected still another question?

Why?

He could not go until she dismissed him. He waited, still with that air of expectancy.

Why? What did he want her to ask?

What was the one question to which she did not ever want to know the answer?

In that split second that the idea occurred to her, she understood what he was waiting for.

And she felt the pain of betrayal, swift and incisive, deep in her vitals: she knew what she had to ask.

"Were you ever with him?"

His bright pale eyes settled on her naked body.

"I am with whoever can afford me," he said at length.

She swallowed hard. "Did you care for him?"

"Not I, my lady."

"Someone else?"

He didn't respond.

"What is your name?" she asked after another protracted silence.

"It cannot matter now. We are finished for the evening." *Forever, he seemed to say. She would never ask for him again; she would never take pleasure in any of the tableaux in which he would participate because he had committed the heinous error of referring to another patron. She might never return to the Seven Pleasures, and there would be penalties to pay for the loss of a well-heeled client as well.*

All of that he knew—and she understood by the resigned look on his face.

She watched as he gracefully sat up.

"My apologies, my lady."

She lifted her chin. "It is no one's fault."

No, the fault is that he is what he is—and he is not Roak.

The thought was stunning.

She didn't even see him leave. She gathered up her dress and wrapped it around her as if it could protect her from that unseemly thought.

To anyone else, this is a game. They come, they perform, they

*derive some release and they go back to their daytime lives. They
are vampires, feeding off each other, sucking the sex-life out of
each other . . .*

*And that was what Arthur had done, perhaps with every man-
jack in the whole of the Seven Pleasures.*

She couldn't do that; she wasn't yet jaded enough to be able
to do that. And yet she had paid for that man and had fully
expected to engage him for the entire night—or until her wanton
nature had had enough.

It hadn't taken long—one kiss that wasn't right from a man
who cared about nothing except the duration of his erection and
was available to anyone who had the price.

Even Arthur.

She could hardly even come to terms with it. So much for her
wanton nature.

So much for anything that had seemed possible the night
before . . .

A woman could not be trusted who had discovered sex.

He watched the whole scene between the lady and the hack
with great interest. She just couldn't keep away. One taste and
she wanted the whole banquet.

And so she had gotten sour milk.

Innocent playing with fire. Even her mother, who had sent him
on these two fruitless quests, knew better than she.

He didn't know whether to be annoyed that she had disobeyed
him or to take the opportunity that lay right within his grasp.

He could not have planned it better.

From the moment he recovered from the blow of the deaths
of the two he cared about most until the moment the lady had
walked in his door and told him her name, he could not have
mapped the thing out better or with more precision than it had
happened.

He didn't like the fact that there was an element of chance, of
luck, of fate—he didn't believe in those things, but the fact the
lady had crossed his path at this very moment, when he had been
so close to that which he had sought for so long—what was it
but fate?

He had been prepared for everything—except his response to her.

And so if she had come to the *Seven Pleasures* seeking something—then so had he.

And he didn't know what it was until he saw her lying naked with that man.

And then he knew.

She was the end game. She was point at which everything he had quested after met. And it didn't matter that the one person to whom it would mean the most would never know.

It mattered only that he would be her savior and then she would be his for the taking . . . and he would know.

"You didn't want him."

His voice pierced the awful silence.

She looked up, startled. *Roak!*

"You know nothing about what I want," she said ruthlessly, resentful of the fact that he had found her in the one place he had plainly told her not to go.

"I proved last night that I did."

Had he not? She didn't want to remember that he was every bit as big and powerful as . . .

"What do you want?" Her voice was harsh with her disappointment.

What would it be like to contain that power?

Why was she thinking like this?

"I will be your lover."

"What?" *He read my mind; he saw inside of me—he is out of his mind . . .* "You are crazy, Roak."

"And you are hungry for sensation and too innocent to play games with the likes of them. I'm safe, my lady—if you must court danger, consider—your life is in my hands already."

She stared into his impassive face. And she could not tell if his proposition were real or if he were making fun of her.

"I don't think so; obviously you are here for some other reason. Perhaps there is someone waiting for you."

. . . waiting for his kisses, his urgency, his ultimate possession . . .

She didn't want to think it or feel it or imagine it . . .

She didn't want him telling her how it could be done; she did not want to know how conversant he was with the details.

She didn't know what she wanted.

"You are waiting for me," he said.

It was so true, she was stunned for a moment into silence.

"Nonsense, Roak. How can that be so?"

"The fact that you are at the very place I expected to find you."

"No—!"

"Where else would you be after last night?"

"Or you?" she said just a little snidely. What was he, really? *Who* was he—except someone who had taken advantage of the situation the previous night?

Deliberately?

"You were not at Green Street."

That sounded too reasonable. Or did it?

"Roak—"

"Not tonight, of course. But the thing is easy to arrange—it is done all the time. We will meet here, whenever you will, my lady. You haven't forgotten, and that is why that man would not do."

"You are talking in riddles." She *had* to get back in control. And she would never tell him why that man would not do. "Of course that man would have done; I was just not in the mood. Not that it's any of your business."

"It will be," he countered.

"And why is that, all-knowing Roak?"

"Because you are already thinking about it."

"The only thing I am thinking about is going home."

He stepped aside as she came toward the door, and as she reached for the doorknob, he grasped her arm and pulled her back toward him.

"Then think about this as well, Lady Genelle—I am the man who can satisfy you."

She jerked her arm away. "And to think I have been satisfied this long without you. Good-night, Roak."

"Good-night, lady—and pleasurable dreams . . ."

Chapter 7

And so—Arthur had bought his lovers from the menu at the *Seven Pleasures*, and there was perhaps someone who might have cared for him, who might have been jealous of his fickle nature . . .

"So—was it as good as you thought it would be?"

Her mother, first thing in the morning, ready to spit kidneys and eggs and spoiling for a fight.

She said the first shocking thing that occurred to her—or was it just that the offer was very much on her mind?

"Indeed, a gentleman offered to become my lover."

"Pah. Useless when Stiles comes knocking on the door—as he will—and reasonably soon, I should think."

"Now Mother, don't go counting your fifteen thousand before I am condemned. There is still much about Arthur's life that must be taken into account."

"The only thing that counts is that you were alone and he was found dead in the hallway. That will be extremely hard to explain away to a jury."

"Nevertheless, Mother, that is why I have hired a skilled investigator who is following every—fragile—clue."

"He will *fragile* you out of all your money before he comes up with anything useful."

"Instead of you," she murmured, lifting a cup of tea to her lips before she said anything she might regret.

There was nothing more her mother needed to know.

There were a thousand things she needed to consider. A thousand questions that had occurred to her as she lay in bed tossing and turning and thinking about the events of the night.

I will be your lover . . .

And that was the least of them, she chastised herself.

Roak, her lover—every time she thought about it, she felt again the thrust and feel of him between her legs—

Using the heat of the moment and the voluptuous sensuality that surrounded them to make her believe that everything was possible and nothing was forbidden . . .

And she didn't forbid it—

And so even this was possible . . .

Roak, whom she barely knew, offering his fertile hard heat to her in the place where pleasure was worshipped . . . but Roak knew her—she had shown him all of her naked self that night when he had possessed her.

He had known what he was doing, and if he had not been the one, there would have been another.

. . . just not that man . . .

Who had—perhaps—been her husband's lover . . .

And so—the question had to be asked: how many others had there been in how many other places?

And how many more pleasures were there to explore?

"Lady Tisne."

Damn, she hadn't expected him. He sneaked up on a person—she had thought for sure that the Yard would not come calling for another week at least.

"Inspector Stiles. Please come in. Have you something more to tell me."

"I am here to report that Mr. Roak has provided us with a list of your husband's friends, acquaintances, business associates, and social intimates, as you instructed, and we are pursuing each lead carefully and thoroughly."

"That is encouraging."

"But we have turned up nothing as of today, Lady Tisne. Your husband was a well-respected businessman, as you well know, who belonged to the best clubs . . ."

. . . who had a secret life . . .

". . . and whose friends held him in the utmost respect."

"Of course they did, Inspector. Nevertheless, there could be so many different possibilities, not the least of which is that he could have arranged to meet someone at the house because he was to be in town."

*Talking too much, too too much . . . what next will you reveal
of Roak's theories?*

Nor was he moved by her little scenario.

"I have spoken to Lord Arthur's mother, who seems to believe
that you and your husband were not on amicable terms and
assured me that you were living separate lives and that Lord
Arthur was providing you with the income to do so."

Damn the bitch . . .

"My husband's mother misapprehended the situation," she
said firmly. "Or she read into it what she wished to read into it.
She was not happy when Lord Arthur married me."

"So she said," Stiles said drily, making a little tick next to a
note in his book. "And yet, Lord Arthur's residual estate reverted
to his mother and you inherited this house and your annual income
for life. Perhaps Madam Tisne's suppositions had some basis in
fact?"

She wanted to gnash her teeth. "My husband was supporting
my mother as well, as I think you know. I felt that to be extremely
generous of him."

"Yet her income died with him."

"Yes. And I wanted for nothing more, Inspector. Surely you
don't think I killed him for fifteen thousand a year and a townhouse in London when the estate, had it been willed to me, would
have been the greater prize. Perhaps Madam Tisne has some
thoughts on that, since she was the legatee."

"Point taken, Lady Tisne. The same might be said of your lady
mother as well—perhaps Lord Arthur's generosity was waning
and she thought that if he died, you would inherit the lot . . . a
neat motive as well . . ."

"My *mother* . . . ?" she said faintly. *Who had barged in the
door with all kinds of expectations and recriminations—* "My
mother was well taken care of by my husband, Inspector. She
had no cause to want."

"We'll have to see about that," Stiles said. "It is true you
were not in touch with your lady mother during the time of the
marriage."

. . . blast him . . .

"I—no, I wasn't."

"Was there any reason for that, Lady Tisne?"

"Divergent lives, Inspector. She had gotten what she wanted—a generous husband for me who would support her."

No, no, no—talking too much—far too much . . . and that last sounded impossibly nasty . . . wretched man, so unassuming that things came out that you didn't expect to tell him . . .

Where is that damned Roak when I need him?

"I see," Stiles said, and made another note. "Well then—many more avenues to explore, Lady Tisne."

Was it irony or did he mean it? She swore she couldn't tell.

"But it does not negate the one true fact: you were the only one home when your husband died. And you found the body. These facts in and of themselves mesh too coincidentally, Lady Tisne. Of course you will not leave town."

"No," she whispered.

"Good day, my lady."

She could not answer. He knew his way out. She had played this scene before. But the telling facts were now being woven into a tight-knit little net from which she would not be able to escape.

She sent for Roak.

It was not yet a full week since he had come to Green Street—and it felt like it had been a month.

She did not make the mistake of taking him to the small parlor. The receiving parlor was more on a scale to contain him.

"You did well to distract the good Inspector," Roak said, after she had recounted the details of his visit.

"Did I? And I suppose you have nothing to report," she snapped.

"I have been very busy on your behalf, Lady Genelle."

"As I indeed have cause to know," she put in—she could not help herself.

"We will concentrate on the business at hand, my lady," he said with the faintest reproof coloring his otherwise expressionless tone.

What a different man this was: she could hardly keep her attention on anything he was saying for thinking of her wanton behavior *that* night with him, willingly with him, which was warring at this moment with her urgent desire to strangle him.

That night—

. . . him . . . in that place of voracious lust, so big, so thick, so filling—how?

She felt the most craven yearning to see him naked suddenly—he was right, he was safe . . .

And he knew her . . .

She didn't know how, but he knew her . . .

". . . I beg your pardon . . . ?" she murmured to something he had said. "My husband was *what?*"

"Lord Arthur was spending his last weekends with a Lady Davidella Eversham in a flat on Oxford Street. And he was known to have several assignations with one Clarissa Bone, whom he was reputed to have met at a house of introduction in Assumption Mews . . ."

Clarissa Bone—Clarissa Bone . . . she sounds like some kind of low-classed woman who would throw her skirts up for anyone . . .

"Don't look away, Lady Genelle. Anything is possible—"

"So you keep telling me," she said bitterly.

"His investments, his businesses are in superb shape, as your lady mother-in-law has good cause to know. However, there is some rumor about the fact that your husband was about to rescind his offer of support to your mother."

"What?" Shock, pure shock. "Had he told her?"

"I believe she was informed of his intentions. It is said she had six months' notice to prepare."

"Stiles—could he have known? The questions—"

"I am not sure. He knows nothing yet about the women—or Lord Arthur's predilections. But that is only a matter of time."

"And the women?"

"No trace of them, yet."

"Dear God—other women . . ."

"Your husband lived in a netherworld of deceit and lies—"

"As does everyone else of his set apparently," she interposed bitterly.

"These small facts are not the end of the story."

"Which you will be investigating nightly at *the Seven Pleasures,* I presume."

"There is only one thing I want at *the Seven Pleasures,* Lady Genelle . . ."

"I'm sure you will find it," she said waspishly.

He paused in the doorway, aware of her eyes, her anger, her needs, aware of too too much, as he took his leave.

"I *know* I will, my lady."

"So Mother . . ."

"So *what?*" her mother said belligerently from the sofa in the small parlor where she was looking through the latest issue of the *Gazetteer*.

"He was going to stop all those lovely payments . . . I wonder why?"

"It wasn't nothing. I sent him some bills I ran up that his puny allowance did not cover."

"I see. Some bills. *Big* bills, Mother?"

"Just some bills."

"For—" She could see the red creeping up her mother's florid face. "For what, Mother?"

"Things."

"Things that your allowance didn't cover?"

"Well, it wasn't fair," her mother burst out. "You got all that money and all them lovely clothes, and there I was, walking around like a pauper because all that money went for the house and servants, and there wasn't anything left for anything else. And anyway, he could afford it."

"He couldn't afford *you*," Genelle said brutally. "What a neat motive you had for murdering him. If he were dead, I would inherit, and you would of course have access to all the money you could ever want. No wonder you were so furious at me when the bequest went all to his lady mother. Poor Mother. Poor *dear* Mother. *Our* money—It comes clear now, doesn't it? No wonder you are praying I get arrested. And to think I felt some remorse for you—in spite of what you did to me.

"Well, dear Mother, I have done as much as I will do for you—you may stay at my house and eat from my table—I'm sure you will have no trouble with your conscience—until they come to put you in jail. And meantime, I am going to enjoy the fruits of my shabby inheritance."

She did not mean to go—she didn't. She needed sleep; she felt as if she hadn't slept in days.

And she felt as if she couldn't keep away.

In spite of that man.

In spite of Roak.

It was the lure of the forbidden and the legacy of Eve.

No constraints . . . how could any woman not respond to the idea of no constraints . . .

And all those naked men—all she had to do was pay the price to summon them . . .

She dressed hurriedly, minimally as before, reveling in the slide of black satin over her bare limbs. Fastening a tiny corset to lift her breasts to fill in the neckline. Rolling up a pair of sleek black silk stockings to her thighs and catching them each with lacy black garters. Wishing her buttocks were as full and flaring as the dress required, but she did not wish to carry the weight of a bustle this night.

She tucked her long black hair into rolls on the side of her head and wound the remaining strands into a chignon to emphasize her long neck. Around her throat she wound a jet choker that was at least two inches wide and matched the long necklace that dangled almost to her knees.

Her heart was pounding wildly as she stuffed money into her beaded bag and headed down the long wide staircase.

Tolliver had already summoned the cab and she climbed in haughtily, waited for him to shut the door and retreat up the steps, and then she gave her orders.

"Dominoes, driver."

"What, mum?"

Damn him—

She rapped tightly against the hatch. "You heard me, driver."

"Aye, mum; just wanted to be sure."

Was she sure? She wanted something new, something different. Someplace where Roak would not be that she could just look and savor all the lovely men and deliciously carnal scenes. A place she would feel comfortable if she chose to participate.

After all, didn't men? Wasn't that their dirty little secret?

And hadn't her husband sampled everything available from the menus of self-indulgence?

Dominoes—what had her mother said? Of course she would

know about those things . . . where had *she met Lord Arthur Tisne in his never-ending round of hedonism?*

. . . you take off your clothes, you put on masks, and you do what you want . . .

"This is it, mum."

The driver opened the door, and she stepped out onto a street of beautifully maintained houses . . .

. . . you'd never guess . . .

Near Regent's Park . . .

No clues. No lights. No clientele . . .

She felt like a fool.

"Mum?"

She looked up at the driver.

"This is it, mum."

She whirled to face the ten-foot mahogany door of the house in front of her, and then, with the sound of hoofbeats underscoring her resolve, she walked up the three front steps and rapped firmly on the door.

Another butler, as ramrod straight as a walking cane, and as disapproving as the Queen.

"Madam?"

Don't let him face you down.

"I wish admittance," she said firmly.

"I beg your pardon?"

Oh damn—there must be a password or a token or something. Now she would have to brazen it out somehow.

"I am Lady Tisne. Tell your mistress or master or whoever it is that I wish to be admitted. *Now.*"

"Very well, my lady." He stepped back and she entered a small reception hall floored in black and white marble and decorated with a gilded center table and a dimly lit chandelier.

One small panel between two doors was mirrored, and she could see herself across the table and through a cut glass vase of fresh flowers.

She looked haughty, nasty. She looked as if she meant business.

The butler disappeared for a moment through the door to the left and reemerged through the one on the right.

"My lady is most welcome. Here is your token." He handed

her a golden domino with snake-eyes indented in its squares. "You may disrobe in there." He indicated the door to the left.

She opened the door. Inside, another servant waited.

"My lady." He handed her the ubiquitous card with the price of the evening's fare on it that was commensurate with the *Seven Pleasures*.

She gave him a handful of bills.

Another door opened, another servant waited to lead her down a long hallway lined with narrow doors—closets with numbers on them.

Hers was down at the very end of the hallway.

She took the key and opened it.

"My lady may undress as much or as little as she pleases," the servant said. "My lady's masque is on the shelf. And if my lady pleases, most of our patrons prefer to wear their keys around their wrists. Ring the bell when you are ready."

Ah now—now she had to perform . . . as much or as little as she chose . . .

If only she had chosen to wear pantalettes—

There was no hiding anything; a little hand-lettered sign made it quite clear that these were the rules by which all played.

If she removed only her dress, she would reveal more to these strangers than she had ever revealed to her husband . . .

Slowly she unhooked her dress and let it fall to the floor.

And there she was in the narrow mirror inside the closet door: clothed in a silk and net corset that barely concealed her nipples, silk stockings, and nothing else . . .

She could not go through with this—

She hung the dress, took the masque, and put her bag on the shelf, closed the door and locked it, and then twisted the black band from which the key was suspended around her wrist.

And then she rang the bell.

The servant appeared instantly. "My lady is beautiful; the men will fall at her feet and worship. Come, my lady. All is in progress already; you have only to join in."

She followed him through another door and down the long flight of steps to the subterranean depths of the house, where he left her standing on a balcony overlooking the main room which was furnished with thick pillows, divans, narrow sofas, caned benches, and jewel-toned rugs like something out of a sheik's dream.

And everywhere, there were naked men and women coupling in every conceivable variation with no care as to who was watching or who might join in.

She watched as a woman walked across the floor, looking, touching, caressing every available male body, touching each thrusting male root as if in search of something—something in particular—

Or maybe not; she stopped suddenly and mounted the nearest man and began riding him into a lather.

And over there, a man grabbed a woman and began fondling her breasts until she melted like butter against him and invited him to enter paradise.

And when she was done, she slipped out from under him and offered her breasts to the very next man, who pulled her onto his lap and began sucking them noisily while she pumped him with her hand for all she was worth.

And when she had done with him, she walked again through the crowd as if she were looking, looking, until another began caressing her buttocks, cajoling her with his hands and she obligingly bent over so he could enter her from the rear.

She seemed to love it, this woman, all the hands reaching for her, feeling her, seeking her; she seemed not to be able to get enough of it. She touched and kissed every man, and let them all have their way with her and then got up in search of another kiss, another caress, another virile male root to ride.

All those beautiful men, just waiting, waiting, wanting . . . she could have any of them, all of them, all that luscious turgid flesh—any which way she wanted it—all night long . . .

That same woman, that same insatiable woman, was now lying on a chaise, her legs spread, inviting a lover—any lover—to take her.

I am not insatiable—I'm scared . . .

She couldn't do this. She couldn't . . .

"My lady." A soft voice at her elbow, a woman, naked, masked, and of indeterminate age. "I'm so pleased you have chosen to join us. Arthur would have been delighted. He spent so many hours. Our men are incomparable, don't you think?"

She bit back an answer, because now that she was not following that siren who was preying on every man in the room, she could see that the incomparable men and women of *Dominoes* were indiscriminate in their choice of partners.

Like that man at the *Seven Pleasures*, they were there solely for the convenience of those who paid the price—or those who wished license to do whatever they pleased.

Men like her husband, who could have been the man in the corner, cuddling a still younger man. Or the two women who lay head to foot in the center of the room.

"You are quite beautiful, my dear. It is a shame you did not join us sooner."

"Is this the whole of *Dominoes*?" *Stupid question? Or stupid words because she couldn't think of a thing to say?*

"Oh no. There is so much more. We are renowned for our *specialties*—ladies and gentlemen with tastes that are outside the norm: we can provide them with access to whatever will pleasure them. As your husband well knew, my lady, and as I hope you will come to know."

"I see."

"It is a bit overwhelming the first time," the lady said understandingly. "One comes prepared to participate, but just what that means must be savored before one decides to *taste*. You are welcome any time, my lady. I know you will find gratification here."

The woman withdrew as silently as a ghost.

And now what?

Her eyes strayed into the pit, and across the room where that voracious woman had abandoned her couch and was prowling the floor again.

She could not be that cavalier. And she did not know how to get out of this snakepit. If she left, everyone would see her go— or at least those paying attention. If she went down below, she would be subject to anyone's whims, because that seemingly was how the game was played.

She took a tentative step down from the balcony.

"Oh look—new nectar . . . !"

Hands reaching for her now—not unpleasant—stroking her, petting her all over and pulling her into the fray.

"God, she's luscious—"

"Get rid of that corset . . ."

They ripped it off of her and tossed it into the crowd.

"Let me touch her—let me . . ."

She pulled away from the hands, slapping away those that were too aggressive, too invasive; she wasn't ready for this, she *wasn't* . . .

She felt herself being spun around and pulled into someone's embrace and then some man kissing her thoroughly, incisively, masterfully.

She could not budge those corded arms or that insistent mouth; she gave into his kisses, hating herself for her weakness, for her need.

She felt him nudging against her, long and thick, and *there,* a beautiful beautiful man, ready to service her at her command.

But suddenly she knew that mouth; she had tasted those kisses. She pulled her mouth violently away from his.

"Roak!"

Dear God, she had to be dreaming—Roak, naked and bursting and in the midst of this orgy—

"Research, I suppose," she said acidly. *All those women—and him among them, urgent with desire for them . . . she couldn't bear it—*

"You are dangerous," he muttered, pulling her body tightly against his.

"I want to get out of here," she whispered.

"No more than I want you out of here. Hold on to me."

She wrapped her arms around him possessively, and instantly his mouth came down on hers with a violence that had nothing to do with his exasperation with her.

She felt his hands down her back, stroking her thighs, her buttocks, her crease; she felt them moving, incremental inch by incremental inch; she felt other hands cupping her, feeling her; she felt his legs, against her own, as he lifted her and carried her further into the unrestrained crowd.

And she felt *him,* long and thick, like a rock, between her thighs, as if he were carrying her weight on the sheer virile strength of it.

She was wet with wanting him, with his kisses, aroused by the idea of all the women wanting him, touching him—

Not touching him—not—she couldn't stand the thought.

"Roak . . ."

He had backed her against a tapestried wall on the far end of the room, the weight of his body cramming against her in the most voluptuous way.

"Don't talk—pretend . . ." he whispered against her lips, as he rocked his hips against hers so that she felt the full-focused power at the root of him.

I don't want to pretend . . .

"I don't . . ." she murmured, shimmying against him.

". . . Here?"

". . . I don't care—"

And she didn't; she wanted him—he was so hot and stiff, bursting with elemental need—

"I will claim you—"

She arched herself against his inflexible body. "Now . . ."

And he grasped her buttocks and lifted her, and slowly entered her, pushing and pushing slowly slowly slowly, deep fathomless, pushing against her deep, until he was at her pulsating center, and he could move no more.

And they were watching, and there was a part of her that loved the fact that they were watching and that it was she whom he possessed in that agonizingly arousing wanton way . . .

And then he rotated his hips and she felt a starburst of sensation radiating outward and outward until with the next forceful thrust, it shattered into a million pieces, leaving her bereft.

He let her down slowly, as slowly as he had taken her, until her feet were on the floor.

"Excellent," he murmured against her eager mouth, his still eager manhood nudging her thigh.

"Oh God, you are so . . ."

"We're not done yet; if I am to claim you, you must show your willingness to do anything I ask—or someone else has the right to take you."

She felt a ripple of excitement rip through her. "Whatever *you* want . . ." she whispered.

"Turn around."

He kept his body between her and the voracious crowd as she obeyed. She was facing the tapestry now, and she could feel him caressing her back and her buttocks once again, and then, unexpectedly, reaching down to feel between her legs.

"Bend over . . ."

She thought she heard his command, or perhaps she knew what to do because she had watched that gluttonous woman; or perhaps his hands had enticed her so completely it was the only thing she could do—

She felt his hands on her buttocks, centering her—and then—oh and then, glorious sensation, he entered her in an utterly new and reverse way . . . she made a sound deep in her throat as he began pumping his possession of her and she hung onto the wall.

There was nothing else—just the ramrod thrust of him, as if he were an extension of her—and her buttocks writhing and wriggling against him seeking the utmost sensation, and the entwined bodies all around her groping for the very same heaven.

It started as just a slide of feeling. Wet, hot, hard, potent, and forceful. Relentless. She couldn't resist it—she had to give into it: he was too hard, too lusty, too elementally male—like granite he was, driving like a piston to master her white-hot desire.

She felt the heat of him and every long hard inch of his brazen nakedness, and then, without warning—the whole jolting explosiveness of his unyielding possession of her.

. . . the little death—it was, it was like dying and instantly being reborn . . .

She heard voices as Roak's possessive hands grasped her hips as he pulled himself from her and then clasped her tightly to his body.

"I want her . . ."

"God, she's wonderful—"

"That body . . ."

"That climax . . ."

"Those nipples . . ."

"I'm not done with her yet."

"Give someone else a chance," someone said resentfully.

"Sure—you want to try everyone, don't you, darling?"

"Look at all these lovely men who are just as expert; they're dying to have you."

"Ask her—ask her if I can just feel her nipples."

"Ask her what she wants," Roak said above the babble as he put one arm around her shoulders and let it slip down over her left breast so that he could finger her protruding nipple. "Go on, my lady . . . tell them."

Oh God—what is he doing now, and why is he doing it in front of them?

She counted five men licking their lips as Roak played with her nipple. And the sensation was unspeakable—like nothing she had ever felt in this night of incendiary feelings she had never experienced before.

She arched her back against him and ran her hands down his hips and thighs.

"I want this man tonight."

She felt him tilt her face toward him and she welcomed his kiss. They stood there, her back to his chest, kissing, with him squeezing her nipple and exploring her body as the disgruntled crowd turned away and began to find other partners.

"Excellent," he whispered. "Now come."

He turned her toward him, and they edged their way through the room, stopping at intervals so he could kiss her and fondle her.

When they got to the steps, the mysterious masked woman was waiting for them.

"That wasn't fair," she said playfully, extending a hand to caress his chest.

Roak ignored her questing hand. "This woman wants everything I can give her. We need a room."

"If you want privacy, it will cost more. If our guests can watch, we can make another arrangement."

"No voyeurs—tonight."

"Very well."

A servant appeared.

"Take them to the bedroom."

He bowed.

"Come—" he beckoned. "I will take you to heaven."

Another door opened as if it were controlled by unseen hands; the servant led them into a cage lit by candles. A door creaked shut.

The apparatus heaved and surged upward and then shuddered to a stop.

"Heaven," the servant said, and opened the adjacent door to reveal an opulently furnished bedroom lined in the omnipresent dim lights.

Roak pulled her into it and shut the door in the face of the servant.

"Hurry—" He pulled the cover back and the sheet off of the bed and wrapped it around her.

"Roak—"

"Shhh—" He wrenched the top sheet out from under the covers and twisted it around his waist and between his legs. "Now . . ."

"There's no door," she whispered, feeling real fear replace her waning excitement.

"No. Just the elevator. Don't talk. Moan, I'm sure she's listening."

He began feeling along the walls and behind the bed. "Damn, there has to be a way out of here—" Crawling on the floor now, peeling back the thick carpeting, gently rapping against the floorboards.

"Get on the bed—bounce around and make a lot of noise . . ."

But it's not quite the same, Roak, or can't you tell? she thought mordantly as she rode the bed like a novice horsewoman and made all kinds of squeaking, creaking sounds that she hoped sounded like a gratified lover.

"Roak—"

"Shhhh . . . the elevator comes—"

They heard it banging and groaning as it came to a stop below their room.

Roak flung open the door to reveal a yawning black hole intersected by thick, rough ropes and cables.

"Come—"

"Oh my God—"

"They'll be up here next; they don't take no for an answer, haven't you figured that out? They will assume I am spent beyond performing and you are in need of lustier mortals with more staying power."

He sat at the edge of the threshold and put a tentative leg down. "We have to be quick—" He slid downward and disappeared.

"Roak!"

Her voice came out in a terrified squeak as she knelt by the open door. She could just see him below her, and as he reached up his hand, she was horrified to see it barely reached her.

"Listen to me, my lady. Don't think. Just put your legs over the side. Take my hand. Close your eyes and just slide your body downward. I will catch you, I promise."

She felt it—the heartbeat of a moment when she wanted to balk and give in to whatever would await her if she stayed.

And then she took his hand, closed her eyes, and—just as the thing began to move downward—she slipped off of the edge of the threshold and into the darkness.

She was going to die. There was nothing there between her and the dark dead air into which she pitched herself and she was going to—

She fell against him as he braced himself against the abrasive ropes and he grasped her around her waist and anchored her against his body.

The thing rattled and groaned and sputtered as it slowly dropped to the next floor and the next, and all they had between them and the darkness was his obdurate strength pinioning them against the mechanism of the elevator.

"We'll never get out of here," she whispered on a sob.

The elevator settled to a stop on the lowest level; they heard the gate open; they heard the muted noise of the carousing beyond the door as someone opened it. And then the gate closed and the noise abated and there was nothing but the darkness and the solidity of his determination.

"There are escape hatches. Get down. Feel around."

She whimpered, but she did as he told her.

"I have it."

Thank God—but it made such a loud metallic sound as he moved it . . .

She held her breath.

"They can't hear anything. I'm going to jump."

Thunk! He was down already before she had time to feel the fear that was encroaching on her very vitals. She could see him below her, reaching up his hand once again.

She swung her legs over the hatch and slipped downward and into his arms.

"Shhh . . ."

He released her and turned to examine the mechanism. "Stand back—let me secure the gate. Now—" he turned knobs and dials and then pulled back on a lever—and the thing moved, as if it were being lifted by an omnipotent being, swiftly, smoothly, up and up and up until suddenly it jolted to a stop.

"I think we're here."

She wrapped her bedraggled sheet around her like a shroud as he opened the gate.

"We don't have time to get anything from the closets. Ready?"

He pushed open the door and they stepped out into the anteroom at the front of the house through the mirrored panel between the two doors.

"Hurry—"

He propelled her across the anteroom, pulled open the front door and grabbed her hand and together they raced out into the black matte silence of the night.

Chapter 8

The dress was too large, the hem was too short, and the shoes were three sizes too big for her and made the most unholy noise when she entered her house in the early dawn hours to confront her mother, who had been waiting for her with an excellent show of motherly fretting.

But of course she had dreamt the whole thing, down to that awful mad dash out into Regent's Park, and the smirking, knowing cab driver who had picked them up and driven them to Roak's flat. And on top of that, the ignominy of having his landlady pay the fare, and loaning her the horrible clothes in which she had finally arrived home.

And then her mother—*really, a dream*—haranguing her about the hour and the state she was in and where she had been.

"Tell me, miss priss lady, there was a cabby now, wasn't there? Did you know they regularly go by all those houses to get them a likely one when things get hot on and some dolly don't want to play footsie? Oh, they'll pay anything then—I daresay your high-priced Mr. Roak had to fork over the dimmock for that little jaunt, and don't think he won't stiff you on it . . ."

Yes, she had to have dreamt that, and the events preceding it as well and that god-awful knocking on the door . . .

She struggled to lift herself onto her elbows and to shake her fogged brain awake.

Yes, the knocking was real . . .

"Come in."

Her mother pushed open the door. "Package for you, fancy lady." She tossed it on the bed. "Go on, open it—"

Genelle eyed it suspiciously. "Why do I have the feeling you know what is in it?"

"Because I do, miss priss," her mother said smugly as she tore into the brown paper.

... my dress—my bag ...

She bit her lip. *And the key? No, she had slipped that off, hadn't she?*

"And that fancy man of yours, that detective, he's waiting downstairs."

"For God's sake!" She jumped out of bed.

"What's he going to tell you that you don't know already?"

... I don't want to see him—I can't—I actually allowed him to ... no, I was pretending, wasn't I? I didn't dream that—

There wasn't a thing in her closet that made any sense.

... the man has seen you naked—what difference does it make?

She couldn't keep thinking like that. She threw on a robe and pushed her way past her mother and ran down the hallway.

... dear God—pounded against the wall ... bent over like ... like—

She stopped in her tracks as she was about to descend the staircase. The memory caught her like a whirlwind—unexpected, vivid, too too vital and real—a tornado of a reaction that lifted her up and crashed her down, leaving her knees weak and her heart beating wildly.

... too real—

She licked her lips. How on earth could she face him?

She started down the stairs on rubbery legs.

He was waiting at the bottom, dressed as always in black, his glowing eyes following her every movement down the steps.

... yes, I want you to be—

... in control now ...

"Good morning, Roak," she said coolly as she gave him her hand and stepped into the reception hall. "Have you had something to eat?"

She turned into the morning room this time, where she usually took breakfast, and sat down at her lovely Regency table with its brass-tipped legs and matching chairs.

"Please—" She motioned to the opposite chair as she rang for Tolliver who appeared at the instant.

... yes, this was better, she was directing things this time, and Roak had actually obeyed her.

"I am ready ..." Her gaze swerved toward Roak for an instant and then she hastily added, "for breakfast—two of everything, please, Tolliver. Thank you."

... idiot—ready, oh yes ... she could not meet his eyes—he saw everything, he already knew everything ... a woman could have no secrets from a man like this ... and she couldn't think of a bloody thing to say either ...

"Ah, tea—excellent—"

Something to do: Tolliver set down the tray and she poured, added sugar and cream, stirred, stared at the teacup, lifted it, blew on the surface and then took a scalding sip.

And looked at him over the rim.

She could have sworn he was amused by the way she put the teapot and a plate of kippers between them, but his expression, as always, showed nothing.

"Tea, Mr. Roak?"

"Thank you, no."

... me, Mr. Roak ...?

She bit into a piece of toast ferociously and looked at him expectantly.

He didn't miss a beat.

"The time has come to tell me who you were with that night."

She choked. "I beg your pardon?"

"Who were you with that night, Lady Tisne?"

She swallowed the lump in her throat compounded of dread and half-eaten toast. "I was alone; I told you."

He stood abruptly, without warning, rattling the tableware with the force of his latent anger. "Then there is nothing further I can do to help you, Lady Tisne."

... out of control again—and she didn't know what to do; she had to keep Tony out of it, she had to ... but she had the distinct feeling he already knew ... dear God, if he knew—

... or had he primed her just so he could use that as a lever to get her to confess ...

Because if he walked out—he would never be her lover ...

Oh God—

That was crazy; that was imputing too much to what had happened between them . . .
All that pleasure—
Coming down to a choice between him and Tony . . . ?
Was Tony that sure of her?

"I don't understand what you mean." *Refuge of the weak and lying, that statement, when she understood only too well.*

And of course he wasn't fooled. His face showed nothing, and still she felt his irritation.

"I must know everything, Lady Tisne. As far as you are concerned, I am omnipotent. Your secrets are safe unless you are going to hang. And even then I will keep them to the best of my ability. Now let's try again. You were with someone that night."

She bit her lip and poured another cup of tea. She had lost every appetite in the space of these few minutes but the need to moisten her mouth before she put her foot into it.

But maybe not—he was the smart one . . . he had probably already figured it out. And then she would not have to confess it—

"And I'm sure you know exactly who it was," she said carefully, setting the cup down and gazing up at him with a limpid look.

"We both know who it was, and you are naive if you think the notion hasn't crossed Stiles' mind that it is a short step from the carriage to the bedroom, my lady."

"Which of course *he* will deny," she put in. "So it is the same as if he had not been there."

He made a dismissive sound. "Gilbert and Sullivan logic, Lady Tisne. The fact remains someone else could have been—and was—in the house with you. Yet another to add to a growing list of suspects."

"I found the body," she reminded him.

He looked at her speculatively. "I wonder if you did."

"Roak—"

"You may make excuses for Tony Lethbridge if you must, Lady Tisne. But not to me. And everyone else knows exactly what he is, if you do not. So you can imagine what was being said when you left the Ball with him."

She felt just a little shocked. "He was being kind."

"Nonsense. And no one thought it. But I expect he convinced you that both of your reputations would suffer if he were dragged through the police investigation."

That was so clearly on the mark, she felt her face flushing.

He went on, brutally, "And after all, it was *your* husband. Nothing to do with him. All he did was offer you a little attention and gratification. And when it got hot, he absconded. Does that cover it, Lady Tisne? You would claim to have discovered the body—you wiped some blood on your nightclothes, I would guess; he probably took his home and burned them. And since the Yard probably could not prove motive or means, you would not be charged.

"Except of course, there is motive and means—a possible inheritance, an empty house—planned well in advance—and a convenient kitchen knife. A note perhaps that you wrote your husband, requesting his presence in your house . . . ?"

"No!"

"No?"

"I gave the servants the night off because I wanted no one to witness Tony's coming home with me."

"I see."

What did he see? Damn him—what could he see?

"We—" She couldn't say it; it was meaningless, nothing next to the previous two nights. "After it was over—a long time after, I thought I heard a noise. Tony went down to see what it was— and he didn't return. So I—went down to find him, and he was at the foot of the stairs, covered in blood."

"He told you he had tried to resuscitate the body."

Again, she was shocked; it was almost as if he had somehow been there.

Or worse—it was a story so common to everyone involved in a murder, Tony could have been reading from a script . . .

"Yes."

"And that you must keep him out of it, citing the scandal if the papers got hold of it . . ."

"Yes."

"And so you and he concocted the story while he smeared your nightclothes with blood before he divested himself of his clothes . . ."

She felt sick to her stomach. "Yes."

He didn't flinch. "He wrapped them up and took them with him."

"Yes."

"And left you with the body?"

"Yes," she whispered.

"And after a while, you went out on the street and pulled in a passerby to notify the police."

She bowed her head. "How did you know?"

"It was the only possible way it could have happened, Lady Tisne. And of course, Tony Lethbridge has done nothing since except breathe a sigh of relief that he got cold away from the affair."

"He paid a condolence call."

"No excuses, Lady Tisne."

"He gave me your name," she said defiantly.

"Well, then all is forgiven, my lady. The bastard."

And he was, but there was no help for it now. She had given in to his demands in the emotion of the moment—how could she not with both of their reputations at stake—and he had given her up in a heartbeat.

"You must not bring him into it."

He gave her a disbelieving look. "I appreciate your candor, Lady Tisne."

Again, she felt that sweeping feeling of dislike; she felt like she was battering up against a wall: immovable, improbable, set in stone.

"Perhaps you are the bastard," she returned cuttingly.

"Dear Lady Tisne," he murmured with his hand on the doorknob, a step away from leaving, "I sincerely hope I am."

How did one deal with the likes of him?

Perhaps she had dreamt that as well. She got up from the breakfast table, having had nothing but a bite of toast and two cups of tea, and wearily went up to her bedroom and dressed for the day.

"A stinker he is," her mother said plainly, echoing her own thoughts as she entered the small parlor an hour after Genelle had settled herself by the window. "You think you can outwit the likes of him?"

"Probably not," Genelle said drily. "But neither can you."

"Nay—I know that world, my lady daughter. You're too high up on the pedestal to see the mud. Believe me, the aristocracy crawls in the mud to feed their needs."

Don't I know it . . .

"Tell me about it, Mother."

"You're too innocent, my dear. *Seven Pleasures* wasn't nearly the whole of it, that much I will tell you; you be careful of every shadow, daughter. You don't ever know what lurks around the next corner."

Oh yes I do—

"Mother—"

But with that cryptic statement, she was gone.

The old shrew—I haven't forgotten, Mother . . . not one thing, not one word, not even the fact you had a far stronger motive to get rid of Arthur than I . . .

It had been—a week, almost two—and it felt like it had been two months since she started crawling around in the underbelly of Arthur's life.

And what had she found out?

That she could be seduced as easily as any parlormaid; that her husband had bought his pleasure from every hellhole in London; and that she wanted Roak to be her lover . . .

Damn . . .

He was too knowledgeable about those places; he had to be a habitué—

Anyway, she knew nothing about him, nothing, except that she was paying him excellent money to find Arthur's murderer.

Nothing should get in the way of that . . . nothing . . .

But what it did was, it left her sitting home doing . . . nothing.

And her idle hands had gotten her into enough trouble already.

She jumped up, seated herself at her desk, drew out a piece of paper and a pen and some ink.

Lists were good. Making lists kept the mind busy and not thinking about *other* things.

She wrote:

About Arthur:
  Frequented houses of pleasure
  Bought many sexual favors from men—possibly women?
  Cohabited with two women in two different places
  *Spent many weekends—one assumes—carousing at the
country houses of friends*
    *Note: list friends—who is in Town, who could be ques-
tioned and or followed*
    Might one of those friends know about the women?
The Murder:
  *Since I did not invite Arthur to the house, how did he get
in?*
  Could he have come to see me?
  Could he have come to meet someone else?
  Arthur still had the key
  *Did not know servants would be out, perhaps thought
they would be asleep that late at night*
  Why would he have come to see me that late?
  Therefore, can assume he was to meet someone else?

She liked that deduction. Arthur had the key; he had not written
ahead to say he wanted to see her—why would he want to see
her? They had settled everything months before and he seemed
satisfied with the arrangement. Yet since he was found in the
house, the conclusion could be drawn that he was there to meet
someone. The question was—*who?*
  She wrote:
  My mother, who was about to lose her support (how likely,
really, that mother would brave the dark of night to meet him
here like this? Or was she that desperate? Could she really have
thought my inheriting everything would solve her problems?)
  His mother (she followed him from Fanhurst, discovered—
what I discovered, couldn't bear it and put an end to it?)
  One of the two mystery women (blackmail he refused to pay
for . . . ?)
  Any one of a number of particular friends (many motives)
  The list seemed to narrow appallingly as she wrote. The idea
that Roak had tendered of a constituent who had traded favors

or money for votes seemed farfetched in this context where everything seemed related to Arthur and his proclivities.

It had to be the bedrock of the motive.

But all those lovers—for how many years back? And two elusive women. And two avaricious mothers.

And you . . .

She watched the day wane through the small parlor window. She felt alone, helpless, restless, and consumed alternately by memories of the previous night that assaulted her at moments when she least expected.

It seemed almost easier to give into them, to think about what she had seen and experienced than to try to subvert and negate them.

She *had* been invited to the orgy on the strength of her husband's name, and she *had* willingly disrobed with every intention of participating. And she *had* let Roak take her while everyone watched who cared to—

And she *did* feel consumed with excitement as she thought about it, and she envied the men who could go about the pursuit of such pleasures with no guilt whatsoever.

Like Roak.

Dear God, what if he were preparing for an evening at Dominoes right at this minute? What if he reveled every night in all those women wanting him, mounting him, riding him?

Like that—like that insatiable goddess?

. . . I could be as insatiable as that sow . . .

. . . I can't keep thinking like this . . .

But all there is to do is sit here and think—

I have to do something or I will go crazy . . .

. . . you are crazy . . .

Roak had said that . . .

. . . oh, do let us canonize Mr. Roak, a man who frequents houses of pleasure, offers himself to his clients, and isn't above a little orgiastic sex himself . . .

What are *you pouting about?*

You are Lady Tisne. Your husband's name among these people is as well-known as the Gazetteer *is among all the population of London.*

You have only to take what you want, and Roak be damned.
And what *did* she want? What of everything so far had given
her the greatest pleasure?
    . . . she knew the answer to that even before she conceived the
question . . . and she knew instantly that she could never control
one of the elements, but she surely could command the other . . .

She directed the cab to *Newbury Arcade* which turned out to
be another building dripping with respectability—this time within
shouting distance of the Palace.

The fee was not exorbitant either—stiff enough to keep out
the riffraff, but affordable enough so that the clientele was as
varied as the *tableaux vivants* inside.

And the Gatekeeper—a wizened older woman with sharp
knowing eyes who was dressed in the highest of style to maintain
the tone of the place—she sat in a little booth in a velvet-draped
entrance hallway. It was hushed, dimly lit, carpeted, swagged in
gold, as rich as the Queen's drawing room, and she, like a queen,
knew the commoners who frequented the place.

Even a stranger.

"Ah, my lady," she murmured as she handed Genelle the ubiquitous masque. "Your husband was a frequent visitor . . ."

Arthur—here, too? Was no place safe from him . . . and did
everyone know who she was—and had they pitied her because
of it?

"We are happy to welcome you. What is your pleasure? Perhaps you do not know—we can accommodate every taste."

"How does one know?" Genelle muttered, slipping on the
masque.

"Oh, I think my lady prefers the usual menu, with perhaps"—
the Gatekeeper slanted a speculative look at her—"perhaps something to whet the appetite. I think that will do, my lady. You
must let me know when you return. And if something strikes your
fancy, that can be accommodated as well. There is no participation
here, as you probably know, but there would be nothing to stop
you and a partner, for example, from acting out a scene. Or, if
you wish, private arrangements can be made.

"Is my lady ready?"

Genelle nodded, and the gatekeeper lifted a baton and struck a series of hypnotic musical notes on some kind of instrument beside her.

A curtain parted on the right, the gatekeeper nodded, and Genelle proceeded through the curtain to find a stairway leading upward.

She waited a moment, in case someone should appear, but there were no guides here apparently.

When she reached the landing, she confronted an arched entryway surmounted by a rich blue velvet curtain which was promptly pulled aside so she could step into the ubiquitous long hallway, on the walls of which were hung huge gilded frames.

There were candles flickering in sconces on the walls and a thick blue carpet underfoot. There was no furniture, not even a chair or sofa to swoon upon.

And there was no one else in sight.

She walked slowly to the first frame on the left wall. It was dark. Beside it, and each of the frames, was a long bellpull.

She reached out and yanked it.

A moment later, the scene was illuminated in every way possible: a woman undressing, all of her clothing piled around her bare feet, her slender arms holding her corset just under her bared breasts, as she bent to try to retrieve her pantalettes which were slipping off of her well-rounded derriere.

She was quite beautiful, in a pose designed to entice a man.

This is nothing . . . this is as tame as a lady's magazine . . .

She moved on and pulled the cord for the next *tableau*.

The lights came up. It was the woman—the same woman, naked now, except for her torn underthings lying at her feet— and she was bending over this time as well, but now, behind her on his knees and clothed, was a man who was holding her buttocks and pressing his mouth tightly against her crease almost as if he were exploring there with his tongue.

She felt a violent reaction to the scene.

. . . I want that—I want . . .

She couldn't take her eyes away from the man and the erotic press of his mouth. She could almost feel it, could imagine how it would feel . . .

And the actors never moved; they held the pose and let her gaze her fill until their muscles strained with the effort and then the lights went down and she was forced to move on to the next setting.

In that view, a different woman, dressed in a camisole that was untied to reveal her breasts, and pair of split, lace-trimmed fine lawn drawers, sat with her legs spread on the edge of a table, facing the frame. The man this time was kneeling between her legs, as if he were worshipping that most feminine part of her, caught in the act of caressing her *there* with his mouth and tongue.

And then he moved toward her, and buried his face in her dark bush and the tableau froze.

She stared at the scene, entranced.

. . . *I love that—I want that—*

—this is the difference between Newbury and Seven Plea-sures . . . this is what my sex looks like—and they let me look as long as I want to, as long as they can hold out . . .

. . . *I love looking . . .*

. . . *I love what he is doing to her—I wish there were someone with me so that we could . . . I would—in this kind of privacy . . .*

The lights came down suddenly and she felt as if she had come out of a hypnotic trance. More than that, she felt liquid with the heat of arousal, and she pulled the cord to open the curtain on the next scene.

They were right next to the frame, the woman's breasts directly at eye level and naked, so that the onlooker could see every detail of those taut stone-hard nipples and the man who held one of them tightly captive in his hot wet mouth while he thumbed the other rigid tip.

Her imagination ran riot, imagining the feel of it; imagining that one rigid tip being sucked until the woman begged for mercy.

And then imagining him moving his mouth to the one he was squeezing, and sucking it with the same erotic fervor.

She loved the scene; she wanted to gaze at it forever. She would never forget the image of that man's mouth pulling at that woman's hot hard nipple.

She wanted *that* . . .

She barely noticed that the lights had gone down. And when she did, she went on, almost dazedly, to the next frame and pulled the cord.

The woman—the same woman—was lying prone in a bed that

was canted toward the frame so that the onlooker could see every detail of the woman's body as she spread her legs and willingly revealed all of her feminine secrets.

She is so beautiful—I am so beautiful . . .

And onto the next setting, across the hallway now. When she pulled the cord, the woman was bent over, her buttocks facing the frame, and Genelle as the onlooker was viewing them over the man's shoulder as he was about to penetrate his partner from this reverse pose.

And then the actor entered his partner, turned them both to the side, and froze the scene.

She caught her breath. He was fully and completely embedded in the woman, leaning over her, cupping her left breast with his hand while he held her hip with the other.

She loved it; she loved the silence and the stillness so that she could revel in every detail.

. . . I want it again—I want it . . .

And the next—now the woman, the same woman, was mounting the man, who lay prone on the bed that was canted backward this time, so that every aspect of her sex was revealed to the onlooker as she positioned her partner beneath her.

So different than watching a greedy sow pop on and off every other man she came across at Dominoes . . .

And then the actress pushed her body down on the hard column of her partner's sex and froze the scene.

. . . embedded again . . . how delicious—

She could almost recreate the feeling of it in her memory . . . and the yearning to experience it again . . .

'. . . I will be your lover . . .'

—yes . . . if you were here, right this moment—I would . . . I would—

In the next scene the woman was backed up against a wall which was at an angle to the frame so that the onlooker could see her naked body in profile. Her arms were secured by a pair of silken ties, and she arched herself so that the profile of her body was perfectly in view as her lover, his male root as hard as an iron bar, came to her, nudged her legs apart and thrust himself into her—and froze the scene.

She almost fainted at the sheer sensuality of it: the woman's legs spread to receive him, his forceful entry to conquer her, the perfect connection of their bodies, with his overpowering hers this time, hip to hip, groin to groin, not moving, not writhing or thrusting or driving to the climax. Just the perfect complement of his body to hers, filling her, mastering her . . .

She could barely breathe, she was so enchanted and aroused by the scene.

. . . I want that—I want it—

She felt her fingers curling in anguish that they could have it and she could not . . .

Not tonight—

I will be your lover . . .

And she had seen less of him than she had of this actor who had revealed every part of his body to her in the course of the scenes . . .

His hips were so narrow, and his maleness so long and large . . . he was perfect, perfect the way he held the pose, long and strong inside her like that, not moving, just wholly there . . . it took her breath away—

And what scenes did Arthur choose to view?

The minute the thought edged into her mind, she felt as if she had been doused with cold water.

Yes, Arthur; the gatekeeper had mentioned Arthur, and she was supposed to be searching for clues about Arthur, wasn't she? Instead of fulfilling every lubricious fantasy she could think of?

And then the scene closed down and the actors, in their naked beauty, were utterly gone.

She walked down the hallway without pulling the other cords, slowly back the way she came.

How many other floors catering to how many other tastes? How many scenes for Arthur to arouse him to conquest?

But never for me . . .

Why, why didn't I know about this delicious place?

She pulled back the curtain and descended the stairs until she reached the room with the gatekeeper's booth.

"You're back," the woman said. "I didn't expect to see you— someone awaits, and you know we maintain the utmost privacy here. Did you like scenes we chose for you?"

. . . I loved them . . . I loved them . . .

Don't talk too much. Don't . . .

"Yes, they were everything I could have wished to see."

"Excellent. Then . . . ?" The gatekeeper paused delicately.

"One question?"

"One."

"My husband?"

"Everything here is confidential, my lady. But I will say, he came often and in the company of that blowsy Eversham woman which I never could understand when he had a lovely thing like you to share the enticements with."

. . . the Eversham woman . . . "I see—"

"I'm sure you do," the gatekeeper said. "Please use the side exit, my lady."

"The scenes . . . ?"

"I'm sure my lady can imagine," the gatekeeper said.

But she couldn't—not if he had been with the Eversham woman . . . she couldn't imagine it at all.

While she had stayed home and refused to share in the "enticements" . . .

Arthur had been rutting and ravishing everything in sight in every establishment from London to the lake district country houses—

She would never get over how much she didn't know—about Arthur . . .

And about herself . . .

Chapter 9

She couldn't find the key and she felt a corrosive panic when she could not remember what she had done with it.

Nonsense—a meaningless key from a house of pleasure where you would never participate again in a hundred years . . .

. . . never . . . ?

She felt as if she were consumed by her appetites and that her burgeoning carnality was a thing separate and apart from the reality of her probable arrest for the murder of her husband.

. . . how else? Who else?

Her clothes felt heavy, cumbersome. She wanted to divest herself of all of them and walk around naked, perfectly prepared for the perfect lover.

The one who would never materialize.

But at Dominoes—every man was the perfect lover, and she could have them all . . .

. . . I don't want them all—

But if the pig-goddess could do it, why couldn't I?

All those men, naked and erect for me—no other pleasures except the pure self indulgent lust for copulation . . . any which way I want—

A luscious way to spend my time until they hang me . . .

"My lady? My lady—"

Tolliver's voice, interrupting her deliciously lewd daydreams.

"Yes, Tolliver?"

"The Inspector—"

Of course, the gods' dose of reality. "Send him in."

He sat himself down opposite her in his usual businesslike way, extracted his notebook, and began without preliminaries.

"You were aware that Lord Tisne had a certain reputation, my lady?"

And so, he had finally come to the subject, just as Roak had predicted. There was the abyss yawning in front of her: yet another motive for her to have killed him . . .

She had to make sure to admit as little as possible—

"I was not aware when we got married," she said finally, carefully.

"And when did it come about that you did?" the Inspector asked, his eyes still on his notes but with a certain alertness that she did not miss.

Traps here, horrible traps—he has discovered the reason for our separate lives and now he knows everything I told him before was a lie—

"I found him with someone," she said deliberately, and that bald statement made him look up at her.

"That must have been painful, Lady Tisne."

She did not answer.

"Since—according to Madam Tisne—he married you to get an heir," he went on when it became obvious that some pain was not describable.

She felt a hot sweeping flush suffuse her cheekbones. "I believe he married me because Madam wished to have an heir and because she refused to believe the true nature of her son."

"I see."

Damn—that sounded vindictive—but then, madam mother had been vicious in her own right. Still, the burden was on the victim, who, knowing the truth, would have done anything to retain her wifely rights—and eliminate the cause of her humiliation . . . ?

Dear heaven . . .

"The marriage was arranged?"

"Yes." *He had all the facts—how could she lie?*

"By your lady mother and Lord Tisne?"

"I believe that is so."

"Why do you think he did not choose among the eligible ladies of his rank?"

Another question designed to lead her straight into the morass of her possible motive.

She did not see how she could avoid sinking into the quicksand.

"I don't know, Inspector. But it would seem that it was easier for him to take a grateful unknown, an innocent, and lift her above her station, than to marry a woman of his own class who would make demands and who would know exactly what he was about. All he had to do for me was give me everything and go on living his life as he had before. If a child resulted, so much the better. Meantime, his mother was satisfied—to an extent—and my mother was provided for, which was of paramount importance to me."

"I see."

Oh God, she hated those words—she hated *them; he saw nothing except that which was necessary to convict—and that she was handing him on a silver salver.*

"What do you see, Inspector?" she demanded, at the end of her patience, and scared by the tightening framework of motive he was constructing before her very eyes.

He took a long time to answer, and again she had the frightening feeling it was deliberate—to make her squirm, to make her think that the thing was hopeless and she might just as well confess.

"This is what I see, my lady. An innocent child sacrificed to her mother's greed and her husband's selfishness. It must have been a shock when you found out the truth. But you could have felt betrayed as well, and perhaps resentful of the fact that this marriage would not be productive, and in fact, that you would always be alone. Perhaps you wished to remedy this."

"I did, Inspector. I made him give me an allowance, promise to live apart, and I decided to take a lover. It was the best of both words—we each got what we wanted, and there was still access to Arthur's generosity should I ever become in need."

"Yes," Stiles murmured, "there is that."

"I knew his largesse could not continue in the event of his death, Inspector—I knew exactly how he had provided for me."

"I find that strange."

"I never thought he would die. It seemed more than adequate at the time."

Once again, the one little trickle of a doubt—how far should she press it? Could he construe it as a crime of passion or a crime for great gain? In either case, there was no passion, and if she had to, she would produce their agreement to prove that she had known all along she had nothing to gain.

"He had many, many particular friends, Inspector."

"I am aware of that. But none of them had anything to gain either." He consulted his notes again. "And it could be said that your legacy and certainty of that income and a house in your name—when added to the humiliation of your knowledge of your husband's true nature—were enough to compel you to take his life."

NO!

She sat still as a stone.

He waited.

"It could be said," she agreed finally, futilely. "Will it be said, Inspector?"

"It is but one of many pieces of the puzzle, Lady Tisne. Here is another of which you may not be aware: one of Lord Tisne's more profitable enterprises is the so-called *House of Correction.*"

She recoiled as if he had struck her.

. . . but of course—of course . . . someone had to be raking in all that money from all those exorbitant fees—why not Arthur, creating a place for himself where all his vices could be served up on a single plate . . .

"I'm sorry, Inspector, I didn't know . . ."

"Just another thread, Lady Tisne. I believe your income is paid from its enormous revenue. And your mother's."

She could not find a single word to say. It was just, appallingly just, given what she had discovered about herself. She might just as well close down this house and go to work *there*—it would be that much more honest.

And it must have tickled Arthur to death to have his whorehouse pay for his virgin . . .

"Is there anything else, Inspector?" she asked faintly.

"My apologies, Lady Tisne. I can see you are shocked. Nothing else today. Please don't leave town."

And again, with that cautionary and unnecessary warning, he left her.

She sat very still for a very long time.

The House of Correction—the worst of the lot, her mother

*had said; she didn't ever want to go there, her mother had said;
they played rough, violent—the girls serviced the prisoners; prisoners were available to the customers, and the girls disciplined
the customers . . . yes, that was what her mother had said . . .
and the customers paid dear for the privilege of watching or
participating in any or all of the events . . .*

*. . . had she been destined to be exiled there after Arthur had
tired of her reticent virginal ways . . . ?*

She knew too much about the House of Correction *just from
that one conversation with her mother . . .*

And who else knew about it?

. . . what about the man who paid her monthly allowance—?

*Oh my God—the lawyer—the Morfit who so benignly faced
her mother-in-law down even when he knew just what ill-gotten
gains were supporting her lifestyle—*

*He must have known everything about her husband—just
everything . . .*

*Well, here was something she could do—she could confront
the pedantic little mole and find out some answers. Who would
know better than the man who had handled Arthur's affairs? And
possibly* all *of them . . .*

"My dear Lady Tisne—"

He looked upset; he had to be upset.

She had burst into his office not an hour after she had had the
thought and demanded to know how much more humiliation she
was going to suffer through the auspices of diligent police work.

"You can have no idea, Mr. Morfit. This very unassuming
Inspector Stiles just laid it on my tea table like a precious piece
of porcelain—and it exploded in my face. I was mortified, totally
ill-prepared, and hardly in any position to defend Arthur or myself.
And I will not have it!"

"Sit down, Lady Tisne."

"I will *not*," she spat. "It is not enough that the tabloids are
ringing a peal over me already; it is not enough that every one of
Arthur's friends have shunned me; it is not enough that this *hound*
of a police inspector keeps intimidating me—now I must find out
that Arthur had an underground life of which I knew nothing
and that it is possible that more may come to light on the subject.

"Well, Mr. Morfit, I *will* be prepared this time. Now—*you* may tell me the whole."

She thought that sounded most excellent—imperious, but not bullying, demanding, but with sound reasoning for her position.

Mr. Morfit wiped his glasses. "Please sit down, Lady Tisne. I cannot talk to a whirlwind."

"You may next be talking to an inmate of the *House of Correction*," she said tartly as she seated herself opposite him. "The case is building quite slowly and quite thoroughly. Now, Mr. Morfit—"

"How shall I say this then? Your husband, as do many men, had a variety of tastes, and he was in a position to indulge them."

Indulge them—oh yes, what an apt phrase . . . you take your bottomless appetite for sensuality and you indulge *it—I must remember that . . .*

He looked at her as if he had perfectly explained the whole and expected her now to thank him and leave.

"Yes, Mr. Morfit? This is about to become a well-documented fact. Tell me the rest."

His face fell.

"Tell me where else the money comes from, Mr. Morfit. How much of the profit of the *House of Correction* lined his coffers? Did he have partners? Did he set it up to *indulge* his desire for a variety of experiences? Explain this to me, Mr. Morfit, and then tell me whether there are any more surprises of this order that I should know about."

"Yes to your questions, Lady Tisne. My lord liked a variety of experiences, and the *House* started out as a piece of ironic humor—Lord Arthur was struck one day by the prison name and thought it would make a wonderful name for a house of discipline, which, as you must know by now, my lady, is yet another variety of sensual experience and one for which my lord had the occasional taste. And then he had the idea of combining the two—in this way serving many palates at once.

"It got rather out of hand. Very popular, tons of money pouring in—what could Lord Arthur do but continue the venue. It made perfect sense—and it kept the inmates in line too."

Her mouth went dry. "I see. What else? Had he partners?"

"He liked it there very well," Mr. Morfit said, deliberately misunderstanding her.

And perhaps to put her off the scent by shocking her . . . ?

"There was—there is—a great deal of variety to be had, and when Arthur went over the top—he was punished, as he expected."

"And in whose name is the place now?"

"It is run by the estate, and I am the executor. This is all outside the residual estate, a private and legal agreement between Lord Arthur and myself, specifically to serve the needs of yourself and your mother, Lady Tisne."

"Except—" she leapt on that, "it was said that he was about to stop her allowance."

"I beg your pardon, my lady, he was tired of the bills she kept sending. He felt it was a form of blackmail and it was easier to cut her off than to keep paying her demands."

. . . blackmail—blackmail . . . *why would he phrase it like that?*

"Go on, Mr. Morfit."

"Indeed, there were many drains on the estate over the years because of Lord Arthur's propensities, my lady. The *House*— once it was established—absorbed them all so that the principal remains intact and producing interest to this day."

"What kind of drains, Mr. Morfit?"

"The kind you can imagine, my lady. From people who wished to use my lord, or take him to court over some imagined peccadillo."

"Such as?"

"My dear Lady Tisne, it must be clear to you that there are many outlets a man with the sophisticated tastes of your husband might choose to explore."

"Such as?" she pressed relentlessly as she saw his reluctance to answer her.

She waited him out as he sifted through all the legalities of telling her what she wanted to know, and then he threw up his hands and sighed.

"Such as—such as? What have we been talking about? His predilection for male lovers, flagellation, the orgies, his penchant for voyeurism and children . . . do you think flaunting the norms of society comes cheap—?"

"I see." *Children too—but then there were men who went*

into transports over young innocent girls . . . she should have
expected this—it just showed how truly innocent she was . . .
    He must have had to expend enormous sums to conceal his
secrets . . .
    "So the *House* paid for all his aberrations—and supplied him
with all the entertainment he could possibly want," she summa-
rized acidly.
    "You could put it that way, my lady," Mr. Morfit said stiffly.
    "Except it could be inferred that he always wanted much,
much more . . ."
    "That is your take, my lady."
    "He supported a woman named Davidella Eversham."
    "I beg your pardon?"
    "I said, it is known that he cohabited periodically with a
woman named Eversham."
    "Known—*known?*—known by whom, Lady Tisne? Certainly
not by me . . ."
    "And not yet by the police, Mr. Morfit, so if there is something
here that I must be aware of, I beg you to tell me now."
    "There is nothing I can tell you, Lady Tisne—but then Arthur
was ever a man of secrets when he wished to be—as you have
cause to know. I have been candid with you, my lady. I will also
tell you that the *House of Correction* will not be dismantled. I
will go on using its profit to support you by the terms of Lord
Arthur's will.
    "What *you* will do is up to you. Perhaps you will find that
you have a taste for the voluptuous, Lady Tisne . . ."
    She froze. *Why was he saying that in such a* knowing *way . . . ?*
    "You might find that the *House of Correction* is more to your
matured tastes too. Perhaps it is not such a bad thing . . ."
    "You may be sure that I will pay a visit, Mr. Morfit. I want
to know exactly what the Yard knows about how my husband
did business."
    "And who knows—," Mr. Morfit said insinuatingly as he
escorted her to the door, "my lady may even find those very
business practices exactly to her liking."

    She returned to Green Street in a fury, unnerved by Morfit's
candor and his smug assumptions.

"My lady." Tolliver as she entered the house. "The gentleman Roak awaits."

Well of course—when he is least expected and never when he is most needed . . .

She rounded on him the instant she entered the parlor.

"This has been a morning to surpass anything since Arthur died. And where were you while Inspector Stiles was informing me that my husband owned and ran a house of discipline and prostitution and used the profits to support myself and my mother—and all of his significant vices? I suppose you knew about that too?"

He was standing by the elaborate fireplace, a black eagle ready to swoop and pounce.

"Of course—I know everything Stiles knows," he said coolly.

She moved closer to him, almost as if she were challenging him. "Then why don't I know these things, Mr. Roak? Am I not paying you to keep me informed so that I am not scared out of my wits every time Stiles comes through that door and informs me that, in spite of appearances to the contrary, I am the only one with a reasonable motive and foolproof means to have committed that murder?

"He is very good at that," Roak said, "like a dog with a bone; he gnaws away at his suspect even while he is appearing to pursue other leads. So it must be clear to you now why it is crucial you do what I tell you."

"Excuse me? *Do* what *you* tell *me?*"

"Exactly—you stay put, Lady Tisne, and you do not go wandering around these hellholes of filthy hedonism in pursuit of sexual thrills."

"I don't know what you're talking about."

"Newbury Arcade," he said succinctly and brutally.

She lifted her chin. "I enjoyed it enormously."

"I daresay you did," he murmured, his eyes sweeping insolently down her body.

She was properly dressed today in black bombazine relieved only by the collar and cuffs banded in rich velvet, and still—still she felt the heat of his knowledge of her in that one telling look.

She wanted to shake his complacency. "I plan to visit the *House of Correction* tonight."

She thought she saw him recoil. "Do you?" he said noncommittally. "Of course you've been told that it is no place for a lady, so I will not try to discourage you."

She smiled, a nasty little smile. Roak was learning.

"Exactly. It is incumbent on me to be aware of whose pound of flesh supports my hearth and home. I went to see the lawyer, you know."

It took him a moment to follow the transition. And then, "Bloody hell."

"But of course you also know everything he told me."

"I can guess," he said darkly. "And you ought to be kept under lock and key, Lady Tisne. The more you go poking around, the harder you will make things."

"Yes, it does all seem to have something to do with sex, doesn't it?"

Now he looked irritated. "The real problem, Lady Tisne, is that you have discovered sex."

He had gone too far. She whirled away from him. "I have yet to see results for my money, Mr. Roak."

"I believe you have had some satisfaction, Lady Tisne."

"I think you are a fraud. What have you brought me but that which I had already found out either by myself or from Inspector Stiles?"

"You have not been hauled off to prison."

"Oh, and is that your doing, Mr. Roak?"

"Let us say it is in part because of my generosity in sharing with the good Inspector."

She stared at him. "That is a likely story—and perhaps nothing more."

He shrugged. "It is your money, Lady Tisne. It is your life."

So he was ready to just let it go—what manner of man was this that he could take her up and drop her down in the whim of a moment—hers or his?

I will be your lover . . .

What was she really seeing in the glitter of those jet eyes— whose bluff? Hers—or his?

"And so you impart this information to the Inspector—and not to me."

Did she sense a release of the tension in him?

"I am here for that very purpose, Lady Tisne. Inspector Stiles was injudicious to approach you so soon."

"Does he know everything?"

"Not everything."

She turned away. "I asked Morfit about the Eversham woman," she said, expecting him to ring a peal over her for heedlessly revealing that little tidbit.

"What did he say?"

"I am still trying to figure it out. He disclaimed knowledge of any such thing, yet—as the man who wrote the checks, surely he would have known . . ."

"Not necessarily. Your husband could have dealt in cash or scrip, or barter for that matter. Anything is possible."

"Perhaps she works at the *House of Correction*."

"I wouldn't think so."

"Or he had taken her there as well as *Newbury Arcade* . . ."

"My lady *has* been busy," Roak murmured.

"Which of course you knew."

"Did you doubt it?"

She wheeled on him. "That is the most self-serving claptrap. I don't know how you convince your clients you are so omnipotent, but I have seen no evidence of it at all."

He lifted his eyebrows and she stamped her foot.

"I am going to the *House of Correction* tonight to search for clues, Mr. Roak, since you seem to be so unwilling."

"While you are so very willing, as everyone is coming to very well know."

"*Everyone,* Mr. Roak?"

He held her eyes. "Everyone, Lady Tisne."

She broke away first. "Then there will be no scandal."

"The scandal will be how you keep yourself out of prison with this irresponsible behavior. Or do you not remember the evening at *Dominoes?*"

"Oh, am I expected to participate?"

"You will have no choice, my lady; entering the *House of Correction* is tantamount to agreeing to play their games. And they devour firm young flesh and they love to corrupt innocence. It was your husband's creation, after all."

Arthur's vision—to serve which of his prurient needs?

She thrust the thought aside.

"There is no way to . . . sample the menu?"

"A little knowledge is a dangerous thing, Lady Tisne . . . there are ways to do anything you want."

"I want," she whispered.

"I know," he said and there wasn't an inch of give in his expression.

She thought she would drown in those fathomless eyes. They saw everything; she could get away with nothing.

"Then I *will*—"

"I didn't doubt it."

"Roak . . ."

"I am not your keeper," he said callously.

She bit her lip, wanting desperately to remind him what he said he might like to be; but she would never say those words.

"Come with me then."

"There is nothing to be discovered there."

"I must see that for myself now."

"It is as I said—you are hungry for sensation and that is all you will find there—and most of it not to your liking."

"How much you know, Roak. From firsthand experience?"

Again she had the sensation—from his very stillness—that he was so vexed with her that he wanted to constrain her somehow.

"I pay your fee, Roak. I want you to go with me."

I need you to go with me.

Their eyes clashed—and she couldn't at all tell now what he was thinking. But she felt his cold displeasure that she would use that underhanded tactic to coerce him.

He didn't say a word as he walked past her and out the door.

But in the end, she knew it was the same—whether she paid the gatekeeper or she paid him—eventually she would get what she wanted.

Chapter 10

The *House of Correction* loomed over the Embankment like an isolated castle—all crenelated towers and forbidding gray stone with shadowy window slits that looked out at the night like cynical eyes.

It stood on the Argyle Embankment, close to the bridge and adjoining the prison, and in the still matte blackness, one could envision it as a tower of terror, behind whose doors the most unspeakable acts took place.

She watched from the narrow cab window as carriage after carriage drew up to its dimly lighted entrance and disgorged a patron who then disappeared behind the massive oak door as quickly as possible.

Gluttons—all of them ... how well Arthur had divined the nature of his patrons. They came in droves; she had been there for an hour and she had already stopped counting.

... Hungry for sensation ...

... she was no different than they, only her own appetites were pitifully pedestrian in comparison to these ...

How Arthur would laugh to see her sniffing around his piece de resistance like a dog in heat.

And how he would feed on her fear ...

... she had to know the worst—and everything else be damned ... this had to be the worst—all those men slinking their way into a bordello that catered to humiliating its patrons.

What kind of man could take pleasure in that?

... what kind of woman—?

She put her hand on the door lever. "Driver—"

"Mum?"

"I'm ready."

"You sure, mum?"

"She is sure, driver."

She recognized his voice, even though she could not see him.

"Damn it, Roak . . ."

A moment later, he appeared at the cab door and opened it for her with a mocking bow.

"It struck me that you are *my* keeper every bit as much as any of the women who frequent these houses, my lady. And I strive to give good service."

She stepped out of the cab disdainfully.

. . . *Good service . . . !* "Go to hell, Roak."

"Brace yourself—we are about to . . ."

It took a minute to cross the deserted road and just another to become lost in the shadows of the building.

"You know too much about this place," she hissed as he reached up to a ledge and removed a wooden mallet.

"Everyone knows about this place." He swung it against a brass plate embedded in the wall and then replaced it on the ledge.

A sonorous gong sounded and the door creaked open.

"My lady—"

She hung back a moment; already the scent of illicit sex infused the air . . . musky, carnal—the perfume of the forbidden.

They entered the antechamber, a great stone-vaulted room with barred windows twenty-five feet above them and fiery torches glittering in sconces high overhead.

Shadows danced over them, copulating on the walls.

Around the room there were wooden doors; there was no furniture, no carpeting, nothing to relieve the starkness or dissipate the sense that something furtive was going on here.

Another door opened and a giant appeared.

"This is Hamat. He is a eunuch who was brought from one of the great harems in Turkey to serve Lord Arthur in this place. Hamat, this is my lord's widow who has come to see what her husband has wrought."

Hamat bowed and turned back into the door from which he came.

"We follow him."

"I don't like this."

"You *wanted* this."

She bit back a response and preceded him into the door which led down a long corridor that looked like the entrance to a dungeon up to and including the spiked gate where Hamat paused and waited for instructions from Roak.

"I can take my lady from here," Roak said, and handed Hamat an envelope.

Hamat gave him a key in return, bowed, and withdrew, and Roak waited until he had disappeared before he went on. "Lord Arthur was a canny man. He did not want the uninitiated to just walk head-on into the *House* and all its variety of experiences. He arranged what one could call a show to exhibit selected events to sell his wares to those who might be hesitant that their needs could be met here."

"You know a great deal about this, it seems," she said acidly.

"My job is to know a great deal about everything, Lady Tisne. In the Great Room, into which we will pass, the ladies and gentlemen who are available for the evening will be waiting for patrons. Since it is so late, a number of them will have been spoken for already. Are you ready?"

"Are you?" she hissed.

He unlocked the gate and they passed through a short corridor this time and into the bright light of the Great Room.

Here it was as opulent as the bedroom of a king. A rich carpet covered the stone floor and the lighting was intense so that the patron could clearly see what he was getting.

There were pillows and thick plush sofas everywhere. There was music, and there were servants with trays offering drinks and tidbits to both the hirelings and the clientele who were lolling in the chairs and on the cushions viewing everything available as intimately as possible.

There were women dressed in leather corsets and nothing else wielding whips and leading away men with thrall collars and chains.

There was a woman dressed in virginal white, from her neck to her toes, being fought over by three men, each of whom wanted to be the one to "educate" her.

There was a naked man, his private part bulging and held in a leather harness, being led off by the one with whom he had consented to spend the night.

There were women already engaged in pleasuring their patrons in the dark corners of the room. There was another fully dressed, except that her nipples were exposed through cut-outs in her bodice, disdainfully dismissing several men who were pleading for her favors.

There was a woman dressed in religious garb walking through the crowd brandishing a switch followed by several men bargaining for her services.

A woman in underwear and stockings lay reclining on a sofa while two patrons fought over her shoes.

In another corner of the room, a naked woman in chains was being auctioned off to a crowd of excited patrons. A moment later, the successful bidder led her away and another woman in chains took her place.

There were men everywhere, looking, touching, begging, bargaining, and ultimately going off through one of the archways at the far end of the room.

"This is the exhibit," Roak said dispassionately. "And now it is time for the show."

He took her elbow and forcibly propelled her through the furthest arch and into yet another corridor which led to still another staircase.

More steps and a labyrinth of corridors, their footsteps accompanied by the sounds of whips, chains, moans, and shrieks.

And then they were in a long hallway with lights far above them and motion overhead.

She felt his hand on her arm pushing her forward, and she felt herself resisting—she did not want to go. She didn't want to know . . . it was too much, suddenly—

"You *wanted* this . . ." Roak's voice, low and gravelly beside her.

But she didn't understand—the sounds of mortification, the commotion—she looked up and she gasped.

"What is this? Where are we?"

"This is the crystal corridor, Lady Tisne, where everything can be viewed and nothing is forbidden."

"*Oh my God—*"

She suppressed a cry. Above her, through the transparent ceiling, she could see everything perfectly: every patron, subjected to pain and humiliation—the dominatrix chastising her class of naked patrons who were chained, writhing, to the wall; the virgin, her dress in tatters all around her, bent over a caning bench, with her teachers above her, punishing her innocence; the nun applying her switch to a class of naughty boys; a chain gang of prisoners in line to service one unwilling prostitute who was being held down by the man who had bought the privilege of being her procurer; men in thrall, on their knees at the feet of their mistress, awaiting her next command as she snapped her whip across each of their backs; a naked man scourging himself while his mistress watched—cubicle after cubicle of mortification and humiliation, screams and cries and begs for mercy; of coy little games that ended in calculated cruelty, and viewed from below, where every detail, every naked flaw, was visible.

She felt sick.

"We have barely begun."

"I have seen enough."

"You *wanted*—" he reminded her cruelly.

All these ones begging for pain, seeking it, embracing it as they spew their seed to legitimize it—depraved, the lot of them, and Arthur had been the worst . . . he had created this hallway so he could be the ultimate voyeur . . .

"It is worse than I imagined."

"This is nothing like you could have imagined. We have yet to pass into the prison area."

"I don't want to see it."

She blanched as above her a body fell to the floor moaning, begging his mistress for mercy, as her pitiless whip and spike-heeled boots thrashed and kicked him.

She could see the whole, from the naked man flat on his face to his engorged erection, to every detail of the mistress's naked body as she straddled him and delivered her remorseless punishment.

She could hear her nasty vitriolic words—

"Well, you limp weed, you piece of vermin—is it up yet? Is it juicy and ready for its mistress? Can you get it up, you mizzy little ant, or do I have to whip you into oblivion to get my ride . . ."

"Anything, mistress . . . anything—"

She rolled him over with a booted foot. "It's not big enough, you piece of shit. Make it bigger—" *Whap!*

"That's right . . ." She spread her legs over him as she thoroughly flogged his flanks. "Now he comes to his lover—" *Whap!* As she lowered herself slowly over the man's elongating member. "Almost there—" *Whap!*

Wriggling over his erection like a dancer. "The little worm stretches to find its home—"

Whap! "It's not good enough, you stinking dunghole—it's not big enough for your mistress, you pissing dog . . . get away from me, get away from me—"

She descended on him in a frenzy of lashes, every one of which could be heard up and down the corridor.

"Get me out of here."

They could not get away soon enough to suit her. They emerged from the arched doorway into the Great Room to find a new wave of patrons examining the merchandise.

And someone whom she recognized, on a couch with one of the naked women curled around him, offering him her breasts.

"Tony . . ."

He looked up from the lush breasts he was nuzzling.

"Well, well—Lady Tisne—who would have thought . . ." he murmured without moving an inch away from his writhing, demanding mistress who was looking at her with resentful eyes.

"Excuse me—" He nosed the thrusting nipple just by his lips and then covered the breast with his mouth and began sucking as if she were not there.

She turned away, horrified by his presence here and what it meant, and incensed by his cavalier treatment of her.

She could not get out of the building fast enough. Even the fresh air seemed permeated with the fetid stench of debauchery.

And that wasn't even the whole, to judge by Roak's dark expression as he signaled to his driver and his carriage came from somewhere in the shadows.

There were still the prisoners who were fair game, he told her, for both the men and women, and who were willing to agree to anything for the money which would pay their freight out once sentence was determined.

"All of that," she murmured disbelievingly, when they were

on their way to Green Street and she finally felt safe, "and he had two women besides. Any one of them could have killed him. Anyone dissatisfied with his treatment in that place; anyone whose mistress get carried away; any felon who was ill-used by any of the clientele—how can they *do* that—*how?*"

"It is their sport and their pleasure; they have nothing to do with their time but dream up ways to take sensation to its utmost limit," Roak said. "Even you, Lady Genelle—you found dissatisfaction in the way things were and went in search of new sensations."

"Nonsense . . ."

It wasn't the same anyway.

I will be your lover . . .

She shook her head to clear it of the impression of the last man as he had rolled over the floor begging for mercy and kissing his mistress's feet.

Could she ever forget what she had seen and heard this night?

She thought it would stay with her forever, and no matter what the resolution of Arthur's murder, by virtue of her marriage to him, she would be marked for life by his vices.

And of course—Tony Lethbridge—she would never forget the sight of him crawling over that naked woman to get at her breasts as if he were a nursing baby—

Maybe he was—maybe that was all he had ever been . . .

She hated the thought. This man was to have been her one great lover, chosen with discernment and pride during the year after she and Arthur had separated—and yet he was no better than the lot of them, chasing after a thrill and a cheap woman who would give it to him.

What else had he been chasing in the House of Correction?

It didn't bear thinking that he too was among those seeking chastisement and sexual atonement with the mistress of his choice.

If she had known that, she would have kicked him in the groin the moment he abandoned her, she thought mordantly. She would have stamped on his thighs, his chest, his manly excesses . . .

Oh, what she could have done—

Except she didn't remember a moment of what she really had done. The memory of her night with Tony was as vaporous as a

*wisp of smoke—you could inhale his essence and enjoy him for
a while, but when you finished, all you wanted to do was crush
him out.*

Before he crushed you—

*And that had been her mistake—she hadn't crushed him out,
so it was no wonder she felt crushed at seeing him so lewdly
servicing some other woman . . . in that place—*

*Oh, that made it so much the worse—what else did a man
like Tony do in a place like that?*

Her imagination could not even conceive of it . . .

"Well, lady missy, so you got your fill of the *House of Correction*, did you?"

"Good morning, Mother. Indeed—and I heard my fill about
your exorbitant bills and attempts to blackmail Lord Arthur."

Her mother sat down heavily at the breakfast table. "A lot of
nonsense. You ask that old priss puss of a lawyer how many
blackmail checks he was paying out in the month—you'll see. A
dress and a bauble here and there—they wasn't nothing in the
scheme of things to keep *me* happy."

She dug into the jam and spread a liberal helping on some
toast.

*Yes—and hadn't Morfit said that? So which unhappy extortionist had met him in the dead of night and pushed a knife into
his black heart?*

*How had Arthur walked a fine line between those for whom
he had contempt and those with whom he shared his depravity?*

Was her mother one of them?

*And then there was Roak, moving with knowledge and ease
from one world to the other . . . it frightened her how much he
knew about Arthur's underground life.*

Roak . . .

I will be your lover . . .

It had been a dream.

The whole thing was a dream.

And she was beginning to think she had dreamt that too.

". . . speaking of which . . . hey, my girl—you haven't heard
a word I've said."

Her mother again—like an annoying insect buzzing around in

her head, looking for the exact right moment to get under her skin and sting.

"I'm sorry, Mother. What?"

"Begging your pardon, your highness, but ain't it time for your monthly allowance? We're running out of money."

"*We*, Mother? *We're* running out of money?" Trust her mother to find the weak spot—how *much* had she spent on entrance fees to the gamey houses?

"Listen, my lady queen—you got bills to pay, you got a staff to pay, you got my allowance to pay—and you got nothing to pay it with. So you have to go to the purse pincher and get some money, you hear? And maybe you've got to sit down and decide what's to do with some of these lazy servants who ain't earning their keep."

"Mother!"

"Trust me, girl. Exact same thing happened to me. Stupid servants—think they got a good thing going, don't think they have to work to get their weekly farthing. And then you—spilling all them pounds into the palms of those drabs who run the shows—stupid of you, girl. What did it get you? What did you learn you couldn't have figured out by just thinking about it? Money gone is what you got, and so you got to grovel to the old priss puss and get some more if it's short of your pay date. You hear? You hear?"

What had she got? An obscenely ungrateful mother; a dead husband, and seemingly a hundred people who might have wanted to kill him; a former lover who had a taste for perversion; a skilled investigator who knew everything and couldn't prove anything; a slow surefooted denizen of the Yard out to prove her culpability; and empty pockets from her own foray into promiscuity.

Twelve hundred and fifty pounds payable and due on the first of the month—a good week and a half away.

But then she had not been so extravagant before this whole business of Arthur's demise. There was money to pay the bills, there was money to pay Roak; there was money to pay for any damned thing she wanted, except for her mother's excesses and her mother didn't have to know that.

"I would not have to grovel, Mother. I can ask Mr. Morfit for an advance on next week's payment."

"Hmph—see if the old sourpuss will agree to that; you know he does everything by the letter of the law."

"Well no, I didn't know that . . ." She stopped suddenly, struck by the notion she didn't know very much about the man who controlled the payout of her husband's fortune.

But then—it wasn't her business, was it? It should be her lady mother-in-law's concern, shouldn't it?

But there was the whole business of the *House of Correction* and the unofficial payouts to those who had threatened to blackmail Arthur. And there was something else from that conversation that bothered her as she thought about it—but she couldn't quite grasp it, something about the arrangement . . .

All that money to anyone who had a claim against her husband. She wondered how much was real and how much was imagined. She wondered if any of the supplicants she had seen the night before would come forward to display their wounds and demand compensation.

How did the damned thing work anyway?

The letter of the law . . . a side agreement between him and her husband—that was the thing. He would run it, and use the money for her support as stipulated in the will—which had not defined where the money was to come from.

Which meant, presumably, that he could close the House and claim there was no more money.

Except that—since the will did not specify the source, she could sue to make sure the allowance was paid out of the estate— the one supported by his legitimate investments and businesses.

Oh my God—still another strike on the side of motive: she could have found out the whole and in a fit of hysteria made sure that Sir Arthur never plundered the lower depths again . . .

Once again she felt the terror, as if somehow Arthur had set this up purely to put her in this position.

The man had been diabolical.

What could be said of his lawyer?

"Mr. Morfit."

"Lady Tisne. I thought we had concluded our business yesterday."

"Well, yes," she murmured, sweeping into his tidy office, the atmosphere of which seemed somehow more menacing today. "But I have since been to the *House of Correction*. And there are some questions I would like to ask."

"I am at your service, my lady."

"May I sit?"

"Of course." Morfit sat himself down opposite her, looking at her over the rim of his glasses disapprovingly. "I had thought all that was settled when you left here yesterday."

"Well, no. It was a matter of your having answered the immediate questions that I had. But now I have had a opportunity to explore the *House*, I have some other concerns."

"Let me set your mind at rest, my lady. The *House* will not be closed down for any reason any time in the near future. All of that is built into the operating expenses. You have nothing to fear in terms of your allowance."

"I see," Genelle said, pretending to give it some thought. "But supposing—just supposing, something should happen and the *House* must close. What happens then?"

"What must, my lady; your allowance continues to be paid as stipulated in Arthur's will, from whatever source will bear the cost."

"Even if it subtracts from the principal in trust for my mother-in-law?"

"Yes."

"Does she know?"

"I believe she is under the impression that Arthur set aside a separate trust to pay your allowance and that it will not impinge on any amounts she is entitled to."

"Shall I have to sue the estate in the event the *House* is closed down, Mr. Morfit?"

He looked hurt. "My dear Lady Tisne, Lord Arthur's wishes are a sacred trust with me."

"What about all the other settlements—what happens to them if the gold mine runs out?"

Now he looked away, taking off his glasses and pretending to clean them. "Their compensation stops the day the *House* cannot operate, and the scandal falls where it may."

She had the feeling, watching him, that this would not be so. That he would lie, scrounge, forage, and protect her husband's legacy however he could rather than let the scandal of his sexual career become public.

But he was the lawyer, after all, and it had been his job to protect Arthur even before he died.

"I hope you are reassured, Lady Tisne," Morfit said, painstakingly slipping his glasses back on. "Is there anything else I can help you with?"

She stared at him for a long minute. "The *House* was beyond anything I could have imagined. And it cost dear too. I need an advance on next week's payment."

"I'll be happy to oblige—this once, Lady Tisne—and only if you heed this word of caution: being a voluptuary is addictive. Your allowance will not support such a lifestyle without your augmenting it somehow, or finding someone to keep you. I do not particularly care which alternative you choose—just bear in mind that your monthly sum can stretch only so far—and there aren't thousands of pounds a year available for you to indulge yourself with."

He handed her a check for a paltry fifty pounds. "Or perhaps you would wish to cut back—sell the house, find a less expensive place to live; get rid of some servants; rein in your mother . . . oh yes, I know about your mother," he added at her startled look. "You are only beginning your career of pleasure seeking, my dear. Plan it carefully so you don't wind up in the cribs or on the streets. Arthur would be positively mortified if that happened to you.

"Now—is there anything else?"

She closed her mouth and tried to get a hold of herself. "I think that is all for now. Thank you for the check—and the advice, Mr. Morfit. I'm sure it is well-meant."

"My dear, Arthur lifted your mother from the streets—he is not here to do that for you."

The door closed behind her.

. . . *from the streets* . . .

. . . *from the* streets . . . ?

Just where had her mother encountered Arthur that she got to know him well enough to offer him her innocent and unsuspecting daughter?

She felt positively constricted, as if her collar were choking her, and her hair weighed too much, and her dress were made of stone.

She needed someplace to sit and think.

But as she slowly descended the stairs, she heard the slam of a door above her.

. . . surely not Morfit . . . someone going to lunch, perhaps—
But what if it was Morfit? Where would he be on his way to this hour of the day?

. . . the House—
Oh heaven—why had she never thought that he too could be a patron of the House of Correction?

She ducked around a corner on the floor below and waited to see who would come down the steps.

Morfit! What luck!

What a stick he is! He's probably on his way to the bank to revel in all that lovely money over which he has control . . .

When he was out of sight, she darted out from her hiding place and ran lightly down the stairs and out the door of his office building—just in time to see him turn the corner.

She made the decision on the instant: she would follow him for no other reason than she resented his annoying condescension.

. . . a man like that at the House—I am delusional. He's probably on his way to have tea with my mother-in-law. That would make some sense . . .

She took a walking stance about a block behind him as he navigated his way from Park Lane over to Regent Street.

He never looked back; he was walking very determinedly until he paused in front of the Cafe Royale which was just opening for business.

A glance at his watch; a impatient tap of the foot, a casual survey of the street, which sent her scurrying into the entrance of a nearby building.

And then a voice greeting him—

"Morfit! Have you been waiting long?"

—a voice she recognized all too well: Tony Lethbridge.

Chapter 11

Of course he would know Tony—who didn't know Tony?
But to lunch with Tony . . . ?

She mulled over this turn of events as she deposited Morfit's check, retrieved some cash, and went back to Green Street.

"Well—did the old swine give you some money?"

Her mother, first out with the questions of paramount importance.

"Yes he did, Mother."

"How much for me?"

Ever the pragmatist, her mother.

"There is enough to keep us going for this week—which means, enough to pay bills and take care of the incidentals. I don't believe my bequest included how much for you."

"Ungrateful bitch."

"So are you," she shot back.

"Wouldn't've had nothing if it wasn't for me—I planned the whole thing, put the whole thing in his head, pushed him and pulled him until he saw what a good idea it was—and do you show me any appreciation? Oh no, you're just like him, you know. All you care about is yourself, and you couldn't give a blue goat for what your mum did for you—you ungrateful brat. You'd be in a brothel now, if it weren't for me."

She stared at her mother. "Just like you, you mean."

Her mother slapped her. "How do you keep soul and mouth together, missy, if you don't have no money? Thanks to me, you don't have to think about those things. But are you grateful? Oh no—you want to swat me away, just like he did. Yes, just like he did. But I made sure, daughter—I made sure he understood he wasn't getting away with it . . ."

She felt like she had turned to stone. "Did you work the *House of Correction*, Mother?"

Her mother's eyes hardened. "I was the matron, and damned good at it I was too. They ain't had a one in there since who could compare to me. I'd go back in the flick of a whip if that old priss puss would have me. But he ain't clinging to the old ways—he made that very clear . . ."

She swallowed. "*You* saw Morfit?"

"I'd get cobwebbed waiting for you, pissy missy. Sure I went and seen him. But it ain't the same; he ain't my lord, and he lacks the finesse. All he wants to do is count the money.

"Well, let 'im. Was me and my lord made something of that place. Me and my lord decided to give himself a respectable air by getting himself married to someone the likes of you. Who thought you'd meddle? Who thought you'd get some backbone, you mewling little piece of garbage?

"And now you can't even find a fiver for your mum now and again. Ain't you the hoity-toity one. Bet you found out last night— you can be dragged down into the mud same as anyone else.

"Same as your mum . . ."

They stood staring at each other for a long hard time.

Now the truth, now the whole of it. She had been a pawn and her mother the master manipulator. So of course she deserved some recompense for her stellar performance.

"All right, Mother. Take this—" she threw a bill into the air and she walked out the door as her mother was scrambling to pick it up off of the floor.

Now it was time for Roak to answer some questions.

She had done it all herself so far—made connections, found out the unpalatable truth . . . everything her *skilled investigator*— whom she should not forget was referred by Tony Lethbridge— was supposed to have done.

And none of it altered the one basic fact: she had been in the house alone when Arthur had been murdered.

And everything else she had discovered was beside the point. *Maybe . . .*

But she had hired Roak to find the maybe that would exonerate

her and what had he done so far but give her a tour of the lewd
underworld with which he seemed too intimately acquainted.

But she wasn't going to think about that—

She took her carriage this time and ordered the driver to let
her off right at the front door.

It was open, as it always was, with his dragon of a landlady
keeping an eye on all visitors from her first-floor flat, whose door
was always ajar.

He met her at the top of the steps.

"Has something happened?"

"Perhaps you can tell me, all-knowing Roak."

He studied her face for a moment before he motioned her into
his apartment.

"Sit down."

His tone didn't brook an argument. She sat.

"What happened?"

"You tell me. In fact, I'd appreciate it if you'd tell me *some-*
thing, Roak."

He braced his body against the edge of the desk and folded
his arms across his chest. "What do you want to know?"

"Who killed my husband."

"I don't play games, Lady Tisne."

"In three weeks, you have overturned nothing that can help
my case, Roak."

"And you've discovered something that has upset you."

She made a mutinous face. "And I'm certain you will say you
already knew it."

"Probably." His jet eyes bored into her. "You found out your
mother was involved with the *House of Correction*."

"Damn you, Roak."

"It was a natural conclusion, Lady Tisne."

She felt like a fool. She felt worse.

I will be your lover—

Why could she not get that out of her mind when she was
sitting across from a man who didn't care a thing about her except
how much she was going to pay him when he finally proved her
innocence?

"And of course you know that the lawyer is now running the

House, and that he had some kind of agreement with my husband, aside from the will, about what was to be done with the profits—"

"Yes, the money was to be used to pay off every claim of sexual perversion that existed against him. I take it you spoke with Morfit again."

"I was concerned about my allowance," she said defensively.

"And he made you every promise that he would carry out the provisions of the will."

"Yes. And then he went out to lunch with Tony Lethbridge."

He reacted—just a minuscule twitch of a muscle in his cheek, but he reacted.

Ah—he didn't know that. He didn't *know . . .*

"Did he? And how would you know that, Lady Tisne?"

"I followed him." She looked up at him innocently. "Isn't that how you do it, Roak?"

"I hope to hell not." He moved away from her abruptly, impatiently. "Foolish and amateurish, Lady Tisne, and you proved nothing."

"I proved that Mr. Morfit and Tony know each other."

"A conclusion that could be drawn by the very fact that Tony Lethbridge and his scurrilous reputation regularly schedule sessions at the *House*. Of course Morfit knows him."

"So what are you saying—that there's nothing to it?"

"There is something to everything, Lady Tisne. And there is still much to be discovered until we find your husband's killer. But that is my job, not yours. We are only at the beginning."

"And you expect me to sit still and wait until you choose to drop tidbits of information in my lap, while I live in fear that they are going to come and take me away to prison? Are you crazy, Roak?"

"No more than you."

"At least I'm doing *something*."

"My dear Lady Tisne—you are getting in the way."

"Then you'll just have to keep tripping over my body, Roak."

"Possibly your *dead* body . . ."

He waited a beat, two . . . three—

She looked horrified. "Roak . . ."

"Did you not think so? Someone has committed murder once,

Lady Tisne. What would he not do to someone who is getting closer to discovering his identity?"

"Like you?" she shot back.

"But that is my risk, my choice. And I am better equipped to deal with the probabilities."

"And I am paying you a exorbitant amount of money to do so."

"Yes, we always get back to that point, my lady. You have bought me, plain and simple."

His eyes bored into hers.

I will be your lover—

He was as negotiable as anyone for sale in any house of perversity—and she must not forget, he knew about them all.

. . . I can satisfy you—

She shook off those disquieting thoughts.

"What value have I gotten for my money, Roak?"

His mouth tightened, the only sign of his growing irritation with her.

"You have not been arrested for murder, Lady Tisne. I assume that is enough."

She felt as if he had slapped her, and she rose, unsteadily, to leave.

She heard his voice, but it was as if he were speaking from a very long distance.

"You would have been better off had you not found out the things you know."

She rounded on him, shaking with disappointment and fury. "But everyone knew—*everyone*—and my husband, a parliamentarian and as well known as the prime minister. How could he get away with those things? Why was it condoned? How could I *not* have known? And why didn't I know sooner? *I* have been humiliated by this affair in every way possible, Roak, not least by being accused of being this monster's murderer—and you tell me I should be content just because I'm not yet in jail.

"Thank you kindly, most wise and condescending Roak, but I am not in the least grateful—for any of it. And I am tired of being manipulated. And tired of being scared. And I'm tired—" She stamped her foot. "I am just plain tired and I will not be a puppet *ever* again."

Her tirade rolled right off of him. "Sit down, Lady Tisne."
She felt like swinging her reticule at him instead.

He hadn't moved a muscle or a inch from the edge of the table where he had propped himself, and as she sat down again, she felt oddly moved by the long lean inflexible line of his body.

. . . a body which had possessed hers in the heat of carnal indulgence—she remembered; at random unwanted times she remembered—

. . . like now—

. . . I will be your lover . . .

—you have bought me, plain and simple . . .

"This is what we know. Your husband was murdered three weeks ago in your townhouse where you had an assignation with Tony Lethbridge, who after having discovered the body, convinced you to keep his name out of the proceedings and left you to report the death and deal with the investigators. We know Lord Arthur was stabbed with a knife, one of a set that purportedly was in your kitchen. His attacker faced him, and this one small fact is troubling because in general it would have been easier for the murderer to have stabbed him from behind, particularly if it were a woman, since it seems probable that Lord Arthur could have overcome his attacker somehow face to face.

"We know that you claimed to have heard a noise and that Lethbridge went down to investigate; how long did you wait before you went after him, Lady Tisne?"

She blinked. "I—I don't know. A few minutes, I think—maybe more. I had to get dressed. I had to—"

I had to have thought that it had been a long time since Tony had gone downstairs, because I really didn't want to move. I wanted Tony to come back and . . . and . . . do everything he had done all over again—

She looked up at him, startled.

"Yes." The word was succinct, as if he had been following her very line of thought. "Tony was gone a long time—"

"He will say not. He will say he wasn't even there." She felt her hard-won control slipping.

And if he said that, and if she claimed he was there, *she* would sound like she was hysterical, and he would seem heroic for being so patient with her.

"And I can't even say how long he was downstairs before I went looking for him," she finished disgustedly.

"We know," Roak went on inexorably, "that the servants were given the night off so that no one else was in the house—to your knowledge—but you and Tony Lethbridge, and that Tony helped you concoct the story you told to Inspector Stiles before he left Green Street. We assume that he burned the incriminating blood-smeared clothing because it is the only sure way to dispose of them. And we know that afterwards he abandoned you totally, and his only attack of conscience was to suggest an investigator and to finally provide you with my name.

"We know that heretofore, you had discovered an aspect of your husband's nature which made it inconceivable that you could live with him as his wife or conceive his child which was *raison d'etre* of the marriage. We know that Lord Arthur was to support your mother, and indeed he did, and that by the terms of your subsequent agreement, he would support you in return for your discretion. You dictated terms that included life tenure in the house at Green Street and an allowance of fifteen thousand a year, which would also be written into his will so that these terms would stand should he predecease you.

"Did you have the agreement in writing?"

"Yes."

"Good. A seemly motive for murder where a young woman is involved with a wealthy older man is of course for her to acquire his estate. Here we know that you had dictated what you stood to inherit should he die, and it is not a critical enough amount to compel you to murder him since you were receiving it anyway.

"However, it might have been a critical enough amount to compel someone else—your own mother, whose allowance was about to cease because of her extravagant ways, and who did not know the terms of the agreement; or Lord Arthur's mother, who had wanted him to sire a legitimate heir, but who did not want him to marry the daughter of a procuress.

"We can assume that he was amenable to the suggestion that he marry you for several reasons: his mother was insistent he get an heir before he died, and he wanted the name to carry on, and his reputation for perversion was endangering his political career and he needed to tone things down and appear to be a respectable husband for a while.

"And lastly, he needed a young and innocent child, who would not question his subterranean life as long as she had everything money could buy, and so he could go on secretly as he always had.

"And as many others do. They all know each other, Lady Tisne, they all go to the same places and do the same things, and they all keep the unholy secret. And their wives look the other way or find amusement elsewhere.

"We know that Tony Lethbridge was in your house the night and time of the murder. We know that he is a regular patron of the houses of pleasure, in particular the *House of Correction,* which we now know was owned by Lord Arthur and in which your mother worked as a procuress. His excuse that he wanted to protect his reputation—and yours—that night seems a little ironic in this light.

"We know that your mother was spending money by the bagful and that Lord Arthur had refused to pay her bills and was about to withdraw her allowance. We know she now lives with you—and we assume her expectations were that you were to inherit the estate should Lord Arthur pass away. Not only that, but she knew to a farthing what kind of money the *House of Correction* took in on any given night. And she must have assumed all of that would come under your control—and therefore possibly hers.

"She was never impoverished, Lady Tisne. She made excellent money at the *House.* But it would not be inconceivable that she saw a way to get more—and even more . . . hundreds and thousands of pounds a month. The aristocracy pays for its perversions, my lady—but surely you've discovered that already.

"And then we can also assume that Madam Tisne has not been idle. Her son had married the daughter of a bawd, and she must have felt she should do something. Perhaps she eventually had to confront her son's true nature. Perhaps she committed a crime of passion—ridding the country of a debaucher and pervert who preyed on the innocent. Or perhaps she merely wanted to find some way to retain the Tisne estate for herself rather than let her son squander it on his dissolute lifestyle. Of course, she could not have known about Arthur's agreement with you nor that a fantastic amount of his income was derived from the *House.* What might she have done had she known?

"We know Mr. Morfit, the family lawyer, was privy to all of this and is now in control of *the House* by virtue of some kind of side agreement he had with Lord Tisne. We also know that your allowance among other things is paid out of the profits of *the House* and that he has assured you that if it is necessary to close it down, the estate will bear the expense. But there is nothing in writing to say he will follow through.

"We know that your husband had, in addition to all his other sexual activity, occasionally spent weekends and was seen in public with, a woman named Davidella Eversham, and with another named Cla-rissa Bone, neither of whom at this moment is traceable.

"This is what we know, Lady Tisne. And this is what we need to know—why was Lord Arthur in the house at Green Street that night?

"Who are the two women who cannot be found?

"What does Tony Lethbridge know about the moments prior to Lord Arthur's death?

"—Did it not occur to you he might have seen someone or heard something? Perhaps your husband's dying words?—

"How much did Lord Arthur's mother know of his business practices and his underground life?

"What is really in the agreement between Lord Arthur and Mr. Morfit as it relates to *the House of Correction*?

"What was the one thing your mother demanded of your husband that made him discontinue her allowance?

"Had your husband been involved in any private scandals which would have provided a compelling reason for murder?

"And this—which is farfetched, but not inconceivable—are there any among those your husband paid for their silence who might have wanted to kill him?

"And finally, the centerpiece of everything: *the House of Correction*: we have established that everyone involved is connected to it in some way, and that it earns enormous sums of money.

"Given that fact, *the House* in and of itself is also a prime motivation for someone to commit murder . . . most specifically, Mr. Morfit, who now controls it and its profits; and your mother, who more than likely had planned to gain control through your inheriting it.

"This is what we know, Lady Tisne, and the fact remains there is still a great deal more to be found out—"

He's amazing, utterly amazing how he has put everything together like that. And my mother ... dear God, my mother— if even a word of it is true ...

But I can't let him mesmerize me. I can't ...

She interrupted him briskly.

"This is all highly entertaining, Roak, and I can see you have spent a great deal of time *thinking*—but what have you *done?*"

His expression never changed; he still hadn't moved and his coal-black gaze raked over her as if she were an imbecile and unable to comprehend a word he had said.

"I have made the connections and asked the questions that have kept you out of prison, Lady Tisne. And now I will take you home and you will decide if you have gotten value for your money and whether you want me to continue."

Dismissed just like that.

His exasperation was unnerving, but he said not one word to try to convince her otherwise during the short journey back to Green Street.

Wordlessly, he took her keys and opened the door and she entered the house to a resounding silence.

She felt an instant sense of panic. There were no lights, there was no life anywhere, as if the servants had all disappeared and left nothing but the shell of the house.

She reached for the bellpull.

No one appeared.

She rang again. The bell sounded eerily in the distance.

"Roak ..."

"Let me look—"

He pushed his way past her and into the interior rooms and she immediately ran after him.

There was no one—not her mother, not a servant, not Tolliver. And their clothes were gone—every servant down to the 'tween maid; Cook, who seemed to have been in the midst of dinner preparations, had just dropped everything; and most particularly—her mother.

"So Roak—deduce the sense of this," she said tartly as they

stood in the middle of the morning room amidst the debris of her mother's mid-morning tea.

She watched him roam around the room, picking up a teaspoon here, a cup with tea dregs in it there.

"An act of vengeance, I should think," he said finally. "There are two cups—she had a visitor. Someone else was involved with her coercion of the servants. My guess is she has found someplace else to live and lured them away with promises of better money."

"She had no money," Genelle protested. "I gave her only fifty pounds before I came to you."

"You forget, Lady Tisne—she had all the money she earned at the *House of Correction* . . ."

"I know you said that; how do you know?"

"There are ways to ascertain such things. One of the things I *did*, Lady Tisne. There is a hundred thousand pounds sitting in a vault in the Bank of England in Madam Alcarr's name."

She felt faint. "A hundred . . . and she was begging *me* for money? I cannot believe this . . ." She sank into a chair. "She virtually *sold* me to Lord Arthur . . ."

"Why would she want to share?" Roak asked quietly. "You had been her burden for—eighteen years? She probably never told you who your father was; she probably doesn't know. More than likely she made you feel as if you owed it to her after all she did for you."

"Yes."

"And still feels that way . . . ?"

"Yes. For setting me up with Lord Arthur so I could make both of our fortunes . . . and furious with me that I didn't make sure I got everything in his will . . . and that I wasn't properly grateful for everything *she* had done."

"And then trying to extort more from your husband by saddling him with the bills for *things*—which wasn't like blackmailing him . . . really—"

He was prowling the room restlessly as he talked, picking things up, examining the tea table minutely, trying to ignore the wounded look in her eyes.

They were all monsters, he thought, and it was always the innocent who paid.

"Whoever was here," he went on, "convinced her it was worth

her while to drop everything, leave, and take the servants with her. And it was someone who could offer her a situation, I would guess, one she couldn't refuse. Perhaps back to the *House*—?"

"No—she said Morfit would never take her back."

"All right—then something new, something irresistible. Someone who has enough money to fund something like that and take her on as procuress."

Deeper and deeper; it was like being swallowed up in a quagmire, all sticky and sopped with ugly noxious things, and you could never get to a bath to wash it all off.

The stench of it might stay with her forever.

"*Who?*"

He didn't answer, and she thought as she watched him prowl the room that he knew—or at least he had some instant list of possibilities at hand—

. . . value for my money—

He theorizes from angles no one else would think of . . . if that were not valuable, what was?

"Why the servants?"

He tossed off the answer as if it were obvious. "So they could not tell you who was here."

"Roak . . ."

"You can't stay here alone."

I don't want to stay here alone—

"Oh, nonsense . . . I—"

He paid no attention to that. "You will do nothing. I will have new servants here by this evening who cannot be bribed or bought by any enemy of your husband's . . ."

"I will need a cook too."

He ignored that. "Secondly, you will not look for your mother . . ."

"You don't have to worry about that."

"I worry about everything, Lady Tisne. You are the variable in this equation. You are feeling scared and powerless, which is a dangerous combination. And now you have some unseen enemy who has stolen your servants and your mother away. No matter how you feel about your mother, it is a invasion of your home, and it was intended to vanquish you.

"Now—you must search and tell me whether your mother

took anything with her besides what was her own. I will return in no more than fifteen minutes. I will take the key, and you will let no one else in this door tonight. Do you understand?"

God, he was scaring her. "Yes."

She ran to the window as he was emerging from the house.

Fifteen minutes? Fifteen minutes—he was going to hire a full staff of servants in fifteen minutes?

He rounded the corner and disappeared.

A magician. A sorcerer. A mind reader . . .

. . . an illusionist—

—with only an audience of one who was perfectly willing to be deluded . . .

She was in her mother's bedroom when Roak reappeared as silently as any conjurer.

And he startled her.

"Have you found anything?"

She whirled, a piece of gaudy china in her hand, ready to throw it at an intruder's head.

And let out a relieved breath. "A lot of litter. Rouge pots. Discarded underclothes in her drawers. No papers. Nothing from my bedroom; nothing from the house—at least at first glance."

"Does she know where you have your accounts?"

"I don't know. She could."

"Where do you keep your papers?"

"There aren't many papers, Roak. My marriage lines. The agreement between Arthur and myself on the terms of our separation. The deed to the house. I keep them in my desk in the morning room in a locked drawer."

"I believe you should check if they are still there."

"We were just in that room—there was nothing amiss."

He turned and walked out the door and she hesitated a irritated moment before she followed. When she entered the room, he was already at the desk, pulling out drawers.

"The drawer was open," he said, moving aside to show her. "Forced open. Here is your marriage certificate; and here is the deed to the house."

"And—?"

"It is as I thought—the agreement between you and Lord Tisne is missing."

"But why?"

"Simple, my lady, and perhaps the object of the whole exercise—now no proof exists that you ever knew beforehand the provision for yourself in Lord Tisne's will."

The cook arrived within the hour, followed by a footman, two housemaids, a parlormaid, and a young woman who would serve as scullery maid and laundress.

"Four house servants should do, with Cook and Joseph Footman," Roak said impassively.

"I need a butler, Roak. One cannot do without a butler."

"I am perfectly aware of that, Lady Tisne. I am he."

"What?"

"You will not be alone in this house at night. These are my people, who are sworn to protect you, Lady Tisne. And I will be on guard at night, and when I cannot be here, Joseph Footman will be my replacement. When you go out, he will accompany you. You will never go anywhere without him."

"You are scaring me, Roak."

"It is never unwise to take precautions, Lady Tisne."

"You are going to *stay* here—*sleep* here?"

"Of course."

Of course—

. . . I will be your lover . . .

. . . I will be your bodyguard—

Nothing else ever happened; nothing else exists but the problem of the moment . . .

She didn't need that; she needed a flesh and blood man, with the sinew and strength to take her and make her his own . . .

Why was she thinking like this?

She was as wanton as any patron who frequented a house of perversion in search of that evanescent moment of release—

And now her mother was the abbess of some retreat—if Roak were to be believed—and wealthy beyond all bounds by dint of her licentious career . . .

And she was her mother's daughter, yearning . . . for what?

"In Tolliver's room?"

"I think so, my lady.

"Roak, this is ridiculous."

"Where would you have the butler sleep, my lady?"

With me . . .

She turned away, not wanting him to see what was reflected in her eyes. "Perhaps you're right. And where do you intend to take your meals?"

"Belowstairs, of course."

Surely he was baiting her. She turned again to face him. "You don't need to."

His jet eyes would not let her escape. "Perhaps not. That remains to be determined. But now that the servants have arrived and you will not be alone in the house, I have to leave you for several hours."

She felt an edgy panic. "To go where? To do what?"

"Lady Tisne . . ."

"Don't *Lady Tisne* me, Roak."

"My lady, I am fully aware of the time and money constraints," he said with an irony which was not lost on her, "and I am at your service. But even the butler is allowed an afternoon of freedom per week—in the *best* households."

Damn him, damn him, damn him—using her words against her, pretending that what had happened was meaningless, and otherwise using her to enhance his reputation.

Why, why was she relying upon him so much?

"Of course—you're right. You may have the afternoon," she said imperiously, playing the game.

I'll just follow you to see where you go . . .

"My lady." He bowed and withdrew from the room.

Where, where would a man like Roak be going on a day like today—and how can I get out of the house without arousing suspicion?

It was a half hour before he left; she watched, hiding behind the tapestry curtains of the morning room window which overlooked Green Street.

It took her only a moment to slip down the stairs and out the door—and then she found to her dismay, almost as if he had divined her intentions, he was gone.

Chapter 12

She dressed for dinner and she wondered why. She had no appetite; Roak had not returned, and she had spent the day wondering what she used to do when Arthur was alive.

But then, before that, she had not invaded the sacrosanct clubs of perversity.

Oh, there was something about the lure of them, that even when you were disgusted or shocked and thought you might never want to return again, you found yourself thinking of them as a last resort to defuse those explosive baser needs which were unaccountably aroused.

And by what? A man's declaration weeks before in the heat of a voluptuous moment, and the memory of his possession "in the line of duty" to save her from her own folly?

But then there was the other part—that visit to Newbury Arcade which had so enthralled her. And her insatiably carnal reaction to both the deliciously explicit scenes at the Arcade and that man at the Seven Pleasures who had not proved his worth other than by his size and his self-indulgence.

Still, she hadn't stopped wanting, and on a night like tonight, where threats and dangers seemed so far from reality, and she was alone with her thoughts and her traitorous memory, tonight she felt the wanting in an overwhelming way.

She picked at her cold layered salad and speared a piece of cold meat with the ferocity she would have loved to have slapped Roak's impassive face.

What was it about a cold empty house and that bone-deep feeling of loneliness that made one yearn for more earthy things?

But again, it was ever a man's world; if Roak were here, he could just pick up and take himself to *the Seven Pleasures* with no feelings of furtiveness or guilt, and spend the evening looking, touching, *embedding* himself in the scenario of his choice.

It was so unfair.

She obviously hadn't learned anything from her night at the *House of Correction*; rather, she wanted to deny that the carnival of perversity was a man's world and that women were only things to satisfy his rutting instincts.

No, she had learned she wanted more—and more—and there were even moments she would be perfectly willing to be an object just to affirm that lust driven satiety.

And knowing Roak would be living in her house did not make things any better.

... I can satisfy you ...

The words resonated in her dreams when she should have been scared out of her wits by the mysterious events swirling around her.

When she should have been curled up in her bed, thankful for the fact that Roak was dealing with the problem and there were people she could trust taking care of her so that no one else could sneak in and steal her papers or her servants.

When she should have been leaving everything in the hands of her *skilled investigator.*

Instead she felt resentful of the limitations Roak had placed on her and annoyed at the fact that he could go out and about and do whatever *he* wanted.

And what could he—any man—be doing at this hour of the night?

What would *she* like to be doing at this hour of the night?

Oh, she knew—she knew ...

... but did she dare ... ?

After all that had happened, after all of Roak's warnings and piecing together of the events so far pertaining to Arthur's death; after this unconscionable invasion of her home by her enemy— did she dare ... ?

Or would she be content just sleeping two floors above the butler's room knowing he was there ... ?

Did she dare?

... did she dare reach with both hands for the same voluptuous gratification as a man ...

... did she dare indulge her senses, and her craving, in the same free and unfettered way and damn the consequences ... ?
... did she dare ... ?
Her mind was suddenly suffused with images of the coy poses of that naked man from the Seven Pleasures, and the final forceful mating of the couple in the tableau at the Arcade ...
She wanted to see it again ... she would dare anything to experience it again ...

She pushed away her salad and rang for the parlormaid. "That will be all for tonight."

"No—fish, mum? Or dessert?"

"No—" *Dessert will be later.* "Clear the table, please."

"Mum."

And now the question of bypassing Joseph Footman. That would not be easy once he was maintaining Tolliver's position by the servants' door.

Nevertheless, her excitement was overcoming all caution.

It was time to change—to divest herself of mourning, and put on the bright gaudy colors of a lady intent on pleasure.

Tonight she would look ... tomorrow she would pay ...

She wore a blue satin gown with a yoke of illusion net which was fitted into panels in the gored skirt, and trimmed with an edging of deeper blue velvet. Under it, she wore a black silk corset and over that, a one-piece undergarment that was corset cover and petticoat both, with narrow black ribbon straps and lace inserts.

Her hands were shaking again as she picked up the dark cloak that would disguise her evening gown and swirled it around her shoulders.

The forbidden is so enticing; no wonder Adam took the apple. No wonder Eve must always seek her Eden—isn't that what I do tonight?

She sent for the scullery maid. "Tell Joseph Footman I would like to see him."

"Very good, mum."

After that, it was easy—she slipped downstairs once again and hid behind the morning room curtains. When she heard Joseph's heavy step on the stairwell, she edged her way cautiously into the hallway and out the door, lifting her skirts so that she could walk quickly to the corner and out of sight.

The traffic on the cross street was light, and dark had descended, but it was not so dark that a cab skittered in front of her without her even hailing it.

"Where to, mum?"

And she knew immediately what he thought: she was a lady of the evening on her way to service a client.

Wasn't she—in a manner of speaking?

"Mum?"

Which one—Seven Pleasures or the Arcade? Whichever one, she could command whatever scenarios would give her the most pleasure.

Oh, it was a hard hard choice—

"*Seven Pleasures,* driver."

"Very good, mum."

No questions asked this time; a butler hadn't called her cab. She had been walking the streets and the driver knew exactly what her business was.

She reveled in it in a way. She was on her way to drown her senses in the naked eroticism of a house of pleasure that catered to appetites like hers.

The butler answered the door as before.

"My lady. It has been a while. I trust that you were not displeased."

"Not at all. Here I am."

"Very good, my lady. And what is my lady's desire this evening?"

"I wish to view something very particular." She was so sure of herself now. "Your best man, naked and ready—and two women. I want him to take the first in reverse and bring her to satisfaction; and then the second, upright against a wall. And I want to see everything. I want to see every detail of what he does and how he does it. And I want this all to myself for however long it takes him to bring the second woman to culmination."

"Does my lady wish a guide?"

"Only to show me to my private room."

"Last time you had Sinbar."

"I would like someone new tonight."

"Very good, my lady. We will prepare."

He withdrew, taking with him her cloak, and she laid out the money on the salver and then entered the arched doorway and made her way down the steps.

A man awaited her there, dressed in cloth that was wound around his waist and barely covered his maleness which was poking insistently against the thin material.

He bowed. "My lady. I am Tomo. Your ecstasy awaits."

As before, the curtains parted, but this time they revealed another staircase.

"My lady . . ."

As they descended, they could hear the intimate sounds of couples sighing and moaning in their mating dances in the private rooms below.

Curtains shrouded every window as they passed; the scent of sex permeated the air, musky, seductive, arousing.

She could not keep her eyes off of Tomo's thickening male root as they approached the far end of the corridor. He was huge, massive, taut and ready, his member thrusting from beneath the fragile cloth as if it were pointing the way.

"Do I please my lady?" he asked softly, insinuatingly, as he slowly unwound his loincloth and let it drop to the floor.

"You please me very much," she whispered as she gazed at his naked, towering manhood.

He was beautiful, tensile and wiry, but with sinewy arms and legs and a thick dark thatch of root hair between his legs that just invited a caress.

"I will perform for my lady."

He opened the door and gestured for her to enter.

It was a spare but opulent room, with jewel-toned drapes on the walls, a rich thick carpet underfoot, and against the wall adjacent to the window was a fat tufted sofa.

"My lady will sit," he commanded softly as he drew the curtains.

She eased herself down into the thick comfortable cushions, and he placed himself before her, his jutting sex just inches from her face.

"Does my lady wish to touch?"

She swallowed; the temptation was so great with his virility flexing alluringly before her very eyes.

"My lady wishes to look. Show me everything."

He was so different from that first man who had loved to pose, and yet the same. This one too loved to show off.

He turned so that she could admire his firm, neat, rounded buttocks. He stroked the long hard length of himself. He propped his leg against the rolled arm of the sofa and showed off the taut sacs between his legs and lush growth of male hair that was so beguiling.

And then he snapped his fingers, and from behind the wall hangings, a naked woman appeared and came to him and put her arms around him and began caressing him.

Her fingers were so explicit, rimming the edge of his erection with delicate precision, and then sliding down slowly, interminably to the hairy base, and under, between his legs to massage and caress him there.

His leg remained canted so she could see every movement of his partner's expert fingers as she cupped and squeezed and slid her hands all over him.

Slowly, he brought her around to his side, and then slapped her buttocks; instantly she bent over and presented herself to him.

He took his time entering her, making sure that every detail was precisely played out before her avid eyes: the stroking of his partner's secret self, the bracing of her arms against the nearby wall, the slow inch by long throbbing inch penetration of her wildly gyrating body, and then the tight filling possession of her which he controlled with his hard hands on her writhing hips.

It took her breath away how deeply and fully his partner encompassed him; it aroused her to see how artfully the woman shimmied and wriggled against him as if she were seeking to pull him farther into the hot velvet of her feminine core. And as he began his relentless thrusts to completion, she was utterly enthralled.

And when his partner stiffened, and began rhythmically rocking her buttocks against him and moaning as she came to culmination, she felt the bursting heat of incipient pleasure wash over her.

He removed himself at the end, slowly, slowly, slowly withdrawing so that she was breathless all over again at how powerful and rock hard he still was, how expertly and perfectly he had pleasured his partner.

How he could pleasure her . . .

She bit her lip as his partner caressed him and left the room. "My lady is pleased . . ."

Your lady is enchanted; your lady can't get enough of watching you. Your lady loves the way you turn this way and that to show off how massive and erect you still are . . . how you stroke it so adoringly while we wait for the next partner to take her place against the wall . . . how you try to seduce me with it, never letting it out of my sight for an instant while we wait—

The next partner came into the room. She was lovely, perfect, dark-haired, olive-skimmed, with perfect breasts and luscious pebble-hard nipples. She splayed herself against the wall, spreading her legs to reveal her thick bush of dark feminine hair, undulating her hips provocatively in overt invitation.

He watched her for a moment, his body in profile so that his jutting member was forcefully in front of her eyes demanding her admiration.

He went to the woman slowly, almost as if he were waiting for a signal to stop.

She did not stop him. She wanted the whole scene: he was so very good at it. He bent and took his partner's left nipple into his mouth—the very taut tip of it, and laved and sucked it intensely while he probed her mound with his hard hot member; and she could have sworn he elongated still more as he pulled the succulent nipple tightly into his mouth.

And then with one savage thrust, he embedded himself deep within the woman's heaving body.

Slowly he released the hot wet nipple from his mouth; and deliberately and painstakingly, he began the slow piston-like drive to culmination.

It was enthralling to watch. He was as precise as a engine, as determined as a lover, and all his partner could do, backed up against the wall, was react.

There were no kisses here, no seven pleasures—it was a pure unrelenting lustful press toward pleasure. And it came suddenly, explosively, erupting in rhythm with the woman's vocal moans.

And then everything was still. He remained joined with his partner for a moment more, and then released her so she could exit the room.

And then he came toward her, still bone-hard and eager as sin.

"Will my lady take her pleasure now?"

She hadn't expected that—but perhaps she should have. To have asked to be on the scene probably was a signal that she would be a willing participant.

And yet as much as she had enjoyed him, she did not want to couple with him. It was a very strong feeling and one she did not quite understand, given her reaction to the scenes.

She looked up at him as he stood poised before her.

It's my money . . . that's all he needs to understand—not my reasons or my fears . . .

"No, my lady does not, thank you," she said imperiously. "You may go."

"But—" he took a step closer to her and she recoiled. "I saved myself for you . . ."

"My lady was not saving herself for *you.*" Another voice. A different voice. The inevitable voice.

Roak.

"As you wish," Tomo said resentfully.

"You may go." There was absolutely no arguing with the tone in his voice.

Tomo withdrew, punching the wall hangings angrily as he disappeared behind them.

And then it was just the two of them, with the murky atmosphere of illicit sex between them.

He circled the room, almost as if he were inhaling it.

"Value for your money, my lady?"

Her hackles rose and her desire deflated.

"Immeasurable," she retorted.

"Immaterial if you cannot use the merchandise, my lady. Or wasn't that the—point of the exercise?"

"I am making very good use of you," she said tartly.

He stopped his prowling and turned to look at her. "Oh, I think not, my lady."

Those mesmerizing eyes . . .

He came closer to her, holding her eyes with that sharp hard gaze that saw absolutely everything.

It was frightening to have someone see into your eyes that way, to see into your soul, to gauge all the lies and deceits—and hold himself above it all.

"I am finished here," she said abruptly, rising from the impossibly comfortable sofa. *All of a piece: the sofa was as seductive as any scene played out in this room; she could have sunk into it and escaped forever.*

"*We* are not finished, Lady Tisne."

"We have never even started, Roak."

"I beg to differ—we started, but *you* were nowhere near ready for the step you were thinking of taking. You are ready now—but not with the likes of *them*. You don't know what you want . . ."

"And *you* know what I want," she interposed contemptuously.

"Do I not?"

She flushed. "This is not the time or the place for this discussion."

"Haughty Lady Tisne. It is exactly the time and place; moreover, you have already paid for my services. And neither time previously did you have any hesitation."

"It was a rescue."

"Deny I can satisfy you."

"This is crazy."

"Deny you came to *Seven Pleasures* seeking satisfaction."

"I will *not* listen." She reached for the door.

"Deny, my lady jade, that you are naked under your dress and only searching for the one to whom you will give your sex."

She froze.

But she was not searching—she knew . . . and he knew . . .

"Everyone is naked under his clothes, Roak—"

"And especially the lady jade who is hungry for sensation . . ."

He had said that before . . . and he was right—he was always so damned right . . . aching for sensation, for experience. Why was she now playing the coy mistress when she had thought about his offer endlessly?

. . . because she didn't want to have paid him for it . . .

. . . because she didn't want him to know so much about these steamy sordid places where sex was a commodity and the partici-

*pants no more than products to be used and discarded like a box
of soap from the grocer's . . .*

*. . . because she didn't know what she wanted as she stood
facing him and his all-knowing eyes . . .*

"I will be your lover."

Her heart began pounding wildly.

*She didn't want him to amplify it—to say again that it was so
easy to arrange, that it was done all the time. She wanted it to
be the first time ever, as if he were Adam and she were Eve.*

"You are my butler."

He ignored that. "It is as simple as this—when you enter this
room to be with me you are no longer Lady Tisne . . . you are . . .
you are Jade, the wanton witch with the green eyes and the insatiable appetite to experience *everything . . .*"

She caught her breath, mesmerized by his words.

"In this room, a Jade can be anything she wants; she can be
naked or she can be a queen. She can be a plaything or she can
wield a whip. She can choose one man—or she can choose a
hundred. She can act like a submissive virgin or she can be a
shameless bitch. Only in a place like this can a Jade explore her
true nature . . ."

*He was so close to her now, speaking of things she had only
imagined in her deepest, darkest thoughts . . . how did he know?
How did he know?*

". . . and only with a man who can satisfy her . . ."

She felt his hands on her shoulders, burning through the illusion
net.

"A provocative dress, my lady . . ." His hands slid down her
chest toward her breasts. "A man wants to discover what lies
beneath all that satin and net . . ." He cupped them and she
thought she would melt at the feeling of him touching her like
that.

*Jade—a jade—how apt . . . what other kind of woman would
choose to spend an evening ogling a naked man and woman
coupling but a lustful wanton who was yearning for excitement
and scared to death she would have to capitulate once she found
it.*

". . . a man would like to think you dressed for him, lady Jade,
in every way possible . . ."

He moved his thumbs across the front of her dress and immediately felt the jut of her taut nipples over the edge of the corset beneath two layers of material.

She made a small protesting surrendering sound at the back of her throat as he stroked her protruding nipples.

"Roak . . ." She could barely breathe his name, she was so overwhelmed by the sensation that just his light touch of her breasts made her feel.

"Let it go—" he whispered in her ear. "You are Jade. Jade is fearless in seeking sensation; she would give her body to any man, but she has found the man she wants—and he wants her . . ."

She could feel it—that hard hot essence of him that had possessed her already . . . if she were Jade, and she could feel him throbbing and pushing against her, she would strip off her clothes and give herself to him in that instant; she would live naked if she could have him anytime ever that she wanted him—

. . . in that room . . .

He cupped her chin and tilted her face back toward him.

"Kiss me like Jade . . ." And he covered her mouth at that slightly awkward angle, invaded it, conquered it, all the while lightly squeezing her hard hot nipple tip through her dress.

. . . how did a Jade kiss—? Like a woman who was hungry to feel, who wanted all the hot wet sensation of being devoured; . . . who felt the lust to possess the mouth that wanted to master hers . . . and subjugate it—

"Your mouth is so hot," he whispered. "You kiss like Jade—"

"I am Jade . . . your kisses are honey—kiss me . . ."

He settled his mouth on hers again, thrusting his tongue against hers with a restrained violence that thrilled her, and she dueled back forcefully, hotly, drowning in the wet heat of his kisses, her body liquefying with mounting excitement as he played with her.

He pulled away from her lips slowly. "Strip for me, Jade."

She lifted her head arrogantly. "You make the effort of finding the treasure."

"I will," he murmured with a faint smile on his lips as he claimed hers again.

And he did—with his free hand—the one that had been expertly massaging her nipple, he reached up, grasped the neck of the dress, and tore it downward.

And then both of his hands closed over her naked breasts, over the support of her silk corset, and he began rubbing his palms against her nipples.

She pulled her mouth away and arching her body into his hands, she shimmied her hips so the dress would slide to her feet, and then she undulated her naked buttocks against his hips as she felt his ferocious erection pulsating through his clothes.

"That feels good, Jade."

"I know," she whispered coyly. "It feels good to me too."

"I want to see you—walk around the room for me."

"I want to see you too—but I don't want to move."

"I know how you can see me and do my bidding at the same time."

"That's a very enticing thought." She gyrated tightly against the powerful thrust of him—just to feel it again. "Why don't you tempt me again?"

"I don't want to stop fondling your nipples."

His fingers were magic on her nipples; her body moved like liquid against him, and she made low, growling, incoherent noises with each telling caress until she thought she would explode from the feeling building up inside her.

"I think you should let me look at you now."

She licked her lips. "I think so too," she said insolently, and she moved away from his seductive hands and strutted her way across the floor, swinging her hips, showing off her firm round bottom, and concealing, for the moment, her taut bulbous nipples.

"Are you ready for me?"

"I'm primed for you, Jade," he growled, and she turned—and he was sprawled on the tuftd sofa, naked and throbbing, ramrod length and all. "I'm waiting for you, Jade. Whenever you choose to get here."

"I'm coming . . ."

"You will—"

She walked toward him, the sound of her booted feet muffled by the carpet, her body encased in that flimsy silk corset which thrust her breasts out exaggeratedly, the thick black bush between her legs contrasting with her smooth white skin.

Eve . . . she was Eve—and every woman who had ever tasted forbidden fruit, and she was as accessible as any.

She stopped just short of the sofa and stood looking at him with her hands on her hips.

He is something—under all that severe black, all that man, all that possibility . . . he's enormous. He's beautiful. I just want to look at him . . . if I could stand it, I would watch him service another woman—but I couldn't stand it . . . there should be mirrors in this room . . . I want to see everything—I want to touch him . . . it's like an iron bar and it just stands there getting bigger and longer and thicker . . . I never want to be with him any other way . . . how will I stand to see him clothed . . .

"Do you like what you see?"

"I do. Do you?"

"I like it a lot better when I can fondle you."

"How can you do that when I'm standing here, enjoying looking at you."

"You'll enjoy it a lot more sitting on my lap."

"I can't imagine how."

"Strumpet—I would wager you can."

"You named me. And I like looking." She felt like taunting him. She felt like teasing him.

She came a few steps closer, and then, spreading her legs, she crouched down to get a better view of him.

"Get over here, Jade; I can't take much more."

"Take *me*—" she whispered, and he leaned over, far over, and grasped her forearm and pulled her onto his lap.

"Straddle my legs—yes, like that, Jade. Now you are just where I want you," he murmured as he ran his hands over her thighs and down the rounded cushion of her buttocks.

"Or perhaps I'm just where *I* want to be," she whispered, rubbing her hands up and down the rock hard length of him which pushed up against her outthrust breasts.

"Stand up."

"Why? I love feeling how hot and hard you are," she breathed.

"I want to feel you another way, Jade."

"I don't know what you mean," she taunted him as she began grinding herself down against his legs.

He felt her there too, she could feel it by the way his body shifted so that she could get the best purchase to spread her legs and rub herself against his rock-ridged thighs.

She loved it—the sensation of being open against him while she was playing with the very heart and soul of him, and denying him what she wanted the most at the same time.

He was licking her nipples as she rode his thighs and massaged and explored every throbbing granite inch of him, all the way into his nest of coarse male hair.

And then he took one nipple into his mouth and simultaneously squeezed the other, and she almost wrung the life out of him as she constricted her hands around the bursting ridged tip of him, and her body spasmed with pure shimmering pleasure.

"Your nipples are luscious . . ."

"I—"

"Jade . . ." His hands were on her thighs easing her up, positioning her, centering her, and then pushing her down.

. . . *down, down onto that gorgeous hot hard male root of him . . . oooo—better than I remembered—ahhh . . . bigger than I remembered . . . ssssst—deeper than I remembered . . . ahhhhh—so far in that I can feel his hair against mine—I don't ever want to move again . . .*

"I want you like this all the time. Meet me here whenever I want you."

"How often will that be—once a month? Once a year . . . ?"

"Every damn hour, Jade," he whispered roughly and took her mouth in a scorching kiss. "I know you want it too."

She wriggled against him, feeling his full thick ramrod possession of her. "You know how I want it."

"How do you want it, Jade?"

She took his lower lip between her teeth and whispered, "I want it rock hard and hot and waiting for me."

"Promise you'll meet me when I want you."

"How will I know?"

"I will get you a message, and I will be waiting for you here."

"And if I don't come—"

"If you want to play coy games, then you won't come . . ."

She made a little sound in the back of her throat as she settled herself tighter against his hips.

"But if you're Jade—and if you want it like you do tonight—" He thrust upward so that he was pressed even more forcefully between her thighs, "—you'll meet me whenever I want you."

She rocked her hips against him, and bent forward to rim his lips with her tongue. His tongue slipped out to meet it and he took control of the kiss and the rhythm of her body.

"Promise you'll come . . ."

She moaned. "I want . . . I'll come—one thing . . ."

"A Jade always has a condition," he muttered, sinking into the kiss again. "You were born to be a Jade." He thrust upward again and she groaned in his mouth.

"Tell me—tell me what else you could possibly want—" He thrust again, "what more than this—*tell* me . . ." and again, and again, until she was wild with his pounding, grinding possession of her.

"I don't care what you want—*promise* . . ."

Her body promised; her body twinged and plunged, riding him furiously, meeting every thrust with her hips writhing and seeking more of his hard surging heat.

"Promise—" As his rhythm began to quicken into short driving thrusts. "Whenever I want . . ." Like a piston, pumping, pumping, pumping, mastering her, pleasuring her—feeding on her rhythmic moaning, driving her to completion.

And when it came, it was soft, it unfurled—and then it exploded into a thousand spangling drops of heat that sizzled all over her body—and melted into his as he pushed one more time and climaxed in a volcanic spending that left his body limp.

And then there was the silence of repletion. He motioned for her not to move, and he shifted his body so that she could lie prone and he could still remain within her.

She lay face to face with him against the back of the sofa, her legs wrapped around him, enjoying the sensation of his hands roaming her body between her buttocks and her legs.

Already she could feel him stiffening again as he began probing more intimate places and she lifted her leg and braced it against his muscular thigh so that he could feel wherever he wanted.

"You haven't promised yet." A whisper against her lips.

"What if I want you?" she whispered back.

His jet eyes flickered. "You have me."

"Same message?"

"Whatever you want, Jade."

"I know what I want," she whispered; he was getting harder

and harder inside of her and she adored feeling him elongating and filling her so thoroughly and completely.

"Then promise."

"I want you naked every time I come."

She felt him spurt again.

"Every time . . ."

Harder and harder.

"I want you naked. I want to look at you and I want to know that that nakedness is *mine*."

Like a rock . . .

"You will always be naked when you summon me here."

Like granite . . .

"I want you naked and ready for me when I come."

Bone hard and so deep inside she felt as if she could just close herself around him forever.

"And you'll come whenever I summon you." A whisper.

"I will come." A breath.

"You love it." He pressed against her.

"You're thick and hard—and I love that . . ." still in a whisper. "Kiss me, Roak."

"Jade," he muttered and leaned into her willing mouth and tongue. "You're so tight and hot and wet, just like a Jade should be—God I want you . . ."

His mouth descended again and he punished her with the ferocity of his kiss.

"You have me," she whispered when he pulled away.

"You excite me." He licked her lips and kissed her again.

"You arouse me. Your nakedness arouses me. You are so hot and hard inside me . . ."

She could have sworn he got harder.

He rocked against her. "Jade," he groaned, and consumed her mouth in a long hard wet kiss as he continued his rhythm against her.

She didn't want him to thrust; she wanted this exquisitely sensual coupling of their bodies, hip to hip, mouth to mouth, fully joined and united as one.

"If we never move, I will never have to summon you."

"You feel so good—don't ever move . . ."

"How good do I feel?"

"God—like iron." Another spurt. "Powerful." A tightening inside her. "Deliciously naked . . ." Another surge. "Perfect . . ."

He reared back and thrust into her and she felt a sinuous uncoiling of sensation, like a slide of satin—rich, creamy, lustrous . . .

"Perfect," she sighed.

. . . Sumptuous and exquisite—one thrust, and then another—in a slow rhythmic cadence that left her breathless . . . and feeling as if she would dissolve with the next voluptuous push . . .

. . . And she did . . . she purely did—her whole body just liquefied into a torrent of feeling that skeined through her blood like molten gold, hot, glittering, gorgeous, and pooling at the very center of her being.

She shuddered violently and grasped his arms as he drove into her one last time and catapulted into a wrenching, wracking release that sapped every muscle in his body.

And then silence again, and his mouth touching hers lightly until a after long long while he could finally speak.

"Promise me, Jade."

"Promise *me*, Roak."

"Whatever you want—whenever you want . . ."

"I promise—" she whispered, "I promise I'll come . . ."

Chapter 13

She left first. She wasn't sure how it happened or what precipitated the ending, but suddenly she was wrapping what was left of her dress and her cloak around her, and Roak, dressed only in his trousers, was escorting her up the steps and into the vestibule and instructing the butler to summon a cab.

It only struck her when she finally arrived home, and was undressed, and lying in bed: she had spent the night in Roak's arms—impassive, self-controlled, cool-headed, imperturbable Roak—

. . . and at the Seven Pleasures . . .

She had dreamt it—she had to have. It just could not have happened.

And any minute he would walk in the door and assume the role of her butler—

It made no sense.

It made wondrous sense.

Her body was still tingling from the shuddering pleasure. She could recreate it—she could still feel it . . .

How could she have him in her house and not want him?

How could she sleep? It was almost dawn already and she hadn't slept a wink—

There was a scratching at her door.

She swung out of bed and ran to open it.

No one was there; a piece of paper lay at her feet.

Jade—your carriage awaits you—come now . . . . . . *whenever I summon you—*

Her body constricted, her nipples stiffened with excitement. She could think of nothing but him waiting for her . . .

She raced down the stairs barefoot, her wrapper over her arm, and flung open the door.

A curtained brougham was waiting at the curb, a patient driver looking the other way as she came down the steps and opened the door.

He was inside, naked, his clothes on the floor, aroused and waiting; she saw the whole in one quick glimpse by the light of the carriage lamp before he slammed the door behind her.

"Jade . . ."

"Oh God, yes . . ." she whispered, pulling off her nightgown and kneeling at his feet. "Yes . . ."

He rapped at the window and the driver cracked his whip.

"How did you know I wanted you again?" she sighed, enclosing his rampant manhood in her hands ecstatically as the carriage moved slowly forward.

"Because I couldn't wait to see you; I wanted you *now*—"

"Take me now . . ." she whispered, running her hands and her tongue simultaneously up and down his gorgeously engorged shaft.

"This is what I want—"

"Anything . . ."

"Turn around, and kneel against the seat. Let me do the rest."

She heard him move forward on the seat, she felt him grasp her around her hips and lift her; and then she felt him probing her in this reverse position, and it was so delicious to feel that hard-ridged tip of him against the flower folds of her sex, nudging and pushing to find her.

She wriggled invitingly, canting her body to let him have his way, feeling him slip and push, inch by long hard torrid inch, deep within her, deep, until she could feel his strong lean hips against the pillow of her buttocks and he was fully, finally and powerfully *there*.

He didn't move; he let her feel his hard virile manhood for a long time as if he wanted to reinforce the strength, the rigidity, and the prowess of it.

And she loved the feeling of it jutting so rigorously inside her. She pushed against it, settling the curvy cushion of her buttocks more tightly against his hips, and then writhing provocatively against the very root of him.

She heard him grunt, almost as if her sinuous movements were too much for him and he was close to losing control.

She wanted him to lose control. She wanted her rocking, writhing body to send him over the edge of all discipline, all sense; she wanted him to lose himself in her, utterly, totally, and mindlessly.

She wanted him at her mercy.

And still he did not move.

She felt his hands feeling the curve and crease of her buttocks. She felt him grasping her hips and pressing himself still more deeply inside her. She felt the sensual motion of the carriage as it moved slowly, slowly, slowly toward ecstasy.

And she felt him, so ramrod and compellingly there.

"Jade . . ."

"Don't move—" she breathed.

"You are so hot and wet . . ."

She gasped as he moved suddenly and thrust his hips forward.

"I want you . . ."

"You feel so good—"

"I named you . . ." He thrust again. "Keep still, Jade—"

"I can't . . ." She undulated her hips to meet his next thrust.

He slapped her buttocks. "Don't move, Jade—let me feel how tight and wet you are."

"I need to feel you—the whole hard length of you . . ."

"Feel it—" He pulled back and drove himself into her forcefully.

"Yes . . ."

"Feel it . . ." He drove again.

She moaned.

"You want it . . ." He lunged again and she groaned. "Tell me . . ." He drove again. "Tell me . . ."

And again.

She gasped. And again. And again.

She sobbed.

And again—that hard, hot, pumping possession of her—that in one fierce lunge, sent her over the edge, crying out in rhythm with her ferociously shattering release.

He eased himself away.

"Jade—"

"Oh God . . ."

"It was good."

He pulled her around and onto his lap so that her legs were dangling against his.

"It *was*," she murmured as he slanted his mouth over hers.

She felt him wedged tightly against her thigh and she took the lush ridged tip of him into her hand and began fondling it.

It was sticky with her residue.

His mouth was wet with hot yearning. She answered him kiss for kiss, whisper for whisper.

"Jade . . ."

"Your kisses."

"I can't stop feeling you—"

"Feel my nipples—they're so hard for you."

"I'm so hard for you."

"I'm feeling you—you are like iron."

"Your nipples are like luscious rock candy."

She caught her breath. *Rock candy—sweet, hard, succulent— like him, like him . . .*

"Suck one . . ." she breathed.

He bent his head and enclosed her lush left nipple in his mouth. She gasped as he pulled at just the very tip of it, pulling as hard as he could between the cushion of his lips, and wetting it with quick tight little flicks of his tongue.

She groaned as he released it.

"Spread your legs, Jade. I want to feel that tight wet heaven."

She felt a dart of pleasure assault her vitals and she wriggled provocatively.

"Only if I can feel yours."

"I thought you were feeling it, Jade. Give me your mouth."

She lifted her face to him and simultaneously parted her thighs.

"I can't live without your kisses," she breathed as he took her mouth and slipped his hand between her thighs.

This part was good too; she was so wet from her pleasure and he was so insistent on probing her there. She spread her legs as wide as possible to ease his way, and she groaned deep in her throat when his fingers penetrated the hot velvet of her sex.

How many fingers—one, two, three—the sensation—his kisses—he is naked for me, I am holding his strength and his sex

in my hands—he is fondling my nipple and thrusting his fingers
deep inside me . . .

Everything—everything . . .

She rode his fingers; she arched her breast into his fondling
fingers; she would not let him stop his kisses.

"Jade . . ." He pulled away from her mouth to murmur. "Come
for me, Jade . . ."

"Yes—" Her body began its insistent ride. "Hard fingers too,
Roak."

"For you, Jade . . . only for you—kiss me . . ."

She opened her mouth to take his kiss and he devoured her,
just devoured her lips, her tongue, the whole tender inside of her
mouth, as she simultaneously bounced against his rigid perfect
fingers.

"It's not the same, Roak . . ."

"I know how it could be . . ."

"Tell me . . ."

"Sit on me—sit on me so tightly I can feel the hair of your
sex rubbing against mine . . ."

"Yes—" She shifted again, still with his fingers possessing her
until she was straddling him, and she braced herself against his
shoulders as she slowly lowered herself downward and felt the
last caress of his fingers replaced by the hard probing tip of him.

Slowly, slowly she settled herself on the rock-hard pillar of
him until she was resting on the very root of him, mouth to mouth
to him, thrilled to her very core with him.

"This is what I want," she whispered. "You, naked, inside of
me."

"I could stay hard for you forever."

"I love it when you're hard for me."

"Jade . . ." he groaned, and reached for her mouth and her
nipples simultaneously. "Don't move."

She gyrated her hips, and he slapped her buttocks again.

"I can't help it," she pouted. "You're so hard you make me
want to move."

"Bitchy Jade—" he murmured against her lips before capturing
them again in a possessive kiss. "I want to pin you to the seat. I
want to ravish you. I never want to finish with you."

"I want you naked for me all the time; I don't know how I got through this night until you summoned me."

"Any time—?"

"Any time."

"You'll stop everything and come and let me possess your naked body."

"Yes," she breathed, shuddering with excitement.

"And I will be naked and ready for you, Jade. I'm the only man who will always be naked and ready for you."

"And hard," she whispered. "Incredibly powerful and hard."

"Feel how hard."

She felt him flex deep inside of her and she kissed his wet lips ferociously. "I need you naked inside me just like that all the time."

He met her kiss again ferociously. "I will be naked inside you Jade, every minute possible. How could any man not want to possess your willing body?"

She caught her breath, excited by his words. "I can't get enough of you."

"I will give you all of my nakedness you can take, Jade."

"I want every hard inch of it," she breathed against his mouth again, flicking her tongue against his lips and letting him take her tongue and suck it with a repressed violence that was thrilling in its intensity.

His mouth closed over hers again and he shifted downward so that he could press up more tightly inside her.

She made a telling sound as he contracted his body and she felt him lengthen. "You got harder," she whispered in awe.

He answered her with another ruthless kiss. "This is what you do to me, Jade. You make me hard, even when I feel like I'm granite."

She groaned. "You make me wet with wanting you."

"No one else has ever made you wet like that . . . ?"

"No one," she whispered.

"Even that naked man who almost took you?"

"You rescued me, Roak. You knew I didn't want his naked body."

"You kissed him."

"It was horrible."

"You were naked for him."

She couldn't deny it.

"I hate that he saw you. Swear to me no one else will ever see you but me."

She ran her tongue over her lips. "No one will ever see me naked but you."

"Whenever I want you."

"Yes . . ." she whispered.

"I want you *now* . . ."

"Yes-s-s—" She sank into his kiss as he grasped her hips and began guiding the motion of her body.

Now she could move, freely and sensually, riding him, her hips undulating, her body writhing against the rock-solid length of him, unmercifully pumping his lust.

And in that last final moment, when she could feel him stiffening wildly, when she could feel her own body ready for that one last sliding downward motion, in that last moment she thought, *I will be your lover* . . . and she plunged downward toward heaven.

She slept. It was well toward noon when she awakened, her body drenched with the scent of sex and the memory of shameless carnal pleasure.

He had brought her home as dawn streaked the sky. She felt like a loose woman; she felt like a woman who had been pleasured by her proficient lover.

She felt like she wanted him again.

She wondered what he was thinking and feeling two floors below.

"Mum?"

The scullery maid, entering the room, having knocked on the door, carrying a tray.

"What is it?"

"A letter, mum."

She slid upright in bed, being careful to pull her bedclothes around her nude body.

"Thank you."

She waited, her hands shaking with excitement, for the maid to withdraw.

She paused at the door. "Breakfast, mum?"

"Tea and toast."

"Very good, mum."

The girl was a dimwit—slow moving and unconscious of *anything* going on around her.

She ripped open the envelope with trembling fingers.

Jade—now; *I can't wait another minute . . .*

She crumpled the note, her body streaming with instant desire.

You'll stop everything and come and let me possess your naked body . . . ?

Yes, oh yes—

She pulled on a pair of boots, and found a wrapper. A cloak over that. Her carriage . . . if Joseph Footman did not stop her . . .

She didn't even comb her hair. She stopped for a moment in the morning room to take a bite of toast and sip of tea.

When she reached the reception room, Joseph was waiting.

"Mr. Roak said to have a cab waiting, mum, when you was ready to go to meet him."

He had thought of everything.

"Thank you, Joseph." She stepped inside the narrow cab and rapped on the hatch.

"Where to, mum?"

"*Seven Pleasures*, driver."

"Yes, mum."

She knew what he was thinking: she had come from a stately house in the best part of town dressed like a drab.

She touched her swollen lips. The interior of the cab was so tiny in comparison to the brougham.

What we could do in this cab—we would be so tight . . . so tight—

The butler met her at the door. "Everything is arranged, my lady. This way."

A new way—a way for clients who were known or who had assignations perhaps. It didn't matter. The musky scent was the same and it excited her beyond all reason.

No, the thought of *him* waiting for her, naked, excited her beyond all reason.

And perhaps he understood that because the curtains were not drawn when she and the butler approached the room, so she could have the pleasure of watching him for as long as she liked before entering.

And she liked.

She liked that he was tall and long and lean, and that his arms were muscular and his stomach was flat. She liked the way he moved, quickly, muscularly, intensely. And she loved the upright ramrod part of him that was just waiting for her.

"Shall I take my lady's clothes?"

"No. He will wish to strip me." *I want him to strip me . . .*

Her guide left her and she pushed open the door.

He turned abruptly and took four steps across the room to take her in his arms.

"Did you drop everything and come?" he murmured, easing his mouth down on hers so that she couldn't immediately answer.

"I couldn't wait," she whispered. "Why did you take so long?"

"Why are you wearing clothes?"

"Tear them away," she begged, offering him her mouth.

He ripped away her cloak and tore off her wrapper, and embraced her naked body. "Yes," he groaned against her lips, sliding his hands over her buttocks. "Yes . . ."

"Kiss me . . . it's been too long . . ."

His mouth melted against hers and he began subtly and slowly moving her backwards and backwards until she was up against the wall and his hard body was leaning into hers, covering her, and pumping meaningfully against her.

"Naked and ready," she whispered, reaching down to fondle his turgid length. "Just as you promised."

"You came—just as you promised."

"I said I would take all of you."

"I'm ready to give you all of me."

"Do it," she breathed, spreading her legs and inviting his kiss. "Give me every naked inch . . ."

She groaned as he entered her swiftly, surely, pushing and pressing until they were hip to hip, body to body, his hands holding hers quiescent against the wall, his mouth wreaking havoc with her senses.

She moaned as he took her.

"Wet, Jade—so wet and ready for me . . ."

"I couldn't stop thinking about you—"

He pushed himself forcefully against her. "Never stop thinking about me. I can't stop wanting you every minute. I want to be naked inside you all the time . . . just like you want it . . ."

"You don't know how I want it. I couldn't stand waking up without you naked inside me . . ."

He covered her mouth in a savage kiss. "I'm naked and I'm inside you now, Jade, tell me how you want me . . ."

"I want you hot and hard," she whispered. "I don't know how to tell you how much I love how hot and hard you are for me . . ."

He groaned and flexed himself against her in a thrilling little lunge.

"I watched you before I came in . . ."

"Did you like what you saw?" he whispered.

"I loved that you were naked for me—and so big . . . so lusty . . . so *there* . . . just for me . . ."

"I get hard just thinking about you, Jade. And I get like a rock when I know I'm going to possess you."

"Then possess me," she begged. "I need to feel you . . . take me—"

He took her, sliding his mouth onto hers and his lusty masculinity deeper into her velvet core.

And then he began a scorching piston-like movement, pinning her to the wall.

"Oh God, Oh God, Oh God—" she moaned as he thrust and thrust with a focused force that took her breath away.

She couldn't move; all she could do was accept his mouth, his tongue, and his naked sex as he surged against her, his hips writhing and undulating, plumbing her to her very depths, and then withdrawing, and driving into her relentlessly over and over again.

This was possession—as hot and wild as anything she had yet experienced with him—he was taking her, she was powerless against his strength even while she reveled in it; she was boneless against the weight of him, and she loved his naked body covering her, his mouth devouring her, and the most primitive part of him pleasuring her.

And then it was over—a sudden white-hot paroxysm of incandescent light, electric, jolting, sizzling that burned into a ravishing swell of sensation and exploded into oblivion.

Done—

Not done—he was coming, reaching for his climax on the edge of hers, driving himself home with ferocious intensity until he ejaculated in a spuming convulsion of release.

And then . . . and then . . .

Slowly he removed himself and they sank to the floor and fell asleep.

She awakened to find herself lying on the floor, her back against the wall, her head pillowed on his arm, and his body pressed protectively against hers.

It was a perfect moment; he slept, and he was totally hers, and she could think of nothing else but the pounding, cramming pleasure of his possession, and her hand crept downward to cup his quiescent sex.

It was quite amazing: it was yielding, resilient, flexible, tactile even in its repose. And yet the moment she began fondling it, she felt it move, almost as if it had a life of its own, and stiffen in response to the caress of her fingers.

Her body reacted instantly, stretching luxuriously in memory and yearning and she sensed that he too had come quiveringly awake as his member stirred to ramrod life.

"Jade—" he whispered.

She answered by stroking the underside of his pulsating shaft.

"Let me take you right now."

"Let me make you bigger," she begged.

"I'm bursting for you already, Jade."

"Let me just—hug you," she murmured, squeezing him tightly. "What's this little dewdrop I feel?"

"You feel my hunger to possess you."

She squirmed as he inserted his fingers between her legs and into her hot velvet center. "Do you like what you feel?"

"You are always wet and tight for me. The Jade wants what I can give her."

"I want *this,*" she whispered, wriggling against his probing fingers and rubbing her hands all over his throbbing length.

He suppressed a groan and she felt him elongating even as she stroked him.

"Remember the first time?" he whispered roughly. "I claimed you then, Jade. I took your naked body at *Dominoes* and I made you mine in public and in pleasure. Don't deny me."

She shuddered at the arousing memory. *In public and in pleasure, pounding at her body with the power of his possession in front of all those people—and some part of her had been excited by the act . . .*

"You were so powerful, so big and so hard. I didn't know how much I wanted it until you pushed me against that wall and took me—"

"Say you want it now," he commanded.

"I want it," she whispered, lifting her leg and opening herself to him. He withdrew his fingers and held her hand as she guided him toward her welcoming fold. "Oh yes"—she groaned as he pushed himself into her—"yes . . . yes," as he kept pressing inch by long, hard inch until he was fully and deeply encompassed by her moist textured heat.

"Jade . . ." he groaned, and flexed his arm so he could get at her mouth.

And this time, it was just his lush kisses and the luscious pressure of him surging into her like a mighty tide. No words— no taunts and teases—just his pure potent possession of her and her willing submission to his power.

He rode her relentlessly, a hot torrid claiming of her by the most voracious and virile part of him. He rode her until she was insensate with pleasure at the feel of his inflexible manhood taking her in the most primitive way possible.

He rode her; she was insatiable in her brazen need to keep him naked and thrusting inside her.

She would not come; he felt himself losing control, and mastered himself with superhuman effort.

She pushed him, demanding more and more with her provocative movements and her greedy kisses.

He grasped her hip to stop her supple body motions, and reluctantly pulled his mouth from hers. "Jade—"

"Stallion," she whispered, and she felt his whole body thrill to the name. "No one else could ride me like this . . ."

"You make me so hard, you make me want to mount you whenever I see you."

"Oh yes . . ." she breathed.

"You made me hard the first time you came to see me."

"I'm glad. I'm glad I made you hard for me."

"I wanted you like this from the day you walked into my flat. Every time I saw you, Jade, I was hot to possess you. And your first night here—I was bursting for you when I saw you, and I mounted you, didn't I?"

"Oh, you did—" she moaned.

"You were naked under your dress and you didn't refuse me."

"How could I refuse a stallion . . . ?"

"How could a stallion not mount a mare in heat?" he whispered roughly, as he contracted his body and thrust himself into her once, twice, three times as her body shuddered with excitement.

"You were hot," she whispered.

"You were so ripe and ready to be taken."

"You were so deliciously forceful. I couldn't deny you."

"You were so wet and willing."

"I'll always be wet and willing for you . . ."

"What if I got hard for you and wanted to mount you someplace else?"

"I will always be ready for my stallion so he can mount me whenever he wants me . . ."

He groaned and pressed against her to claim her lips in a succulent kiss.

"I want you naked under your clothes all the time," he whispered. "I want to know you are naked for me even when you are not with me. And then I'll know you are always ready when I want to mount you."

"I hate clothes. I want to be naked all the time—I want you all the time."

"I'll never stop . . ."

"Never . . ." she sighed as he began the slow beguiling movement that would drive them toward culmination.

She wound herself around him and gave him her mouth, and as the intensity of his thrusts increased, she lost herself in his melting kisses and in the torrid sensation of his rhythm.

And after a long, long while, she felt the break of feeling deep within her, and the sudden keen lust for completion. One moment it was there, building into a volatile crescendo of excitement—and the next—the next, she fell off a cliff and into an avalanche of pure, pounding, heart-stopping pleasure.

An instant later, he followed, drenching her in the frenzied geyser of his climax, sinking into her so tightly, so deeply, she felt as if she were bound to him forever.

Chapter 14

In the morning, like the punctilious butler that he was supposed
to be, he served her her breakfast in the morning room.

He brought her what little mail there was and then spent the
rest of the early hours belowstairs, directing the servants in their
work.

And the work got done: the fires got laid, the silver was pol-
ished, the rooms were cleaned and the beds made, the dusting
accomplished, and dinner was always served on time.

But in the ensuing week, when she inquired, she was always
told, Mr. Roak is unavailable, mum, and so she never knew
exactly what he was doing at any other time during the day.

It lent a deliriously intriguing intensity to her days: nothing
seemed real except the presence of Roak in her house and her
unbearable razor-sharp desire for him.

It was especially impossible at night, knowing he was sleeping
two floors below—she would lie awake all night thinking about
just creeping down those stairs and entering the forbidden sanctum
of his room.

And then his message would come—this one delivered to her
practically at the crack of dawn.

Jade—I need you now . . .

Her cab was waiting; Joseph Footman asked no questions. The
driver understood her nature. She flew down the steps to the
private rooms at *the Seven Pleasures* within the half hour, into
their room, into his arms, into his kiss.

"I couldn't stand it," he whispered, as he pulled off her cloak
and skirt.

"I was awake all night . . ."

"I needed to feel you"—his hands were busy, all over her back and her buttocks, and then he cupped them and pulled her tightly against his rampaging erection, as he slid his hand down her bottom and between her legs so that he could insert his fingers from behind—"right *there*—"

She wrapped her arms around his neck and invited his kiss. He lifted her up against his body as he met her mouth, and then let her slide back down so that his throbbing member was pillowed between her thighs.

And then he moved slowly back toward the sofa and eased himself down with her on his lap so that she straddled him and she could press intimately against him as he kissed her and probed her from behind.

The kiss was endless, wet, lush, deep. Her body responded, rubbing against the ramrod length of him, fitting against it as if she were made for it; she strained against him, undulating in a mating dance that was heightened by the feeling of him exploring her sultry sex in that exciting reverse way.

She couldn't get enough of it or his kisses, or of pressing her provocative femininity against his rigid member.

"Hot wet Jade," he murmured against her lips. "Even with my fingers in you, you are so hot and tight, and your body moves so enticingly for me."

"Only my stallion has such vigorous fingers—"

"Only a wanton Jade would let me feel her like this . . ."

"I am your wanton of the evening . . . the afternoon, the dawn . . ." She bore down on him tightly and commanded his kiss.

It was a long, savage, turbulent kiss, intensified by her gyrating motions and his carnal penetration of her.

She pulled away from him and rested her lips against his. "I love being naked for you so you can feel me all over—"

"If I just think about fondling you, I get hard for you. I want to tear off your clothes and mount you. I can hardly stand waiting for you to come to me."

"I can't stand wearing clothes any more; I want to walk around my house naked . . . I want you hard for me every minute of the day—"

"I never stop wanting to possess you . . . ."

"I can't sleep, knowing you're lying two floor below me, naked and hard for me."

He took her lower lip between his teeth and sucked on it forcefully. "At home you are the prim and proper Lady Genelle . . ."

"At home, at night, I am the wanton Jade, naked in my bed and waiting for my stallion to come and mount me."

"Maybe . . . maybe he *will* come . . ."

"Maybe if he knows I am hot and willing and want him . . ."

"What does the wanton Jade want now . . . ?"

"She wants your kisses, and she wants the pleasure that only you can give her . . ."

Slowly, he eased his mouth onto hers, and ever so slowly, while his fingers still possessed her, he eased them both onto the floor; he removed his fingers and spread her legs, and then, with one long torrid thrust, he embedded himself in her to the hoarse sound of her ecstatic moan.

It didn't take long; she met each thrust joyously, surging her hips against his, rolling her body shamelessly to his rhythm, building the feeling and building it until her final glittering tempestuous surrender.

He didn't want to—but the thing overtook him almost by surprise; he spent himself in one volcanic spasm and collapsed on top of her, certain he would never have the stamina to possess her ever again.

He took her again that morning, and later that afternoon, and still later that night.

She floated on a buoyant orgy of pleasure and endless consummation.

But she could not convince him to come to her room.

"My dear Roak," she protested one afternoon as he served her tea.

He looked at her and his eyes said, *I see you naked . . .*

"We will not speak of these things, *Lady* Genelle."

"But I want to."

"There will be time to talk. Now it is time for tea. And you forget the most important point: we are here to protect you."

"There hardly seems anything to protect me from; my mother

has all but disappeared off the streets, the servants are well and truly gone, and Stiles hasn't come up with any reason yet to haul me off to prison."

"You are being naive, Lady Genelle. Your mother was *bought* away from your home; your servants were bribed and perhaps offered better stations; a valuable piece of paper has disappeared; and Stiles may very well decide that there was some hidden motive that is not explicated by your knowledge of your inheritance— which is now an arguable point since your agreement with Sir Arthur to all intents and purposes does not exist—or the fact that it would have made more sense if you had stabbed your husband in the back.

"There is an evil lurking out there that is not finished with you, my lady. Don't get comfortable just because it appears nothing is happening."

She felt like stamping her foot; the man had two personalities, and it was as if her lover did not exist when he was in the guise of her *skilled investigator.* Or her *butler.*

"What *is* happening, Roak?" she asked waspishly.

Again that long measuring look, and this time it had nothing to do with his sensual appreciation of her.

"You are being kept safe . . ."

"Even as I roam the streets at night," she put in tartly.

"We are searching for the two mysterious women. We are monitoring the events at the *House of Correction.* We are looking for your mother, for only she can tell us who paid her and who is your enemy."

"I will find my mother."

"You will stay put, Lady Genelle."

"Except, of course, when you summon me."

His expression got tighter and more forbidding. "As you say, Lady Tisne."

"I hate sitting still," she said peevishly.

"No," he said impassively, "you can't keep still."

Her bright green gaze met his for one long deep moment, and then her mouth tightened.

"You may go, Roak."

He bowed—and she just hated him for playing the game to perfection.

"My lady."

She watched expressionlessly as he withdrew.

And under all those clothes is the man who claims he can't stand being away from me for a minute . . .

I can't believe it . . . I can't believe that that man is real, and what just transpired in this room is real—

I am playing the wanton for him—and willingly too—dear heaven, I love it . . . I want it . . . I want it all the time—how can he just turn it off and on like a spigot?

But she knew the answer to that: she had hired him to take action, and her role was to sit and wait.

Women will wait, she thought mordantly. *Women die from waiting . . .*

But she didn't quite know what she wanted to do—what she could do, beyond trying to find her mother.

In aid of what? And what could she do more efficiently than Roak, with all of his talent and his connections?

She had no connections whatsoever: Arthur's set had cut her off completely. And she wasn't sure if part of it wasn't her mother-in-law's doing.

How powerful was the Madam Tisne who sat on her throne at Fanhurst and presided over her son's empire?

How much did she know? How could she not know?

Of course, if the lawyer just deposited her income into the Capital & Counties Bank as he usually did with her own, her mother-in-law had no need of knowing anything beyond that all her investments were making money.

But if Arthur were still alive, she would still be installed at the Dower House, a covert witness to his vices. So how did anyone know how much of her son's secret life his mother had ever discovered?

It was such a far stretch to even involve her mother-in-law.

And he had said nothing about Tony Lethbridge—

It was as if Tony had dropped off the face of the earth, and all of those months she had flirted with him and challenged him and finally taken him as her lover—all of that was another dream, one that had ended in a nightmare.

. . . Roak had talked about Tony's reputation . . . Tony was a

habitué of the House of Correction . . . Tony had no reputation to protect—and he was as self-centered as the day was long.

If she could be cool and unemotional for a minute, she might ask herself just why Tony Lethbridge had gotten involved with her.

. . . well—why?

She sat uncomfortably still while she considered it. She knew why she had gone after him: he was handsome as the devil, he was personable, he had been said to be an insatiable lover, and—most of all—every other woman wanted him.

And he treated every woman as if he wanted her.

So why had he succumbed to *her?*

She had been no more beautiful, no more forthcoming, no more dissolute than any other woman of Arthur's set.

Maybe less so . . .

. . . men of that set loved to deflower virgins—

Odd thought—she didn't know where it came from.

. . . they used to take bets on how many girls they could poke in one night . . .

. . . and the women thought it was an uproarious joke . . . even Arthur went in on the betting—lost terrific sums of money . . .

. . . he couldn't even poke his own virgin—

. . . so he got someone else to do it for him?

She caught her breath in horror.

. . . could he have?

. . . would he have?

. . . she knew the answer—Arthur would have done any-thing . . . and if he could fund an establishment like the House of Correction, what depths wouldn't he stoop to?

No—no . . . it wasn't Arthur . . . it just couldn't have been. She and Tony had been intensely attracted, overwhelmed with lust . . . she had not been so innocent that that had been impossible.

Only now the memory was like a puff of smoke drifting away from a chimney—dark, untouchable, illusory, leaving a faint stench in the air when it was gone . . .

And a sour taste in her mouth.

* * *

Everything was illusory, nothing was real—perhaps since the moment she consented to marry Arthur.

Everyone had a secret life—and now, even she . . .

And it was quite one thing to split one's life between waiting and wanting, and quite another when a thousand ideas felt as if they were splitting her brain.

And her mother missing, and her servants mysteriously vanished. And a vital piece of paper gone . . .

All of that after she had solicited her mother's counsel and dismissed her advice about illicit houses of pleasure. All of that *after* her mother had started to reveal little tidbits of truth about her experiences in those places.

Troy Street—The Barracks . . . *soldiers wanting you-know-what . . . Fox and Hole—men and woman all laid out—you take your choice—Wolf's Den—she couldn't quite remember . . . an introduction house? Who to whom?*

Where might her mother have chosen to hide? And was it reasonable that since she had been so knowledgeable about those same said places that she also might have worked at one of them—?

Before the *House of Correction?*

A place that no one would know about—a place that might cater to the lowest of the low instead of the highest lords and ladies with their exceedingly salacious tastes . . .

Was it even possible that her mother had deliberately mentioned places she had been involved with?

Troy Street—Fox and Hole . . .

. . . did she dare?

. . . wretched clothes—and maybe she could pretend to be a streetwalker looking for more steady work . . .

She knew something about it now—

. . . just smudge her face, wrap some of her torn clothes around her body, and somehow sneak out into the night . . . ?

She rang for Joseph Footman. "Where is Roak?"

"Mr. Roak is unavailable, mum."

The very words she wanted to hear. "Thank you, Joseph."

His note came an hour later.

Jade—come . . .

Perfect.

She encased herself in the concealing cloak and went downstairs.

"Your cab, my lady."

Yes . . .

She rapped against the hatch. "Troy Street, driver.

"Mum?"

"You heard me."

She heard the edgy aggressive note in her voice. And she knew why—Roak was waiting—and for the first time in days she did not care.

Troy Street—dingy, dusty, ominous, crowded with beggars and brahmins both.

It was where they came seeking fresh faces, untried lambs.

"Ah, here's a flower—"

And there was a gentleman in his carriage.

"Come with me, beauty—I'll give you a shilling if you let me touch. I'll give you another if you'll touch me . . . easy money, my lovely, and all you have to do is let me have my way—"

The exchange was as brazen as sin: she saw it going on all around her as she pushed through the evening crowds.

"I'm savin' meself for the nunnery, mister," she called back with an apt replication of her mother's accent. "I don't want no truck with the likes of you."

"It would be a pitiful waste me darling, when I would give a sovereign to poke at your pretty twim."

She turned her back on him and immediately another man grasped her arm.

"A half crown for your favors, pretty."

She wrenched her arm away and turned in a different direction, only to find, to her dismay, that both men were in hot pursuit.

Stupid idea—stupid to think you could act the part and someone wouldn't take you up on it . . .

How desperate was she?

She didn't even know where she was going.

In a panic, she stopped an older woman with tired eyes and rough-looking clothing.

"I want—I want . . ." she couldn't even choke it out.

The woman looked her over for a long careful moment. *"The Barracks* is that way. They'll take you on—yer young enough . . ."

Soldiers wantin' you-know-what . . .

The Barracks you know . . .

She caught back a sob; she had given up her pleasure for *this*—

She started running through the crowd, elbowing people out of the way . . . surely there was a cab to be had *somewhere?*

She bolted across Troy Street to the opposite side and whirled to find her one admirer shaking his fist and cursing at her—and the man in the carriage already approaching a new conquest.

She looked frantically around for a cab. And then she began running again.

This time, people moved away from her; it was almost as if they thought she was crazy, contaminated, and they wanted no part of her.

No one, in her mad flight down Troy Street, stopped her or propositioned her, and when she finally reached Edgecomb Banks, she was out of breath, hot, scared, and utterly unsure of what to do next.

She walked, slowly now; the Banks were much less crowded, and she could make her way with a little less galling fear as she scanned the stream of carriages and coupes for a cab.

And then one appeared—and she fairly jumped over the man who had hailed it and dove onto the seat.

"I need to go to hospital, sir—I'm expectin' and somethin's gone wrong—"

He looked utterly petrified. "Go—go . . . Driver—the Alms Hospital . . ."

The cab lurched forward, wheeled around in the opposite direction, and took off at a fast clip.

But I don't want to go to Seven Pleasures yet . . . I'm not finished—I can't let that scare me—I want to go—to—

"Driver—take me to the *Fox and Hole* . . ."

"But—the gent said—"

"Do what I tell you," she said commandingly, settling back into the pillows.

One quick look at the most licentious of houses . . . surely there was something to be discovered there—

"Mum . . ."

The driver opened the door.

"Wait for me," she said, stepping down, handing him some money, and looking around uncertainly.

It was the most quiet unprepossessing street in the whole of South Bruxton, and lined from front to back with tenements and forlorn looking homes that had seen better days.

"Straight ahead, mum," the driver said patronizingly, pointing to the building across the street.

There was nothing to distinguish it from the row of apartment houses that made up half of the block.

She walked forward hesitantly, and then with a stronger step until she reached the door.

It was open. Inside the vestibule there were two doors, side by side, distinctly labeled: *Fox* and *Hole*.

From somewhere in the distance, she heard raucous laughter and loud goading voices.

She girded herself and pushed open the door marked *Fox*.

Stairs again—there were always stairs in these places, dimly lit, and going nowhere.

She climbed the stairs gingerly; the stairwell reeked of urine and other more erotic excretions, the noise was almost grating, and as she came closer to the landing, she could hear the individual conversations.

". . . 'ey, 'ey lovey—put it there, put it there . . . oh, and ain't you a pretty young thing . . . oh my, oh my—what's yer name, dolly?"

The answering voice was high-pitched, cracking slightly under the weight of its emotion. "Gemma—Gemma Hardstone—"

"Ever so hard stone, my pretty . . ." the other voice said, and faded away to be superseded with another thick deep voice.

"Ooo—and 'e got the sweetest thing, now didn't 'e?"

"You don't need a special friend tonight." A woman's voice, calm and reassuring—and *not* her mother. "Try them all. Let everyone be your special friend tonight . . ."

Her voice receded for a moment—and then came back strongly.

"Marcus—come—Athena awaits you, and quite eagerly too . . ."

And at that point, Genelle reached the turn in the staircase and climbed the last five steps with her heart pounding, not knowing what to expect.

It was a hell she could not have imagined: the dingiest room, outfitted with the shabbiest sofas and threadbare chairs and muddy-colored carpeting, and lounging around the room were boys and young men in various stages of undress, and a dozen or so older men trying out the "merchandise."

" 'Ey," one of the men shouted as the woman came back into the parlor. "This one don't want to play the game."

"Oh, but you *must* play the game," the woman said chidingly, approaching the recalcitrant boy, "otherwise how could you earn all those lovely pounds this dear is going to pay you. Now tell 'im your name, dearie . . ."

"Penelope," the boy mumbled. "Penelope Longbow . . ."

"Ah, there's the thing. Now, Bonham, ain't that sweet? Don't you want to take this sweet thing and show your appreciation? Do you want her?"

"If she wants to go . . ."

"She wants to go," the woman said with a vague threatening tone underlying her words. "Tell him, Penelope."

"I want to be with you," the boy said mechanically, but it was enough to satisfy Bonham who shoved a fistful of bills into the woman's hand and claimed his reluctant prize.

And then the woman turned and noticed Genelle standing there.

"You're in the wrong place, lovely. The women go into the *Hole* next door. Ooo—" she came closer and tilted Genelle's chin up to the near nonexistent light. "Ain't you a looker. They'll go crazy for you in the *Hole*. But why you'd come here and not up to *Seven Pleasures* . . . except if you just want it all the time— they'll keep you busy here. They'll love you here. You been on the street long? You'll make a lot of money down in the *Hole* if you've got the strength to go at it all day and all night. Wears the girls out fast—some of 'em—and some of 'em stay for a year and build up the money until they can get out comfortably. Then they take 'em on at *Seven Pleasures* or the *Arcade*—but you don't get no tips there. Downstairs then, girl—and next door. And take off your clothes before you get there. Give the mates something to lust after while they're waiting. They'll want you naked and on your back the minute you walk in the door."

She turned away then to watch a scenario in the corner where the client couldn't seem to keep his hands or his sex away from his conquest.

"Money first, mate—and then you can have all you can get . . ."

Genelle turned and fled.

So this was it—the other side of the coin for those who could pay shillings instead of crowns to vent their lust . . .

. . . and those children—those poor, sad, greedy boys . . . pawns, the lot of them . . . and how demoralizing to encumber them with female names . . .

And this too had been Arthur's world—had not Morfit told her—?

She felt sick with the knowledge of it and the sight of it . . . she would never understand it.

And what selection must have awaited a client who chose to go down the Hole? Young girls? Willing virgins claiming male names to satisfy what prurient desire? Nubile young things or weary and experienced harlots?

Or both ?

What was she?

Her mother's daughter—the woman who had married a pervert and become a jade . . .

Full circle—really, because if she had not come here this night, she would have been on her back anyway, and willingly lusting after Roak's incomparable sex.

And it wasn't any different from the strumpets at the Hole.

She wanted it as avidly as they—

She wanted the goading, provoking games and she wanted the kisses and caresses; she wanted the pleasure, the opulent feelings, and the ultimate orgasmic delirium.

But with him—*only with him . . .*

And she had given him up without an instant's remorse to explore this venality, and on the next to non-existent chance she might find a clue to her mother's whereabouts.

She was no better than her name . . . and as the cab proceeded

toward Kingsbridge, she debated whether to continue on to the
Seven Pleasures or just go home.

It was so late—too late, she thought as she redirected the cab
toward Green Street.

And eerily silent as she paid the driver and opened the door.
The house was deadly quiet, the servants asleep—not even Joseph
Footman guarding the door.

And Roak—?

Asleep—or awaiting her?

She crept up the steps furtively and into her room, and sank
down heavily onto her bed.

. . . down in the Hole, even at this hour, the drabs are spreading
their legs to accommodate anyone who wants a fast frot for a
quick five and a tip . . . while the inverts at the Fox hunted their
prey till the morning—

. . . every vice, Morfit had said, paid off and purged with the
profits from the too aptly named House of Correction—

. . . House of Reparation as well . . .

Dear heaven, there was no end to Arthur's perversions or the
sinkhole of his vices . . . and she was intent on probing into each
and every one . . .

There were some things she was better off not knowing—

But she knew—sometime deep in the night—and the scent and
the feel of the weight of Roak as he forcefully held her down,
and the sound of his voice whispering harshly in her ear.

"*Where were you?* I waited, damn you, and I waited—and I
hope you never have to wait like that, you bitch, for *anyone*—"

She bucked up against him furiously. "Get your hands off
me—I couldn't come . . ."

"That wasn't the agreement, bitch . . ."

He was seething in a hot, controlled rage—she could feel him
through the sheets, she could hear it in his voice, and she could
sense herself rebelling against it even as she thrilled to the degree
of fury she could arouse in him.

"Where were you? Who were you with?"

"No one—and I don't have to explain myself to you."

"Damn you—you have to explain every damn thing, you wanton. If you're not with me, then you're with someone else, and

you didn't mean a bloody word you ever said . . . which is just what one expects from a jade . . ."

"Roak . . ."

Dear heaven, he was wild with anger—and something else—jealousy . . . lord, he was jealous that someone else might have possessed her . . .

"I won't be in thrall to *you,* damn you—"

Yes you will—yes you are . . .

"Roak—" she whispered, writhing under the sheet. "I want your kisses."

"You could have had them six hours ago . . ."

"I want to feel you naked against me—"

"You could have done that six hours ago . . ."

"I feel how hard you are for me."

"I was hard and hot for you six hours ago."

"I want you to mount me and let me feel you inside me."

"You could have—"

She clamped her hand over his mouth. "Roak . . ."

"Damn you . . ."

"You want me . . ."

"I never stop, damn you."

"Then take me—"

"Where were you?"

She stopped her provocative movements. Here was the moment of truth—would it be honesty or a whore's lies?

Her choice to tell.

"I went searching for my mother."

There was a dead silence and then he rolled off of her.

"Jesus. *Where?"*

"Troy Street—"

"Goddamn . . ."

"Fox and Hole—"

"Bloody *hell* . . ."

"And then I came home."

"After you had a round at the *Hole—"*

"For God's sake!" she snapped, bolting upright and pushing herself back against the headboard. "You're acting like a spoiled child."

"And you're acting naive and stupid—to go to *Fox and Hole—*

for Christ's sake." He was silent for a long hard moment. "And what mystical insights were revealed to you?"

She didn't answer at once.

Nothing was revealed—and everything was made murkier. Don't you understand?

But he didn't need to understand; he only needed to be her ready and able stallion . . .

"It was awful. The boys. Those horrible men. The procuress—"

"You went into the *Fox?* Bloody brave of you, Jade. They eat women there."

"I thought that only happened down the *Hole.*"

"The artless Jade got educated, I see. And what did it prove?"

"Mother wasn't there. So—nothing," she whispered. "Just stinking nothing."

He let the words sit between them for an awful long time.

Nothing . . .

Nothing—

"Go to sleep, Lady Genelle," he murmured finally. "The games for tonight are over."

"Your tea, my lady."

He was at the morning room door, his expression severe and his coal-black eyes hard with decision.

She hated that face—it was the one that would reveal nothing, the one that would keep its own counsel, do what it wanted, and leave her out in the cold.

It will not . . .

She braced herself for a confrontation.

"Good morning, Roak."

"My lady has recovered from her nocturnal foray," he murmured, setting down the tray, infusing the tea with water, and his tone with heated irony.

"Your lady awakened alone this morning, and she has not recovered from *that.*"

"Duty called."

"Indeed, you are nothing if not dutiful," she said scathingly. She picked up her cup for want of something to do. "Tell me, Roak, which nefarious threat are we circumventing today?"

"Your unbridled stubbornness . . . my lady."

"I see no risks."

"You have seen too much. The dangers are real and your ingenuousness is unnerving . . . my lady."

"So I'm to draw up the bridge once again and stay immured within the castle walls."

He sent her a shimmering look which said plainly she knew the answer to that.

"Except when you send for me."

"I believe you have summed up the program for the day."

He turned to leave.

"Roak—"

"My lady . . ."

"I hate what you're doing."

"I truly understand your position—"

Like arguing with a wall.

"You may leave," she said, waving him away. She did like dismissing him—especially since he was a man who could not usually be dismissed so easily.

And, all she was left with, was a lukewarm cup of tea, cold toast, a rasher of bacon, and some cloying egg dish—and cold memories of the night before.

The summons came mid-afternoon.

Jade—to the castle tower . . .

Her heart leapt. *In the house—he was in the house . . .*

She raced up the stairs to her room and flung open the door.

He lay sprawled naked on her bed, his engorged sex jutting toward her in an invitation as old and primitive as time.

She closed the door behind her and locked it, and then slowly and deliberately moved toward the bed.

"Shall I undress for you?" she whispered, kneeling beside him and running her hand up the rigid length of him. "Or shall I just lift my dress and let you take what you want . . . ?"

"I want you naked . . . all the time. I never stop thinking about your naked body . . . I could hardly stand it last night not being able to have you. I was bursting for you. I could explode right now with wanting you."

"And you were in my bed this morning . . . you could have mounted me and taken me this morning . . ."

"Waiting is a virtue—it whets the appetite for all the delectable things to come—"

"Yes . . ." she breathed, stepping out of her dress to reveal her breasts shrouded in a thin lawn camisole, against which her nipples protruded in taut, dusky bulbs, her naked hips and thighs and her long legs encased in silk stockings.

His glittering eyes narrowed. "The Jade is ready to be possessed. Lie down."

She climbed onto the bed and kicked off her boots, and then stretched out one stockinged foot toward him and rubbed it against his throbbing erection and down the inflexible shaft and in between his legs.

"Jade . . ."

She swung her body opposite his and lowered herself so that her head was facing the footboard and her silk clad foot could still slide easily between his powerful thighs.

He didn't move as she caressed him there; he held himself quiescent with superhuman control to give her the pleasure of stroking the taut sacs between his legs and the ramrod object of her desire.

She propped herself up on her elbows to watch him as her foot played with him. She felt her body liquefy into a luxurious quickening.

And as she watched him and stroked him, she felt an explosive urgency to be possessed by him.

"What's that I see, Roak? A delicious little drop of surrender?"

He thrust her leg out of the way and levered himself over her. "It is time for the Jade to submit to her master."

She undulated her hips, lifting her body to brush provocatively against his thrusting member. "Take me."

He took her—in one jolting forceful drive, he rooted himself deep deep inside her. "Tight—you are always so wet and tight . . . put your legs around me; I want to feel the silk of your stockings against my skin . . ."

She lifted her legs and wrapped them around him, and he pushed even tighter inside her.

"I need this Jade-naked body ten times a day," he growled, beginning to slowly circle his hips against her in short sharp little thrusts.

She slid her legs down his buttocks and massaged the backs of his legs before she braced her legs against them.

"I want your Jade-naked body so that I can mount you like this every time I get hard for you."

"Oh, yes," she breathed, thrilled by his words.

"Every time I think about you I get hard . . . I want to rut with you all day long just like this—possessing you as many times as I want you . . . just like this. I want to finish you now, and take you all over again. I want—I want . . . uhhhhhhh . . ."

His words tailed off in a protracted groan and a shuddering spasm of climactic release.

"*Jade* . . ."

"Don't move," she whispered. "Don't do anything."

They lay, he with his weight totally resting on her, his surfeited manhood still thrust deep within her intimate heat, and her body bathed in the luxurious cream of his ejaculate.

It was enough to hold him and to know his erotic craving for her could not hold him, even with his iron-willed control.

Her excitement heightened as each moment passed in a sultry silence, and finally, as she felt him stir to life again, she whispered, "Now Roak . . . Let me feel how hard you get for me." She wriggled her hips against him and she felt him swell. "I feel it, I feel it getting harder . . ."

Another spurt, and she gyrated against it. "Give me more, give it to me . . . yes . . ." as he elongated again. "Let me have it, let me feel it—I need it, Roak, I need it big and hard . . ."

Rock hard now and potent as sin.

"Cram it into me now tight—tighter . . . every inch, Roak. Every thick, long, hard inch . . . like that—I feel it real hard, real hard . . ."

"Jade . . ." he whispered hoarsely, wedging himself against her.

"It's hard, Roak, it's so deliciously hard . . . take me—take me now—"

He moved; she moaned—every sensation was magnified by the ejaculate-wet of her velvet sheath—he felt it, he felt her, slippery with his juices and wet with her own.

Her body surged in rhythm with his; he rode her, he took her in long powerful lunges with the perfect cadence of a long-time lover; he found an inexhaustible reserve of stamina as he possessed her spangling body, her erotic need, her elusive culmination.

But it would come; he could have pumped it all night—but even she was stunned at the staggering explosiveness of her release—a cataclysm of sensation skyrocketing like fireworks and bursting like a comet and tailing off into hot fire.

He thought after that he could just go all night. He thought he would let it rest and let her recover and cradle himself neatly and tightly until they were both ready again.

He had thought it was a matter of just rocking gently against her until she calmed down. He had thought that everything was over.

And then he wriggled his hips to force himself deeper inside her—just one telling little movement and his body contracted, his manhood spoke, and in one mighty convulsion, he went hurtling over the edge, spending himself in a shuddering moan of completion.

Chapter 15

They lay side by side, her hand enfolding his forspent member.

. . . mine—

Three times now and I awaken in the early morning hours yearning for more—

It was a most distinct sensation: her body felt lubricated as she stretched languidly beside him, her movements slow, deliberate, sensuous, hovering between wanting him and wanting to prolong the burgeoning pleasure of arousal.

Her nipples felt sensitized, stiffening into taut bulbous nubs as her desire was kindled by the mere fact she was lying naked with him in her bed.

This is mine—

I want to make it mine . . .

I want to hold it inside me forever—

She rubbed her hand against his pliant length and he stirred.

I want to hold him like this forever . . .

She felt the urgency in herself; if only she could capture this most elusive part of him and make it her own—she played with him, lifting, patting, squeezing, stroking his elongating sex—if only she could bind it to her, constrain it somehow, label it as her possession and hers alone . . .

Ah now, now—he is so upright and right—stiff as a poker and ready to ram himself home . . .

She ran her hand down his jutting length to the nest of hair at the base and with her fingers circled his thick hard root.

There . . . I would ring him right there with my token so he would know this is mine—

. . . mine—

She covered him with her hands in the darkness, and, as always, in awe at the magic of him, at how much she wanted him, and at how easily and completely this gorgeously male part of him aroused her.

Every time.

She had only to envision him, naked and thrusting, and her body went wet with longing. She had only to remember the penetrating feel of him and she could almost recreate the hot slick slide of pleasure.

And it never abated; the more he possessed her, the more she wanted him.

And now I want him to wear a symbol of my lust for him . . .

She trembled at the thought, excited beyond all measure at the idea of her possessing him in some tangible way when they were not together.

She would invent it—some wondrous item that would fit around the thick root of him and encompass him when he was in repose and when he was rock hard and ready for her.

. . . that wide . . .

This pliable—

Made of wire to hold its shape and still expand as he does; gold coated to make it silky satin against his tender flesh . . .

. . . so he knows that I hold him there all the time . . .

. . . and he never forgets who makes him hard—

Her fingers writhed against him and her body undulated in a voluptuous swell of desire.

Tomorrow . . . tomorrow I will commission the thing and have it made—

"Is it hard enough for you, wanton Jade?"

His voice was hoarse with tumultuous excitement, almost as if he had been awake and aware and waiting for the perfect moment.

She grasped him tightly. "It's naked enough for me, Roak."

She felt his hand slide across her thighs and she turned toward him and angled her one leg outward to give him her naked heat.

His fingers found her welcoming fold and he instantly inserted them into her honey. "Is it hard enough for a Jade?"

"It's getting harder," she equivocated coyly as his fingers probed her just the way she liked. "It's getting longer and thicker and more powerful . . ."

"Is it hard enough?"

"It is ravenous to possess me . . ." she whispered, spreading her legs still wider apart so he could explore her hot satin sheath with expert intimacy.

"Is it hard enough?"

"It is vigorous with wanting me . . ."

"Is . . . it . . . *hard* enough?"

She gasped as he twisted his fingers erotically deep within her. "It . . . is . . . like . . . iron—"

"Ah, the Jade says I am hard enough for her . . ." he murmured, moving closer to her and nudging her leg over his own. "The Jade is very particular about how hard she wants her master to be. Tell me, Jade"—as he slipped his fingers from her lush yearning center—"tell me if *this* is hard enough for you . . ."

She felt him pushing against her, nudging at the creamy coral beneath her thick pubic hair.

And he waited, poised at her entrance point, with just his thick-ridged tip inserted within her.

She gasped as she felt him crown her velvet cleft. "I can hardly feel you . . ."

". . . *this* . . . ?"

He pressed inward another inch.

She groaned.

". . . this?" Another inch.

"Or this," he moved again.

"Or *this*—" the last forceful drive into her wet and welcoming sex.

She made that guttural sound at the back of her throat.

"*Now* is it hard enough for the Jade? And now—and now . . ." as he thrust into her fiercely and without restraint, that whole hard part of him wild to pin her to the bed.

She couldn't move—she could only feel; she wound her arms around him and hung on as he pounded at her, as he muttered thick incoherent lust words against her lips, as he pushed her into a twisting, lunging, plunging fervor for completion.

He's mine he's mine he's mine he's mine . . . the words shimmered in her mind; her body responded ferociously, surging up to meet him exultantly, glorying in every hot hard thrust of his possession.

"Is it ... hard ... enough?" he panted as he plunged vora-
ciously into her fecund heat.

And at his words, and with that last driving motion, she came;
there wasn't a building of feeling, there wasn't a silver slide of
sensation; there wasn't a moment when she thought her body
would surrender with such tempestuous finality to the power and
the virility of his.

For one tantalizing moment, she hung between command and
culmination, and the next, she was engulfed in a dazzling, bone-
crackling torrent of pleasure ... swallowed by it ... drowning
in it ... enslaved by it ... yielding to the utter force and power
of it ...

Beyond her—it was beyond her, and she was its slave ... it
rippled all over her, spiraling out of control.

And he came with her, erupting into a volcanic ejaculation,
shuddering with the force of it, succumbing to the raw hot need
to possess her still again. And to remain the hot hard force within
her, as wordlessly they fell asleep in each other's arms.

The idea obsessed her from the moment she awakened alone
in her bed: a symbol to claim him—something simple, golden,
elegant and *there*.

She spent the morning thinking about it, sketching ideas, refin-
ing the physical look of it, explosive with excitement at the very
notion of it.

"Well, Roak—may I do some shopping today?" she asked him
as he served her breakfast and she watched him keenly.

*Oh, he was there for her, and it was no accident that she was
stretched out languidly on the couch as he marched to and from
the kitchen bringing her whatever she imperiously demanded.*

*It was part of the game—Roak as servant was a ridiculous
idea—but still, she loved him at her beck and call, and she especially loved the coiled bulge between his legs that neither his frock
coat nor his serving apparatus could hide.*

*He was so there for her; even after such a glorious night, he
was there, reaching for her. And she wanted him. She ached with
wanting him.*

"It is as I told you, Lady Genelle—"

... am I hard enough for you ...

"Joseph must go with you everywhere."

. . . am I hard enough for the wanton Jade . . .

"I will take Joseph," she promised. "One little errand and then I'll return." Another promise, with the hope that he would be waiting for her—that he would summon her to relive the pleasures of the night before.

Maybe two little errands—she wasn't at all sure she had enough money to squander on such a fancy.

But she was going to do it—nothing would stop her from doing it.

Joseph's expression revealed nothing as their carriage stopped on Bond Street at the Hulston and Featherbaugh jewelers.

"You can wait," she instructed him and hurried inside.

Mr. Featherbaugh, a tall, elegant, gray-haired gentleman, greeted her. He prided himself on being able to smell a parvenu from a hundred yards away. And here was this gorgeous lady whom he had never seen before and yet who seemed to know him, his establishment, and precisely the golden ornament she wished to have him design.

And then her name—Lady Tisne. Who did not know of the notorious Lord Arthur? But dead now. And she—this glorious creature—his widow, dressed sedately in black silk edged with satin bands, and a proper lace cap on her head, and asking him to design the most outrageous bracelet.

He just didn't understand, and she patiently explained it all to him one more time.

"It is to be a wire coil—it must be malleable, but it must hold its shape. It must be expandable, but it must also retain its shape. I envision it wrapping around my wrist three times; I want to be able to stretch it out lengthwise and compress it to one thin gold ring. It must not constrict my veins. It has to float on my skin, and it must accommodate my whim to wear it at my wrist or up toward my elbow.

"That is why, Mr. Featherbaugh, it must be able to expand or contract, and it must be as thin and delicate as possible, yet as strong as possible.

"Now, can you make me something like this or shall I find another house to fill my order?"

He was absolutely nonplussed. "And you want it coated over with gold?"

"Exactly; the thinnest, finest layer of gold that can support the bracelet."

"I see." He looked at her for a moment, and then down at the sketch she had brought him. "I see. Well, we have never done such an . . . object—I cannot even calculate the cost until we make a prototype . . ."

"How long will that take?" she interrupted.

"Several days—I will send word," he said, still eyeing her uncertainly.

"Excellent, Mr. Featherbaugh. I leave my design in your capable hands."

He watched her as she walked out the door and into her well-sprung carriage where her footman was waiting.

The accoutrements were all there. But still—one never knew.

He called for his assistant.

"Digby—please check on this patron—a Lady Tisne. See if she has enough money in the bank to afford this ridiculous whimsy."

"Where is Roak?" This time to the parlor maid.

"Oh, he is about to leave the house, mum."

"Is he indeed?" she murmured. "Well, isn't that interesting?"

And where did he go every afternoon and evening in the hours before he summoned her?

. . . women will wait—

How could she wait when she was consumed with curiosity about all things connected to him?

And where was the danger if she were following him?

. . . crazy—

How could she sit and wait?

She went into the entrance hall and surreptitiously opened the door to the servants' stairwell.

She didn't even think—she slipped in behind the door and darted down the steps to the servants' hall.

She could hear his voice issuing orders, and then the slam of a door. She hurried down the little hallway that skirted the kitchen, dining room, and wine cellar door.

At the far end of the basement had been Tolliver's private

room, the room to which Roak had assigned himself and returned every morning after their nights of splendor.

This room, isolated from the others, the door now locked, the inhabitant now gone . . .

Damn him, he is as slippery as a shadow and twice as hard to pin down . . .

There had to be an exit door somewhere down here. She tried them all frantically until she found it, located practically near his bedroom door.

She flung it open and raced up the stone steps to a stone parapet at the rear of the house.

There was the fence, the gate still swinging. She pushed through and emerged in the carriage house drive.

Which way? Why did one never know the fine points about one's home?

She ran up the drive and out the narrow entryway to Green Street just in time to see Roak climb into a cab.

She heard his voice—"Deepditch, driver,"—the slam of the door and the ominous sound of the cab rolling away.

Deepditch?

She walked slowly around to the avenue to hail her own cab.

What on earth could be in Deepditch?

She wasn't going to ask him—she was going to find out . . .

It was a neighborhood to the north of the city, peopled by immigrants who lived in tenements or small, inexpensive houses and ran specialty shops along the shore road.

It was an area of narrow cobbled streets with three-story brownstone buildings with cheap office space which housed lawyers and doctors who could not afford to set up on Harley Street.

And it was a bustling little community with peddlers rolling their wagons and selling food and wares and children swarming around them; a place of churches and sinners, of workers and streetwalkers—

She saw them all as her cab rumbled through the streets at her directions as she vainly tried to discover why Roak had come here.

There was no sign of him as the afternoon sun lowered toward the horizon.

For all she knew, he was back at Green Street, and her summons awaited her.

She couldn't think of that now.

She scanned the streets—looking—looking—

Looking for what? A likely candidate to question.

Because it stood to reason that if Roak had come here, he had found a connection to her husband somewhere in Deepditch.

Perhaps there was an illicit house of pleasure in Deepditch—

Or more than one, she would wager, as she spotted some ladies of the evening beginning their parade.

So easy, suddenly, to identify the women who *would* . . .

The question was, *would* they talk?

She opened her purse and hastily counted her money. Enough to pay for information and the cab?

She had to take her chances.

"Driver—stop . . . by those ladies, if you please . . ."

She opened her window and motioned to one of them.

"Mum?"

She knew what the question was, too; the only successful ploy—a newcomer seeking "work"—even here . . .

"I'm new to town and I'm looking for a place."

"What kind of place, mum?"

"The kind where a girl can have some fun and earn some money at the same time."

"What kind of place is that, mum?" the woman asked sharply.

"The kind with good money—you know what I mean."

"I'm a good girl and I don't know nothin'," the woman said tightly and flounced away.

Genelle stared after her as she began walking quickly down the street, with the other girls, save one, following behind her.

That one sauntered over to the cab, taking her time, assessing the situation.

"Well, well, well—" she said, twirling a scarf around one long pointed finger. "A newcomer to town looking for fun. Why didn't you go up to London?"

Good question—and by the look in this one's eyes she was as smart as the street and more wicked than sin.

"I'm down from Bickley and I was looking for something

slightly bigger and a lot better. More men, you know? I'm not nearly ready for the likes of London proper."

Did it sound right? Did she sound right?

"Where did you work?"

Dear heaven—and what if she knew all about the cathouses in Bickley—then what? It didn't matter; she still had to lie through her teeth.

She crossed her fingers and launched into her story.

"There was a place called *The Ottoman House.* And then another called . . . called *Seven Veils* . . ."

Lord, where did she drag these names up from?

Her inquisitor nodded. "We have a place here called the *Veil.* Maybe you want to try there. Down by the waterfront; rough part of town, but lots of business, lots of action."

"That's what I want—lots of money," Genelle said fervently, debating whether to offer her some money.

"Good luck then." The woman turned away, and Genelle warily watched her follow after the others who had long disappeared.

Now what was that about? She was too friendly, that one— took too much on faith—or was she being paid to look for likely candidates and steer them in that direction?

"Driver—the waterfront . . ."

The cab moved forward, skirting the traffic, edging its way through the narrow streets until it came to the docks.

The streets were well-nigh impassable here, except for drays and flat trucks to convey cargo. The buildings that lined the waterfront were red brick, no more than three stories with dormers, and they housed everything from shipping offices to warehouses to merchandise stores.

On a side street, there was a broad brick plaza from which radiated out more buildings, stores, consignors, factories, and merchant banks.

Somewhere, in that maze of streets and buildings, there was an illicit house of pleasure catering to seamen called the *Veil.*

She might just as well look for a ha'penny on a heath as find this house amidst all this noise and bustle.

"Driver—turn around and—"

As the cab swung around, she had the full wide view of the

adjacent street, and in the lowering light, she caught a glimpse of black in motion climbing into a carriage far off down the street.

"Driver—that way!"

She leaned out of the window to get a better look—but the carriage was gone.

The impression wasn't—she knew that body all encompassed in black and just the way it moved . . .

The cab pulled up at the corner to avoid a pedestrian, and Genelle shifted to the opposite side to get a better look at the row of buildings from which he had sprinted.

She hadn't imagined it: Roak had been there. There couldn't be two men who had that particular muscular movement when they walked—and he had bolted from one of these doorways— none of them identified and all of them looking every bit the—

She broke off the thought as the cab inched forward and simultaneously one of the doors opened and a woman peeked out.

And for one stunning moment before the door slammed shut again and the cab moved on, she found herself face to face with her traitorous mother—in the last place she had expected to find her.

That was my mother—and that was Roak emerging from that building . . . but how do I ask him, how, when I wasn't supposed to be there—and never supposed to know?

She lay in his arms that night after two rounds of exhausting lovemaking, floating on an orgiastic cloud of desire and deceit.

When is he going to tell me? How can I tell him I know?

She hated the fact her pleasure was tempered with a lie. And she was grateful when she awakened alone the following morning.

And she determined as she dressed to prise some information out of him over her breakfast scones.

"So Roak," she murmured as she poured her tea into a delicate cup. "Where do things stand?"

"I answer that question every night, my lady," he said, his tone rigidly restrained.

She gritted her teeth. "I see no forward movement in my case."

"You have seen much upward movement, Lady Genelle . . ."

"Roak . . ."

"It is for the best, my lady, that you know as little as you do."

"The question is, how much do *you* know? Nothing has changed in the last week. Nothing at all."

"Something has changed."

She looked up into his fathomless dark eyes. "Yes . . ." And she almost added, *what did you find in the house at Deepditch . . .* and she bit it back just in time.

It would spoil everything if he knew—just everything . . .

She choked down her scones and washed away the brittle feeling inside her with gallons of tea.

Alter all, now that *she* knew her whereabouts, she could go question her mother herself—anytime she wanted.

Maybe today . . .

Maybe her mother had the answer to everything in one little word.

Maybe . . .

She needed money—a simple matter of having Joseph accompany her to the bank. And then she needed to duck out of the house and grab another cab.

This time, though, this time, she would know where she was going and what she was doing.

She was getting so proficient at dealing with cabs and lies.

The driver this time was amenable and voluble, keeping up a running commentary on all the sights of interest from outer London to Deepditch Lay.

In the morning, everything looked different. There was a silence at the waterfront which belied the bustle of the day before.

And she didn't quite remember the street; they stumbled around across the maze of back alleys for more than an hour before they accidentally came upon it again.

And then all the houses looked the same. There was no way to identity the door from which her mother had emerged for that flashing instant.

But she was determined. She started at one end of the street and she knocked on every door.

And she asked the same question: "Is there a woman here, gray-haired, stout, green-eyed, like me—a businesswoman perhaps, who keeps house for working girls—do you know her? Does she live here?"

And at each and every doorway the answer was no until she

reached the building in the middle of the block on the opposite side of the street.

"Ah yes, that'd be mother Maud," the old man said who answered the door.

He eyed her knowingly. "You just missed her, young lady. She moved out yesterday, bags and baggage—in spite of her signing a lease for a year. Still, she paid me for six months, so who's to lose? You interested in a place to let? The whole building except the basement. Ten rooms, dining, parlor, and kitchen. Lots of space to set out your baggage—if you know what I mean."

". . . Missed her?" Genelle could barely comprehend it.

"She took the place not three weeks ago; I don't understand it. But you could take in a lot if you've a mind to set up here . . . the men all know where to find her and the word's not out yet she's gone. The apartment is furnished too—all good beds and covers . . ."

"I—no, thank you," she said, gathering her wits. "I'm looking for mother Maud. I don't suppose—if you ever find out her where-abouts—you could send me word?"

"I might do," the man said cautiously. "But who's doing the asking?"

She rummaged around in her reticule for a piece of paper and a stub of pencil, and then scribbled her name and direction.

"Oh," he said meaningfully as he scanned the address. "A London swell. Down on your luck, are you? Want the old mother to take care of you?"

. . . *dear God—did everyone know?*

"Something like that," she said caustically as she turned to leave. "Except I really *am* her daughter and I really need to find her."

Her mother was like a ghost, vanishing and appearing at will, haunting her with truth and evasions.

She felt weary when she finally debarked at Green Street and paid off her cabman. There was no end to this business, there was too much secrecy, and endless debauchery.

Something had to explode.

She thrust open the door to find Joseph Footman standing there reprovingly.

"My lady."

"Yes, Joseph," she said in her haughtiest voice—the one that brooked no argument and deflected confrontations.

But he wasn't about to criticize the fact she had gone out without him despite Roak's orders.

He handed her a card.

From Mr. Featherbaugh—the gilded coil is ready to be approved. Oh, very nice, very, very nice . .

"Call the carriage, Joseph."

In and out, in and out—too apt. I have to stop thinking like this . . .

She allowed Joseph to assist her into the carriage.

The thing is ready—it took only two days to fashion . . . how clever they are . . . how delicious it will be to encircle him with it and make it mine . . .

"Mr. Featherbaugh—" she said flutily, holding out her hand as she entered the jeweler's shop. "I knew I could count on you."

"Lady Tisne. Do follow me so we can have a little privacy." He led her behind the counter and through a rich velvet drape into a little anteroom off of which there were several cubicles concealed by curtains.

He pulled aside the curtain of the first one and invited her to have a seat.

There was a small mahogany tea table inside, and two densely upholstered chairs.

She sat, and a moment later he returned, carrying a velvet pillow which he set on the table as he took the seat opposite.

The object was covered with a gold-trimmed, black velvet shroud, as if he were presenting it to royalty, and there was a kind of reverence in the way he solemnly lifted the cloth.

"There it is," he whispered, and there it was, placed at the exact center of the black velvet pillow, a gleaming coil wound into a snake-like golden circlet.

"A most interesting project, Lady Tisne. To get the tension of the spring just right, and then to make sure that the gold coating was both thin enough and satiny enough for a lady's delicate skin . . . Pick it up, my lady. There is just enough spring to it so that it maintains its shape."

"Yes—" She rolled it between her fingers, feeling the sleekness of it, testing it against her bare arm, and finally stretching it to encircle her wrist and watching how it eased gently back into shape. "Yes. It's so light, and yet it's very much *there*. And the ends—you gave the ends a tiny little nub that I can just barely feel . . ."

That he will just feel . . . I want him to feel every minute of the day when he's not with me . . . this is so perfect—so perfect . . .

"This is perfect, Mr. Featherbaugh; this is exactly what I wanted."

"Thank you, my lady."

"But—if it turns out there is any trouble with it—can there be adjustments?"

"Oh certainly, my lady. You have only to ask."

"I may take this then?"

"Most assuredly. There is only the matter of the bill."

"Would you send it to my solicitor, Mr. Morfit? He will have the bank issue a draft tomorrow and deliver it to you."

"Thank you, Lady Tisne. A pleasure to create a distinctive piece of jewelry for you. I'm sure it will be noticed and commented upon."

"Oh yes, I am too."

He bowed—they understood each other, this well-heeled little provincial widow and he. He escorted her to the door with all the deference he would have shown a peer of the realm, and then immediately he called his assistant.

"Digby—" he handed him an envelope in which he had prepared the bill. "Take this to Morfit in Fitzwilliam Square. And make sure you get the check today."

When she returned to Green Street, there was a package waiting for her.

She took it to her room and opened it with shaking hands.

There was a note:

Jade—dress for me and come . . .

And inside layers and layers of tissue paper, she found a corset dripping with pearls.

Her heart accelerated. She ripped off her dress and her underthings and took the beautiful thing and hooked it around her waist.

*Oh, it is gorgeous, gorgeous—look at those festoons of pearls
swinging so seductively from the bottom edge . . . I just need to
turn it and lift my breasts into the upper part . . .*

*How cunning the way it reveals my nipples . . . and that long
apron of pearls that just covers my navel . . .*

*And a choker with a long pearl-beaded extension that just falls
to my breasts . . .*

"Jade . . ."

She whirled and he was there, locking the door behind him.

"I couldn't wait—" His eyes glittered as they rested on her
and he began removing his clothes. "Get over here—"

"It's beautiful—"

"Get over here—" His coat and shirt lay at his feet, and she
stepped over them as he shucked his pants. "Over by the table."

He followed her and lifted her onto it and positioned her the
way he wanted to see her.

She arched her back and exaggerated the bend of her leg to
give him a better view of what he wanted to see as he removed
the final obstacle to what she wanted to see.

He came closer to her and closer until he was nudging her
feminine fold. Until he inserted himself there.

She looked down at the ramrod length of him partially embedded in her and she thrilled to the sight of him penetrating her like
that.

She didn't want him to move; she wanted to feel him like that
just inside the wet heat of her cleft and she wanted to watch him
elongate with the hot need to possess her.

He rotated his hips and pushed slightly against her. She spread
her legs further apart to bear down on that thick-ridged tip of
him that delved into her.

She moved against it, arching her body and shimmying against
its heat and the pliant hardness of it.

"Your nipples look gorgeous in pearls."

"My nipples love how hard you are for me."

"The Jade loves what I'm doing to her."

"I love how you adorn me with your nakedness. Don't move.
I look wonderful with the thick hot jut of you just inches inside
me." She bore down on his sex again. "Do you love how I look?"

"I never want to see you any other way but with my naked heat between your legs."

"You're so deliciously big; you fill me between my legs with just the very tip of you." She wriggled her body against him again. "It feels so good, so thick . . ." she groaned as he contracted his muscles and pressed against her.

She spread her legs again so that the aroused nub of her pleasure was in direct contact with the hot press of his male corona.

"Oooo—I could ride you like this all night, Roak," she breathed as her hips ground down rhythmically against him.

"Ride it," he growled, and she moved again, this time intent on achieving her completion with just those hot hard inches of him inserted between her legs.

He watched every voluptuous movement as she wriggled and writhed and gyrated against the thickness of him.

And she loved him watching her. The thought of him being able to see himself inches deep inside her excited her still the more. It was that he could see and she could not.

Next time, next time I want to see it—I want to see him inserted in me just that little bit . . . just that, just that—just . . . that—

She came, slowly, creamily, dreamily, opulently, her body pumping against the hard pliant tip of him, her hands grasping his rigid shaft as she rode him rhythmically to a climax.

"Jade . . ." A whisper.

"Yes . . . ?" A breath.

"I want you."

"I can't—it's too much, too much . . ."

She still held him, her hands like a vise between them.

"I have to possess the Jade. Right *now*. Lie down."

"On the table?"

"Lie down."

She eased herself down and he lifted her legs so she could brace them against the table top.

He positioned himself at the edge, and moved her lower torso closer to his body; she grasped the edges of the table as he centered her against him.

She gasped as he drove into her once, twice, and then again, his member utterly bursting with his need to claim her.

And then again—one deep longing plunge, drowning, drowning in a spume of a release that gushed out of him like a geyser and eddied away into a cool feeling of relief.

He pulled her toward him gently and lifted her, and then, still inside her, he carried her to the bed.

He slept; she lay awake thinking about the pleasures of this bold new way he had possessed her.

I need a pier glass in this room; I need to see how he possesses me—why do men always get to see the delicious things and women close their eyes and submit . . .

But I have never submitted. And I am a jade at heart, and I want to surround him with the symbol of my *possession . . .*

It still encircled her wrist, as light as gossamer, a reminder of all the potent pleasure he had given her.

She slipped it off and ran her fingers over the sleek silky coil of it, and then she felt for his sleeping member and deftly wound it around the root of him, and pressed it tightly against his rough pubic hair.

She had never felt so aroused by anything. She turned her body against his so that her taut tipped nipples were pressing hard into his arm and hair-roughened chest.

She began rubbing her leg against his thigh, and then her foot against his groin, stroking his sleeping manhood and scrotal sac with her toes and finally her fingers as she massaged him to a glorious tumescence.

She felt for the ring; it nested neatly at the base of his erection, expanding just that much to accommodate his thickness, the little nubs separated now by an inch of space and resting one on the underside of his shaft, and the other above, lost in his thick male hair.

Perfect—it is perfect . . .

She stroked the pulsating tip of him, and finally he stirred.

"Jade . . . ?"

"Your naked Jade is worshipping her pleasure . . ." she whispered. "Even when you sleep you get hard for me."

He turned toward her and reached for her.

". . . What's that?"

"What's what?"

"I feel something . . ." he muttered, sliding his hand down to his erection. "What the hell . . . ?"

She closed her hand over his. "Don't touch it. It's my ring of pleasure. I want it there. I want to know it's there when you possess me—I want you to grind it against me so I can feel it when we couple. I want you to feel it there all the time as the promise that I am always naked and waiting for you. I never want you to take it off . . . unless it is uncomfortable and until I do not please you."

She felt his fingers stroking it, pushing it, twisting it, testing the feel of it against his tender manhood.

"I will wear the ring," he whispered, "and you will never ever put on a piece of clothing again when we are together—except what I give you to wear."

"I want to wear that gorgeous hard part of you between my legs. It is the perfect size . . ." she breathed as she enclosed him with her hand and measured him. ". . . the perfect fit. Give it to me."

"I can't wait to give it to you, you naked Jade. It's so easy to slip into."

"It just . . . slides right into place . . ." she gasped as he crowned her and drove deeply into her, and then rocked his hips against her so she could feel the ring.

"Nice . . . tight . . . fit," he growled.

"Always . . . in fashion—"

He groaned as his manhood stiffened and ejaculated suddenly, purposefully, explosively just on the pure erotic play of words between them.

"Damn . . ."

"Roak . . ."

"No . . ." He rolled off her. "Spread your legs."

She did as he told her, and he levered himself on top of her and inserted his fingers.

It was so intense—one, two, three fingers twisting and probing inside of her; her body reacted, bearing down on the pressure.

Her hands cupped his manhood as she shimmied against his fingers, her hips undulating, seeking her release.

She felt him spurt into life as she drove toward her climax, her fingers writhing involuntarily against his stiffening length.

Hard, harder—*harder* . . .

She was lost in a haze of sensation as his fingers pumped her toward completion. She found it—she squeezed—hard, harder—*harder* . . . and she came, her body bucking violently with each rhythmic wave.

And then she came down, slowly, slowly, slowly, still grasping his now jutting erection tightly in her hand.

It was the most erotic little tension around the base of his root. He could just feel it, but his awareness of it made the feel of it seem more intense.

It felt smooth, like satin, and slippery like silk—like *her;* he wanted her again and she was asleep.

He crept out of bed in search of a mirror; it was not enough to feel the thing—he wanted her to see it nestling against her hair, against her wriggling bottom.

There was a mirror in the armoir, just beside the chair.

He experimented with the chair: which way to position her and which way afforded the best possible view of him taking her.

She watched him, from beneath her lids, as he moved this way and that in the soft bedroom light, his manhood jutting upright like the bough of a tree, the circlet flashing as the gaslight hit it.

She stretched luxuriously to let him know she was awake and ready for him.

"Get over here."

"I'd love to." She swung her legs over the bed, slowly and deliberately, taking her time. "Here I am—and you are all there . . ."

"Don't be a coy bitch, Jade. Bend over; I want your nipple."

She caught her breath and leaned her right shoulder toward him.

She watched it in the mirror, how he cupped her breast, nuzzled her nipple, and then took the taut bulbous point of it between his lips—and pulled and sucked on it . . .

. . . *like the Arcade—like I loved it at the Arcade* . . .

She shifted backward slightly so that he would have to suck harder and she watched it all in the mirror.

She felt him take her left breast in his hand; she felt him squeeze the tingling hard tip of her nipple in concert with his sucking.

She heard him groan; she saw his manhood flex with arousal. "Sit . . ."

She straddled his legs, easing herself down, watching her every movement in the mirror as she encompassed every last hard hot inch of him into her satin sheath.

And then they were joined, and she could not see her symbol of possession—she felt it pressing against her bottom and she wriggled against it, her eyes on her every movement reflected in the mirror.

"Ride me, Jade—"

She rode him—she watched him—she goaded him—and he blew—cupping her buttocks and sucking her nipples, and feeling her body taunt and tease him, he just blew, rolling and jolting against her as his climax engulfed him.

"Bitch, bitch, bitch—you stick a ring around me and then you want to prove I can't possess you any more . . . shit—get off of me, Jade. Get *off.*"

She slipped off of him silently. "Or maybe the idea of it excites you so much you just can't hold it in."

"I'll hold *you* in, bitch. Give me an hour and we'll see who can hold it in."

"Make sure I'm the one holding it in, Roak. Because I want it and you had better be ready to give it to me."

Chapter 16

"I love the ring."

"I knew you would love it—"

It was the aftermath of another two rounds of lovemaking, each of which had culminated in simultaneous completion.

"It excites me . . ."

"It arouses me just to think of you wearing it . . ."

"Then you'll always be aroused and ready for me—"

"Oh yes . . ." she whispered. "And I loved the mirror."

And I love you—no, I love what we do . . .

She mentally shook herself. She didn't have any feelings like that for him. It was lust, pure and simple. And nothing to do with men and women and how they could feel about each other.

. . . loved the mirror . . . when had women ever been able to see what their sex looked like . . . ?

When could she feel free to ask him how he had found her mother—?

No, no, no—why spoil it? Why did she want to ruin the night when she lived for the night and glorious pleasure of abandoning herself to him . . .

She nestled against him, feeling faintly aroused and secure. Every part of him was hard—arms, thighs, belly—*that . . . already —and it had not been an hour since the last coupling.*

And if it stopped? If it were over?

She couldn't think that far ahead. She could only think in the moment while she wrestled with her feelings of dread.

And then he whispered against her, and she turned in his arms and opened herself to him and gratefully abandoned herself to his might.

* * *

Daylight—the end of month one.

She sat in the morning room assessing how little Roak had found to help her case.

The two mystery women; Arthur's ownership of the House of Correction as motive for someone else to have killed him; her mother's motive of greed, now disproved by the fact that she had put by her own little fortune by dint of her "career"; her mother's disappearance and reappearance in a small river town near London—why? The theft of her written agreement with Arthur that she would inherit only what he was giving her in separation; the disappearance of the servants.

Amorphous things—

Those awful places that her husband had frequented when the House of Correction was not enough for him . . .

And Tony Lethbridge, who was assiduously protecting a reputation that did not exist . . . and lunching with her husband's lawyer, whom he would have no reason to know—

And no reason not to know if he were part of the vast circle of Arthur's "friends"—

Arthur's particular friends . . .

Shadows, all of it—shapeless, formless things with no substance, nothing that could be touched or molded into some kind of alternative theory.

The facts stuck: she was alone in the house when Arthur was murdered; and to all intents and purposes, Tony Lethbridge had never been there.

And there wasn't a single place in that web of suspicion which surrounded that she could find a weak spot or a tear.

She had to find her mother.

Mother Maud . . .

Mother to a thousand other girls but her . . .

Damn it—damn it . . . damn it—

She yanked on the bellpull.

The parlormaid responded to her summons.

"Where is Roak?"

"Oh, Mr. Roak isn't available, mum."

Of course not—he was only available when he wanted to be . . .

"Thank you."

She didn't feel like thanking anybody.

Why was it in the light of day, everything good and exciting seemed unreal and misbegotten?

She bit her lip. This kind of thinking was not helping her. She was paying Roak too much money not to have confidence in his abilities.

On all fronts . . .

. . . so to speak—

Stiles had not yet come for her. She had another day in which to unearth a vital clue.

". . . Mum? Mum?"

The parlormaid again, interrupting her thoughts.

"What is it?"

"Someone to see you, mum."

Her heart dropped to her feet. *Stiles already, just when she had convinced herself he had no reason to come . . .*

She took a deep breath. "Show him in."

But it wasn't *him*—

It was her mother.

"So you found me, Miss Priss—ain't you the smart little girl . . ."

"Why did you leave—*Mother Maud* . . ."

"Ooo—clever girl—found out about that one, eh? Well, I'll tell you what—you tell that fancy nancy detective of yours to keep out of my business. You tell him—I know somethin' he don't want me to know—"

She felt an awful chill. "You know something about Roak?"

"You just tell 'im, girl. I know somethin' he don't want no one to know."

She felt like shaking her mother. "You have to tell me."

"I ain't gonna tell you nothin' . . ."

She had to change her tack even while her heart was sinking to the floor. What could she know about Roak? What could she get the old bitch to tell her?

"Who bribed you to leave? Who broke into my desk?"

"Stay out of it—you'd be better off if they took you away."

"Damn it, Mother! When you have thousands of pounds

banked away, and you walk out my door and take away my servants and the one thing that could clear me of murder . . . ?"

"How'd you know about that?"

"I hired a *skilled investigator,* Mother, you remember. He's dug up lots of interesting things. All that money all those years you made me believe we were living in poverty . . ."

"We was—I put it by . . . I wasn't going to have a frugal old age, my girl . . . and I didn't think that nosy son-of-a-bitch would ever ferret that out. Well, you tell 'im, you hear, and he'll stop his damned snooping. And anyway, you was young and beautiful enough to marry well."

"And didn't I just—to a man who stooped to every perversion and had women on the side . . ."

"Do you think so, eh?"

"And probably *you,*" she spat. "Who paid you to leave here, Mother?"

"I thought of it by me own self, daughter."

"He had to have a *lot* of money, Mother, to make it worth *your* while."

"Ohhh, a lot of money—"

"Maybe you had better make a will, Mother. What would happen to all those lovely pounds if something happened to you?"

"I know which bodies are in which crypts, my girl, I'm safe as houses."

"So why did you run? Why did you leave the waterfront? Why did you come here?"

"I come to tell you to leave it alone—leave *me* alone. You can't get nothin' back, girl; your money-sapping detective ain't goin' to find nothin'; and I come to tell *you* somethin' . . ."

"Tell me what?" she demanded sharply.

"Tell you—tell you you're looking at things straight on instead of how they really be. You ain't thinkin', girl. If you'd've been smarter about it, we could've had *everything* . . . and you wouldn't've needed no spoon lickin' investigator with his own wheel to grease . . ."

She felt a sense of pure terror. "You mean we could have had the *House of Correction* . . ."

Her mother swung around to stare at her.

She jumped into the silence as her mother was caught off-guard.

"Who is Davidella Eversham, Mother?"

Her mother looked taken aback—and then she started laughing—a huge booming laugh that rocked her whole body.

"Who is Clarissa Bone?"

Her mother stopped laughing abruptly. "So he got that far, eh? Well, when you tell 'im, he'll stop—he'll stop before he figures it out."

She hated her mother; she hated her intimations, her gall, her betrayal. "Who bribed you to leave, Mother?"

"I did the best I could," her mother said with a righteous tone in her voice.

"Who stole my papers? Who is my enemy? Who killed Arthur?"

"It wasn't you," her mother said and started laughing again as she moved toward the door. "Remember, daughter—look at things how they really be . . ."

She edged out of the morning room, and Genelle jumped up to follow her.

"I ain't tellin' nothin' more, girl. You're on your own. Don't come lookin' for me—tell that detective—neither of you ain't gonna find me again."

She watched helplessly as her mother bolted from the hallway out the entrance door and slammed it in her face.

She had never felt such pure fear.

Her mother had come to warn her not to pry.

Pry into what? What could she not know that they hadn't uncovered already? And the House of Correction was the worst of it—

Wasn't it?

And what could her mother possibly know about Roak?

She had to find him . . .

She felt like running—she went to her room instead—her room that was redolent of sex and desire, and things she would rather not think about.

She had to find Roak.

She pulled out her clothes and hurriedly dressed, kicking the beautiful pearl-encrusted corset into her closet and closing the door on that memory.

She almost jumped out of her skin at the sound of the knock on her door and she flung it open violently.

"Joseph," she gasped.

"My lady." He handed her the envelope she would have expected had her mother not destroyed the day, her night, her mood.

"The carriage waits."

"Thank you, Joseph."

She didn't even read the note until she settled into the seat and the carriage was on its way.

Jade—I am in a state of permanent arousal.

I need you now . . .

I need you too, she thought; she could not get to him fast enough.

And everything was as it had been before. He awaited her as always, naked and rampant, with the symbol of her possession ringed around the base of his erection.

He took her breath away, as always, and when she burst into the room, he came to her.

"Look at what you've done to me. It is like having your fingers around me all day long. Don't deny me . . . Lift your dress—I want you . . ." he walked her backward toward the wall. "I want you . . . now."

Her fear melted away. He was so strong, so *there*, so indelibly hers; he slipped into her quickly and easily and pinned her to the wall.

"Let me take you—in spite of what you want right now . . ."

How did he know?

"Yes," she whispered. "I promised—any time, anywhere . . ."

And he took her, slowly, easily, quickly, in short pumping thrusts; she didn't expect to find culmination. She had thought her worry would prevent it.

But she gave herself over to the feel of him, and the sensation of his tight hard thrusts, and her body responded for her—a long slow slide into a molten pool, and he came with her, diving explosively into his climax as he poured himself into her.

And then there was rest; he pulled on his trousers and lay with her on the sofa until the pleasure subsided and reality had to intrude.

She told him the whole.

"And that was all she said: she knew something I didn't want anyone else to know."

"That was what she said."

"A bluff," he said. "And the rest—grains of truth. *Her* truth. And she has been living a lie for so long, she probably can't distinguish what *is* the truth."

"She knows who those women are, the two Arthur was with."

"I don't doubt it."

There was a tone in his voice that made her look at him.

"Do you know?"

He hesitated a split second. "No."

"And you have no idea what she was talking about?"

Another fractional hesitation. "No."

She didn't know what to think. She moved out of his arms, away from the scent, the feel, the seduction of him.

"I'm going to go back to Green Street."

"I think you should; you are not in the mood to play."

"Are you? Will you find someone else with whom to play?"

"You own me, Jade. Isn't that what this means?" He was erect again already.

She got up to leave. "I hope you never forget it."

Joseph met her at the door.

"You have a visitor."

"Indeed?" She handed him her cloak with a feeling of foreboding. "And who might that be?"

I don't want to know . . .

"The gentleman from the Yard, my lady. I've shown him to the small parlor—he seemed familiar with the way."

"Thank you, Joseph. You might bring some tea."

She waited until he left her and then moved toward the small parlor with trepidation.

The Inspector was seated by the fire, consulting his notes.

"Inspector."

"Ah, Lady Tisne. You haven't left town."

"My dear Inspector, how could you think it?" She seated

herself opposite him, prepared to spar with him, word for word, insinuation for insinuation—and *not* to get caught in any of his traps.

"The household staff were not apprised of your absence."

She looked at him as if to say, *so?*

He held her gaze for a long awful moment and then turned to his notes.

"So, Lady Tisne, you have hired the estimable Roak to find the proof to clear you of suspicion in your husband's death."

"Yes."

He waited; she didn't elaborate. He said, "I see," in that flat noncommittal tone, and went back to his notes.

"Well, my lady. We are at an impasse."

She waited.

He waited.

Finally she said, "How so?"

"Nothing has emerged from our investigation, my lady, that could be helpful to you. You are the only one who could have killed your husband. And the only thing that has held me back from arresting you is the fact of your inheritance—that it is unusually modest, given the size of the estate, and that was confirmed by Madam Tisne—and that you knew the terms of your bequest long before your husband's death. So, Lady Tisne, I need to see the agreement that you and your husband signed."

Her heart dropped.

In the space of six words, everything changed.

"I—" she nearly choked on the words. And there was no way she could dissemble. "I don't have it."

"Is that so, my lady?"

His tone of polite disbelief stunned her.

"That is so, Inspector," she said coldly. "It was taken from my house—" she stopped short as she realized how the thing would sound.

How did she explain to him about her mother—about Roak? She had to get hold of herself and present the information in a way he could not discredit.

She took a deep breath. "A week ago, Inspector, I came home to find that my mother, whom—as you know—I had taken in, had utterly disappeared—and so had my servants. I searched the house to see if anything was missing. Mr. Roak was with me, and it was he who discovered that the drawer in which I keep my important papers was forced and that the letter of agreement was missing."

"I see. Did you report the theft, my lady?"

"No I didn't."

"Or that your mother was missing?"

"She might have disagreed that she was missing; she might have said she had decided to live apart from me."

"Or that the servants had, as a body, just vanished from your home?"

"No."

How bad did that look—that she hadn't been worried enough or cared enough . . . how did it sound in light of the fact that something valuable had turned up missing?

It sounded like a story cut from whole cloth, and she could see by his expression that that was exactly what he thought.

"Mr. Roak can corroborate that the agreement was missing?"

Another trap . . . Roak had never seen the agreement—and he had only her word that it existed.

"He can testify that the drawer was forced open," she said finally, reluctantly.

"You had not shown him the agreement," the Inspector concluded.

"No."

He made a note, and then looked up at her. "So, my lady. It is now arguable that there even was an agreement, which means that you might well have thought that the whole of Lord Arthur's estate was yours for the plucking. A tidy motive, Lady Tisne."

She tried not to let the terror show in her face.

"And yet here I sit with fifteen thousand a year and my mother-in-law reaps the harvest."

"You could not have known what the provisions were—if there had been no agreement. Lord Tisne was not a man to reveal those kinds of matters casually."

"I suppose not," she said reluctantly. "And it would not matter if I had found out by snooping since there were no witnesses to the fact."

"Exactly. So now we have motive. We have opportunity. We

have means—except we have not found the weapon. Nor can it be explained why Lord Tisne was even in the house that night, unless it was at your request, Lady Tisne?"

"I did not summon him."

"And yet that is the only likely explanation."

"I had no reason to summon him; I bore him no ill will. I was content with the situation as it was arranged."

"Possibly you wanted more money, Lady Tisne . . . ?"

She sent him a skeptical look.

"Perhaps you found out just how much money Lord Tisne was pulling in from his various . . . investments and you felt you had shortchanged yourself."

"Inspector Stiles . . ." she said impatiently.

"Lady Tisne—there is no other explanation. Perhaps my lord disagreed that you were worth more, as perhaps you expected he might, and you decided then and there that you would take the whole: it was just the matter of ridding yourself of the one encumbrance—and you had planned for that by having the knife with you when you confronted your husband."

"A fairy tale," she said succinctly. "I found him like that. I did not summon him. He was here for some other reason. He could well have assumed I would be out all night; I quite enjoyed the Landower Ball the several years he and I attended together—and he knew it. He could have arranged to meet someone in what he thought would be an empty house—to which he still had the key. That is a possible explanation, Inspector, and it makes just as much sense as my killing him to insure the bequest I had already arranged by the terms of our agreement."

"And if the agreement were available to corroborate your story, it would be quite another thing, my lady."

"It was taken, Inspector—either by my mother when she left, or by the person who convinced her to leave."

"And you never found out what happened to your servants?"

"No."

"And you haven't heard from your mother since?"

"No . . . I heard from her today."

"With what explanation?"

"She gave no explanations."

"And where is she now?"

"Somewhere in Deepditch."

"I see. So it's possible she could confirm that there was an agreement . . ."

"Really, Inspector—? And confess that she was an accomplice to its theft . . . ? I shouldn't think so . . ."

"I see," he said noncommittally. "So we are right back at the beginning, my lady."

She bit back her terror. "And you have come to arrest me for my husband's murder."

"I am here to fit the facts together to make a coherent whole, Lady Tisne. Everything is circumstantial except for the two facts of the matter: you were home alone in this house and your husband was murdered in this house during that time."

So there it was; so all she had to do was tell him that she had been with Tony Lethbridge and that he had found Arthur's body—and she would perjure herself and implicate Tony who could verify her story . . .

There was no end to it: it would be either Tony's lie or her lie, and neither could be disproved.

And yet, Stiles was making no move to arrest her . . . why?

"Those are two independent facts, Inspector. And there is nothing to connect them," she said carefully, as a thought suddenly occurred to her, "because you surely must have questioned Mr. Morfit and Madam Tisne and found out that my inheritance came as no surprise to me when the will was read."

There was a silence and then he stood up. "That is true, Lady Tisne. Mr. Morfit confirmed it and right now, it is the only thing that is keeping you out of prison. You know, of course, not to leave town. Do not call your butler, Lady Tisne. I will show myself out."

. . . look at things how they really be . . .
Her mother's advice—how ironic . . .
Nothing was how it really was, not even she.

She sat in the darkened small parlor after a light dinner of vegetable soup and crab salad, a glass of currant wine in her hand.

Mother and the Inspector, all in one day—and I'm still here, no matter what either of them thought would be the end of it.

And he was no closer to finding Arthur's murderer . . .

And neither was Roak—

Dear heaven, there has *to be a way this fits together to make sense—*

She felt hot—she put her hands up to her cheeks and they felt burning hot.

I lived in this house with Arthur for three years before he agreed to the separation. I knew nothing about him—nothing . . .

A man like that—what wouldn't he have done? He had done everything and more, and created an outlet to spend his prurient lust.

And still, it hadn't been enough. He had frequented the houses; he had preyed upon anyone who was susceptible . . .

Everyone knew who he was and what he was in that tight circle of the debauched elite; they kept his secrets—and he kept theirs.

So many secrets . . . men, women, children, seductions, prostitutes, orgies . . . those poor, poor boys . . . those awful men, those horrible names—that terrifying tunnel with the glass ceiling—there had been no end to Arthur's perversions . . .

And that had to be why someone wanted him dead.

All those places Mother had known . . .

Mother knew his secrets and lusted after the House of Correction. And Mother knew who those two mystery women were . . .

If Mother knew . . .

. . . if Mother knew—

There was a thought there—she tried to grasp it, she sensed it was important, but she couldn't quite formulate it.

. . . if Mother knew—

Who else might know?

Morfit—

Tony Lethbridge . . .

Oh yes, Tony dear, would you be kind enough to give me a list of the women that Arthur poked? Oh—and you too?

But Tony was so beautiful—every damned woman in the whole of London and the country heaths had been after him. And he had loved every minute of it—and every woman who would succumb to his charms.

Sad that she had been one of them.

Strange he had lunched with Morfit. Or maybe it had just

*struck her the wrong way. Or maybe it was because she had seen
him at the House of Correction and every last one of her illusions
about him had been shattered.*

*He was a selfish sot, and he didn't care if she hanged, as long
as his hands didn't get dirty.*

And he would deny being with her till his dying day.

*. . . dear lord, she wished she had paid more attention in those
early years of the marriage . . .*

Or maybe there was something she was not paying attention
to now.

Her mother's ominous hints?

Her refusal to admit anything?

*The fact she had laughed when she had been asked if she knew
the two mystery women?*

The mystery women . . .

*Who had money to pay her mother to leave this house—some
mystery woman they knew nothing about?*

Morfit? Tony?

*Tony could have charmed her mother right out of her own
little fortune, he could have . . . Tony had no money that wasn't
tied up somehow in family trusts and bled from his mother.*

Not Tony.

Maybe not Tony.

And Morfit lived on the bounty of Arthur's deviant pursuits.

Who had bribed her mother to leave her house?

She was going around in circles again. But it all had to do
with money—nothing else would have moved her mother.

But maybe the object wasn't to move her mother.

*Maybe the object was to remove the one thing that proved she
had no monetary motive to attack her husband.*

So that she would be arrested for his murder . . .

The net, the net—closing tightly around her with just one little
opening that had not been knit shut: Morfit's testimony about
the reading of the will.

. . . Morfit—and not Madam Tisne . . .

*—who would always want to paint me in the worst light
possible . . .*

—who had money . . . pots of money now . . .

—and who wouldn't be averse to having fifteen thousand a year more?

Absurd!

Picture her sitting in that moldering pile of stones, Fanhurst, plotting and planning against the likes of me—or my mother . . .

When it was Morfit who had the side agreement about the management of the most profitable house of illicit pleasure in the whole country—

How much money might he be siphoning off and not reporting to Madam Tisne?

How desperate was he to maintain control of this secret fortune, a man who had always been her husband's lackey?

Who had gone to lunch with Tony Lethbridge, a man not of his social station whom he would not have contact with in the normal course of events . . .

Unless he had met him through Arthur—

Or that heinous House of Correction.

Or he had become Tony's lawyer as well . . . ?

Her brain hurt from trying to conjure up all the permutations of these relationships. And her mother's intimate involvement with any or all of them.

There was no sense to it, and there were missing pieces from the equation she might never know.

Or that Roak might never tell you . . .

The thought brought her up short. Why would she think that?

Because he hesitated today. Because you asked him and he thought carefully just how he was going answer your questions about the mystery women and about the nefarious secret your mother hinted at . . .

No—no he was right: my mother has no truth but her own; she was trying to shake my faith in him—to deflect my questions, to obliterate her guilt . . .

Everyone knew about Rulan Roak; his exploits had been chronicled on the front pages of the newspapers for years.

And Mother herself called my attention to him.

What secret could Roak have—but one?

And he has sworn to wear it as a constant reminder that I am always willing and waiting for him.

But still, he had not summoned her again today.

And this has been a most unsettling day.

She set aside her wineglass just as Joseph Footman entered the room.

"Is there anything else tonight, my lady?"

She shook her head. "Joseph? Has Mr. Roak returned?"

"I am not aware of it, my lady."

"Thank you, Joseph. Good night."

He took her wineglass and withdrew; she went to the window and looked out onto the street—a fruitless exercise because it was very late, she had been sitting a very long time, and now the street was dark but for the intermittent gaslight, and there was no moon, and most especially, there was no Roak.

She walked slowly up the stairs as Joseph moved through the rooms, making sure that windows were closed, doors were locked, and all lights, save the one in the downstairs hallway, were extinguished.

She paused on the landing to look back at the shadows pooled just outside that circle of light.

Illumination and obscurity—if I take one step in any direction, I plunge into shadows . . .

It was as if there was no one in the house. It was eerily silent; she could hear her own footsteps, she could almost hear her own thoughts.

She could just see the thin line of light from underneath her door as she came up the steps, and she paused, reluctant to enter an empty room.

. . . a night without Roak . . .

She pushed open the door.

He lay on the bed, naked, her golden collar glowing around his towering erection.

"I was savoring the pleasure of waiting for you," he said, and she felt a spasm of intense pleasure. Nothing mattered but *this;* everything that existed outside that door could be subjugated to *this . . .*

"I wanted you," she whispered, kneeling on the bed to reach for him.

"Then take off your clothes because I have been *rampant* for you all day long."

. . . clothes—she hated her clothes when it took this long to remove them . . .

She kicked off her shoes, pulled off her petticoats, unfastened her buttons with her fingers fumbling over every one, watching him greedily as he swung his legs from the bed and moved a chair near the armoir mirror.

Then he came to her and tore away the fragile cambric underthings that hid her body from him, and took her breasts in his hands.

"I've been aching for you all day, Jade. Everywhere I went, you were with me. I could feel you surrounding me, and every time I let myself feel it, I got hard for you. I was like a rock all day, waiting until the moment when I could possess you."

"I thought about you too," she whispered, arching her body against his hands. "I wanted my ring to make you hard for me. After I left you, I wanted you all over again."

"Your nipples are ready." He stroked the taut tips. "Your lips are ready." He brushed them with his lips. "Is your body ready for me, Jade?"

"The minute I saw you naked on my bed, I was ready for you."

"Let me see how ready . . ."

He sat her in the chair facing the mirror.

"Spread your legs for me."

She parted her legs so that they both saw, in the mirror, the lush feminine hair that crowned the opening to her cleft.

. . . And that is how I look—like that goddess at the Arcade who revealed everything to me . . . I'm a goddess too—

She caught her breath as he knelt in front of her and propped her one leg over the arm of the chair.

. . . Oh my lord, oh my lord—who would have dreamt his tongue could be so wet and possessive—so long and strong and firm . . . how does he know where and what and how to . . .

She was moaning with pure unalloyed pleasure, watching him, watching herself as he sucked at her and explored her and lifted her body against his mouth for his expert carnal kiss.

She saw it all, she felt it all; he was there—there—there, and she bore down on him and let him take her until the last flashing twinge of ecstasy subsided.

"The Jade loves it every which where," he whispered against her belly, against her breasts, against her mouth so she could taste the fragrant perfume of her body.

She cupped him between her hands now that she could reach him and stroked his shaft until she could feel the gentle caress of the golden coil.

Immediately her body reacted. "You are so potent; all I have to do is feel you and I want you all over again."

"Get up on the chair and bend over the back. Can you see me?"

"Oh, yes," she whispered breathlessly as she presented her rounded bottom to him and saw him, in the mirror, probing her, and then slipping inch by inch into her until his entire shaft was buried in her and all she could see was the gleaming golden coil against the cushion of her buttocks.

His hands grasped her hips. "Watch how I possess the Jade."

She watched; she loved watching the way he contracted his body and thrust into her, and how she writhed and shimmied and curved herself against him as she taunted and tempted him to surrender to her voluptuous nakedness.

He ground his hips against her to punish her for her brazenness. She felt the ring, hot against her buttocks, and the hard, blasting thickness of him possessing her.

She saw him, his hands flexing involuntarily on her hips, embedded deep within her body from this luxurious reverse position, and she felt like an extension of him and as if he were powerful enough to thrust her into the universe.

The connection was intense, physically and visually. She didn't want him to move; she wanted to look at the two of them in union for the whole night and into the morning.

And she wanted to excite him to the most explosive completion of his life.

She wanted both—she wanted neither . . .

She wanted him. Of its own volition, her body began the pumping drive to finish, straining against him, inviting his thrusts.

He jammed her buttocks back against his hip. "Feel me, Jade. Feel every inch of me wanting every inch of you. Feel the ring that makes me hard for you. Feel it . . ."

"I feel it . . ." she gasped. "I feel you. I want every inch of you . . ."

"Feel it—" He pulled himself away from her as she watched in the mirror, and then drove it forcefully home.

"It feels so *big,* so *hard,*" she moaned as she felt him take her. "More . . . yes—more . . . *yes*—more . . ." in rhythm with his taut thrusting body as his movements became urgent, overpowering, explosive.

His body rocketed against her with long powerful strokes; he held her steady, imprisoned in his powerful grip as he took her, and he felt her body easing into her climax, almost like she was riding a pounding wave that crashed on the rocks, and broke into foaming breakwater that slowly eddied away.

He dove into the backflood of her release, spewing himself so deeply into her, he thought the flood of her juices would wash away in the impact.

And curved into each other's body, they sank down off the chair, and onto the floor.

It felt like hours later.

She was half asleep; he was kissing her and idly fondling her right nipple which had burgeoned into a pebble-hard nub.

He was hard as a rock beside her. She could feel him flexing and nudging her and she slipped her hand around the base of him just above the golden coil.

"Ah Jade—" he whispered, licking her lips. "I'm hard for you again."

"I feel it."

"Tell me you want it."

"I always want it," she breathed, feeling a blooming excitement engulf her.

"Tell me how much you want it."

"It's so big and hard, how could I not want it?"

"Now that I wear your ring, I'm always big and hard."

"Then I always want you because you are big and hard for *me.*"

"I want to mount you—now."

"Why are you taking so long?"

He positioned himself over her. "Jade—"

"I want it . . ."

He pushed himself into her tight wet haven.

"You've got it . . ."

"I know it . . ."

"So wet . . . so ready for me."

"So deep I can feel the coil. Rub it against me, Roak."

He pushed himself against her so that the golden coil was buried in her feminine hair and she moaned with excitement.

"Take me now," she whispered, wriggling against the feel of it, the feel of him so thick and strong and powerful once again.

He took her.

And it didn't take long; they climaxed together on a long wet slide of sensation: he drowned himself in her; she was immersed in hot silver that shimmered all over her body and settled like a blanket between her legs.

And then they slept.

He came awake slowly; it was still dark outside and the flame was guttering in the gaslamp wick.

She lay curled up trustingly beside him, and he stroked the long sensuous curve of her body.

He was already hard with wanting her. He propped himself on his elbow and began to stroke her, loving the fact that her naked body was always available to him whether she was awake or asleep.

She stirred in her sleep as she felt his invasive hands.

"Roak . . ."

"I can't stop, I need you again . . ."

Her leg moved, angling so that she was open to him.

"Come . . ."

He came, thrusting himself into her welcoming fold and instantly and decisively erupting into a volcanic climax in one galvanic lunge.

He collapsed against her. "Perfect, Jade. Perfect . . ."

"Ummm . . ." She liked him inside her like that, hard, used-up, pliant, vulnerable, and on the verge of retraction, with her as his vessel.

She felt the sticky pour of his ejaculate between her legs, sopping them and the mattress with the juice of his passion.

She liked that too.

"Jade . . ."

His fingers now, replacing his wilted manhood, as long and probing as he was, seeking her center to bring her to climax.

She bore down on him. "Yes . . ."

"Now—"

"Yes-s-s—"

His mouth closed over her breast, rooting after her nipple.

"Ah yes . . ." she sighed as he began pulling and sucking it in concert with her movements.

And then—and then—

Lightning . . . bone-crackling lightning radiating from the very center of her, rippling up her spine and into her bloodstream, pumping, throbbing, thunderous, inundating . . .

And gone.

He held her tightly for a long long time.

". . . what was that?"

"What?" She was floating on a cloud of luxuriant satisfaction.

"I heard something."

"The servants. Joseph—they start . . ."

"It's too early." He relinquished her and swung his legs over the bed.

From that angle she could just see the shadow of his inflexible manhood standing at the ready, and his impatient hands grabbing for some clothes.

"I'm going to go see."

"Roak . . ."

"I'll be back in a minute." He was out the door before she could protest again.

She rose slowly on her elbows and then to a sitting position. *It's not the same—it's not . . .*

She padded over to her closet and rummaged for a wrapper.

Roak will be back in a moment; it's only the servants. They start early. I heard them sometimes very early in the morning . . .

She turned up the wick and the room brightened.

He's been gone for so long . . .

She bit her lip and pulled open the door.

Silence.

She stood at the head of the staircase and hesitantly took the first step down. And then the next—and the next . . . all the way down until she saw him kneeling on the reception room floor.

He looked up at her, almost as if he had sensed her walking down the steps, his eyes inscrutable, his face impassive.

And then he rose gracefully to his feet, his hands covered with blood, and she could see the whole as if it were a nightmare being played all over again.

Only this time it was clear: the body with its lifeblood seeping onto the floor was her mother—and she would never be found again.

Chapter 17

Oh my God oh my God oh my God—

She sat shaking in the morning room while Joseph plied her with tea she did not want, and Roak sent for the authorities.

What am I going to tell Stiles? What am I going to tell Stiles?

The horror of it was unrelenting. Her mother in her house, bleeding to death from a knife wound in her chest, and the knife by her side.

The knife that had killed Arthur.

She shuddered violently and reached for the teapot to pour another cup just so she could warm her hands around it.

Mother—dead . . .

And her skilled investigator was not going to abandon her . . .

Oh my God . . . Oh my God—

How had her mother gotten into the house?

Oh my God—all those questions that Stiles would be asking . . . and after their interview this afternoon—

And she hadn't even told Roak about that . . .

The net was tightening. Someone dearly wanted her put in prison for murder.

She couldn't see any way out.

Stiles would find out everything; her mother's past; her association with Arthur; why her mother left Green Street; why she would want to kill her . . .

But no—there was no motive; there was no motive . . .

No, Stiles would dig up some motive.

There was no end to this . . . no end—

Her head was spinning.

Look at things how they really be . . .

Here's how they "be," Mother—you're dead . . .

He'll say I hated you because of your past. He'll say I resented the way you arranged my marriage. He'll say I finally got my revenge . . .

. . . but why here, why now?

The saving grace?

No reason. No reason . . . yes—no reason. She wasn't going crazy. There was no reason she would have wanted to kill her mother.

"My lady—" Joseph, politely, at the door. "Inspector Stiles and Mr. Roak."

She nodded and they strode in, Stiles taking his usual seat by the fireplace and removing his notebook from the inner pocket of his coat, and Roak taking a chair behind her at her desk.

"So Lady Tisne," Stiles murmured. "Your lady mother has been killed."

There was just no answer to that.

"Now my lady—tell me just what was what. Where were you?"

Oh God, it was the same story, the very same words . . . how could he believe that? How could it happen twice, within a month, in the same house with the same scenario?

. . . no, almost the same scenario . . .

She took a deep breath. She couldn't see Roak—maybe he had done that deliberately, maybe Stiles had suggested it, she didn't know, but she felt as rudderless as a sailboat without a wind as she fought to quell her fear and to think of the best way to answer his questions.

Don't talk too much.

But instantly it got complicated: *she* hadn't heard the noise; *she* hadn't investigated.

What had Roak told him?

The truth . . . ?

What was the truth? She was rolling around in bed with a man who was almost a stranger who was supposed to be proving her innocent of murder, and instead he had become involved with another . . .

Dear heaven—who in life would believe that story?

"Lady Tisne?"

"I—yes, Inspector, I just needed to collect my thoughts."

"I'm sure. No, Mr. Roak—say nothing. Lady Tisne is quite able to speak for herself. My lady?"

Damn it—damn it . . . if she could just look at Roak she could get some idea what she should or should not say . . .

But Stiles won't let me; he pins me with his eyes. He dares me . . . and so the only recourse is the truth.

She swallowed hard. "I—we were upstairs . . ."

He jumped on it. "We, my lady?"

"Mr. Roak and I, Inspector," she said frostily, wanting desperately to put him in his place.

"So late at night, my lady," Stiles murmured, making a note in his book.

"*Very* late at night, Inspector," she amplified, just hating him. "We heard a noise. Mr. Roak went downstairs to investigate. I followed. My mother was there, at the foot of the steps, like Arthur . . . and the blood—the blood . . ."

"There was lots of blood," the Inspector agreed. "Now, who found the body?"

Her eyes flickered; she wanted desperately to look at Roak.

"Mr. Roak." *Don't tell him too much.*

"And how exactly was it when you finally came down the stairs?"

Damn it, bloody damn him, trying to get me to incriminate Roak . . .

"Mr. Roak was kneeling next to my mother—" She stopped, quelling the temptation to impute a motive to Roak's actions. He could do that himself, all that she needed to do was give Stiles the facts. Only the facts.

"He got to his feet when he heard me come down the stairs and then I saw it was Mother."

"I see."

Once again, his patronizing cover phrase that could mean anything—or nothing.

"Mr. Roak immediately sent to inform the Yard."

"Most promptly," Stiles said, nodding his head.

She said nothing more.

"My lady?"

"That is all I know, Inspector."

"I see."

She felt like strangling him, and breaking those competent fingers that were making who-knew-what notes in that little book of his.

Violence to the Inspector—an excellent recommendation for a woman who claims to be innocent of committing murder . . .

No—not this time—this time he would try to make it stick.

Stiles consulted his notes.

"This is what Mr. Roak tells me—that sometime during the night, while you and he were together in your room—" He recited the fact flatly as if it had no import whatsoever—"he heard a noise, dressed, and went downstairs to see what it was, and he found your mother at the foot of the stairs, covered in blood with the knife by her side.

"He knelt to see if she had a pulse—which accounts for the blood on his hands—and when you came down, he sent Joseph Footman to notify the police.

"Neither he nor you, he asserts, knew your mother was in the house or where the knife came from. But I can tell you it is either the same weapon or one from the set of knives with which your husband was killed, Lady Tisne.

"And he further asserts that you both were upstairs together all night. So in order for one or the other of you to have committed this murder, one or the other of you had to have left the room, gone downstairs, and having been expecting Mrs. Alcarr, committed the murder in a minute, washed, and resumed your place in bed.

"Am I correct, Mr. Roak? Is that how it could have happened?"

Roak must have nodded because Stiles went on, "Did either of you fall asleep any time last night?"

Silence. And then Roak: "Of course."

"And so, theoretically, that scenario is possible?"

Roak said, "No. Under those conditions, Inspector, when one awakens, the other is aroused as well. Neither of us was asleep while the other was awake without either of us knowing it."

"I see," Stiles said. Another note. "No reason you know of for your mother to be here?"

"I told you this afternoon, she had come to see me today." *Don't talk too much, don't talk too much . . .*

"And why was that again, Lady Tisne?"

Why was that, Lady Tisne?

She wanted to be left alone, Inspector.
Why would she want that, my lady? Did something happen?
Yes, someone bribed her to leave my house; remember, I told you.
... oh God—deeper and deeper—how did she explain her mother's actions and her own?
"She wanted to . . . she wanted to—"
Gloat—she wanted to goad me and trip me up and make me angry—and she did that, Inspector; she did a bloody good job of it . . .
"She came to tell me not to pry."
"Pry, my lady?"
. . . Talking too much, talking too much . . .
"She had left my home, Inspector, and gone who knows where. I tried to find her. She didn't want to be found."
"She was in Deepditch, I believe you said."
Even she felt Roak's reaction behind her; what had the Inspector seen?
"Yes. But she wanted no interference from me." *Talking too much—*
"Interference, my lady?"
Damn—damn . . . "She did not want to return to Green Street, and she wanted me to understand that."
"I see. She had gone away to Deepditch and she did not want to return here, no matter what you wanted?"
"Yes."
"And how did you know she had gone to Deepditch, Lady Tisne?"
Uh-oh—a trap—another chasm of a trap . . . and time to throw her skilled investigator to the wolves . . .
"Mr. Roak had found her, Inspector."
"Had he been looking for her?"
. . . blast him . . . another lie—or maybe some version of a truth—another sacrifice in any event . . .
She wished she could see Roak's eyes.
"Inspector, she left my house unexpectedly; my servants disappeared, and my desk was broken into. Is it any wonder I—or Mr. Roak—would have wanted to find her and question her?"

"And yet you said," he consulted his notes again, "she offered no explanations."

. . . those bloody notes . . .

Don't tell him too much . . .

"No, she didn't."

"Why was that, Lady Tisne?"

"I don't know. I asked her the relevant questions."

"What *did* she say?"

More traps—what did she say?

"She offered advice. She told me she did not wish to return. She laughed when I asked why she had left and where were my servants and my papers. And she left without telling me anything except not to come searching for her again."

"And before this—what was your relationship with your mother?"

"I didn't see much of her between the time I was married and Arthur's death."

"And after?"

"She was living with me, Inspector, and I welcomed her into my home."

"I see. And then she just upped and left."

"Yes. And I don't know why."

"And now she's dead . . ."

"Yes." And he was looking at her keenly to see if she felt any grief. "And I feel numb, Inspector," she added for good measure. "I cannot believe this has happened."

"Of course," he said instantly. "We can leave off questioning now. Mr. Roak and you each provide alibis for the other, and that will stand for the time being. Your mother should have been taken away by now, Lady Tisne, so you'll want to make arrangements in the next day or two for burial."

. . . for burial—

. . . two funerals in the space of a month—and who would attend this one?

"Thank you, Inspector."

"Please don't leave town."

She watched him as he exited the room.

. . . tenacious—she felt as if she had been gnawed at by a bulldog . . .

Behind her, Roak said nothing, nor did she turn to look at him. There was nothing to say that would not seem superfluous. *... he is in for fifteen thousand pounds,* she thought mordantly, *whether he wants it or not. And I don't want to know what he thinks—this time.*

And then there were the tabloid papers. Oh dear lord, the papers which had already made mincemeat out of her when Arthur died. The *Tittle-Tattle* would come after her with a razor and dissect every aspect of her life. And *The Black Book* and *Town Tattler . . .*

And it would be worse now, because Roak was involved— with all of his reputation and his much-vaunted discretion . . .

No more . . . no more . . . it will be all over the papers just where Roak was when someone was committing murder in the downstairs hallway—

Her head felt like it was going to burst.

Mother is dead . . .

Dear heaven—my mother is dead—

Her body suddenly felt shaky and weak.

Not much of a mother . . .

Murdered while her daughter was copulating in the room above with a man who was supposed to be ferreting out proof she hadn't killed her husband . . .

A bloody tabloid story with shrieking headlines and notoriety from Bedlington Heath to Belgrave Square . . .

She couldn't hide forever either. They would find out what her mother did, and they would rake up the whole story of Arthur's murder, and they would try her right on the front pages for as long as they could sell that sensational story to the public . . .

And what had *she* ever done but listened to her mother?

Her tears started then, just pouring down her cheeks, a storm of tears that shook her whole body in spite of her effort to suppress them.

No one should ever see a woman cry.

She stood outside herself, watching, as if she were analyzing a stranger.

But she was a stranger to herself. What she had done in the past month since Arthur's death, and her intense and erotic liaison with a man she barely . . . she would never in her life have believed she could do these things.

And now she could do them no more, and her feeling of loss was almost greater than that she felt for her mother.

"You'll have to leave," she said finally, when her tears had diminished.

"You need to sleep," Roak countered.

"You can't—"

"You will."

"I don't—"

"This is not for discussion now, Genelle. You'll go upstairs and go to sleep. And that is all. There is nothing that Stiles can hold against you: you were in your room, *I* was the one who heard the noise, who went downstairs—"

"Like Tony," she whispered.

"And found a body . . . those are the facts, nothing more, nothing less, and whoever killed your mother—it was not either of us."

The Inspector came back in the afternoon.

She had slept; she didn't know what Roak had done in those intervening hours, but when she awoke, she was told Stiles was waiting. She found him in the small parlor, seated by the fire with his ubiquitous notes in hand, and Roak nowhere to be seen.

"Inspector . . ."

"My condolences, Lady Tisne. I was remiss in not offering them to you last night."

"That is very kind, given the situation. What more can I tell you, Inspector?"

"Tell me about your mother as abbess of the *House of Correction.*"

She caught her breath; he had found out so soon—or had he always known?

"I cannot tell you much, Inspector. I only recently found out about this aspect of Mother's career."

He sent her a skeptical look. "And yet you went there."

There were no secrets. Not a one.

"My dear Inspector, I went to see Mr. Morfit after *you* revealed Arthur's connection to that place. And what do I find but that my income is derived from the profits from that place. Of course I would want to see it. It never occurred to me that my mother had worked there, until she herself told me shortly after that."

"What did you think your mother did?"

"I never thought about it, Inspector. She educated me to marry above my station, she found the eligible *parti* and I married him. I never asked where she met him. I never guessed until after he was gone and she moved in with me. And that is all I can tell you."

"Lady Tisne, your mother was the fabled Queen of the Night in those years when she was abbess of the *House of Correction*. She was the most notorious madame in all of London. She started at the *Veil* in a little town called Bickley—"

No . . . no—I didn't dream it up?—There really was a Bickley and the Seven Veils . . .

"And made her way very quickly to London after she established her reputation. My lady, do you know who was your father?"

Crazy questions.

"No, I don't. Mother never said. There was always an atmosphere that suggested she did not ever want to be asked."

"Were you ever curious?"

"Of course I was, but it was easier to make up fantasies than to ask my mother. We lived in boardinghouses, Inspector, and the landladies would take care of me when Mother went out to try to earn a little money . . ."

Did that sound right? Yes, that sounded right; she hadn't known, and she had to remember that she hadn't known . . .

"A *little* money, my lady? Hundreds of thousands, my lady—"

She tried to look shocked, horrified, innocent, and she was certain none of it came off.

"In the Bank of England, directly in her name, my lady. And you didn't know?"

"I didn't know."

He made a tick on his notes. "So now we have a possible motive."

Oh no . . .

"But you didn't know," he added, hoping to catch her off-guard.

"Inspector, I swear to you, she was always crying poverty and her one great dream for me to marry a man above my station so he could provide for her. Why? Why go through that charade if she were already that wealthy?"

"You tell me, my lady."

"She literally sold me to Lord Arthur for a yearly allowance and a fashionable address. And she spent money like water and sent him the bills. Why? Why, if she could afford all of this herself? And why would I want to kill her? Lord Arthur was kind enough to me in his way, and when it became clear we could not cohabit, we entered a mutual agreement to separate and that he would continue my allowance. Why would I want to jeopardize the only security I have ever known?"

"Greed," Stiles said succinctly.

"I am not that clever, Inspector."

"Oh, I think you are, Lady Tisne. And capable of deep passion and great rage. You must have had deep anger at your mother for managing your life as she did. And deep resentment that the husband she had chosen for you could not give you that which every young wife expects: a loving home and children. You have had many years to plot out a revenge, my lady. It's not inconceivable that you might have finally chosen to carry it out."

"To what end, Inspector?"

"Money."

"I have none of it."

"Yes, it does come back to that, does it not. You were not expecting it. You haven't got it, and yet two people now who were endowed with it—the two people closest to *you*—are dead."

And it sounded horribly suspicious—terribly damning . . .

She could not dissemble or back down, not now.

"Yes."

"Exactly."

"All of this is conjecture, Inspector."

"Indeed. But the connective tissue is there, Lady Tisne. It's just a matter of the surgical procedure to put it together."

"Then you will understand if I say that I cannot give permission for you to operate on *my* body."

"I perfectly understand, my lady. All the signs seem to suggest you might survive such a blood-letting—but there will come a time when you might well want a tourniquet. I won't take up any more of your time today, Lady Tisne. Of course, I am not done, and I strongly suggest you do not leave town."

"It hardly need be said, Inspector."

"I will show myself out."

She sat preternaturally still after he left.

... *It was clear.*

Someone was intent on hemming her in and tying her up in tidy little knots so that she could never get free, even if her innocence were proven.

But who? Who?

She sat so still, thinking; she thought if she never moved again, no one could ever accuse her of anything, and she would die, sitting at the small parlor window that overlooked Green Street.

She could not move a muscle if her life depended on it and she didn't know if an hour had gone by or a minute when Joseph interrupted her reverie.

"My lady."

"Yes, Joseph."

"For my lady."

He was carrying a silver salver on which there was an envelope, and he extended it toward her.

But I never get mail these days—never ...

She took the envelope and held it in her hand, staring at it for a moment before she remembered to dismiss Joseph.

"Thank you, Joseph."

"Very good, my lady."

He withdrew in his usual unobtrusive way and she turned to the envelope.

The handwriting was not familiar.

She tore it open and unfolded two sheets of paper, from which two keys dropped into her lap.

The top page was a letter.

Daughter—

I got a lawyer to write this up for me, right and tight; I did what you said and good advice it was too. Now you do what I told you. Look at things the way they be—not how you want to see them. Everything happens for a reason—

even Roak. Everything is tied together. And I don't want them to get anything more so here are the keys.

Your mother

Under it was a legal document:

This is the last will and testament of Maud Alcarr who, being of sound mind and body, gives, in the event of her death, to her daughter, Lady Genelle Tisne of Green Street, London, the key to her lock box in the vault of the Bank of England; and the premises at Skirling Vail in the village of Bickley, Cheswickshire with no restrictions attached.

Signed: Maud Alcarr
Witnessed: Thomas Law
By: Walter Adcock, Esq.

She dropped the papers on her lap in horror—and then snatched them up and read them again.

And now, she thought bitterly, *now I am dead . . .*

Chapter 18

No one could see these papers—*no one* . . .

She felt frantic; she knew she had to be calm. She folded them up slowly and deliberately, tucking the keys back inside the folds, and put them back in the envelope.

No one would have to know Mother ever executed a will—she just wouldn't file it—who would know? Not even the solicitor . . . yes—she went right back to Bickley so that someone she did not know would keep her secrets . . .

No one can know—not even Roak. . . . Oh God, Roak— that horrifying suggestion in Mother's letter—the hints . . . the interminable fear that something outside herself was working to destroy her . . .

She could not show this to Roak . . .

She didn't know what to do. There was no place to put it that he wouldn't find it . . .

She had to calm down. She had to *think* . . .

Things were closing in on her too fast. She needed time, she needed to be able to adapt to circumstances as they changed— and on the instant.

She needed to save herself because it was obvious Roak was not going to do it . . .

She needed . . . money—

And she needed to plan very carefully. Stiles would be following her every move, her every footstep. She had, perhaps, only this morning to accomplish anything—

Like hiding these papers. Like getting some money . . .

She had to stop thinking and move—now . . .

She lifted her hand to summon Joseph.

No—Joseph cannot be a part of this. They'll haul him onto

*the witness stand so fast—and she did not need him to testify
about what she would be doing this morning . . .*

She had an idea—a very brazen idea about where to hide the
will.

The first thing she had to do was burn her mother's letter.
And she had to find a chain on which to hold the keys around
her neck. She had to get some money, and then—the boldest
part . . . she wasn't sure she could carry it off.

She had to dress the part too, and there wasn't much in her
wardrobe that would make her look matronly.

*My mourning gown will probably do it. And a large hat with
a concealing veil—do I even have one?*

She put one together and she had it tucked in a bag when she
finally and furtively crept out of the house.

It was well before ten o'clock in the morning; traffic was light.
She put on the hat and its swathing veil, got rid of the bag, and
then hailed a hansom cab.

She hesitated for one full minute, after she climbed in and the
driver asked her destination.

*I can't do this; they must know my mother in this place. All
that money—a valued customer . . . I have to do it—*

"The Bank of England, driver."

It took up a whole corner of Threadneedle Street, a huge gray
stone building with fluted columns decorating the long entrance
side. There was a low iron fence surrounding it, and nowhere, in
the rush of carriages, drays, trucks and cabs, a place to park the
cab.

She got out finally across the street, and it took five minutes
at least to dodge the traffic, which only made her all the more
determined.

She pushed open the brass doors to enter a marble-walled
anteroom with a ceiling at least twenty feet high. The floors were
marble, the ceiling was ornately plastered, and there was an iron-
bannistered staircase.

And straight ahead, between two marble columns, were the
teller's stations—all walnut and etched glass, each with its own
light over its white marble counter—and behind matching screens
fitted out with etched glass and brass fixtures, sat the clerks and
officers of the bank.

It was busy; patrons swarmed in and out, clerks and runners were going to and fro; well-dressed gentlemen and ladies were being led to more private inner sanctums to discuss business; and here and there a clerk asked those coming in if they could be of service.

She needed a young clerk—a very young clerk, one who would not have known her mother, and then she needed to bluff her way into the vault.

She saw someone likely a moment later. "Excuse me? Excuse me—"

The young man turned and headed in her direction.

Pink-cheeked, sharp-eyed—she wasn't sure—but it was too late now.

"Can I help you?"

Say as little as possible . . .

She handed him the key.

"Ah, Mrs. Alcarr—"

Her heart dove to her feet.

"Yes . . . this way—"

But he didn't question her; he led her to a broad marble staircase with shallow steps which descended in a curve to the lower level of the bank.

It was noticeably cooler here—there were no windows, no doors, no way to leave except by the steps, and there was only one other person: the guard at the vault gate who opened it as they approached.

"There you are, Mrs. Alcarr. I will leave you to it. Fifteen minutes, say?"

"That will be fine."

She stepped into the vault and knew he was watching her. The number on the key was an ornately scripted *35D* and she saw immediately that boxes were stacked and arranged in alphabetical rows.

So it was easy enough to go unhesitatingly to Row D and find the box.

She placed it on one of the narrow tables that were between every row, and waited until he withdrew and she heard the clang of the gate.

Her hands were shaking as she unlocked the wooden box,

which was about eleven by fourteen inches in size and almost four inches deep.

Deep enough to conceal the deepest secrets.

Big enough to conceal the darkest lies.

She lifted the lid slowly.

There was a white paper lying glaringly on top of several other items.

She bit her lip and picked it up.

Daughter—the solicitor wrote this for me; I was busy these last two days getting everything ready because I knew eventually you would need the money.

Your mother

Dear dear heaven—

Under the letter there was a stack of bills neatly tied up. There was an envelope in which there was the deed to the house at Skirling Vail and her certificate of birth which provided every vital statistic except her father's name. And there was a wig. A long dark wig made of what looked like human hair.

Time was almost up.

She took the money and made a quick count. Enough to last her a year—enough to last a lifetime the way things were going.

She tucked them in her bag. And the wig. She took the wig. And she left in the box her mother's will.

And then she closed it, put it back in its space, and went to the gate to have the guard signal her clerk.

Five minutes later she was out on Threadneedle Street, searching for a cab back to Green Street because there was nothing more to be done.

The excursion had taken less than an hour, and when she was finally sitting in the morning room, waiting for her tea, she felt a severe reaction to the chance she had taken.

And it wasn't nearly over. For all she knew, Stiles had had someone watching the bank just waiting for her to come waltzing in and claim her inheritance.

For all she knew, that fresh-faced young clerk was telling him right at this moment that Mrs. Alcarr had come to visit the vault that very morning.

But then, her mother must have been there within the last day as well. The note, which she had taken and burned, had said: *I knew eventually you would need the money* . . .

Could her mother have known then that her own life was in danger?

She felt sick at the thought; her mother had been preparing for the eventuality that someone would lure her to this house and shove a knife into her?

Who? Why?

Don't leave town . . .

She had hidden the money; she wore the keys on a long thin chain between her breasts. She had burned both letters.

And she would not allow Roak to come any closer to her than across the room—where he was now standing in the doorway, watching her out of those implacable black eyes.

"Stiles was here already this morning," she said finally, "but I suppose you know that."

"And you were out—and I wasn't supposed to know that."

She decided not to explain. She was telling too many things to too many people. "Have a cup of tea, Roak. It will do wonders for your digestion."

"Where were you?"

She looked up at him as she handed him his cup. "Out looking for clues. Where were you?"

"Making sure Stiles doesn't hang *you*. Joseph said you got something in the post this morning."

Terror—

"A bill—past due—I forgot all about it in the aftermath of Arthur's death. Surely you didn't think it was a condolence letter."

She held his eyes, hoping against hope that he could not detect the lie.

Whatever he thought, he decided not to pursue it—not yet at any rate.

"Where will you bury her?"

More problems—she hadn't even thought about it . . . "I—"

She bit her lip as she tried to hurriedly think of a solution.

Yes— "Bickley, I think. She was originally from Bickley. It's pretty over there—I think she would like that."

"You might send off a note to the parish priest. I'll get someone to ride over."

"Yes, I'll do that."

"Good. And now we must consider your situation."

"There isn't much to consider, Roak. My mother is dead in my house, presumably by the same hand that took my husband's life. And Stiles obviously thinks it was mine and is going to great lengths to give me enough rope to hang myself.

"He said it himself this morning: the motive is money—I have none of it and yet the two people closest to me who did, are dead."

"But the fact remains, you gained nothing and Morfit confirmed your bequest did not upset or shock you. And insofar as you know, your mother made no provision for the money deposited in the Bank of England. So you could not have immediately claimed her fortune if you had killed her because you would have had a protracted court hearing to prove you were next-of-kin."

Except that there was a will.

She couldn't tell him—she just couldn't . . .

"Well, that all sounds well and good, but Stiles has come up with a secondary theory: revenge."

"Excellent man, Stiles. His thinking is obvious—and it doesn't answer the obvious question: why wait all this time to carry it through?"

"Then who did, Roak? Where are you in this investigation?"

"On your side," he said sharply, as though her question and the implied lack of faith nettled him.

"And what have you come up with?"

"You know very well I tracked your mother to Deepditch. I am sure you don't know she had a little bank account there for the two weeks she lived there—ten thousand pounds—removed the day before yesterday and taken . . ."

. . . into my pocket this morning . . .

"And the account closed and she disappeared altogether."

And came to see me, throwing around hints and threats and goads—and could not tell me anything forthrightly . . . why, damn her? Because she knew she was going to die?

By whose hand?
Who—of everyone involved—had that kind of money?
They all did . . .
"No, she came here, remember, and refused to tell me anything."
"Someone was tracking her."
"How do you know?"
"Because she had nowhere to stay in London. She had closed up in Deepditch—gone by the next morning. So in order for her murderer to have found her, he had to have been stalking her. He had to know where she was in order to get her to come here."
That makes such perfect logical sense . . .
"But Stiles would argue that all I would have had to do was ask her to come back the next night. And since there were no witnesses to our conversation, he has only my word once again about what she said to me.
"So you see, there is an answer for every point, and every possibility leads back to me . . ."

She buried her mother two days later in the church cemetery at Bickley. It was a small procession: herself, Roak, Stiles, all saying little or nothing during the more than two-hour trip with the coffin wagon.

The eulogy was brief, the priest respectful and comforting. He was young and he was filled with the enthusiasm of his calling. He offered them some tea and cake, which they refused, and they were on their way back to London within the hour.

"A large woman, your mother," Stiles commented, when they were a half hour into the return trip. "As large as a man . . ."

"I never noticed," Genelle said curtly. *Her mother had filled a room with her presence . . .*

And after she had embarked on her career—she must have filled a lot of rooms . . .

. . . don't even think about it . . .

She appreciated the fact that Stiles was courteous enough not to try to make conversation beyond that or to pursue the course of the investigation.

But still, she had the distinct feeling he didn't trust her. And he didn't trust his instincts about her either.

"I won't leave town, Inspector," she told him, when she alighted at Green Street.

"I'm sure you won't, Lady Tisne."

No, I'll just sit in my parlor and wait for you to dig up the proof with which you can arrest me . . .

She was shocked to find Mr. Morfit waiting.

"Merely a condolence call, Lady Tisne."

A condolence call or a checking-up call?

"I was horrified to hear of your mother's death under such similar circumstances."

"I'm not feeling sanguine myself, Mr. Morfit."

"They haven't found anything?"

"Oh, no, Mr. Morfit. They have *me.*"

She didn't startle him in the least. She thought he looked hopeful. Or maybe she wanted to be able to detect that he was suppressing some guilt or some evidence—or *something.*

"Thank you for coming by, Mr. Morfit. Of course, I'll expect my check deposited next week."

"Oh—yes, yes—next week as usual, Lady Tisne."

She showed him out the door and summoned Joseph.

"Where is Mr. Roak?" *Mr. Roak the shadow; the man who was never around when you needed him.*

"Mr. Roak is unavailable, my lady."

"Excellent. Thank you."

So Roak had just slipped away upon their return to Green Street when she was so taken up with astonishment on finding Morfit in her parlor.

". . . Joseph?"

"My lady?"

"How long had Mr. Morfit been waiting?"

"I apprised the gentleman of the fact that you were burying your mother today, and it was impossible to calculate when you might return. Still, he insisted on staying. He was here an hour or more—perhaps two."

"Two hours, Joseph?"

"Yes, my lady."

"And how did he occupy himself"

"He had the newspapers, my lady, which he asked me to remove shortly before you returned."

"I see. Thank you."

So they had printed up the whole sordid mess already, had they?

". . . Joseph?"

He paused at the door.

"May I see the papers?"

"Very good, my lady."

He brought them back a few minutes later and spread them out on the table she had arranged by the sofa. She did not need to hunt for the relevant stories—they were emblazoned right on the front page.

And every last scandal and tidbit of gossip had been dragged up out of the cellar and into print, worse than she could ever have thought possible.

Death of the Infamous Queen of the Night
Death of the Prima Diva Disciplinaria
Death Whips the Abbess at Last

Her heart sank. It was all there—all of her mother's exploits at the *House of Correction* where, for more than ten years, she had invented and controlled every punishment, penalty, and chastisement.

She turned to the *Gazetteer* for some fairness in reporting, but still, under all that dry prose, the story screamed scandal.

In her heyday, Madame Alcarr was the most sought after procuress in the country; she was known to get the best girls, to institute the most rigorous training, and to present the most compliant companions. Her fees were the highest among the brothels, her standards the most stringent. When she went to the notorious House of Correction, her loyal clientele followed without a caveat. And when she put them to the test, they all failed and received with pleasure their exacting punishment.

In recent years, Madame Alcarr had retired and was living in London. She was found two nights ago at the home of her daughter, Lady Genelle Tisne of Green Street, who had recently been widowed when her husband of five years, Lord Arthur, had similarly been found dead in her home.

The Metropolitan Police are not commenting on the cases or whether they are investigating them in tandem. Lady Tisne claims an alibi for the night in question and no motive for the possible suspicion of murder of her well-known and well-respected husband. But it must be asked whether these two deaths are related since it was common knowledge that Lord Arthur was a habitué of Madame Alcarr's establishments and it was he who brought her to the House of Correction when it was first opened to the public.

Madame Alcarr achieved her most famous title, Queen of the Night, when she was the Abbess at the House. It is said she was merciless and challenged any man to take the test. It is said that those who were squeamish about participating could pay to walk down the infamous Crystal Corridor, through the ceiling of which they could clearly view every possibility the House had to offer.

It is said Madame Alcarr never admitted to having a daughter so the news of her engagement to marry Lord Arthur Tisne created a minor sensation. No one knows where the girl was or who her father was; she appeared on the scene as if she had been born from her mother's head and married Lord Arthur five years past, and separated from him two years after that, an amicable arrangement by which he gave her his townhouse and an allowance. When he died, he provided a continuance of the same in his will.

The night of her mother's death, Lady Tisne was said to have been in the company of Rulan Roak, the estimable investigator of some local fame.

Roak came on the scene some six years ago when he provided the Yard with the solution to the knotty problem of The Lydgate Truffle, a case of poisoning that had baffled the police. His most recent foray was to bring to a successful conclusion the case of the missing Holcomb artifacts, and he had been had been hired by Lady Tisne after that to investigate her husband's untimely death. He had been living at Lady Tisne's townhouse to provide her with protection at the time her mother's body was found.

Succinct, to the point, and never glossing over one prurient detail. And the others were written even more sensationally. Her mother had worked the docks; her mother had sold herself when she was thirteen; her mother had ten illegitimate children scattered all over the countryside; her mother was a *man*...

...*Stiles had made some similar comment*...*what was it?—Yes—her mother was large enough to be a man*...

...*there was something*...*something about that—she felt again as if she ought to be connecting something, but she couldn't*...

...*large enough to be a man—*

...*woman as man*...

...*woman as man—*

...*man as woman*...?

...*she almost had it—she almost had it—*

...*the boys at that awful Fox and Hole*...?

...*the boys with—those girls' names*...*called "she" by the Madame—how could she ever forget?*

...*but what—why?*

—*large enough to be a man—*

—*maybe* was *a man?*

Her mother? No...*no*...*man as woman*...*that was the thing—man as woman*...

...*they pretended to be girls*...*for the patrons—obviously not girls, just the names—just the names*...

So—

—*if the boys could, why—not—the—men?*

—*Oh dear heaven—no*...*yes—*

—*the mystery women*...

—*not—women*...

Who?

No...

Yes—

No! *That was insane—that was reaching for solutions where none existed.*

Exactly—the women didn't exist because . . .

Because they were men.

She was crazy; she was going crazy because she felt so desperate.

She stared at the paragraph with the scandalous speculations.

Her mother was a man . . . her appetites were too intense and gargantuan for a woman . . .

What about her daughter?

This is off the track.

Whereas the other is major deductive reasoning. And reasonable. Arthur reveled in the perverse—not the common. The clues are all there. Two women who could not be found with names— did one think about it—that sounded as patently false as the idea that her husband would do something as ordinary as take a mistress.

No—she was stretching it . . .

No—how could she find out?

How?

Someone had mentioned it—besides Roak—weeks ago. Years ago, it felt like. She felt as if she had always been drowning in this morass of depravity, and that she could have succumbed to it herself, given more time.

Look at how she had enjoyed her discoveries. Look at how she had been perfectly willing to go further and further and finally take the ultimate step with Roak.

But someone had mentioned the woman's name—Eversham—sometime during her explorations and she had not given it a second thought.

And now—

She closed her eyes. Now—

. . . the Gatekeeper . . .

At the Arcade. Arthur had come there, she had said, with the Eversham . . . yes—yes . . .

She glanced at the clock. Late. Yes. She would sneak out again, and take a cab. She could wear her wig. Perhaps that was what it was for.

Her mother had provided for every eventuality.

Fog. It drifted in opaque patches across the landscape as she slipped from the house and flew down the street wrapped in a dark cloak.

Too simple to elude them, she thought, pulling the hood tighter around her head. But there was hardly a cab to be had.

It took longer than she would have wanted, and she had to pay dearly to bribe him to wait.

And on the ride there, it occurred to her that the Gatekeeper might not be the woman who had passed her.

All these variables that ruled the twilight world that Arthur had inhabited and on which her defense might depend—

Oh yes, you've got them taking you to prison already and putting you before the bar . . .

What if that woman isn't there—

Her stomach was in turmoil by the time the cab deposited her at the *Arcade* and then turned to park across the street.

She moved swiftly into the entrance, closed the door, and turned, as she removed her hood, to face the Gatekeeper in her booth.

"Ah my lady . . ."

Was she the same—or someone new?

"Welcome, my lady. We have not seen you in a long while. I hope last time you were not disappointed."

The same—the same—with that wizened face and that knowing tone of voice, she looked like she was a daughter of the ages with all the wisdom a thousand years could imbue.

"No," she answered carefully. "Circumstances have prevented my return."

"Ah yes, we understand."

"And now I must approach you on a matter of some delicacy, with the knowledge that the preservation of privacy is of the utmost importance to you."

"Yes, we know you appreciate that," the Gatekeeper said,

nodding. "So it is not that you wish to partake of what we offer tonight."

"Not tonight."

"What *does* my lady want?"

"The answer to a question."

"We told you last time, my lady—"

"I remember. And I would not wish you to violate a confidence. But what I want to know might well be common knowledge to everyone—but me."

"My lady—"

"I am willing to give a full evening's fee for the answer to my question."

The Gatekeeper's eyes flickered as Genelle pushed the wad of bills across the counter of the booth.

"One question, my lady."

"Possibly two."

"My lady . . ."

"No more than that."

"We can see our way to *listening* to the questions you have," the Gatekeeper said, taking the money. "Two minutes, my lady. No more. Speak quickly. Someone is already waiting."

"You told me my husband had come here with a woman named Davidella Eversham. Who is she?"

"She was a particular friend of Lord Arthur's whom he escorted here every now and again to view that which interested them the most. What is your next question?"

Nothing—she had told her nothing. She felt a mounting frustration and anger that she would have to ask the question she had not wanted to ask, and as baldly as possible.

"Is Davidella Eversham a man?"

The Gatekeeper looked down at the money and then back at her, nodding just once, and then holding her gaze steady.

"One protects the privacy of one's patrons who are free to choose and act out any alternate life choice they wish, my lady. *What* gender Davidella Eversham is has no meaning here."

"Thank you," she whispered.

"Please—leave from the exit behind me, my lady. It is time for my next patron."

She ducked behind the curtain, and listened for a moment.

"Madame—"

Oh, the voice—the voice . . . it was Roak, and if he ever found her here—

But she had to listen . . .

". . . information about . . ."

She couldn't stay—she couldn't chance it . . .

"Lord Arthur Tisne . . ." She heard just that much and then she darted down the narrow corridor that exited to the street and ran out into the foggy night.

Look at things the way they really be . . .

Oh Mother, did you know about that as well?

She must have done—she knew everything about Arthur— everything, but surely knowing everything was not enough to get her killed . . .

Or was it?

Everything had to do with everything else—that was what her mother had said . . . even Roak, she had said; Roak with his secrets and mysterious comings and goings . . .

And the power to make her dissolve in his arms—

Roak who wore her ring as a symbol of her desire for him . . . but she wasn't going to think about that.

How had things gotten so complicated, so intense?

And now that one small mystery had been solved, nothing was any clearer than it had been twenty-four hours ago.

A door slammed and she heard footsteps on the stair. A moment later Roak burst into the room.

"What the hell were you doing at *Newbury* tonight?"

"The same as you, I expect," she said carelessly, "asking questions, getting answers . . ."

"Did you get the answers you wanted, my lady?"

"Did you?"

They stared at each other. He broke first, a fact she did not like.

"Perhaps my lady wishes to handle the rest on her own."

"I have told you already, I cannot sit still and wait for you to feed me tidbits of information."

"And so, having figured out that tidbit of information, you decided to confirm it."

"Yes," she said curtly. "And you?"

"I was after something else, my lady. The other was pure coincidental; I knew it already."

No—he had said not . . .

"You told me you didn't."

He hesitated. "Perhaps not then."

"Oh, and so you chose not to tell me otherwise?"

"How upsetting would it have been?"

"How can I know—now? What else have you *chosen* not to tell me?"

"Nothing that makes any difference to your situation, my lady. I have identified Clarissa Bone as well."

"Another gentleman, I assume?" she asked caustically.

"Your husband," he said flatly, and that did shock her.

But why should it—why had she assumed that Arthur hadn't played those games?

"I see."

"You don't. There is a house of accommodation in which the gentleman regulars take the names of women. Your husband was a frequent customer and he took the name out with him in public. It amused him to rent a room and install *Clarissa* as its tenant. The landlady never guessed; she thought *he* was Clarissa's lover, and had some hopes in that direction herself. Most amusing."

"Is that all?" she asked coldly. *She didn't want to know these things, she didn't. And she couldn't see why he hadn't told her the whole the first time she had asked.*

"For tonight," he answered, matching her tone.

"Then you may go."

"Lady Tisne." His tone was as formal as any butler's ought to be, but it was tinged with irritation and impatience as he acknowledged her and left her with the gnawing questions answered—to no purpose—and the certainty that tonight she would not lie in his arms.

Chapter 19

What did she know about Roak?

That question seized her and she could not sleep.

She knew of his reputation as a *skilled investigator*. She knew he was renowned in higher circles for taking cases which seemed impossible to solve.

She knew he kept his own counsel. She knew he worked in ways she did not understand.

She knew he was her perfect lover.

She knew he had told her one small falsehood.

And she knew that her mother claimed to know something about him he would not want to become public.

Faint faint clues to the man in whose hands she had placed her life—and her sex. A man as reticent in daylight as he was voluble at night.

A strange combination of man—

How many other of his clients had he pacified in bed?

What?

Oh no, oh no—she was not going to start thinking like that just because she was scared, and because Roak had found nothing viable—yet—to prove her innocence.

There still had to be prospects for a different solution. There were three other people—four if you included her mother—whose motives and actions had not been explored.

And they all had secrets . . . her mother especially—with her money and her years in service to Arthur's pornographic vision.

But what about Morfit, with his sly side agreements with Arthur to take care of his most obscene creation, and Tony Lethbridge, who knew every truth about Arthur, was patron of his

*illicit houses of depravity, consorted with Morfit, and denied he
had been with her the night of Arthur's death?*

*And then there was Madam Tisne. What secrets was she hiding
in her gilded ballroom at Fanhurst?*

*No—too fanciful by half . . . and where did one go from there?
Did she confront her mother-in-law with all the vile details of
Arthur's life just to see her reaction?*

*Or did she demand that Morfit tell her the details of Arthur's
estate as it pertained to his mother just to see how much the old
bitch did know . . . ?*

How much did *she* know?

She raked through her mind to sort through the details, and
it seemed to her that there was nothing, just nothing, and that
was the point she had been avoiding with this exercise.

She knew now of her mother's sordid past, that she had started
in Bickley, that she herself had been born in Bickley; that her
mother was a wealthy woman by her own hand; that she had
probably been the Abbess at the *House of Correction* when she
concocted the idea of soliciting Arthur as a husband for her
"secret" daughter.

And she herself had never been aware. They had lived in boarding houses all over England and had finally settled in one just
outside of London when she was about ten.

The landlady took care of her at night—not an onerous job
since she slept through—while her mother was scrounging around
the local pubs to earn a few dollars to meet expenses.

That was what she knew.

Was that what she knew?

*Had she never wondered just what her mother was doing?
Had she never questioned anything?*

*She thought not. Her mother, in those London boarding house
years, sent her to school and talked incessantly about her marrying
well. Yes, that had been Mother's dream, which she had been too
cowed to deny.*

*She was going to marry someone with money and then she
could take care of her mother too, because the gentleman would
have to promise.*

And she seemed to remember one or two likely gentlemen

having come to meet her—with no results, and no interest on her part—

And then—Arthur. And the threats. And the scurrilous wedding.

And then Arthur setting her mother up in a house in London.

Nothing about "retirement"—everything about how she deserved this respect from her one and only daughter.

Yet somewhere it had been said that her mother retired . . .

And then she remembered: the article in the *Gazetteer*. Her mother had "retired" when Genelle married Arthur because Arthur had been willing to support her as well.

But—if she had been working for him, he must have had some idea of the money she was pulling in . . .

Why had he agreed to give her money?

And why had he suddenly withdrawn that support not more than a week before he died?

Odd . . .

And she had known nothing about any of it.

And Arthur's interminably secret life—all those crass little secrets stored in the vault of Mr. Morfit's office. All the blackmail; all the deceit; all the flaunting of his dissolute fantasies . . .

And strutting around town as Clarissa Bone . . .

And Eversham—being seen in public with . . .

. . . Just who had played Davidella Eversham?

The thought almost knocked her off her feet. No one knew *who* Eversham was, only that it was a man and that Arthur had been seen with *her* so that it could not have been Arthur in still another identity.

Or could it?

Surely Morfit would know . . .

And certainly he was cagey enough not to reveal too much . . . but perhaps not with her.

Perhaps this was just the right time to confront him and coerce him into admitting something more.

He made her wait.

There was something about small mean men who suddenly ascended to power. They became petty and vindictive. They seemed to like to put people in their place.

Or perhaps it was just women.

She waited.

She knew there was no one in the office with him; she was fairly certain he had no other clients but Madam Tisne and herself.

She was also sure that he was not a very good solicitor, and that it was possible that Arthur had chosen him because he had very few scruples.

It took him an hour to open the door, and even then he met her with unprofessional ungraciousness.

"What is it now, Lady Tisne?"

"I need to talk to you, Mr. Morfit," she said pugnaciously. "If you please—" She stepped right up to the door and waited for him to let her pass.

He moved aside and she entered his office and went right to the most comfortable chair.

He seated himself behind his desk. "Well?"

She had chosen her attack long before she walked in the door, and she bent to it in her most forceful and belligerent manner.

"Well, Mr. Morfit—you have lied and I have been placed once again in the most untenable position."

"How is that, Lady Tisne?" He wasn't a bit fazed by her bald accusation.

"You told me there was nothing else I needed to know about my husband's so-called affairs, and that his involvement with the *House of Correction* was the worst of it. And so now, I am confronted by the police with yet another embarrassment: that my husband was known to dress as a woman and maintain a residence in Town; and moreover, that he was often seen in the company of another woman, whom the police assume was a man. Now how am I to respond to *that*, Mr. Morfit, when they are on the verge of arresting *me?*"

He didn't look in the least shocked. "It was one of his little . . . *foibles* . . . Lady Tisne. Nothing to take account of."

"And who was the other *woman* then, Mr. Morfit? His mother? Another *wife?* You?"

"Lady Tisne—you go too far . . ."

"Oh, I don't believe I have gone far enough; the Inspector is certain I coveted my husband's wealth, and meantime, here are a host of characters behind the scenes who presumably had greater emotional investment in him than I and could have done away with him in a trice, and no one the wiser once they disrobed and became men again."

She could see him getting angry, slowly, slowly, like embers in a fireplace suddenly flaring up.

"And how many of their secrets did my mother hold to her bosom that she deserved the same fate, Mr. Morfit?" she added for good measure, watching the flame of fury stain his pale cheeks.

"Your mother was a greedy slut, Lady Tisne, no more, no less. And she had her secrets too. Arthur's little *quirks* have nothing to do with your case or his death."

"Who is Eversham?"

"The person has left town."

"I'm sure he has, Mr. Morfit. Especially now that it is known someone is seeking him. Easier to disappear when all one has to do is wash off some makeup, remove a wig, and step out of a dress—"

. . . the wig—

"Lady Tisne, this avenue of inquiry will not profit you."

"Who will it profit then, Mr. Morfit? Isn't it true—if I am incarcerated, my allowance is restored to the estate? And there is no provision for reclamation?"

"If you were imprisoned, and if you were subsequently proved innocent and released, of course the estate would do the right thing, Lady Tisne."

"I see. I begin to see . . ."

"You are looking in the wrong place, Lady Tisne. Everyone who knew Arthur loved him. There was no question. Perhaps what really happened is that your mother killed him and then when she realized the golden goose was dead, she turned her hand on herself."

"After she had been bribed away from my home, and my servants with her? I think not, Mr. Morfit, and it makes me wonder who you are so desperate to protect."

"I have nothing to hide, Lady Tisne. I have given you everything and told you everything you want to know. Perhaps you ought to look elsewhere. Perhaps someone closer to you has a better motive for murder than you think."

"What do you mean—*what* could you possibly mean?"

"I mean that it is no accident that the man handling your investigation is Mr. Roak. Mr. Roak has his secrets too."

She felt a horrible twinge of fear.

"Tell me one," she challenged him. "Tell me—in your zeal to reveal everything I want to know—why haven't you told me this?"

"You didn't ask my lady. I have told you already that the profit from the *House of Correction* provides your income as well as a source of reparation to those who—unjustly I think—felt the need to pursue a legal course of action against Lord Tisne. Ten or twelve years ago, Mr. Roak was such a one."

"What do you mean? What can you mean?"

"I mean that Lord Tisne was much taken by Mr. Roak's young son, a boy of—oh, ten or so years, and showered him with presents and such—all with the consent of the mother. Mr. Roak saw it differently, especially after the boy died. Collusion and corruption, he called it, with the mother, his wife, being seduced as well by Lord Arthur's generosity. The boy died; the woman could not live with what he made her feel that she had done: she killed herself. Lord Arthur generously provided redress, in spite of the fact he was innocent of any wrongdoing, and it was with this lavish settlement that Mr. Roak embarked upon his present career.

"One could say he profited at the expense of his wife and child—but one would not be so unkind. Or it might be that he had been looking for the moment to avenge the deaths in his family—but that might be taking it too far as well. It would make him an inordinately patient man—and how many men have that kind of persistence?

"Or perhaps he is only what he maintains he is—a private investigator of extreme ability and great mental gifts, and he *can* eventually prove you innocent of murder."

No, no—no . . . that couldn't be true—it was just a diversionary tactic he was using to distract her from pursuing the question of Eversham . . .

She wouldn't let him get away with it either—even though her hands had turned to ice and she half believed him.

"So what you're saying, Mr. Morfit is—what? That Davidella Eversham could be any one of a number of people, even those I mentioned to you?"

"Lady Tisne . . ."

"Perhaps Mr. Roak? He would make an awfully tall woman . . ."

"I have no more to say to you, Lady Tisne. I have fulfilled all my obligations relevant to you. Now if you'll excuse me—"

She ignored him.

"Who paid my mother to leave my house, Mr. Morfit? Who stole away my servants? Who stole the agreement that Arthur and I signed that would prove I did not kill him for his money? Who killed Arthur, Mr. Morfit—you? Tony Lethbridge? He was there, you know . . . Mr. Morfit—Mr. Morfit—"

But he was gone. He rose up from his chair without saying a word or protesting any of her accusations, and he walked out on her and into his inner office.

She sat there, shaking.

This was too much; whenever she entered this office, she learned something she wished she did not need to know.

And now Roak.

No, she wouldn't take Morfit at his word: he had too much to lose and too much to protect. Anyone could make up a story . . .

. . . *something he would rather not be made public—*

. . . *a child who had been corrupted; a wife who had committed suicide over her lapse in judgment* . . .

. . . *a man seeking vengeance—by doing what? Killing the violator—or defiling his wife—*

Or both . . .

Her blood ran cold.

It couldn't be true . . .

. . . *came onto the scene eight years before* . . .

She jumped up out of her chair and walked around to the other side of the desk.

An unnaturally clean desk; you would think the man would have papers or legal documents strewn all over it, at least to give the impression that he was busy and had a lot of clients.

There were some sheets of paper piled neatly to one side, the topmost one blank.

She lifted it curiously.

My dear Madam Tisne,
Enclosed is the quarterly investment report . . .

She lifted the next sheet. A jumble of figures, attached to various symbols, signs, and abbreviations. And then the word: *other,* with a modest figure written in next to it.

The House of Correction? Other? With that little money against it? After her allowance was paid? Or after Morfit took his management fee?

She lifted the sheet. A letter.

My dear Tony—everything—

She heard him rattling the doorknob.

"I hope you are not still there, Lady Tisne," he said from behind the door. "I have nothing more to say to you. Your money has been deposited, if that is what you came to find out, we have no more business today."

"I daresay we are *not* finished, Mr. Morfit, particularly if the police come to me with any more of Arthur's shocking *eccentricities.* But it will do for now."

She moved away from the desk reluctantly and finally, as the inner door slowly opened, out of the office altogether.

Now what?

Her head was spinning.

Secrets . . . what was Morfit's secret?

He was siphoning money from the House of Correction into his own pocket . . .

A natural inclination, wouldn't it be?

He was writing letters to Tony Lethbridge . . . or maybe some other Tony?

He and her husband had paid Rulan Roak thousands of pounds twelve or so years before to buy his silence in the matter of the deaths of his wife and son . . . ?

Secrets . . . no one was immune from secrets.

Even she had one—Roak had been her lover . . . but no more— no more . . .

Where could she find out the truth about Rulan Roak?

Where had she first found his name?

In the papers, of course; in the papers. And they would have

some place where they stored back copies of their publications—
wouldn't they?
So that someone could look it all up?
Really—she felt sick and dizzy and scared—and she didn't
know what else.
But she was going to find out.
Before the day was over, she was going to find out.

Everything in the whole of London that had to do with money
or anything illicit was invariably housed underground in dimly
lit rooms that one reached by traversing long dark corridors.

She felt like she was entering a tomb—she probably was: news
long dead and buried was housed here, in a room where the
temperature stayed at a constant so that the fragile newsprint
would not crumble.

Fifty years worth of the weekly tabloid paper was bound into
leather folios with the years stamped in gold on the spine. And
these were the copies for public perusal.

In the center of the room there was a long reading table that
slanted on both sides so that up to ten people could be reading
at a time by the light of the three stained-glass fixtures that hung
above.

The clerk, who was tall, slender, and ascetic looking, took
down the binders encompassing the years she had requested, and
cautioning her again to be careful with the newsprint, he left her
to her discoveries.

It was a fascinating way to pass an afternoon. The *Gazetteer*
missed nothing in the way of scandal or sin. Every iniquity was
chronicled; every crime, offense, atrocity, and degradation was
limned in the most matter-of-fact prose possible, which did nothing to diminish the vice and wickedness that abounded in its
pages.

And nothing had changed. Men's lives were still bounded by
dishonor and disgrace to this day—as ten or twelve years before,
Roak's family had been dishonored and disgraced.

She was now in the first book, dated 1883, and going slowly
through the mid-months—May, June, July—August . . .
September . . .

Tragedy at Plumford Wye

An article that detailed the drowning of an unidentified child in the Plumford Rapids.

And the following week:

Boy Identified in Tragic Drowning

The article named Frederick Rulan Roak, aged ten, as the victim of the mysterious drowning at Plumford Rapids the previous week. His parents, Rulan Sr. and Violet Dawes Roak, had been vacationing and the boy had spent the day visiting with a maternal friend, Lord Arthur Tisne, at his nearby estate, Fanhurst. Lord Tisne expressed himself as shocked and grieved that such an accident could have happened. The parents were in seclusion.

So there it is. Arthur involved, and the child gone, twelve years past and counting.

Her hands were so cold she could barely turn the pages.

A week later:

Reward Offered

An article detailing the generous offer of a reward made by Lord Arthur Tisne to anyone providing information about the shocking accidental drowning of Frederick Rulan Roak, aged ten, the previous week in Plumford Rapids.

How public spirited of Arthur. What a humanitarian he had been . . . or was that too coming from the profits of the House of Correction?

Three months later:

Mother Commits Suicide Over Loss of Son

The contents of the article chilled her.

The body of Violet Dawes Roak was found this morning, the day after Christmas, three months after the tragic accidental drowning of her son in Plumford Rapids.

She was discovered in the hallway of her home in Hampstead Heath by her husband, bleeding from a wound to her chest. She had been despondent and distraught over the loss of their son and had apparently taken a knife to her person. She was pronounced dead by the village doctor who was called on the scene. Her husband is in seclusion.

A month later:

Police Investigate Death of Violet Dawes Roak

Some question then about how she died and whether she could have stabbed herself with the force required to kill herself. Roak, submitting to the infamy of the police inquiry which was painstakingly detailed over the next three weeks and coming away with a cloud of suspicion hanging over his head.

And then:

Improprieties Alleged
A case of misconduct has been brought against Lord Arthur Tisne by Rulan Roak whose recently deceased son he accuses Sir Arthur of molesting. Roak's wife committed suicide last month.

And then—nothing.

Nothing until the spring of 1889 when suddenly the paper was full of the story of the Lydgate Truffle and the miraculous solution devised by one Rulan Roak.

After that—every several months, there was a mention of his name in the most oblique way possible, usually at the end of a story about Lady This-or-That or Lord So-and-So who was eternally grateful to the skilled investigator, Rulan Roak, for saving him or her from a fate worse than death.

One had to look, but if one were sharp, one could find the whole of his career in London between the lines of the most scandalous stories topping the most notorious incidents, down to and including the case of the substitute Royal jewels, and the problem of the Holcomb Artifacts which he had found by deducing the unbelievably unlikely place they had been hidden.

He made miracles, his admirers claimed; he was a magician, finding substance where there seemed to be nothing, conjuring up illusions when there was absolutely no hope.

And all this sleight of hand in aid of someday avenging the deaths of his wife and son.

By whatever means possible.

She felt sick.

His wife and son . . .

Connected to Arthur . . . motivation to kill.

And Arthur's naive wife—whom he had conveniently seduced—on whom to pin the blame.

She felt paralyzed with fear when she finally left the newspaper offices; Green Street was the last place she wanted to go—and the only place possible.

The house was quiet when she entered. No bodies on the entrance hall floor. No sounds of servants going about their daily business—a reminder of the day she had returned and they had been gone.

Maybe they had disappeared again. Maybe the whole thing was happening all over again.

And then Joseph appeared as if out of thin air.

"My lady; Inspector Stiles has called."

Terror . . .

"Is he still here?"

"He said he would return, my lady, and would you be so good as to wait."

Oh I'll be good—I'm always bloody well good . . .

"Thank you, Joseph."

What else was there to do but sit and wait for the final disposition? Stiles would arrest her tonight and the thing would be over.

And she was tired; she wanted it to be over.

She would just pack a bag so she would be ready when he came. And then Morfit and Madam Tisne would dance a jig over her grave.

She climbed the steps wearily to her room and thrust open the door.

Roak was waiting, dressed and impatient, pacing the room.

She took in the picture of him striding back and forth and the bundle of bills she had not taken with her strewn on the bed.

The minute she entered, he wheeled on her.

"*Where* did you get that money?"

He could be her enemy . . . he had every reason to want Arthur dead—and her mother . . . well, her mother—he knew everything about Arthur; how could he not have known about her mother?

It would have been a twisted and violent vengeance to kill the molester, corrupt the wife and destroy the madame.

And he had done it—he had done it to a turn.

She quelled her nerves; she had to deal with him as if she knew nothing, as if he knew nothing.

"From the bank," she said noncommittally, "and now I must pack. I understand Stiles is coming for me."

"Oh, yes, Stiles is coming all right. They got into the bank today, into your mother's lock box, and what do they find but a right and tight legal document that names *you* her heir."

She feigned shock—not very well either. "That is impossible. My mother never would have . . ."

"Your mother did, and what's more—someone had access to the vault box three days ago, the day after your mother was buried—Lady Genelle, claiming to be her. And now you turn up with all this money—"

"*My* money; Morfit just made my monthly payment."

"*Five thousand pounds?*"

"I have lived very frugally."

"Not in the last month, you haven't," he said stridently, and she turned away and scooped up the bills and shoved them into a bag she took from the closet.

She wasn't going to answer that and she wasn't going to think about one brazen thing she had done in this last month with a murder charge hanging over her head, and a possible murderer in her bed.

But she had to say something.

"Is that why Stiles is coming?"

"Stiles now has motive number two, my lady. Money, money, money."

"And Stiles has looked no further than that."

"It seems likely to him. Once the will clears the court, you will be a wealthy woman, all on the ill-gotten gains of your mother's performances for Lord Tisne. A tidy little circle, don't you think?"

"With chinks here and there that no one cares to account for."

"My lady has been sleuthing again," he said mockingly. "What now, Lady Genelle? You just cannot leave it alone."

His tone made her angry; *he* made her furious the way he paced around the room as if he had no connection at all with the whole. She could not look at him with equanimity any more. He had taken money from Arthur. He had waited to take some kind of revenge.

She thrust clothing into her bag without much thinking about what she was doing. The point was to be ready. The point was for him to face the accusation.

"All right—my *skilled investigator*—here are some questions for you to answer while I am in prison. Who is Davidella Eversham? And why, when Arthur knew what kind of money my mother was pulling from the *House of Correction,* why did he agree to support her and furnish her with a house? And why does Morfit underreport the profit in his quarterly statement to Madam Tisne? Why does he write to Tony—Lethbridge, I assume—and finally, which well-known private investigator has finally got his revenge for what Lord Arthur Tisne did to his family . . . ?"

She waited for the explosion. She expected him to deny it. Perhaps someplace deep in her being, she hoped he would.

"So suddenly, out of the blue, there is *you,*" she said, after a long hard silence. It was a parlor game, she supposed. She didn't know what else to do in the face of his impassivity and hard silence except try to make some sense of what she had discovered.

"And someone else has a reason for wanting him dead. You must have wanted to drag Arthur's name through the mud after your son's death. He must have bought you off handsomely— there was never another word about it in the papers after your initial threat to take him to court."

"It was a monstrous amount of money," he agreed expressionlessly.

"Enough to buy your virtue, Roak?"

"Enough even to buy yours, Lady Genelle."

She flushed. "Everyone has a price. Mine was fifteen thousand a year; yours was enough to do what? You could not ruin him monetarily . . ."

She paused, and looked at him speculatively. *No—he would have taken the money all right, but for someone like him the matter would not have been over.*

"So you took the money as a means to a end—you were going to find some other way to destroy him. You"—she reached again for some inference that made sense in the context of what he had become and what he had been to her—"found out about the *House of Correction* . . ."

He was very attentive now; she sensed his alertness, his interest in the intuitive way she was edging around the truth—and maybe he was just a little alarmed she might be getting too close to it . . . ?

What truth?

She went on doggedly: "And you probably could see that one way or another, you could get to him through that. And you were willing to wait until the right moment, when the perfect opportunity walked in your door . . ."

"And after all that—it came too late," Roak said, and there wasn't a ounce of emotion in his voice.

"I don't think so," she interpolated bitterly. "I think it amused you to corrupt your enemy's wife; you must have been overjoyed at how innocent I was and how easily led."

"How easily enticed to what you had always wanted to do— my *lady.*"

"Perfect revenge . . ." she said slowly, as a stunning thought suddenly struck her with the force of lightning.

It couldn't be—it couldn't—not even he was that devious . . . or maybe he was; what did she know about the passions of Rulan Roak outside of a whorehouse?

"Perfect," she reiterated numbly, as the whole horrible possibility blinded her with the elegance of its solution.

And it explained everything—their affair, his seeming lack of progress, everything that had happened to her . . .

. . . she didn't want to believe it—and yet . . . and yet . . . she had to try it out on him—she had no other choice . . .

"You seduce your enemy's wife, pretend to help her—and let her go to prison for a murder you know she did not commit . . ."

The words reverberated between them, lined in a awful truth.

"Oh my God—oh my God . . . all this time, and you've done *nothing . . . nothing—*"

"*Genelle . . . !*"

"Oh, no, oh no—it makes perfect sense: the noose keeps getting tighter around my neck, and you've come up with nothing I couldn't have found out—you said so yourself. And everything else all along was secondary to . . . to—"

She couldn't say it—she choked on the words and the betrayal.

He had planned it from the moment she walked in his door like a gift from heaven . . . manipulated everything as a means to his end . . . which now came down to this last final moment when Stiles would arrest her.

There was a knock on the door and her heart plummeted.

"Inspector Stiles is here," Joseph announced.

"I'll be right down."

She snapped the bag shut and looked at him.

He wasn't going to say a word. He wasn't going to do a thing to help her. And Stiles would never believe the truth.

She turned on her heel and walked out the door.

"Well, my lady, we are here again."

Stiles was waiting, and a moment after she settled herself across from him, Roak entered the parlor and took a seat behind her.

"Yes, Inspector?"

"The news is not good, my lady. Your mother left a document in which you were named her heir. It was found this morning in a lock-box in her bank, along with the astonishing revelation that someone calling herself by your mother's name had access to the box the day after your mother was interred."

"That is very upsetting," she murmured.

"It is time to fit the facts together, Lady Tisne, and when one does, one comes to the whole picture: the only one who could have wanted either your husband or your mother dead was you. In both cases, you stood to inherit a lot of money. There is no proof that you did not have that expectation in either case; your mother-in-law claims you were extremely and violently upset in the first instance, when the disposition of Lord Arthur's estate was laid out; and in the second, you claimed not to know your mother was wealthy, and to have had a break with her whereby she mysteriously left your house along with your servants, and then returned to tell you not to pursue an inquiry relevant to her.

"In your favor, Mr. Morfit substantiates your story that you knew what your inheritance would be and so it would not have profited you to murder your husband; in the second instant, Mr. Roak was with you and found your mother's body, and gives you an alibi for the evening. However, he could have fallen asleep and you certainly would have had time to commit the murder.

"In both cases, large sums of money were at stake; you were in the house; both murders were committed in this house in similar circumstances; and I find all these facts taken together make a strong case to warrant your arrest."

"I see." Her turn to utter those enigmatic words she hated so much.

He was deadly serious about it too. He would not be put off with alternate theories and unrelated probable causes.

"What do I do now, Inspector?"

"You engage the best solicitor you possibly can—but tonight, Lady Tisne, you come with me."

So that was the end of it; Roak was witness to the artful success of his scheme. And she would face prison utterly alone. But hadn't she always been?

"May I pack a few things?"

Oh God, what if Roak tells him I already have?

"In fifteen minutes, Lady Tisne."

"Thank you, Inspector."

Fifteen minutes? Fifteen minutes? She could barely get down the stairs and out the door in fifteen minutes—

But she was going to try—

Carefully up the steps after leaving the room without even looking at Roak . . . carefully into her room—lock the suitcase, grab her cloak, her reticule with the rest of the money in it—she had the keys; the letters were gone—there was nothing in that room to link her to anything but a libidinous lust for the man who had betrayed her.

But that was over now too—

Down the servants' staircase, into the servants' hall, bypassing the dining room in case they were eating . . .

"Mum?"

The damned scullery maid.

"You haven't seen me." She pressed a five pound note into the bewildered girl's hand.

"Yes, mum."

Past the room that Roak had occupied . . . no thought for that now. Not to think about that until later . . . days and days later . . .

Out the basement door and up the stone steps to the little terrace—God, the house is so lighted up . . .

Past the hedges . . . Oh God, a minute more, just another minute to clear the view from the house . . . yes—

She ran. She hoisted the bag over her shoulder and she ran. She ran into the traffic, looking for a cab, a carriage, a likely looking someone who would drive her out of town.

She had enough money—she could buy anything—

"Here, you!" she hailed the uniformed driver of a passing carriage. "I'll give you twenty-five pounds to take me to Hampstead Heath—tonight."

"Get in."

A chance—a huge calculated chance that the driver belonged to one of the wealthy townhouses around Green Street and that nothing more would happen than he would deliver her just where she wanted and still get back in time to pick up his master— wherever he might be—twenty-five pounds richer and none the wiser.

"Drive past Green Street, will you?" she called up to him.

"Aye mum."

The carriage wheeled around and turned a corner.

She saw it all as she passed: the lights—the motion—Joseph racing out of the house from the servants' hall to see if he could catch her; Roak and Stiles pounding down the street in either direction; the parlor maid standing helplessly at the door.

The carriage clipped smartly by all the commotion.

A moment later, it turned the corner toward Bennington High Street, and then they were gone.

Chapter 20

And now that she was on her way, she felt almost overwhelmed by the logistics of her flight.

She had thought she would go to Bickley, that she would go to the house at Skirling Vail for which she had the key. She had thought she could hide there, and they would never find her.

But of course Stiles had seen the papers in the lock-box—he had seen her birth certificate and the title to the house . . . *how stupid of her not to have taken it*—and now Bickley could not be a refuge for her because it would be the first place they would look.

But she could search the place first. They would not start there until morning most likely; they would try to discover if she had taken a train or a cab tonight to get out of the city, and where she had gone.

She had some time—but so very little . . .

Nor could she travel from Hampstead this night. She would need a place to stay. But at least she would be an hour closer to Bickley . . .

The driver let her off at the train station and she paid him handsomely for his time and trouble.

And then she took a moment to assess the situation.

The worst thing she could do was ask the stationmaster where she could find accommodations for the night; the police would leap all over him like a bull on a cow.

She needed someone innocent, someone unlikely, like the carriage driver. A worker at the train station perhaps, or someone from town. Preferably a woman, but that probably was not a possibility this time of night.

But—what about a . . . boy?

There was a young one, crawling around on the tracks, picking up coal and who knew what else and squirreling it away in a bag.

"Boy!"

He jumped, paralyzed into inaction.

"Hey, you—boy!" She got to him quickly. "Listen, I'm a stranger in town, passing through for tonight. You know a place I can buy a bed for tonight, and maybe hire a carriage tomorrow to take me where I want to go?"

He couldn't even speak he was so frightened.

"I won't tell, I promise. I just need a place to stay tonight and someone to take me up to Bickley tomorrow. I'm willing to pay."

"You one of *them* wimmen?" he asked finally, hoarsely.

"No. I just—I'm just in a little trouble and I have to get to Bickley tomorrow, real early. Can you help me?"

"Mebbe—if my mum says all right."

"Could you ask her?"

"How much?"

"Ask your mum how much she wants."

"You stay here."

"I won't move; I wouldn't know where to go."

But she hated the darkness, and the eerie stillness of a night in a strange place, where she was surrounded by unfamiliar country sounds.

He was back in five minutes.

"Mum says ten shillings for the bed; twenty-five for the wagon and my time. Five for some supper and a breakfast."

"Done."

He led her past the tracks and down a long dirt road—which ended at a small gabled cottage that could not have been more than two rooms big.

A careworn woman waited within, her sharp eyes examining Genelle the moment she walked in.

"She'll do," she said to the boy. "Don't need to pay, missus. Glad to help a stranger."

The boy slept in the loft. The woman in a separate bedroom which she turned over to Genelle. "I'll put a straw mat up with the boy; don't make no nevermind to me. I'm up with the dawn anyhow."

She slept—with her clothes on and her bag under her arm,

and she too arose with the dawn, and sat with a steaming cup of tea and some eggs and bacon which the woman had prepared.

"You with child?" the woman asked point-blank at one point.

"Not that kind of trouble. And you should not know any more than that—not my problem, not my name. Nothing."

"Your choice," the woman said phlegmatically. "The boy'll take you over."

"And you will take this." She pressed a handful of bills into the woman's hands. "You must; I don't want the boy sweeping the tracks. You understand?"

The woman nodded. "Only for that."

Genelle smiled and climbed into the wagon. The boy snapped the reins and they started off for Bickley as the sun rose over the rooftops.

Bickley—it seemed such a small sweet *common* place to have spawned someone like her mother. There was a town common surrounded by the wealthier houses and then the long main street filled with shops that petered out into horizons that led to nearby farms and smaller homes clustered around the church.

She gave the boy some extra money when he left her in the center of Commerce Street. Here, there was a bank, some stores, a tobacconist's shop, a dress shop, a ticketing booth, a post office—*the post office* . . .

She pushed open the walnut doors.

A small office—with one teller dispensing postage and information to a line of five people waiting.

She got on line. Ten minutes later, it was her turn, and she was about out of patience.

"Skirling Vail, please—how do I get there?"

"Oh, easy mum—down Commerce Street toward High Church, left at the crossroads which is Holland Road, and follow it down to Skirling Vail. But no one is at the house, mum. It's been empty all these years."

She was here. She pulled the key out from under her shirtwaist and stared at it for a moment. She had a hour—maybe two before Stiles might be on his way.

The cottage didn't look all that big; what secrets could it hide?

Resolutely she pushed the key into the door and turned it in the lock and the door swung open on squeaking hinges.

It was dark inside, gloomy, with what furniture there was covered in holland cloth. There were shades at the windows pulled low with just a crack of light showing through on which dust motes danced.

And there was the musty scent of disuse pervading the whole house.

She dropped her bag and threw open two windows at the back of the house.

Now she could see the sparsely furnished room with its bed, dresser, and desk along the far wall near the fireplace, and table, chairs, and cupboard close by the little ell of a room that was the kitchen.

There were shelves in there lined with long spoiled condiments and jellies, a small stove with a cache of wood still beside it, and several pots sitting on it; a rack of cracked dishes, and a sink in which there were cups and plates covered with mold.

Out the window she could see a pump close by the house, and to her right, there was a crude wooden door.

The stench in here was unbearable, from rotted food and the spoilage, and she closed the door behind her and went back into the main room.

So here is where mother lived . . .

At least it was her own.

She prowled the room, looking under surfaces, running her hand over the crude fireplace, lifting the rotting mattress, feeling under the bed, and pushing aside the chamber pot with its fetid remnants, shuddering at touching the evidence of the presence of mice.

There couldn't be anything here—

She opened the desk drawers—

Crumbling papers as if mice had come in and had a field day . . . what could these have been? Probably the answer to everything—

She searched the dresser next, but there was nothing but chewed-up material as if the mice had made nests out of it.

She chewed on her lip.

Her mother had been gone for years from this place. What

had she expected—that she would hide her secrets in the one place no one knew about?

Yes . . .

She got on her knees and looked under the table and chairs, and then began on the cupboard. It was a decent piece of furniture, painted, with glass doors behind which were some china plates—the "good" dishes probably, two drawers and a lower cabinet with double doors that latched together.

There was nothing in the upper shelves. Nothing in the drawers but some worn silver plate and not much of that. Nothing in the lower cabinet except a cracked ironstone tureen, and that was empty too.

A latched cabinet though—

A safer place to conceal something . . .

She ran her hands all over the interior of the cabinet, under the drawers and shelves.

Damn and damn . . .

. . . wait—

She put the flat of her hand against the inside panel of the cabinet doors.

One was made of a different material than the other, and painted to look the same.

She grabbed a rusted knife from the drawer and began hacking at the door. The thin wood splintered and cracked at her first assault and she tore the rest away with shaking hands.

Behind it was a thin packet of letters tied with a piece of twine, and as she removed the barrier, it fell into her hands . . . just as she heard a sound outside like someone wading through the overgrown bushes that surrounded the house.

Terror . . .

She eased the cupboard doors shut, and crawled across the floor to her suitcase with the packet in her hand.

Money—she had to get the money; everything else was inconsequential . . .

She edged into the shadows near the fireplace and dug for the money, listening, listening—the stillness was unnatural—

Someone is watching . . .

Someone is waiting—

She stuffed the money into her bulging reticule, and the packet of letters, and then she broke the handle and retied it around her waist so that her hands were free.

And then—and then—

She waited . . .

There wasn't another sound.

It could have been a dog—an animal . . .

But it had sounded like a hurricane through the dry leafy bushes, and for all she knew, someone was waiting out there . . .

But who?

It was too soon for Stiles—even if he had begun at the break of dawn, he would still be on his way.

Who?

She couldn't sit still. She had to move. The window shades to the front and sides of the house were still closed so her movements would be screened from the outside.

And there was that kitchen door—

Or was he smart enough to be waiting there . . .

She had never felt such terror. There was just nowhere to hide in this house. And her adversary could be anyplace between the two doors waiting for her to emerge.

She had to calm down and think . . .

The sound had come from the side of the house closest to the kitchen. Which meant that her adversary was closer to the back door, but still within pursuing distance of the front and she had inches of a chance to get out that door.

Inches . . .

There was another little rustle of a sound as if he had shifted or moved one way or the other.

Clever opponent—

But maybe she could create a distraction . . .

. . . if she broke a window on the opposite side of the house— would he come?

She had to time it perfectly—absolutely perfectly. And she had to be one step away from the front door the moment the window crashed . . .

And of course, anything she could throw was in the cabinet across the room . . .

Except under the bed—bless the fates—

... the chamber pot ...
She wasn't too squeamish now—
She crawled that few feet to the bed and pulled it out from
the corner where she had pushed it during her first search.
... now—which window?
The one on the far side of the fireplace ... and closest to the
back of the house ...
It would work—it had to ...
And she wouldn't just throw it ...
... had she left the door open? ... and she would have to run
in the opposite direction of the road back to town—hide in the
bushes ... just get out of that ...
... house ...
She swung the chamber pot and sent it crashing through the
window; she waited an instant to see whether her pursuer had
taken the bait, and then, hearing nothing, her heart in her throat,
she darted to the door, flung it open and dashed out into the
sunlight and dove into the nearest copse of bushes.
She thought she had died; her dress was dark and probably
eminently visible through the dense leaves and he would see her
immediately when he came out of the house.
But he didn't come—
She heard the sound of a door being forced and the rip of
metal away from wood.
She crept further into the bushes, hunkering low, clutching her
bag. She could have run a half mile by now, and in any direction.
And he—if it were a "he"—when he momentarily emerged
from the house—he would have to choose a direction as well.
She waited, frozen with fear.
He was taking too long, too long. He had found her bag and
probably was rummaging through it. He would find nothing,
nothing.
Who was in that house?
She squeezed herself into a tiny ball, absolutely certain that
the sun was shining right over her and he would be able to see
her instantly.
She heard the crash of something against wood and a loud
curse—and her nemesis running out the front door ...
Tolliver!

* * *

Racing this way and that, beating the bushes around the house, muttering under his breath, cursing, calling her—

Calling *her*—as if he had known she would be there . . .

She wanted to bury herself in the ground, and all she could do was watch in horror as he searched for her, with murder written all over the expression on his face.

Tolliver . . . ! How had he known? Where had he come from? He was tenacious—unrelenting . . . too thorough for words . . .

And then suddenly he disappeared, and she waited, waited, certain he had gone . . .

And then abruptly he was there, loping down the Holland Road, astride a huge stallion, looking, looking—

Stopping and debating which direction she could have taken . . .

She didn't move; she couldn't breathe.

She prayed . . .

Her dress—so *black* against the leaves . . . how could he not spot her?

His hard gaze shafted through the trees and bushes, looking, looking, certain she could not have gotten far, trying to analyze her thinking and which way she would have gone.

Howp! He made a decision, wheeled his horse, and took off back up Holland Road.

She waited . . . waited—she could not wait too long . . .

There was silence—dead still silence. Chittering birds. The hot sun. The rustle of the faint wind through the tall grasses.

She crept out of her hiding place with cold shaking hands and into the shadow of a tree.

If he came back now . . .

She turned and started to run, not even knowing where this dirt track led.

It led to hell.

No, it led through this dense forest with not a soul in sight; what kind of place was this? And why hadn't she thought to get some water?

And what if he was behind her, pounding through the under-growth?

Her body felt so tight and hot, she thought she would die.

She had to rest.

No, she had to go on. She had to get out of here and find a place to hide.

Where? Where?

The thought of that just might keep her sane.

Deepditch . . .

No, Stiles knew about Deepditch . . .

But he didn't know about the Veil . . .

God, she was crazy—in the midst of a witch-dark wood trying to make sense of what she was doing and where she was going?

There was no sense . . . because if there were, she would understand what Tolliver had been doing at her mother's house in the Vail and why he wanted to kill her.

It felt like hours before she finally fell to the ground and rested. Or slept.

And heard voices suddenly that jolted her out of her sleep.

"Hey, lookee here—a princess in the woods . . ."

"Runnin' from the evil witch, she is. Burnt on her face and all . . ."

A woman's voice that, and somewhat reassuring.

She opened her eyes.

"Hello dearie—are you fine and all?"

She struggled to sit up. "I'm lost. I've been walking for hours, and I'm lost."

"Easy go," the man said, helping her to her feet. "Not a problem. We'll take you where you want to go."

They were farm people, she could see by their clothes and the faint smell of manure than emanated from the woman's skirts.

"Wagon's over here. The wife caught sight of you—thought you was dead."

No, I'm very much alive.

Still . . .

Such kind people—

"Where you be goin'?"

"To the train station at Bickley?"

"Oh, now—and you're turned in totally the other direction. Happen as we are goin' to Bickley, so you wouldn't be puttin' us out . . ."

It was a jolting ride; she sat crouched in a corner of the wagon bed behind them, so there wasn't much conversation.

That was good and well, since her bones were rattling from the jouncing she took along the back roads to Bickley.

But they got there eventually, and she offered them some money—which they refused, and just bid her good-bye at the train station, saying they were happy to help her on her way.

And now there was no help for it.

She had to go in and buy her ticket, and so make herself conspicuous. But she didn't have to go directly to Deepditch.

There was a map and she stared at it for several minutes. All the little towns in Cheswickshire along the London line, laid out like a string of pearls. And Plumford Wye above Bickley, and Deepditch below. If she bought a ticket to Plumford, she could then backtrack to Deepditch and put that much more distance between her and Stiles.

She bought the ticket to Plumford and went out on the platform to wait. It would be an hour and a half at least until the train steamed in from London.

No little time to wait, when time was of the essence.

But finally it came.

She was at the very end of the platform and still she saw him: Inspector Stiles and two of his men exiting from a car further forward.

She darted into the last car, her heart pounding, and chose a seat on the opposite side of the car, deep in the shadows where no one could see her.

And as the train chugged out of the station, she saw them, Stiles and his men, making their way determinedly toward the stone steps that let out into the village, no doubt to inquire the location of Skirling Vail.

She made Deepditch at sunset after interminable hours of waiting at Plumford for the return train to come; she ought to have just stayed on the line except for the prohibitive cost of it.

She did manage to find something to eat. And she had decided not to touch her mother's letters until she was certain she was safe.

So what she did was conceive a plan: she was going to take over her mother's business—if it still existed.

But it must—someone had to be in charge because the girls would want to be working, no matter what her mother was doing.

But Deepditch at sundown was another matter altogether. It was like a vision of workingman's heaven, especially down at the docks: rowdy, noisy, crowded, girls everywhere, and men looking for a good time, their beer in one hand and a couple of pounds in the other to buy twenty minutes of pleasure.

And somewhere in this wallow of alcohol and fast women was the house of the *Veil* . . .

And she wasn't too hoity-toity to push her way through the middle of it to find the answer.

"Coo-ee, here's a pretty one—" A hand reached for her and she brushed it aside.

"I got better ones than you lining up for me," she retorted.

"I'll pay double."

"You couldn't find the money or the time."

She shoved her way into one of the pubs along the dock street.

"Bartender—"

"The girls work the tables only, lady," he said brusquely, shooting a pint of ale across the counter with the expertise of a bowler.

"Oh she can work my table any day," a voice said in the midst with a howl of laughter after.

"The *Veil*. I'm going to work at the *Veil* and since Maudie hired me, she moved it, never thinking a girl from Cheswickshire wouldn't know the ropes . . ." Well, it was a chance, and a somewhat legitimate story—she thought he might buy it.

There was a huge burst of laughter.

They all knew; they all damned knew . . . like there was some kind of underground network that disseminated this information. Which of course there was . . .

"Now how do I know that's the real story?" the bartender asked patronizingly. "Everybody knows Maudie . . ."

Her heart sank.

"I'm here; I want to work. I was over to Shore Street, which is where she told me to come. They told me she left, lock and stock and didn't know where she'd gone."

"That sounds right," someone in the crowd said.

"Give 'er the address—give us a chance . . ."

"Dock Street, over the *Dock Ferry Pub*," the bartender said reluctantly, yielding to pressure. "Ask for Dirty Annie, 'cause they don't where Maudie's gone."

Perfect.

She shoved her way out of the pub, followed by the jeering comments of the men.

Dock Street had to be close by.

She dodged horses and errant hands with equal asperity rather than ask for directions, and in the end, she found it, a tiny narrow side street, not visible, not easy to locate unless you knew where it was—or you stumbled upon it.

It was two doors down from the *Dock Ferry Pub*. There was a bell, and the door, she was glad to see, was locked.

It was opened by a young girl.

"I want to see Dirty Annie."

"She's busy."

"I'll wait."

"You kin come upstairs," the girl offered.

"Then I will," but she had a feeling of being thrown back to the horrors of the *Fox* as she climbed the stairs.

And how different was it? The girls were lounging, waiting for the evening's fare.

There were two floors, she estimated, and the bedrooms were upstairs. Down here, in the reception area, were sofas and chairs, some tables on which there were empty glasses, a piano, some lamps.

Tawdry . . .

All of a piece—she could easily picture her mother holding sway here, returning to her roots, hoping to build something up with the reputation of the House of Correction.

Ever the optimist things would come round.

She could have started it with the money she got to leave Green Street. Next to nothing would operate this place, and the whole of her ill-gotten fortune would still be intact.

Why would she have done it?

"Waiting for Dirty Annie?"

Oh, and here she was, tall, limber, blonde, frowsy—a girl you
knew had been rutting in the haystacks by the time she was ten . . .
And dressed in a pair of drawers and a camisole out of which
her breasts were hanging unabashedly.
Dirty Annie indeed . . .

"Yes. Did Maudie have an office in this place?"

"Shit, what do you know about Maudie?"

"Lots. We need privacy." God, she was bold. She never would
have thought she would have the guts to walk in and take over,
but that was just what she was going to do.

And she could see by the look in her eye that Dirty Annie was
going to let her.

"Maudie's dead."

"I kind of knew that."

"Good. I'm her daughter."

"Shit."

"Exactly. And they think I killed her."

"And you think you can hide out here?" Annie said skeptically.
"You're an innocent, you are."

"I'll run the place."

"You're bloody crazy."

"Who is in charge?"

"Me," Annie said rambunctiously.

"Well, then . . . that's why."

They stared at each other.

"You ain't made for the business, your ladyship."

"And you'd rather be made flat on your back. I can do it. And
if I can't, I'll turn it back over to you."

Annie got up from her chair and sauntered to the door. "Yeah,
all right. Maybe you'll give the place some class. By the way,
what do we call you?"

She thought a moment and then a wry little smile twisted her
lips.

"You can call me Jade."

So now she felt safe . . . for the moment.

The next day she took over the office, she talked to the girls,
she reckoned the money, and she made everybody clean the house.

"There has to be someone who would come in twice a week and do that," she said to Annie.

"Oh, your ladyship, we got hordes of ladies who can't wait to do the blinkin' work. See that line down there? For what kind of money? I knew you was an innocent."

"For the same kind of money you make."

"Bloody crazy. *I'd* do it for that."

"Well, then—?"

"You can't run a brothel like a bloomin' Buckingham Palace, Jade. Your mum never did."

"I'm not my mum and I want a clean place."

"They want a dirty place, the dirtier the better—like them fornicatin' houses in London . . . you know about them, your ladyship? They want to sink themselves into it and wallow. So you give 'em the wallow and the stink and all the muck they can handle and you rake in the money as fast as they can pay it out."

She didn't have to do much of anything, she found that out the first night; the house was a well-oiled machine where every man and woman knew his place, and the girls went up the stairs like clockwork.

Her mother's dream, spawned in the farmland of Bickley— and all led back to this.

How?

That night she took out the meager packet of letters and stared at them for a long time.

Here was the ending—or the beginning—and she wasn't sure she wanted to know which.

You don't have to; you could stay here forever and never have to know . . .

She pulled at the twine and untied the letters.

There were five in all, tucked into envelopes with no addresses, and worn thin with handling, folding, and refolding, and so fragile she thought the first one would tear as she removed it from its envelope.

The ink was so faded in places it was hard to read the writing.

But not the salutation.

And once again, her blood ran cold.

Dear Arthur . . .

She had known him then? But why not? Fanhurst was barely a
half-hour trip from Bickley.
Still—that was quite a step up for one such as her mother.
She read on.

*Don't you worry none; these ain't letters that'll ever get
sent. Just a place to put a piece of my heart now that you
broke it.*

*You didn't want to hear again from me—that was made
perfectly clear. And I ain't never gonna know if it was your
mother's decision or yours. But I tell you, it ain't necessarily
so that we wouldn't meet again sometime, somewhere.*

And until then, I keep hoping.

Maudie

Her mother and *Arthur?!*
She pulled open the next letter.

Dear Arthur . . .
*It's been a month since I put down on paper about what
happened between us. I went and drove to Fanhurst to see
if maybe I could get to see you and all I got for my trouble
was the gameskeeper firing a shot at me.*

*It was your mother who brought us together—why should
she keep us apart? She* wanted *it—she wanted us and we
was good together and that was what she wanted to see.*

*You might tell her it wasn't worth the money she paid me.
It was only worth something to me.*

Maudie

The next letter, a month later.

Dear Arthur . . .
I'm not pining, mind you, for something I now know I can't
have; rather I was looking to remind you of something you
might have lost.

They tell me you're going up to London now; I'm thinking
to meet you there, when this particular crisis is past. And
then maybe, without the presence of your mum, we can find
what you lost in the Vail.

Maudie

Six months later:

Dear Arthur . . .
Well, the thing is done and I'm ready to come follow you
and make my fortune. Won't you be shocked if I turn up
on your doorstep? Do you remember the days at Skirling,
when your mum would drive you down and leave you for
hours on end, days on end; was it any wonder a girl like
me felt some hope? And didn't a man like you?

But now I got a whiff of what my future is to be. We can
work it out between us—you'll see. I wasn't stupid, you
know, just a romantic. Bickley is too small to hold us.

Maudie

And the last, dated two years later:

Dear Arthur . . .
You'd be so proud; I started the business, and all because
of you. I can support myself and any little thing that comes
along. So I guess I'm ready for London because the police
are getting suspicious and I don't want no trouble.

So look for me soon, Arthur. It's not a threat—but I'm just
not ever going to let you forget.

Maudie

And she hadn't . . . she hadn't. She had gone from being an obnoxious country girl of dubious reputation to the most notorious madame of London, and under his sponsorship, for all those years.

And now she herself was starting out exactly the same—the small house in the small village where her mother had thought to reinvent herself.

It was so incredible it was almost unbelievable—except her mother was dead and she was wanted for murder.

And she sat up here reading these scurrilous letters while she had told them to call her Jade.

Why had her mother saved them?

What could they have meant to her?

And what did they tell her daughter except that her mother and Arthur had been lovers—

Yes—but paid for by the haughty Madam Tisne . . . oh, interesting—interesting—and her mother still sought to see it as something real. And Arthur couldn't possibly, so Madam got rid of Mother . . .

That's what it sounds like. And it sounds too like Mother wanted to strip off her own pound of flesh into the bargain.

How patient was Mother . . . it took . . . almost three years by the dates on the letters for her to get the wherewithal to go to London.

And that had to have been the original house of the Veil.

So what does it mean—she blames Arthur for starting her on the path to ruin? That had to be nonsense. Surely Madam Tisne chose her for her son because she already had some sort of reputation among the farmers' sons.

And picture it—the desperate mother looking for an earthy cow to make her effeminate son come to heel—and my mother, with the brazen confidence of youth, thinking she had done it . . .

. . . they had known each other that long ago . . .

And so she'd gone up to London and made a career with him and then married him off to her daughter, knowing perfectly well he could never perform.

Thank you, Mother.

And now both of you are cohabiting in hell—and Stiles is looking for me . . .

There was a knock at her door.

"Jade?"

"Come in, Annie." She was just tucking away the letters as Annie opened the door. "What is it?"

"Kind of strange is what is it. There's a gent out there askin' for you by name."

. . . oh God . . .

Don't panic . . .

"That's not possible."

"That's what I thought, you being so new in town and all . . ." But the look in Annie's eyes belied her words.

"What does he look like?"

"Oh, real flash in a quiet strong way—you know what I mean—the kind that seethes and bubbles like a cauldron and always shows a smooth top . . ."

Roak!

She slammed her hand down on her desk. "Damn it. Damn it . . . damn it—Annie—I have to go. That man cannot find me . . ."

"That man *has* found you."

Annie whirled, but she could see clearly who stood in the doorway of her seedy office.

Roak . . .

Once again seeking her out in a house of pleasure.

How perfect.

The inevitability of it was stunning: wherever she would run, he could find her merely by tapping into her weakness, her frailty, her desire.

And now that he had finally cornered her in a place where no one would ever find her, he would drown her screams in an orgy of blood.

How could one ever escape him?

"Roak." Her voice was so calm; her hands were trembling and cold as death as she motioned to Annie to leave them alone.

He looked like death—impassive, implacable, unmoving, never-ending.

"Jade . . ." his voice was mocking. "You're a fool."

"I believe we came to that conclusion in London. Surely you're not going to try to convince me to return?" *Too daring, in the face of what she knew . . .*

"It's obvious I can't convince you of anything."

"My dear Roak—you convinced me you were on my side when all along, you were playing your own little game. In retrospect, I think it was masterful. You managed to seduce me *and* manipulate an airtight case against me into the bargain. You took an innocent fool and turned her into a foolhardy dupe. No man was ever more—*convincing.*"

"Bitch." His expression was murderous and she knew she didn't dare push an inch more.

"Get out."

"I don't think so—*Jade.*"

And now her name was a sneer on his lips as he began to walk toward her menacingly.

She bolted out of her chair and across to the opposite side of the room.

"What do you want?" Her voice couldn't be shaking like that.

"God, what do I want—what do I want? I can't have what I want, Jade. What do you think I want?"

"You want to see me hanged for murder," she spat, "so you can have your revenge and no one will ever be able to touch you."

. . . touch you . . .

The words hung in the air between them, resonating in ways she could never have expected. She didn't want to feel them; she wanted to kill her feelings for *him.*

Nothing made sense, nothing.

She had to get out of there and leave him behind forever.

"Genelle—"

Oh God, when he used her name like that, so softly and lovingly . . . it was enough to melt a stone—

"Just get out."

"You'll be on the run forever."

"I suppose I will. Or I'll follow mother's footsteps—I seem to have a talent for it . . ." She couldn't keep the bitterness out of her voice.

"Jade—"

That was Annie's voice from beyond the closed door. She pushed it open and barrelled into the room.

"Oh—not done, are you? Sorry to interrupt. Problem with a gent, needs a soothin' talkin' to from the mistress." She flashed an interested eye over Roak's inscrutable countenance.

"I'm coming."

"I'll stay if you like," Annie offered.

"*Annie—*"

She whisked Annie through the door a step before Roak realized that she was not going to return.

She heard his footsteps as she slammed the door behind them.

"Lock the door!" she whispered, and Annie fumbled for the key and inserted it in the lock just as they heard Roak turning the knob.

"Now wasn't I clever?" Annie murmured as they raced down the hallway in concert with his ominous effort to force the door.

"You don't have a lot of time. Oh God, what'll we do without you?"

"You'll do fine. And I can give you some money. But I have to get out of here—*this minute*—and you're going to have to do the acting job of your life to convince that man I'm taking care of your mythical customer. Can you do it?"

"Do I want to?"

"I think you will." She pulled a handful of bills out of her pocket and shoved them into Annie's hands. "I think you like me enough to want to help me."

Annie pocketed the money. "You're a deep one, you are. Sure, get yourself out of here; I'll take care of your flash gent. And I say we'll be lucky if he doesn't do something drastic when he finds you've disappeared."

Chapter 21

And so now she was going to wander around Deepditch in the dead of night with Roak hot on her trail.

She was out of her mind, and she wasn't going to find some well-heeled carriage driver to take her where she wanted to go.

Where did she want to go?

She couldn't go back to the Veil, not now. Roak would wait her out until he was sure she wasn't coming, and then—blast him—he would somehow figure out her next move.

No, how could he? Even she didn't know her next move. But she knew it could not be a return to Bickley or to London—or anyplace in between.

That was just a little frightening, almost as if Stiles were narrowing down the corridor of escape.

There was nowhere else to go . . .

But—as long as her money held out, there was always someplace to go; but she could be on the run for the rest of her life.

And it wouldn't answer any of the questions—

And Arthur's sins would follow her too . . .

She had to calm down. She had to *think*.

She would find *something* . . .

Any conveyance would do—

You can't drive a carriage . . .

I would ride a horse if necessary to get out of here—

She was among the crowd again, pushing, shoving, prodding, protecting the bag around her waist as she was shuffled back and forth along the streets and further and further away from Dock Street and the *Veil*.

And closer to houses and the possibility of escape . . .

. . . Safe as houses . . .

Her mother had said that on her last visit—safe as dead, rather . . .

She was getting desperate.

There had to be something . . .

Straight ahead of her there was a side street, and she ducked onto it—a long dirt road of small houses tucked away behind overgrown hedges. Hardly any light at all except from the upper stories of the buildings—it was like walking blind—and maybe not a good idea, she was beginning to think, when she saw the buggy.

It loomed up in front of her like a nightmare—the back end of a small buggy that was still hitched up and standing in front of one of the houses on the right hand side of the road.

You know nothing about horses and buggies.

I know enough to climb in one of them and snap the reins, and whatever happens—happens . . .

She eased herself into the vehicle slowly so as not to distract the horse who was contentedly chewing on the side grass.

The reins were wound around the dash rail and she untied them with one easy pull. Immediately the horse became alert, waiting for her next command.

She took the leather reins in her hands, lifted them, and gently snapped them down against his rump, and he took off like a shot, almost dumping her out of the carriage in the process.

It was all she could do to maintain her balance and keep the reins in her hands as the horse raced down the road blindly.

And it took all of one minute for her to give up the idea of trying to control him. She couldn't do it—she could only hope he would head for some open road and run until he got tired and then . . . and then—

An hour later, long away from the outskirts of Deepditch, she felt him slowing down.

By then, her hands were raw from pulling on the reins, and she had no strength left to even try to get him to the side of the road.

A half hour later, he stopped of his own volition; just dead stopped in the middle of the road—and she decided she wasn't going to get out of the buggy to move him.

She lifted the reins pulled them—and him—to the right. He moved, reluctantly and only with insistent tugging until he was finally on the side of the road, and close to a sheltering tree.

She looped the reins over the dash rail and huddled back against the seat with a sigh of relief.

For the moment—she was safe.

And another moment later, she was sound asleep.

She awakened to the cold and the whickering of the horse.

Dawn now, and she was shivering—and lost. And there was nothing familiar in sight—just a long country road edged with trees and bushes and wide swaths of fields.

This was worse than if she had stayed in Deepditch. She felt herself engulfed by the terror of the unknown.

She could die out here and be buried forever along this windswept road.

Or she could get the buggy moving and go someplace else . . .

She snapped the reins and the horse bolted forward again at breakneck speed and she just hung on with all the willpower she could muster.

He raced down the road and over the next rise, and just as she caught a glimpse of roofs over the trees, he took a corner in the road and the buggy swerved on one wheel and toppled onto its side, and she was thrown onto the road and landed on her back.

All she could do was watch the horse drag the buggy another two or three hundred yards before the weight of it pulled against his speed and finally slowed him down.

Painfully, she got to her feet and began walking; she could feel the bruises on her arms and a nasty ache in her back, but she would go on forever if she had to rather than mount that buggy again.

The damned horse and the damaged carriage were about two hundred yards beyond her, near a sign on a tree, and as she got closer, she read:

Entering the village of Plumford Wye

. . . the very last place she wanted to be . . .

* * *

She changed her mind about that after; she sat in the train station taking stock of the situation, and counting her money.

She had wanted to find a murderer, not run for her life forever. The money would not hold out that long.

And maybe it was provoking fate to keep it all in one place. What if someone stole her reticule which was already tattered from so many days on the run?

She felt like a gypsy herself from wearing the same clothes for the last few days. Nevertheless, it made sense to divide her money and tuck some into her corset. Just in case.

Just in case . . .

Just in case—what? Roak catches up with you again?

She ignored that thought and shifted the money around and tucked the rest—and the letters—back into her reticule and fastened it around her waist again.

Think about it—you are that close to Fanhurst.

And now this new information, from mother's letters, sheds all kinds of interesting light on the subject because apparently Madam Tisne was not a retiring dowager twenty-some odd years ago; and she certainly was not at the reading of the will.

So why have I thought it is impossible that she has known all along what has been going on?

In fact, it is possible to infer from what Mother wrote that she was very well aware of Arthur's orientation.

. . . so it is also possible that she has always known more than anyone thought . . . about everything—

And if she did . . . if she did—

She couldn't carry the thought an inch further.

. . . if she did . . .

. . . if she did—

. . . and Roak was on the scene—

No, the thought was inconceivable . . .

Fanhurst was awfully close to Plumford Wye. Plumford— where Roak's son had died . . .

And Roak had gotten a fortune from the thing—

And conquered her when Arthur turned up dead—there was no other way to read it—and he was so good at it too—

—too good, too perfect—

Everything had gone his way . . . up to and including the murders.

And she had fallen too hard . . .

About as hard as she had from the buggy and she had gotten every bit as injured and bruised.

So—maybe it was time to visit Fanhurst and ask her mother-in-law some questions . . .

Especially since she was already here . . .

The train rolled into the station and suddenly all manner of conveyances appeared.

She hailed one—a wagon with seats built into its wagonbed.

"Fanhurst."

"Certainly, me lady."

He took on two other passengers and delivered them in due course to the Inn before taking her out into the country where Fanhurst was located.

She stood at the gate, looking up at its imposing architecture. It looked like a medieval fortress, closed up and inaccessible.

But the gate was always open, she remembered, and she knew exactly how to get into the house from belowstairs from having lived there as a newlywed for six months while Arthur went off on his lewd pursuits.

And perhaps she ought—there was a carriage parked to one side of the house by a copse of flowering bushes.

Someone was there, someone with expensive tastes; the carriage was brand new and highly decorated with stripes in contrasting colors and panels painted with miniature scenes; and the bloodstock was the finest at point and panting from exertion.

This visitor had come a long way.

She ducked behind some hedges and slipped around to the long side of the house, behind the parked carriage.

From this side, it looked like a prison, with cuts in the stonework that looked like mean little eyes.

Like Arthur's eyes . . .

And she knew that further along the wall, there was a door cut into the stone, one of those arched heavy wooden doors with strap hinges, and that door was always open so the servants could attend to chores.

She flattened herself against the wall on the hinged side of the door and waited.

The sun pounded against that wall; she felt like a crow waiting to pounce on its prey.

There was silence against that wall, and after a little while, she felt confident enough to move to the other side, depress the latch, and open the door.

Darkness then—cool, musty, forbidding . . . just as she remembered it. And no different from the surroundings Arthur had created for himself in the *House of Correction*.

She eased into the vestibule and closed the door.

Not even a candle to light her way, but she knew the corridor to the kitchen was straight ahead, and that a second hallway veered to the right and led past the work rooms and the store rooms, and she would probably be safe enough there.

She heard a voice suddenly, and she ducked behind a stone arched column.

A maid, young, artless. "Oooeee, her la'yship don't want no interference nohow when she gets on like that—"

"Mind yer business girl . . ." A snappish voice in response, faintly familiar.

The voices drifted away, and she didn't hesitate for a moment: she headed for the servants' staircase, which gave into the main hall of Fanhurst.

She listened at the door, and then opened it a crack. Dim, dusty, musky air—a preternatural stillness—no one was about . . .

She crept into the entrance hallway.

Everything as she remembered it: the winding stonework stairs, enclosed in gothic fretwork; the high, high walls and ceiling with only one small window for light and air shedding dusty beams of sunlight on the balcony above.

The opulent carpet on the floor, anchored by a rectangular table on which was a massive silver candelabra.

The arched doorways leading off of the entryway to the various downstairs rooms. And the massive oak doors through which one entered.

They were magnificent—and threatening—all at the same time.

And the silence. The hard, harsh silence.

She pressed open the doors to peek into the surrounding rooms.

There was no one in the parlor, the dining hall, or the small reception room.

So quiet.

And then a loud raucous clanging that almost made her jump out of her skin. She darted into the shadows of the reception room door just as a maid came scurrying out of the servants' entrance.

"Coming mum, coming . . ." the maid called as if her mistress could hear her as she ran frantically up the steps.

She knew that voice.

She knew that voice . . . her servant—her maid at Green Street—she would have sworn it.

And the voice belowstairs—

And—

"You stupid chit—you stupid little chit; barging in on my lady in such a way when she is with her gentleman—"

She heard a slap, and the maid's shriek . . .

"Bring your mistress what she requires and lay it by the door . . ."

She knew that voice—that voice too . . .

. . . Tolliver . . .

Dear lord—Tolliver . . . and what—all of her servants—mysteriously transported to Fanhurst?

How could it be when she had left Tolliver searching for her at Skirling Vail?

She felt faint; she heard the maid tumble down the stairs in her haste to escape Tolliver's wrath, and she peeked around the edge of the arch to get a glimpse of her.

Yes—that one—that was Enid . . . scared as a rabbit . . .

She twisted back into the shadows and waited. A few minutes later, she heard the servants' door open, and a heavier step.

She looked again.

Oh lord—Mrs. Pepper . . . the housekeeper, the one with the common sense . . .

She pulled back into the shadow of the arch, her heart pounding painfully.

Oh my lord, oh my lord—my servants are here, my servants are here . . . what does it mean? What could it mean?

And my mother-in-law—upstairs with . . . whom?

At her *age? What* gentleman?

She almost didn't want to find out.

She waited until long after the housekeeper had returned from her errand and a deep still silence enveloped the house.

She had to go up there. She had to find out.

She edged her way out of the doorway and the safety of the shadows and paused at the bottom of the stairs.

Once she was on her way, there was no hiding.

Once she found out her mother-in-law's secrets, there was no turning back.

She flew up the steps, a long endless flight of steps that ran straight upwards with no landing.

At the top of the steps was the balcony which overlooked the entrance hall on all four sides, and off of this were the doors to the many bedrooms, and to the right, another corridor that led to another wing of guest rooms.

She and Arthur had lived in that wing.

Her mother-in-law had had a guest room to the left in the corner of the balcony, a big corner suite of two enormous rooms.

The tray lay in front of the door to that room.

She tiptoed down the hallway and listened at the door.

Yes—noise in there, voices—laughing . . .

Now or never—

She knocked at the door.

"Your tray, my lady," she called, and then brazenly she pushed the door in.

It was like a scene from her past life, except the players were different sexes.

On the bed in a tumble of sheets and covers and not much else lay her mother-in-law and the elegantly muscular Tony Lethbridge riding her into a lather.

Everyone froze, and then her mother-in-law shrieked over Tony's hard-bitten curses as he climbed off of her body, "Get that bitch . . ."

And Genelle turned and ran for her life.

Across the balcony, down the steps, she pounded; she heard Tony shouting, and her mother-in-law's loud harsh voice—and then the deeper tones of Tolliver's voice and the heavy tread of his boots as he took off after her.

Down she flew as bells sounded everywhere and servants came running from the upper hallways and the lower, and Tolliver screamed instructions that no one could hear.

Down she ran the last several steps pushing servants—*her servants*—out of the way in her frantic need to keep moving and moving—

Across the entrance hall, into the servants' stair where she toppled someone who was just behind the door as she pushed it in . . .

Down and down into the maze of arches and storerooms, with Tolliver hot on her heels . . . and the servants rallying after . . .

. . . *terror* . . .

To the outer door with the kitchen maids staring at her as if she were daft, and yanking it with all her strength even though her arms were sore with fatigue—

Out the door—out—slamming it in the servants' faces who had gotten to it ahead of Tolliver who was just behind her—

And then what? Then—*what?*

The carriage—another carriage—God, Tony's carriage, most likely—perfect vengeance if she could get the damned thing going . . .

"There she is!" Her mother-in-law's vampire shriek rending the air as an army of servants burst into the daylight.

She was already in the carriage, snapping the reins. She would run them all down if she had to—

Her servants—

Her mother—

Her life . . .

The horse jolted into motion, the carriage tore off toward the crowd of servants as she jumped out into the bushes on the other side.

Everyone was running after the carriage now as it coursed down the long driveway to the back of the house.

Yes . . .

She slipped out of the bushes and raced for the gate.

Tony Lethbridge waited for her, his arms crossed over his manly bare chest.

* * *

"So," he said softly as she stopped dead in her tracks.

Instantly she felt like a hunted animal.

"It is time to end the game, Genelle. The thing is over. Whatever you thought you would find here—it doesn't matter. They will have you anyway for the murders of Arthur and your mother. So come along peacefully now, and everything will be taken care of."

"Monster," she hissed, wrenching her arm away as he made a move to take it. "Don't touch me."

"Oh now, Lady Genelle—I remember a time when you couldn't wait to have me touch you."

"That's funny—I can't seem to remember . . . but the old lover never survives the new when it comes to comparisons."

His expression darkened at that.

"And of course," she pressed, "if you are desperate enough to take that old woman—she must be *very* easy to please . . ."

She didn't expect him to slap her. She felt it from her cheek all the way down to her toes, a reverberation of pain.

Oh yes—pain. She mustn't forget Tony was an acolyte of the *House of Correction* . . .

"Maybe you'll learn your place by the time we get through with you," he said nastily. "Go on, in the house with you. Tolliver! The room next to Madam's with the bolt and chain."

He marched her right back up the stairs again, and pushed her into the adjoining room.

This was no guest room—it contained just a bare narrow bed, a chair, a dresser—and bars on the windows.

"You should be comfortable here," Tony said, with no irony whatsoever. "I'll take that pouch around your waist."

"I think not," she retorted, girding herself to defend it.

But he was quick—quicker than she could imagine—he swiped it with one long reach of his arm and ripped it open.

The money and the letters fluttered to the floor.

"Well, well, well—what have we here?"

She dove for them first—scooping the letters—just as he fell on top of her and pushed her to the floor.

"I'll take those—damn you . . ." His hands were everywhere, beating at her, pulling and tearing at her.

She had them in her hands, crushed against her breasts, and she shredded them into chunks as she bucked his relentless hands.

"*Let me go . . .*"

"Bitch—I want those letters."

"I'll give you the letters," she panted, as she pulled them into little pieces, irretrievable pieces she folded into her hands.

"I don't believe you."

"Don't hurt me—" *God, it killed her to beg, but he wanted her to and she wanted to win this skirmish.* "Don't . . ." as he pulled her head back by grasping her hair and straddled her. "Don't hurt me . . ."

"Give me those letters . . ."

"I will. Let me go. I will . . ."

He climbed off of her, and still holding her hair, he pulled her to her feet.

"*Now . . .*"

She opened her hands and threw the pieces, like a handful of rice, into his eyes.

"Bitch—bitch, bitch . . ." He slapped her so hard she fell on the floor, and when she was down, he kicked her. "Bitch—you won't get away with that, I'll tell you. Tolliver!"

The butler appeared at the instant as if he had been waiting.

"Pick up that money. My lady has decided to stay."

"Very good sir. May I say the lady looks quite fetching lying on the floor."

"Yes she does, but we have in mind a more public forum for her. Needless to say, she will pay for making us work."

"You never would get your hands dirty," she said goadingly.

"You never got dirty altogether, you stupid virgin. And there was only one reason why you got me in your *creche.*"

She stared into his eyes—his flat dead eyes, the handsome, flirtatious Tony Lethbridge whom everybody coveted and everybody wanted.

How many everybodies—men and women both—and Arthur's mother too . . .

She caught her breath as she read the truth in his eyes.

Not Roak—

"You killed Arthur."

"Did I? I wasn't even there, Lady Genelle. Didn't you tell them? You were there alone. You found him yourself covered in blood."

Not Roak . . . "You killed Arthur."

"It worked perfectly too—didn't it?"

"She bought away my servants—she bought my mother—again . . . and you were the one who stole the agreement between Arthur and me—"

Yes—she saw it in his eyes—a kind of triumph that he had bested her all these months.

"Why? *Why?*"

"I'll tell you why."

A new voice—Madam Tisne now dressed and moving in for the kill.

"Because *I* wanted you arrested for murder."

She was alone in the dark, her wrists manacled to the bed, with her mother-in-law's confession ringing in her ears.

I wanted you arrested for murder . . .

Not Roak—

Why why why?

It could only have to do with Arthur, solely and only Arthur . . .

She wanted Arthur dead.

She wanted me arrested for murder.

Not Roak . . .

But why?

She wanted the money he had agreed to pay me . . .

It was hardly worth committing murder for—

Clever Tony, convincing me not to tell . . .

How stupid was I—what a gullible fool . . .

And me thinking Arthur had paid him to deflower his little virgin—and the actuality was Mother Tisne had paid him to kill Arthur and set me up for murder.

Paid him to make love to me too . . .

Because why—because he was her lover as well—and they were after every penny of Arthur's estate before he squandered it on his vices?

It sounded so improbable and so reasonable at the same time.

And with so many missing pieces.

But it wasn't Roak—it wasn't Roak . . .

She pulled at the cuffs futilely. Tony had wrestled her to the floor on that one too, and Tolliver had held her while he snapped the barbaric things around her wrists.

They were leather, and wide and studded with metal buttons and fastened together with a chain which was locked onto the bedframe.

She wasn't going anywhere tonight, maybe not ever. Tony looked like he wanted to beat her to a pulp for the delectation of Mother Tisne.

But Mother Tisne wanted her in prison to hang for Arthur's murder.

What had set Mother Tisne off after all these years?

Had she not absorbed all the nuances of his aberrations, paid to have him "cured" by her mother when he had still been young and malleable; stood by while he explored every possibility and invented others; been aware of the shakiness of his political life; and so, hardly protested when he got married; hadn't quibbled when they separated; and then played the grieving and outraged mother when Arthur turned up dead.

By her arrangement.

What could have changed that made such a difference?

Or had she been planning it for much longer than that?

After all, the flirtation between herself and Tony Lethbridge had been building for all those previous months before their final explosive union.

And supposedly Mother Tisne had encouraged it . . . ?

Why?

. . . so that they could have a convenient scapegoat . . . ?

But what had changed to make it necessary?

Her head was spinning; her wrists were raw from her wrenching at the cuffs, and there wasn't any way that she was going to sleep tonight—

Chained in the Fortress—

Like some medieval princess in a romance of lust—or a scenario from the House of Correction . . .

. . . oh yes—exactly—

So who was to say Mother Tisne knew nothing about it when she was practically living it in the middle of the Cheswickshire farm country . . .

It made the most awful sense. They were all depraved, the whole lot of them, and she had been thrust into the midst of it, the virginal innocent, by the greed of her mother.
And she was going to be the one to hang for murder.

They came for her in the morning, bringing her some food and a basin of water so she could wash.

"We're taking you back to London, little girl," Tony said, as he followed Tolliver into the room, and Tolliver began unfastening her one hand so that she could drink her tea and use the washcloth "We love your company, we think we'll keep you for a while . . ."

"We do not," Mother Tisne said, as she entered the room. "We want to give her over to the Yard as soon as possible and put closed on those cases."

"One night," Tony said playfully. "Maybe two. No more. We should have our fill of her by then."

"Maybe," Mother Tisne said, looking her over critically. "She seems none the worse for wear. You have been remarkably durable, my girl. I was sure you would fold up like a deck of cards."

. . . shriveled up old bat . . .

"Perhaps I now hold the winning hand."

"My dear—I've been leading the play and taking trumps for months." She settled herself into the one chair in the room. "Starting with granting Arthur permission to marry you. A trump card, if ever there were one, something to distract his detractors and keep your mother quiet. But that lasted all of about an hour. There is something about those village-bred cows—they can never get enough cud to chew on. She would have been fine if she had just taken the money and stayed in her manger.

"But oh no, she had one more flag to run up the pole, she did. And look where it got her. But still, nicely thought out, don't you agree? Got you alone in the house—and all that money of hers just lurking in the background waiting to be discovered by that tenacious Yard man."

. . . shock upon shock . . . but it wasn't Roak—it wasn't . . .

"You knew about . . ."

"I know everything. I managed everything. Arthur couldn't do anything but flit around town playing his little games. When he wanted to start the *House,* he came to me; I set it up, I got the patrons, I made it what it was, and I paid your mother to run it. Are we clear on that? Arthur was good for absolutely nothing but getting into trouble and having me pay to get him out of it."

. . . oh lord oh lord oh lord . . .

"The servants at Green Street? Mine. Of course they came when I bid them to. Naive of you, my girl, not to get rid of them and train your own. Ingenuous of you to hire Roak without checking at all on his background. I dare say Morfit gave you an earful . . .

"So you see, it's all worked out splendidly. Arthur is finally at rest where he can pursue his proclivities forever and I will never have to pay another cent to expunge them; and in you, we have the perfect dupe—a woman with pure and powerful motives to eliminate her wayward husband and greedy mother. And that, I think, should answer all of your questions."

"No—!" she was shocked her voice was so hoarse and emphatic. "No! I want to know why. Why now? Why kill him now?"

Madam Tisne looked up at Tony Lethbridge and smiled, but it was a particularly nasty smile, and not a communication between conspirators.

"I don't particularly want to answer that—but I see Tony will if I don't. It's as simple as this: Arthur had finally gone too far. He was parading around Town dressed as a woman, seducing naive young men, jeopardizing everything, and not giving a fig that his whole career could go up in a cloud of makeup powder. And he was furious that Tony was flirting with you, and already in a rage that Tony and I were lovers. So of course he was willing to meet Tony and discuss it. The timing was perfect. Tony was wonderfully convincing, wasn't he? You were avid to protect him—you couldn't do enough for him . . ."

. . . a pawn—she had been someone's pawn all along—and she had thought that only Roak was devious enough to dream up such a plan—

Her mother had done this to her, starting from the first moment when she had accepted money from this debased old woman to make her son right . . .

Oh, Mother must have made them pay and pay and pay for having done that to her . . .

And she would make them pay—somehow, someday . . . not least by giving her all the answers—all of them . . .

"Who is Davidella Eversham?" she shot out at them.

Madam Tisne blinked; Tony started laughing.

"You're amazing," he said finally. "Just amazing. The silly virgin turned into a veritable Rulan Roak. Do you want to tell her?"

"Please—enjoy yourself . . ."

Tony chuckled. "Davidella was variously Morfit, Arthur himself, Madam Tisne"—his tone turned deadly—"and me."

"What?!"

Could it be—something Madam Tisne did not know . . . ?

"Oh, yes," Tony said blithely. "We had a go at it for a while. It was fun while it lasted, but I liked your plans better, Madam, and I know where the power lies and when to align myself with it."

"And who will make you pay for your perfidy."

"I am ready and willing, Madam."

. . . and now it sounds like a set piece—something they threw out to shock me . . . and they'll find out—I'm not so easily led now. . . . And I will get away . . . I will . . . I need one day in this mausoleum, just a day . . .

But it wasn't to be quite that simple.

"Today," Madam Tisne pronounced, "my new life begins. We will return to London, and we will finally end the farce when we turn this pretty one over to the Yard."

They were to travel in Tony's carriage. They had bound up her wrists again, and when they got her settled against the cushions, they put a gag around her mouth.

"It's only for three hours, my dear," Madam Tisne said with artificial kindness. "You do understand."

Three hours—three long awful hours to look at the faces of conspirators to murder. And they would get away with it too. Who would suspect—who would guess the motive was as simple as a long-suffering mother fed up with her son's destructive behavior?

Long-suffering . . . she was a monster—plotting and planning the right moment to liberate herself from his tyranny.

Three hours with them—listening to them gloat and make plans for the future . . .

For true, how much of a future could a raddled old woman like Madam Tisne have with a butterfly like Tony Lethbridge? He was a commodity, available to the highest bidder; he had no morals, no judgment, no loyalty.

And Madam Tisne was as deficient as he; worse than that, time was not on her side. She would collapse and die—or he would kill her—before too long. She could see it in his flat speculative gaze that came to rest on her periodically as the carriage jounced over the country roads.

A matter of time; he was probably calculating just how to do it—get the money and get rid of her . . .

It is not a pretty sight—

She swung her gaze out the window as the carriage passed through the streets of the next village and proceeded southward toward Deepditch.

There has to be a way I can escape from them—even if I have to dive out the window—I will . . . I will . . . I will not let them win . . .

London seemed like it was years away. The carriage swayed on relentlessly; at one point, she thought she fell asleep, a dangerous precedent with two murderers sitting opposite her.

And the whole trip long, she could think of nothing but what Madam Tisne had told her.

Tony had done it. Her mother wouldn't leave things alone. Eliminate two nuisances with two murders and one scapegoat. They both obviously played into Madam Tisne's hands. They both were predictable. If Madam Tisne had left them alone all those years ago, they might have stayed with each other and accommodated each other.

So maybe Madam Tisne's interference was the real causal effect of all that had happened.

But no matter, the thing still ended with *her*. She would go to prison, and she probably would hang.

They came into London in the late afternoon into streets swarming with pedestrians. Here, the carriage had to move slowly to make its way through the city . . . *and here, it might be possible to take a chance . . .*

Her interest quickened as the carriage sat for an indecent amount of time at a pedestrian crossing.

The next time—the very next time . . . I can slide up to the window and throw myself into the crowd . . . somebody will help me—

She prayed now that they didn't notice her alertness or the way she watched the crowd.

They were coming in toward Whitehall from Fleet Street and there really wasn't much time.

Just at the juncture of The Strand, she saw her opportunity. Traffic had crawled to a halt; there were carriages everywhere, and better than that, there was a crowd outside of St. Mary's Church.

This was the moment—she levered herself up and thrust her head and shoulders out of the open window, making horrible honking noises from behind the gag.

Behind her, Tony was yanking her and beating at her, and almost succeeding in pulling her back into the carriage.

Her muffled shrieks were lost in the din of carriage wheels on cobblestone, and she felt a tearing frenzy that she wouldn't succeed, and she lifted her foot and shoved it up against Tony's nether region with all the strength she could muster.

And then, without another thought, she bent through the carriage window, closed her eyes, and launched herself head over foot into the oncoming traffic.

Chapter 22

. . . I'm dead—
No . . . I'm—paralyzed . . .
No—
I'm in hell . . .
No . . .
She looked up at the ceiling which seemed to be a pristine white with a simple cove molding. Nothing ornate, which meant she wasn't at Green Street.

No bars—so it wasn't the jail.

No antiseptic smell, so it wasn't hospital . . .

She couldn't remember a thing.

No, she did . . . somebody saw her dive out of the carriage and traffic stopped as she took a good hard tumble onto her back again . . .

And then one of the drivers leapt down to see if she were still alive. And then all that commotion when they realized she was bound and gagged and she had to convince them not to summon the police, that it had been a very bad practical joke—her husband, pretending to kidnap her as part of the sensual games that they played—

And then the discovery that Madam Tisne, Tony, and Tolliver had totally vanished and left an empty—and expensive—carriage standing plumb in the middle of Whitehall.

And all those nice parishioners rushing to her aid.

And what had she done—idiot that she was? She had asked to be taken to Piccadilly Circus and Roak's flat—her "brother's" place, she told them—which she knew was nearby . . .

Any port in a storm, after all.

And why? Because she was counting on Roak not being there and the landlady helping her.

Which was not a wise decision because, of course, he had been there and he knew all about things like locks and picks and arcane handcuffs and was able, without saying a word, to dismantle the awful cuffs and thank all those who had been so kind to his "sister" and reassure them that she was perfectly safe with him.

Like being perfectly safe with a tiger.

Who had caged her in a small guest room someplace in his flat and was off doing who knew what . . .

And anyway, she was feeling a lot better—a very lot better, and all she needed to do was—what?

She eased herself up out of the bed, moaning at the painful battering her body had taken.

All she needed to do was find something concrete to prove that Tony and Madam Tisne had conspired to murder her husband.

Except it sounded like an accusation she had invented to save herself.

And only Roak would believe it because he had been so intimate a part of it.

A very intimate part of it . . .

She stood up; her legs felt shaky and there was a horrible ache in her hips.

She couldn't stay here, and she didn't know where she would find the energy to get away.

Maybe—maybe not tonight. Maybe tonight she would just rest and plan what to do. She still had some money—she touched it to reassure herself it hadn't dislodged and was still tucked deep down into her corset.

There! All problems solved except how to prove her innocence.

She slowly sank back onto the bed.

No, most certainly—not tonight . . .

She was being watched. She lay with her eyes closed, her hands curled into fists, her mind sharp and her body ready—*well, not quite ready*—for the attack.

She hadn't slept; she had tossed and turned in that narrow bed where there was barely room to stretch her legs, and she had gone over in her mind for the thousandth time how neatly her *mother-in-law, not Roak,* had framed her for murder.

And how nice and tightly Mother Tisne had arranged the whole thing so that there wasn't a single opening through which she could escape.

The web she had felt being woven so inexorably around her. Strong enough to catch its prey—fragile enough to be wiped from existence with the swipe of a broom—

All she had to do was figure out *how . . .*

Roak was watching her.

She figured that out almost immediately. He was sitting some-place beside the bed, relentlessly patient, waiting for her to move or say something.

She couldn't think of anything to say. How did one elaborate on the obvious?

And the thing wasn't over, and she couldn't begin to guess what he was going to do.

"I know most of it," he said abruptly in that deep rich imper-sonal voice. "But perhaps there are some things you don't know."

"I doubt it," she said sourly, her face turned toward the wall.

"Perhaps you were not aware that Lethbridge and Morfit are *particular friends,* and that both of them separately took the Eversham name when they were out with Arthur—and sometimes they used it with each other . . ."

Tony and Morfit—having lunch—Morfit writing him let-ters . . . and shortchanging the quarterly reports to Madam Tisne . . . so who was in the way? Arthur—gone; my mother—gone . . . and Tony a killer . . . who is left besides me?

She felt a cold wash of fear. She had seen it in the carriage as they came down from Plumford—Tony's eye on Madam Tisne, plotting and planning—

No—no, he put this plan in motion when Madam Tisne involved him in hers. And there is only one way he can get her money, her estate, her assets, and Morfit in the bargain. He's going to marry her.

And he's going to kill her—

She could see him watching her, almost as if he were follow-ing her thoughts; but how could he? How could he know the steps that got her from Eversham to the probable death of Arthur's mother?

"Oh my God—Roak . . . Tony—and Madam Tisne—he's going to kill her . . ."

He wasn't even surprised.

"He won't do it yet; you have to be disposed of. Lord Tisne's file has to be closed. He has to marry Madam Tisne and if he were smart, he would wait—he would wait a very long while before he attempts anything like that."

"He's not smart," she said rudely.

"Oh, but he is. He convinced you to lie for him, and Madam Tisne that he wants her, no matter what other carnal distractions may sidetrack him. I think that is very smart indeed, Lady Genelle."

"Smart enough to keep the Yard on my trail in any event," she muttered, turning her back to him again. "I suppose you've summoned Stiles?"

"No, I haven't. But that was ill-conceived, running away like that. What did it do but put you in the hands of the murderer and almost get you killed."

"And yet things came to light that even my *skilled investigator* could not have unearthed. So perhaps it was worth it. There is more substance to the story now; it didn't just *happen* for no reason, and perhaps that will be of some consolation to me as I stand trial for murder while Tony and his elderly bride watch from the balcony."

She couldn't hide her bitterness. "There is no way to convince them that I didn't kill my husband unless Tony confesses."

"No, there isn't. It was really quite a tidy plan."

"And when Mother interfered too much, they got her too."

"But they didn't factor in that someone might be with you that night," he reminded her.

"Neither did Stiles."

"He may come around on that."

"And then he'll discover you were in the midst of your corruption campaign—which was working quite nicely—and that will shoot that alibi in the foot. No thank you, Roak. I've had enough help from you already."

"Yet you came here first."

"Your flat is practically around the corner from where I fell. I was hoping against hope your landlady would help me."

"I see."

Bloody "I see" . . . *if she never heard that phrase again—*

"I have to get out of here," she said abruptly, struggling to a sitting position. "You can't hide a murderess. It isn't good for business . . ."

"You have nowhere to go; no more information to gain; nothing you can do even if you left here. You're in sorry shape, and very likely Tony Lethbridge is combing the whole of the surrounding area looking for you and probably has someone watching this building as well."

"So they've got me hemmed in once again. Why don't you just summon Stiles and let him take me away?"

"Didn't you know? He's out of town; gone to Cheswickshire on your trail. Probably he has remembered Deepditch by now and traced you there . . ."

"Oh, that . . ."

"You have been damned lucky, finding people who were willing to help you . . ."

"I suppose next you will say you are one of them," she retorted.

"Oh, no, Lady Genelle. I'm not one of them. You're *paying* me to be helpful."

"And you took it a giant step further."

"Value for your money, Lady Genelle. You've done a lot on your own, after all. But the end is the same: Tony Lethbridge murdered your husband in collusion with his mother, and most likely because everything was being endangered by Lord Tisne's rash behavior. And my guess is, she was tired of paying to silence his victims. Yes. I see it in your face. You didn't have to run all around Cheswickshire to find the answers, Lady Genelle. You had only to look at the facts, the actions, and the predictable ramifications.

"Madam Tisne had to have known everything about your husband's secret life; he was just not capable of either discretion or dealing with the consequences of his indiscretions and his marriage to you was a sop to his constituents. But you know all this already and that your husband's murder was no spur of the moment thing; it was well-plotted out, timed exactly right, and precipitated by your husband's dangerous behavior and your mother's relentless greed.

"Which is why Madam Tisne decided to kill her; she planned that very carefully too—she took back her servants—oh yes, that was an easy conjecture; why else would they go?—offered your mother a bribe to leave your house so that you would be totally alone the night it happened; got hold of the one thing that could prove you would not have killed Lord Tisne for his money; and then, lured your mother back to your house and killed her."

"Madam Tisne?" She felt shock; she had been so sure it was Tony, it had never occurred to her there was any other possibility.

"I think so. She had the emotional strength and cold-blooded need to do it. She probably thought the Yard was taking too much time building its case against you, and she saw a way to get rid of one problem and cement your guilt too.

"Look at what is at stake: the money the estate pays to you every month—over a thousand pounds. The value of this house—which can only come back to the estate if you die; the various investments of Lord Tisne, the legitimate ones, and then, the golden calf—*the House of Correction.*

"You don't think she is aware that Morfit has been siphoning money from the profits? Believe me, she counts every groat, and she knows to a ha'penny what the bottom line is. She is biding her time, Lady Genelle, and Tony Lethbridge is not going to pull the wool over her eyes."

"And all of that you deduced from looking at actions and facts and consequences? You hardly need to move a foot from your desk, Roak. You could sit here like some mystical potentate and have them lining up outside for an 'inference' reading."

"Thank you, Lady Genelle. It's easy when you know how."

"This is what you don't know," she snapped. "Twenty-odd years ago, Madam Tisne paid a local country girl to seduce her son. It didn't work—or at least it didn't work fast enough to suit her. And so, two years later, this country girl followed him to London to expand her career . . ."

"And she milked it until the day she died."

His bald comment was like ice water on her anger. Even giving him the details diminished the import of it because it didn't make a difference in the end.

"I suppose you could say that," she admitted, her voice subdued.

"That is exactly what you could say, and you could easily conclude your mother had known Lord Tisne in the past just from the tenor of her relations with him. You asked exactly the right question: why *would* he have agreed to support her when he knew she had all that money. Inference, Lady Genelle: something in his past left him open to blackmail; deduction—since she seemed to be holding the cards, it must have had something to do with her. Conclusion, something happened between them in the past. One almost doesn't need to know what."

... *Look at things the way they really be* ... she could almost hear her mother saying those words.

Simple, really, when you knew how.

"So there is nothing to stop Stiles from arresting me for Arthur's murder."

He didn't answer; he didn't need to.

"This is going to destroy your reputation, Roak."

"We both know the solution, it's a question of whether a jury would accept it."

"Then I have to keep searching; there has to be something—what if the Yard demands Morfit hand over the profit statements on the *House of Correction?*"

"On what grounds, Lady Genelle? He is not implicated in the least."

"They know Arthur was the patron. Why can they not ask to see relevant items?"

"On what grounds?"

"The possibility someone else might have had a motive."

"They don't operate on possibilities when the clear facts point to a conclusive solution."

"Then I'll implicate Tony."

"It is too late; way too far after the fact."

"Then I'll keep running."

He made no comment—which was a deadly statement in itself.

340 / Thea Devine

It was an impasse, there was nothing else she could do and she had nowhere else to run.

"Genelle . . ." The voice of reason.

She resisted it. There was still that small niggling doubt in her mind—he had just painted her into a corner from which there was no escape, none, and no hope.

And he was not going to do anything. Once again, it was obvious. He had the facts at hand and they all pointed to her arrest, and she could not resist that little shadow of a doubt that clouded her thinking: he wanted her arrested; he wanted that final judgment against Arthur for what he had done to his family.

He moved; he held out his hand.

She looked into his eyes. So deep, so implacable. Formidable in his strength of will. From whom was she really in more danger—Stiles or her own emotions?

She didn't know. They had parsed out the solution and still she came up guilty with no way out.

She had to find a way out. She could not go down at the power of someone else's machinations.

She had to save herself.

She didn't know how much energy she had—or how much guile.

She put out a tentative hand and just as he reached for it, she dodged him.

He lunged at her. She rammed her foot against his most vulnerable spot.

He doubled over and she thrashed her way off of the bed and out of the room and into a little hallway.

Doors everywhere, and she didn't know where to run; she was always running. She hadn't stopped running since Arthur had died.

She flung open one door—his room . . . she slammed it shut; she wrenched open another—she could hear him coming—and she dashed through it into a dining room and then an arched entryway into his reception room.

The door—the door . . . she prayed it wasn't locked; she reached for the knob, turned—it opened and she bolted into the building hallway and down the steps.

Oh God—it's so dark—it's so dark . . .

It's raining; too much traffic . . . one prison for another—he had never done a thing—she had escaped even his final revenge: to destroy everything tainted by her husband—

She was panting now, running down the block and toward the Whitehall and St. Mary's Church.

Somebody will help me there; they can't all be in collusion to punish me for Arthur's sins . . .

Somebody was pounding hard behind her; she heard the steps, she pushed herself to run harder just when her body wanted to collapse.

She felt herself giving in, slowing down—she felt a hand reaching for her and she girded herself for a renewed burst of speed.

But too late—too late. The hand grabbed her, pulled her off balance and sent her toppling to the ground.

Something fell over her head—something thick, dense, and then hands, rough as they pulled her to her feet, and wound what felt like a rope around her arms.

"Ah, lovely lovely to see you all tied up and quiet for a change."

The voice was hateful, muffled, the hands prodding her and thrusting her suddenly upward and into a carriage; she could smell it, she could feel it.

The carriage moved and she rolled to the floor.

The horrible hands beat at her shoulders.

"Naughty girl. You didn't think you'd get away without being punished, did you? Poor little fool. Now you're going to have to do what *I* say."

It was beyond a nightmare.

Finally, finally, the carriage reached its destination, and she was hustled out of it, still encased in that smothering blanket, and pushed blindly by her captor where he wanted her to go.

Oh God, the reek and stench . . . and the shrieks of the doomed . . .

She was enveloped by a terror as tight and as choking as the blanket.

Hell—her captor had sent her to hell, and there was no redemption anywhere . . .

And corridors again; the hands pushed her forward violently and then up shallow narrow steps, endless steps, and she kept bumping into the side wall and the hands kept shoving her forward as if it were her fault she could not see.

Finally the steps ended; she stumbled over the last one and fell to her knees.

Immediately the hands began again, beating at her, pulling and pushing her, wrenching her to her feet and poking her forward again.

The noise was almost unbearable here—shrieks and moans, strapping sounds—*punishment . . . just as her captor had promised—*

She knew where she was, and she could infer who would want her there.

The House of Correction—
The refuge of the damned . . .

The hands coerced her to a halt; she heard the scrape of a lock being opened, the creak of a door.

The hands pushed her and she staggered forward and dropped to her knees.

Her captor kicked her, booting her against her bottom and then her thighs.

"I love it when I have you under control," the hateful voice said coyly. "Not so strong when you're on the floor, are you? Not so high and mighty a mistress are you? There comes a time in every woman's life when she needs chastisement. She has to understand—she must pay for her crimes—all of them—in one way or another. And so you will, my pretty. So you will."

She felt the rope around her body give, and as she wrestled with the blanket, she heard the door shut heavily, and when she emerged from its tangling folds, she was alone in a room that was as spartan as a monk's cell.

There wasn't even a bed—just a pallet of straw, a candle on a small table, and chains suspended from the walls.

"Take off your clothes, my pretty . . ."

The hateful voice reverberated through the chamber, as if the speaker were somewhere above her and watching her every move.

"Take off your clothes . . ."

Now the voice meant business.

Oh God, my money—my money . . . where is he—how much can he see?

"If you don't obey, I will have to see you are educated. . . ."

She moved her stiff arms and began to unfasten the buttons of her bodice.

"Faster, my pretty . . ."

Which of them was it? Which? And how much time could she buy with defiance?

"Why don't you show yourself?" she shouted.

"Ohhh, the bitch never learns, never never learns . . . her master shows himself when he is ready."

"He is a coward."

"He is going to teach you the exquisite pleasure of pain, my pretty. *Get naked . . .*"

His voice was like the crack of a whip.

She pulled apart the upper half of her dress and shrugged out of the sleeves.

"So many stupid layers and impediments . . ." the voice, musing now, as she unfastened her skirt and let it drop to the floor. And the petticoat. And the corset cover . . .

Damn, damn—the money . . . what do I do about the money?

Her stockings; the drawers . . . a quick sleight of hand to palm the thin wad of bills she had secreted in her corset . . . a wiggle of her bottom to distract him as she lay down her drawers and pushed the money under the rough blanket that she had laid on the floor.

And now the corset . . .

Oh God—now the corset when she could hardly bear to turn around and reveal the rest of her.

"Exquisite, my pretty," the voice said cajolingly. "What other treasures have you yet to reveal?"

She was shivering with fear and the dank coldness of the room.

"Take it off now, my pretty, your master will not wait on your whims . . ."

The voice was positively threatening now, and she reached behind her back and slowly began unfastening as much as she could of the corset bindings.

"What a obedient little bitch. Are you ready for me now, my pretty?"

She slipped the garment off of her shoulders and turned it around to get at the laces.

"Tiny little breasts for such a high and mighty one. Very disappointing, my pretty . . . I expected more of you . . ." the voice chided her as the corset fell to the floor and she crossed her arms over her chest.

"And now, my darling little Nella will get you ready to meet your master."

The door opened, and a woman walked in carrying a tray. She was naked except for the black stockings and boots she wore, and the expression on her face bordered on reverence.

She moved aside the candle on the small table and set the tray in its place.

"You will dress for the master."

She unfolded the garments. A pair of long leather gloves. A thrall collar. A pair of long leather boots. A long thick golden chain with a lock appended to it.

"I will dress you," Nella said, and she came toward her like she was a marionette and someone was manipulating her strings. "Take—" Nella handed her the boots and then knelt and slipped them on. "Take—" Nella handed her the gloves and then helped tie them on. "Take—" Nella gave her the collar and then fastened it around her neck.

"This—" Nella said, "this I do . . ." as she lifted the chain.

She wound it around Genelle's waist and between her legs, and hooked it together and locked it behind her back, and then surveyed her handiwork.

"Master will be pleased," she said, and picked up the tray and exited the room.

Genelle was but a step behind her—but the solid door was quickly locked and she could not move it.

I look like a pornographer's dream. Who is doing this to me? But I can guess who is sadistic enough . . .

"Are you ready, my pretty?" His voice came through the door, hoarse with excitement, and she jumped back in horror.

And then the door swung open, and Mr. Morfit stood on the threshold stroking a whip through his hands.

* * *

And he had warned her.

He ripped out the door of his townhouse not two minutes after her—and two minutes too late.

And whoever had gotten her was a master at doing it.

It could only be one—or all—of the three.

And physical force was not the solution for dealing with them.

The end would come now, and far differently than either he or she could have envisioned it.

Elegant solutions—vengeance *would* be his in the end—and in mysterious ways he never could have foreseen.

He walked slowly into the room, savoring the moment.

"So, my high and mighty lady—" he murmured, extending the whip, touching her chin, and running the end of it down between her quivering breasts. "Not so high and mighty now."

He was crazy—she was sure he was crazy . . . his eyes burned with the lust to hurt—the man who had always been overlooked now wielding the power . . .

She backed up against the table. "Why? Tell me why."

"Because you're so pretty, and I'm so strong, and you always thought you could run right over me, my lady; just poke your nose where it didn't belong . . . just barge in on me any time you wanted and take my time, my money, my information as if it were your own.

"So you can see—the house was a revelation for me. I had Arthur, I had Tony, I had Madam Tisne's excellent business sense, and I had all this flesh to expend myself upon.

"And then *you* . . .

"You couldn't stay quiet and cowed the way you were when Arthur married you—oh no, *you* had to go sniffing around, discovering sex, using it like you had invented it.

"And *demanding*—oh my dear, as if you had some special place in Arthur's life. He thought of you as a doormat, you stupid girl. He thought you were ugly, useless except as a smokescreen. Unendurable for more than ten minutes at a time.

"So naive you were. I did so like you better that way. If you had just kept out of the way, and taken your punishment like a good girl, none of this would have happened.

"None of it. But no—you had to know where the money came from, who would own the house if you were imprisoned, who was Eversham—God, you can't imagine what a nuisance you were.

"But those days are over now, my pretty. It's my turn; stupid Tony could not keep you pinned down for more than a couple of hours. And Madam—well, all she cares about is Tony and ending the Arthur affair with your conviction for murder.

"It will just take a little longer than she planned. I decided to keep you for myself for a while, to give you a taste of your own medicine. What you've been waiting for, my lady bitch."

He snapped the whip for emphasis inches from her naked hip.

"A little pleasure, my lady? A little submission to my wishes for a change?" *Snap!* He cracked it again, this time just at her feet.

"You should get down on your knees to me. I told you things I should never have revealed just because I pictured that one day you would be in my power. You became a very forward woman when you discovered sex, my lady. It was both repulsive and fascinating to watch you run off every night to meet your lover . . ."

She choked back her revulsion; nothing had been secret—nothing sacred. In the midst of her turmoil and her ecstasy, some-one had been watching, a witness to her surrender and his betrayal.

"So I decided to lock you up, my lady, so you will be as chaste for me as you were for Arthur. Dear dear Arthur . . . he might have done very well with your body if he could have suppressed his repugnance. You really are not all that rounded.

"Ah—" The whip snapped again as she started to make a move. "I am perfectly content for you to stay right there without moving. I am contemplating what joys I wish to sample tonight.

"Just the sight of you chained, with a thrall collar around your neck, galvanizes me. It makes me yearn for your submission. It makes me want to chastise you for all of your provocations. It makes me want to teach you a lesson you'll never forget . . ."

Crack . . . he snapped the whip again, this time laying it right against her right arm.

And it hurt—it hurt like the devil, a narrow red weal that appeared like a bracelet around her upper arm.

"Did you feel it, my pretty?" He did it again, this time against her left arm. "A lovely mark—not too sharp, not too flaying— I'm sure you'll agree I'm quite an expert at this.

"Now *kneel . . .*"

She knelt; one did not argue with a madman.

"Face down on the floor . . ."

She lay down in front of him. She felt the whip, teasing her buttocks.

"That's better—"

His foot pressed into her back.

"Yes, I like the submissive you much better. I wished I could have bent you to my will every time you walked into my office demanding something. But you're not demanding now, are you, my pretty? No, you are obeying *my* demands, aren't you? How do you like submitting to your master?"

She wanted to tell him; she really wanted to tell him, but she wasn't going to be foolhardy at a time like this.

"I hardly know what to say," she choked out.

His boot caught her just below her hip.

"You say you have lived for this moment, my pretty. That all your life you have dreamt of submitting to your master."

"All my life," she said fervently.

"You have dreamt—"

"My only dream . . ."

"On your hands and knees begging for punishment . . ."

She made a hissing sound. "I think not . . ." *Stupid, unruly, unwise . . .*

She felt the crack of the whip across her buttocks.

I'm dead; now I am dead. He will kill me before the morning, and no one will come to rescue me. The case will be closed and they will all get away scot-free . . .

"I think yes," he shouted. "I think you don't understand the situation, my lady mouth. Here is the situation: I am the master and you are the slave who submits to my every whim. You tell me what I want to hear, and you accept and bear the punishment when you don't. That is why one comes to the *House of Correction*. Do you understand?"

"Yes," she whispered, feeling the shocking pressure of his boot on her stinging buttocks.

"And when I am done with you, I will hand you over to the others so you may have your just punishment from whoever wishes to choose you as his vessel. Is . . . that . . . clear?"

Sickeningly, horribly clear . . . and she didn't know how much more she could take.

"Ah my dear Morfit—" a new voice, instantly recognizable. "You have beautifully humiliated her, my dear . . ." *Tony* . . . "One could not have asked for better. Absolutely genius of you to think of keeping an eye on Roak's townhouse. And look at her now—genuflecting to her superiors. A painting—a Renaissance painting—although her body was never rounded enough . . . I can't tell you how onerous it was to take her to bed . . ."

She felt great waves of rage consuming her. "Then Madam Tisne is the ideal, I suppose," she interposed, her voice sharp, resentful, controlled, goading in a way that she knew was not smart.

And she reaped the immediate reward: discipline from Tony this time, shoving her head against the floor with his foot and beating down on her buttocks with his hands.

"Always a bitch this one. Worse and worse after Arthur died. Used to be gullible and tractable. So here is where you wind up, my dear, when you choose to be willful. A day or two with us and you will beg to be taken into custody."

He hadn't removed his foot and her cheek and jaw were jammed painfully into the floor as he bent over and pulled her hair so that he could look into her eyes.

"The time has come, my lady bitch. It is time to introduce you to the acolytes. I *know* you are yearning to meet the acolytes." He yanked at her hair. "Tell me!"

"I—I am ready . . . to meet the acolytes," she said through her teeth. *Nothing more—I can give them nothing more . . .*

"Very good. You still can learn; it is a excellent sign. And the acolytes are ready to teach you . . ."

They led her down yet another of the interminable hallways to a large hall with trestle tables lined up against the walls which were festooned with chains and medieval heraldic flags.

They were holding her, one on either side of her, grasping her arms and making lewd comments about the size of her breasts.

"Fear," Morfit said, "is excellent for stimulating the nipples. Look at how hard they are . . ."

She wanted to kill him.

She balked at the door, and they pulled her into the room. It was redolent of sweat and sex and some other indefinable scent. Fear, perhaps.

She looked down at the floor and her knees almost buckled. The floor was transparent, and below, like insects, there were patrons moving slowly, looking upward, savoring all the carnal revelations.

"They want to see you, bitch." Tony now, with no patience because he didn't care. "Spread your legs."

He nudged his boot between her legs and kicked them apart.

"That's better; we give the customer what he wants, bitch— and you'd do well to remember that when the acolytes come in."

"What happens with the acolytes?"

She never should have spoken. Tony slapped her sharp and hard.

"Bitches don't ask questions; they just do what they're told."

Her cheek stung like it had been burned.

"You see?" Morfit said. "That's just what she's like. Always coming into my office and asking questions. Where's my money? Who is Eversham? Why didn't you tell me—as if anything were her business . . . I can't wait to see her humiliation; I can't wait to hear her beg for mercy."

She could not stand it; she couldn't keep her mouth shut— and she knew she would never learn.

"What are they going to do?"

Tony slapped her again ruthlessly. "She is a damned one. The acolytes like a little resistance. Let's get her on the table. It's almost time . . ."

The end was almost near, and it was curious to him that the execution of it was the only thing in his life he was going to plan carefully.

It was going to *be*—like a force of nature and he would be the instrument of corruption.

He was good at that.

And she had been closer to the mark than even she knew.

He had never been involved before.

He had always consciously never gotten involved. It was always a given that one or another of his clients would fall in love with him.

It was never a possibility that it might work the other way around. He was too clear-sighted for that. Too aloof and removed and focused for that.

Nor did he even know if he could call it getting involved. It just *was,* in spite of its start.

And it had to be because now he was going to exert himself to play the hero instead the mystic potentate.

And he had never ever done that before.

The ironies were appalling.

And the ending was clear: she would be free; her enemies would be vanquished; and he—he . . . would be the one begging for mercy.

Chapter 23

He had no time to lose. The vampires were circling for the kill, and not even a stake to the heart would prevent them from sucking the lifeblood from their victim.

He was out the door after her not fifteen minutes after her abduction.

He didn't need to follow her—there was only one place she could have been taken; and it was just midnight when the hansom cab let him off within walking distance of the Embankment.

There it loomed, the house from hell, the epitome of all the places in which he had spent his sap since he had come to London looking for monsters and mistresses.

He took down the mallet and struck the gong.

He had learned this lesson: one only had to know how to open the doors. The rest was provided on a golden platter.

The question was, who had her and where to look . . .

He hadn't even allowed himself to speculate about who. But he would have wagered Lethbridge was the most likely, and in one of the rooms along the crystal corridor where he could see or be seen—

Damn him to hell . . .

He raced down the steps to the corridor feeling the pressure of time. Anything could have happened within the last half hour—anything—because they weren't desperate.

They knew they had won and they had in their hands the sacrifice to their devil.

She lay on the table, her legs and arms bound to the trestles, watching the acolytes file in the door.

They were dressed in long black robes and they were barefoot;

they could have been postulants or pretenders—but they all were eager and erect and none of them could keep their eyes from her writhing naked body.

"And there she is," Morfit pronounced, his voice high-pitched with excitement. "The one whom you are commanded to worship. She waits for you; she willingly abases herself for you. And all you need do is offer yourselves to her and she will take you all the way to heaven."

"Surround her," Tony invited.

No—no . . .

"Touch her. See that she is real and that your initiation will be repaid in your possession of this glorious creature."

She closed her eyes; she couldn't bear to see the lechery, the bestiality; she could hardly stand the feeling of their hands tentatively stroking her as if they couldn't believe that she was real or that Tony meant what he said.

"Step back!"

Morfit now, his voice like the crack of a whip.

"Now we come to the mortification. Each of you—one at a time—reveal yourselves to your masters and bear the punishment for wanting this female creature . . . you first." He pointed to one of the men who stepped forward with a degrading eagerness and quickly untied his robe and let it fall to his feet.

"Lovely—just lovely," Morfit murmured, stroking his whip. "Turn around against the wall, my lovely—it is time to begin the passion play . . ."

And finally he found her, spreadeagled between Tony and Morfit—Morfit!—and struggling to get away.

Vipers—bastards . . .

Damn them, damn them, damn them—

There were ways out of the crystal corridor but they were few and far between; the patrons who elected a heaven of voyeurism were meant to stay and enjoy the whole thing.

It took more time than he wanted to find the outlet to the main staircase.

No one in the *House of Correction* rushed anywhere.

He could hear the pulse-pounding shrieks as punishment was

instituted in rooms along the corridors; it penetrated the staircase and floated up with him into the floor of private fantasies.

Somewhere here they had her prisoner.

He crept along the hallway, pushing at doors, reckoning the distance from the staircase to the place where she was being held.

In the distance, he saw a parade of men heading toward one of the rooms and he followed at a discreet distance.

A door opened for them, beyond which he could see the table and a woman prone on top.

Genelle . . .

Goddamn—

He edged closer to the door—a thick wooden door, slightly ajar because the hem of one of the robes had gotten caught in it.

He heard the benediction; he saw them all move toward the table at Tony's bidding—and he saw the first of them step forward to accept his chastisement.

When he heard the crack of the whip, he burst through the door, pushing the communicants out of the way, and leaping over Genelle to get to Morfit.

And Morfit lashed out—cutting him across the cheek with the whip, and raising his arm to strike another blow—as Tony moved behind him to immobilize him.

He caught the shaft of the whip and twisted it out of Morfit's spineless grip, and instantly wheeled around and rapped Tony against the neck with the handle.

"Everyone out! *Everyone* . . ."

"Everyone stay—" Morfit, above his roar, "or you'll . . ."

Roak didn't hesitate—he swirled the whip above his head and swiped it across Morfit's face.

". . . be sor—*ahhhh!*"

"Get out—get out—get out—" He pushed them out, rapping the whip against the wall to emphasize his words. "Out—you . . . Lethbridge—"

"A gorgeous performance, Roak," Tony said languidly. "Positively virile. I never did understand why you wouldn't join our games—"

"Get out."

"She's really not worth it, are you my virginal darling; you look so much better than you perform—" He strolled past the table and her virulent eyes, and ran his hand from her thigh to her breast in a gesture of disdain, and then he left the room.

So there was only Morfit, staring at him with poisonous hate.

"Untie her."

"I made her."

"I'm going to make you into mincemeat if you don't untie her."

"Sounds delicious, Roak—a feast . . ."

He lifted his arm and struck, wholly unconscious of the force, the anger, or the feeling behind the blow.

". . . for the senses . . . *ahhhhh!* You bastard . . ."

"Do it."

"I love the pain."

"You might like death too . . ." Roak said, his voice utterly devoid of expression.

Morfit's head snapped up.

"I'll throw you through that floor if you don't untie her— *now* . . ."

"You're a gorilla, Roak."

"You're the animal, Morfit. Now do it—"

She felt faint as Morfit's cold fish hands worked at the ropes.

Roak was the last person she would have cast in the role of knight-errant. And Tony was the last person she would have thought would cave in.

She flexed her wrists as the ropes were cut away, and Roak shrugged out of his frock coat and draped it across her shoulders as she sat up.

And then her legs were free and Morfit turned and scuttled out of the room.

Roak watched him, his skepticism reflected in his eyes, and then he tucked the whip into the waistband of his trousers—just for good measure.

"We have to get out of here now."

She slipped off the table onto wobbly legs. "It can't be too soon for me."

"Put that on."

She slipped into his jacket as she stamped her legs to get the feeling back into them.

"Ready?"

"Ready."

They ran down the hallway to the nearest stairs.

Downward again, running again, her boots and her shaky legs hobbling her.

"They won't let us get out—you know that. Lethbridge has already sounded the alarm and every exit will be blocked."

"And business will go on as usual. What are we going to do?"

He smiled grimly at her use of the word *we*.

"The unholy three had better prepare to meet their maker— whoever it is. We're going to blow this place to kingdom come."

They secreted themselves in a stairwell near the reception room so he could make his preparations.

He had brought with him a parcel of nitro powder, a half box of ten-gauge white felt wads, a ball of twine, and enough matches to burn down the city of London.

They worked by the dim light in the stairwell, separating the felt wads and laying them on the steps, and then carefully sprinkling a healthy amount of the powder into the center of the felt.

She then pinched the felt into a ball and he tied it with a length of twine cut with his pocket knife, leaving a long leading piece that would burn slowly, enough to give them time to set each explosive.

They left one nitro ball in the stairwell and put the others into the box that had contained the felt wads.

"We'll start at the top—as many on each floor as we can."

It wasn't easy: every floor, every room was occupied, swarming with patrons—and guards.

And they were looking: Tony Lethbridge had left no stone unturned. He wanted them, and everywhere they looked, there were guards unobtrusively searching for them.

"We'll have to take the chance," Roak said. "If we could find other clothes . . ."

They edged their way out of a stairway—the third outlet on the top floor, and emerged into a relatively empty hallway that was suffused with sounds and scents and moans and begging.

They left one in the stairwell, unlit, and then inched along the top floor walls, pushing at doors, looking for possibilities.

Roak, in a whisper, three doors ahead of her: "In here . . ."

They ducked into the room, which was adorned with the usual paraphernalia, and, bless fate, a silk robe she could wrap around her body to hide the obvious trappings she wore.

They left a felt ball in that room, lighted, and they found one other place on the floor before they scurried back to the first stairwell, lit the twine fuse, and scrambled down the stairs to the next floor.

It was busier here, almost as if the patrons were between scenes and rushing to the next. Easier to get lost among them, and to find an unobtrusive spot to set the balls and light the fuses.

"*Damn*—a guard—stay back . . ."

They flattened themselves against a wall in the midst of a crowd as one of the eunuchs marched by, his eyes passing over the crowd looking for a naked woman with a thrall collar and a chain girding her waist, and a tall dark man in shirtsleeves.

"He's gone . . ."

They moved again, carefully, warily back to the stairwell, and lit the fuse there, and raced down to the next floor, set only one felt ball and that in the stairwell, and emerged finally on the main level.

"I want the crystal corridor."

"But there are so many people there," she protested.

"One at either end, and then we'll go."

She wasn't sure—it wasn't right—but neither was the business of the house or what had made it possible.

She trailed after him into the anteroom and down the stairway underground.

Too many people—this was real. What they had done on the floors above was too real . . .

They mingled with the crowd, strolling down the corridor— "Look up occasionally," he whispered, and she girded herself to act as one of the crowd and look at the scenes being played out above.

It was a long corridor, encompassing many rooms; she counted the escape outlets as they proceeded, until they reached the opposite end.

He set one ball in the stairwell there. Another midway through. And third in the stairway through which they had entered, leaving two other stairwells free for escape.

They came out into the anteroom again, and pulled back behind a column as patrons and eunuchs wandered in.

"We have to get out of here . . ."

He pulled her out from behind a column into the reception hall.

Instantly the eunuch called Hamat appeared, conjured up like a genie, the guardian of the gate, the one who had first admitted them so many weeks ago.

"Mistress? What is your pleasure?"

"It is time to leave," she said imperiously.

"One is ordered to keep everyone in while the Masters search for a Disobedient."

"It is not I."

His obsidian eyes rested on Roak. "No one is permitted to leave."

"My lady is ill."

"My lady looks very well to do."

"You are not qualified to tell," Roak said, keeping his voice even, and cursing himself that he could not reach the whip that was propped like a backbone under his coat.

"My Masters dictate the terms. You may be seated in the waiting room."

There was yet another room, in a veritable rabbit warren of rooms, off to one side of the reception room, and in here there were chairs and a table.

Hamat showed them in politely and shut and locked the door.

"He has gone for Morfit or Lethbridge, damn it. And the first wads could blow at any minute."

So it was over; her life would come to an end in the infamous House of Correction . . . and Roak will have been the agent of her demise, as she had supposed all along . . .

She sank wearily into one of the chairs. "Morfit will chain us to the walls."

Roak pulled out the whip. "One still has *this*—" He cracked it experimentally. "As effective as ever."

They heard Morfit outside the door.

"Oh my darlings, you managed to get caught anyway. Open the door, Hamat, I can't wait to see my loves . . ."

The door swung open and Morfit pranced over the threshold.

"There you are—how naughty of you when we were having so much fun—"

Roak snapped the whip in his face. "Stay back."

"Stupid of you, Roak. Hamat—"

Hamat lunged—Roak cracked the whip—and simultaneously there was a thunderous *boom* from somewhere above—

"My God, what was that?" Morfit screamed, wheeling around and dashing out the door.

Hamat wavered, torn between duty and necessity, when another *boom* reverberated through the building, and then he turned and ran after Morfit.

"Now—"

Roak grabbed her hand and they ran into the reception room and to the door, inches ahead of the crowd exploding from the interior rooms.

"Open that door—"

"Get that door open . . ."

"Get him out the way—"

"Let me out, let me out—"

"The key—where is the key?"

It was Roak, levering himself upward on the shoulders of a scared but willing patron, who found the keys on a ledge nearby the door.

"Hurry, man . . ."

"Oh God—Oh God—" as another explosion went off.

And another—

They pulled the door open—Roak grabbed hold of Genelle, and together they and the panicked crowd stampeded out into the early morning air to the accompaniment of thunderous explosions, choking smoke, and flashing fire.

They watched the *House of Correction* burn.

Inside—everything was gone inside, and outside, as day broke, they could see the scorched and blackened walls.

The habitués had fled, like rats from a sinking ship.

And somewhere in the ruins, one of the ungodly three was probably still trying to salvage something.

"They'll rebuild," Genelle said, shading her eyes and trying to catch some movement from within. There were firefighters inside now, and the police, and she marveled she could stand there so calmly when Stiles could appear at any moment and arrest her.

"*If* they live," Roak said.

His words chilled her. *Vengeance was his against the unholy triumvirate if any of them had not survived the conflagration* . . .

"There is nothing more we can do here," she said, but her voice was tentative.

"No," he said. "Everything has been done that needed to be done. It is time for you to go home."

Back to Green Street, he meant.

Joseph Footman answered the door, and without blinking an eye, murmured, "Good morning, my lady. It is good to have you back."

"Get the housekeeper. I'm going to get her to bed. To bed, Lady Genelle, without protests. Everything else can wait."

He bustled her up the stairs to her room. She was too tired to think about the ramifications of that—

Actions, motives, consequences—he had rescued her from the House of Correction and then he had burned it down . . .

She toppled onto the bed before he could pull back the covers, and she fell soundly asleep.

So here was the end of it—she was back exactly where she had started from, encased in chains and collars, and nothing, with all her effort and discoveries, nothing had changed.

Joseph brought her breakfast to the bedroom. "Of course it is afternoon, my lady, but I ascertained that you had not eaten either this morning or last night, and I thought you might like something that was not too heavy."

"Thank you, Joseph."

She indicated the table by the bed, and he set the tray down and poured her tea.

I am forever drinking tea, and forever having breakfast. This past month could have been a dream for all that things feel different.

But she was different. She felt it, and it wasn't that her experience at the *House of Correction* had scarred her; rather she felt fatalistic, as if she had travelled this circle for some reason that was meant to be.

She swung herself off the bed. Someone had removed the boots and the leather gloves, but the collar and the chain encircling her lower torso—those remained.

The collar had a little lock, she realized as she fingered it. She hadn't known. And the chain—the thin fine chain that outlined her womanhood—she could break it with a twist of her hand.

Maybe she didn't want to do that; maybe she wanted to wear the apparatus of chastisement when she was taken away to prison.

And she would finally go. Perhaps the events of this month were meant to show her that, that evil could live and the innocent would suffer.

She slipped off of the bed and went over to the armoire whose doors were both open as if someone had been rummaging in her closet.

Roak?

Slowly she closed the doors so that she was facing herself in the outside mirrors.

And she froze.

Behind her, at the threshold of her door, stood Madam Tisne, her smoke-smudged face a mask of utter hatred, and a riding crop twitching ominously in her hand.

"They are dead."

The words dropped like stones in the silence of the room.

"Everything is ruined. *Everything.* Between you and your strumpet of a mother—I have lost everything."

She couldn't say a word; her mother-in-law's face looked like the very devil.

"Would you like to know how, little girl? Would you like to hear what heinous crime your mother perpetrated so she could wring every last cent from my son and from me? So her daughter could ultimately destroy my life, my peace, and my security? Would you like to know, Genelle *dear?*"

"Madam Tisne—" she managed to get out from behind her clogged throat.

"Shut up!" Madam Tisne thwacked the crop on the bed. "I will kill you, daughter-in-law. There is no help for it. It's over—everything is over—and I too will die, if that is any consolation to you. But you will die first."

"Madam Tisne—don't . . ."

"Damn you!" The crop crashed down again, this time on the bedpost, and it cracked a little seam in the woodwork. "They went back in to try to save something, and walked straight into the explosives; goddamn you—*how did you do it?* Who helped you do it? No—I know—that Roak. That bastard Roak. Never satisfied. For years I told Arthur, the money wouldn't be enough, it would never be enough for the likes of him.

"Or your mother—born of a kind those two—always wanting more and more and more and so everything got destroyed because *they* wanted *more. I* just wanted to be left alone—no more threats, no more payments, no more embarrassments, no more—no more . . .

"And there came your mother with her big fancy ideas and Arthur agreed to everything. *Everything*—marrying you, even, which for a time I thought might be a *redeeming* idea—not that anything could change him, but at least he would be perceived differently. And then she came back with the idea of him support-ing her. And then all the bills. You have no idea. Every last thing, from the servants to her hairpins—

"And do you know why, little girl, do you know why he said yes—*I* said yes? No, you don't know why—but I can see that you wondered. You understood how unseemly it was—all the money she got at the *House*—and then *that* . . .

"So after Arthur died, she had to go too. To rectify my mistake, so to speak. After all, I was the one who brought her into Arthur's life all those years ago—and we have been paying for it ever since.

"And then you—spineless—couldn't put up with Arthur's eccentricities and had to demand your own house, your own allowance, your own inheritance . . . and he did it, didn't he? Did you ever wonder why, little girl? Or did your mother teach you that it was your right, your due to squeeze all of that money from *my* family? Hmmm? Hmm?

"No answer, eh? Not thinking too clearly yet, are we? It must be the shock of Tony's death. I'm not over it myself. But I'm thinking very clearly now, and I know you have to die.

"But not before you understand why, my girl.

"Tell me, why do you think? Because Arthur was so generous? Please—it wasn't Arthur; he couldn't think past the direction his nether parts led him. Except for that scurrilous agreement you made him sign, everything was me—me—me; anything that was done, *I* said yes to it. Any money that was spent—*I* wrote the check for it. Anything your mother wanted, *I* was the one who agreed to it.

"Why—why do you think?

"No ideas yet, little girl? Think back—think back . . . you went to Skirling Vail, didn't you? Could you picture your mother as a young girl there, as placid and bovine as a cow, chewing her cud, perfectly natural and earthy in the way that peasants are.

"And Arthur, ascetic, aloof, removed from those sorts of pursuits—oh, it was a match made in the haystack—she fell for it; she fell for him and I made him leave her the moment I realized that he sustained some feeling for her.

"Imagine my shock when she showed up in London two years later, talking about her great success in the Vail, doing Arthur-would-know-what with local customers. She liked the money I gave her; she never got so much after. And she was burdened with other problems, so it took her much longer to leave the Vail than she had originally planned.

"Are you beginning to understand, little girl? Yes—I see by the look in your eyes you know some of this.

"Think about it—think about the ramifications of her having a brief affair with my son . . ."

Facts, actions, ramifications—why was she shaking all of a sudden? Why was this ugly little woman frightening her like this? Why couldn't she get the memory of her mother's never-sent letters out of her mind?

This particular crisis . . . her mother had written three months after the affair.

And six months later—the thing is done.

And two years after—I know I can support myself and any little thing that comes along . . .

"I don't know what you mean . . ." she whispered.

"I'll spell it out for you then—" her mother-in-law said kindly, her voice just overflowing with glee.

"No—"

"Yes, yes, my dear. Yes, yes. Your clever mother; she hid you, you know. For years and years. Kept you out of town and out of sight until Arthur got even more out of control, and then she came up with this delicious idea that he should get married to save his reputation, and she *happened* to have this beautiful and innocent young daughter who would ask him no questions and tell him no lies. Arthur was quite taken with you, my dear—I must say. He envisioned a joyous future of proper appearances and improper liaisons.

"He was even more innocent than you. And then your mother—with the truth . . . the whole insane truth—"

"No . . ."

"What, you think she didn't scheme to punish him—punish *me* for what I had done to her? Oh, she succeeded quite well, little girl. She foisted my bastard granddaughter off on me as my daughter-in-law. And she thought she was damned clever about it into the bargain."

"No! No!" Did she whisper or did she scream? *Unnatural— unclean . . . facts—actions—ramifications . . . all the reasons why—the inutterably horrible scandal of it—Mother . . . Mother—*

"And so we met her every last demand. Is it any wonder she had to be gotten rid of? Can anyone blame me for wanting to stop the cycle of disgrace with my son? And now you, little girl. Now you . . ."

"No—no . . ." *The dates on the letters—cursorily noted . . . twenty-some years ago—twenty-some . . . she was twenty- some—and it never ever connected . . . why? Because it was too horrible to contemplate? Because it just didn't seem possible? Ah—ah . . . Mother— Spawn of Lord Arthur Tisne, given to him as a wife . . .*

She felt sick; all the money, all the secrets, all the lies.

"Spineless little thing you were, five years ago. Now look at you—a killer—think of it that way, little girl: the existence of you killed my son, your mother, my lover, my solicitor, destroyed my fortune and my life. You have a lot to account for."

She started to edge slowly toward Genelle, who was paralyzed with shock.

"I believe in an eye for an eye, little girl." She rapped the riding crop against the footboard of the bed. "If you hadn't existed, none of this would have happened."

She was coming closer and closer.

My grandmother—this horrible ugly woman is my grand-mother . . . my mother lied and cheated and manipulated every-one, and the end result is, we are going to die . . .

"You should have just let them arrest you for Arthur's murder, little girl. You shouldn't have hired that interfering Roak. Then at least you'd still be alive—everyone would have been alive—"

No—no . . . none of that is my fault, none of it—she's crazy; she's as crazy as Arthur ever was . . . my father—dear lord, my father . . .

Maybe I'm crazy too . . .

Her mother-in-law—no, her grandmother—came closer, her face twitching with fury, rhythmically beating the crop against the palm of her hand with the force she wanted to attack Genelle.

She could see it in her grandmother's eyes: the pure lust for destruction centered on *her* as she came closer and closer and closer.

"I didn't know about Roak . . ."

"Naive little girl; just took everything for granted—the hus-band, the money, the house, the servants, the mother, the investi-gator—you have to pay for mistakes like that, Granddaughter, and now that your mother is dead, who else is there to teach you?"

Closer . . .

How did you handle a madwoman? There was no reasoning with her, no deterring her determination . . . everything had been taken from her—just everything, by her own design or by that immovable force, Maudie Alcarr . . .

Her mother must have dogged her like a she-devil . . . two years after the event of her liaison with Arthur, and her mother was on his tail, and probably just when Madam Tisne was feeling comfortable that he had escaped that trap . . .

. . . her father . . . her father—her father—the man with whom she had fumbled for one night in a bedroom, accomplishing noth-ing, and her mother had sold her off to him deliberately and willfully—almost as if she had conceived her with that objective in mind.

It was more horrifying that she could comprehend and the

*more she played the words back and forth in her mind, the less
real it became.*

It wasn't real; the whole awful plot was not real, and yet her
mother had planned it, executed it, died for it.

And all that from a country girl who had been bought by the
aristocracy on a whim for a night . . .

"So now, little girl, now you know. And now it's time to pay
for your sins . . ."

The door flew open.

Genelle looked past her grandmother's distorted face, and a
knot of fear constricted in her belly.

Tolliver!

"Did you think I would be so dull-witted as to come alone?
You *are* a stupid little girl; I have always had the keys. I had the
muscle. The minute it was clear the *House* was a lost cause, I
came here. Tolliver . . ."

He came toward her now with a man's economy of movement;
her grandmother had said everything that needed to be said. He
had only to wrestle her into a position where the old woman
could beat the life out of her with that riding crop.

She saw the blood-lust in her grandmother's eyes.

She saw Tolliver lunge for her out of the corner of her eye.

She dove for the bed. He scrambled across and caught her leg
and pulled her toward him.

She hung onto the edge of the mattress and tried to slither
away from him as he jumped on the bed and straddled her.

She felt the throbbing blows of the riding crop against her legs,
and she screamed and bucked her body to escape them.

He was strong, so strong; she tried to hike her legs under her
body to unseat him, and he grabbed her hair and pulled.

She felt the blows raining down on her shoulders, her head,
her face, and she desperately, blindly, grabbed for the riding crop
to wrest it from her grandmother's hands.

She grasped air; the crop kept coming down, whacking her
thoroughly on her rebellious hands.

"It's time," her grandmother panted. "It's time—I'm tired of
these games; I want her gone. I want it over—"

Tolliver grabbed her by the thrall collar and pulled her backward off the bed and twisted her up to her feet.

Her grandmother had opened up the french windows that gave onto a small balcony and she was standing just outside, waiting for Tolliver to wrestle her onto the balcony.

Terror . . .

The harridan meant it—she was going to have her thrown off the balcony—

Instantly she began to struggle, to use any means at her command to distract her captor. His one arm was like a vise around her, and with his other hand he pulled at her collar, choking her, immobilizing her—

Killing me—he's going to kill me before he throws me off the balcony . . .

She gasped for air, trying to prise the collar away from her throat; she wrapped her legs around his as he pulled her toward the window, trying to trip him or slow him down.

She felt the air swirling around her head as he yanked her across the sill of the balcony.

She felt death but a step away as he hauled her over to the little wooden balustrade and tipped her over the railing.

She felt his strength overwhelming her as he pushed her forward and she wildly flailed her feet trying to get a toehold anywhere, anyhow.

She heard her grandmother cackling in the background and saw a kaleidoscope of colors in the garden below as Tolliver's hands began to pressure her further and further over.

She felt his impatience with her resistance, with her furious will to live.

She felt her grandmother beating at her legs to keep her from finding any kind of balance.

She felt the moment of reckoning was near and she had to do something, anything, or she would be dead in another minute.

She couldn't see, her hands were disabled, her body was half over the edge of the railing . . . but her legs, her legs, so cracked with pain from her grandmother's riding crop—still free, still moving . . .

All she had to do was thrust a leg forward and pray that she punched the old bitch in the gut—

Last chance—last minute . . . hardly any breath—

Pounding sounds coming from the bedroom—

Can't get balance ... can't ...

"Good-bye little girl," her grandmother sang, coming in for one more blow on her legs.

I can't do it—I can't—no breath—

She lifted one leg with the last ounce of strength she could muster as Tolliver shifted to better thrust her over—and she drove it into the air—

And she connected right with her mother-in-law's face.

Her scream was unearthly—

And she felt Tolliver's hold loosen—

And she wrenched herself violently away, catching him off-balance as he turned to her grandmother—

And she levered herself upright and twisted herself so that she threw her body against his . . .

And she felt his body buckle at the unexpected assault—

And she heard the screams and the pounding and voices and—

She watched, as in slow incremental motions, Tolliver lost his balance and tumbled over the railing into the garden below.

Chapter 24

She heard something breaking behind her and she whirled.

Her grandmother stood there, a piece of broken porcelain in her hand, looking like an avenging fury.

"Clever little bitch," she snarled. "Look at what you did to my face, little girl. Insult to injury I call it . . . and I'm going to gouge your face to pieces before I kill you."

"Grandmother—"

"Don't you call me—family—" her grandmother growled, jabbing her weapon at her.

She backed up against the bed to support her wobbly legs.

The pounding on the door started again, and her grandmother moved to bar her way.

"You'll never get past me," she shouted even as the banging got louder, as if whoever was out there had a battering ram. "Those bastards won't get a foot near you, little girl. I'm going to carve you up good with this—" She waved the shard of porcelain. "You're going to bleed your life away right on this floor."

Her grandmother was a panting, heaving animal, as feral as a jungle beast, waiting for the moment to move in for the kill.

She can come get me; I have no strength to resist. I can't move, I can't move—my legs are like jelly, there's no power in my arms—oh lord, oh lord, oh lord, such hate, such insane incredible hate . . . and she could overcome me—she could just blow on me and I would fall on the floor . . .

Her grandmother sensed it. She looked as if she were ready to pounce. She took a step forward, and then another—

And then the door burst open, knocking her aside and Joseph and Roak came hurling into the room.

She was already up, shoving them aside with superhuman

strength as Genelle bolted from the room and fled into the hall-way.

And she was right behind her; her grandmother was steps behind her, an inhuman beast intent on destruction.

And then her body gave out, and her legs folded, and she toppled to the floor just in front the staircase.

Her grandmother came barrelling toward her in pursuit, could not check herself as Genelle went down, hit her foot against Genelle's inert body and went tumbling over her and down the steps, her banshee scream echoing to the very rafters of the house.

And then there was silence—a matte, dead, anguished silence, and Genelle looked up at Roak and began to cry.

She was in bed for days.

The story was a ten-day wonder in the papers, but she didn't see any of them. Joseph kept them from her, and probably rightly so, she thought later. All they would have done was dredged up the past, the scandals, the relationships, barring the one that no one would ever know about, and they would speculate about what would happen to her now that the Yard and her past had finally caught up to her.

Roak was nowhere in sight.

Two weeks after her grandmother's death, Inspector Stiles came to see her.

When she entered the small parlor, she found him seated as usual by the fireplace, his notebook in his hand, and when he looked up at her, he nodded as if to acknowledge the fact of his familiarity.

She sat down opposite him. "Inspector—I suppose you've come to inquire whether I am well enough to be taken off to prison."

"How are you doing, my lady?"

"I'm better." *No, I'm just existing, waiting for the guillotine to fall* . . .

"It was no easy thing to see your lady mother-in-law fall down a flight of steps."

"No . . ." *Or my grandmother either . . . God, my grand-mother—I still can't quite believe it . . .*

"And so we come back to my original purpose, my lady, with

several important considerations. Witnesses who could have testified are dead. And we have the fact of your mother-in-law threatening to kill you which was overheard by both Mr. Roak and your butler Joseph. Moreover, Joseph alleges he heard the greater part of your interchange with your mother-in-law and that she talked extensively about her part in the death of both your husband and your mother.

"We have taken his statement and I am here to ask if you are willing to make a statement as well as to what was said so we may compare what Joseph alleges to have heard with what you say actually happened."

She closed her eyes, relief washing over her like slow heat. *It's over—it's finally over . . .* "Yes, I will. But it is an incredible story, Inspector."

"I have some inkling of that from Joseph's testimony, Lady Tisne. It remains for you to corroborate it."

But how much had Joseph heard—and how much had he told?

"Whenever it is convenient of course," he added as a afterthought, "but sooner would be better than later."

"Tomorrow, Inspector?"

"Will be fine, my lady. Eleven o'clock at the Yard?"

"I will be there."

And still no Roak.

The next day Joseph accompanied her to Whitehall where a stenographer took her detailed testimony in Inspector Stiles' office, and when she left, she felt as if she had been to confession and all her sins were absolved.

Not all—and none of the memories either. How did one expunge the lies of a lifetime, and secrets meant to be taken to the grave?

But still the shocks were not over.

Stiles ordered that Yard-appointed solicitors go through Morfit's papers and those of his clients.

"He had only two clients, my lady—" Stiles told her two weeks later. "Lord Tisne and Anthony Lethbridge, which of course ties into the facts of your statement. Moreover, you are your husband's sole surviving relative and there is still the residue of his estate to be dealt with. I believe you will be the legatee."

Oh my God . . .
"And your mother's as well—"
Dear lord—all that money . . .
"And the official verdict in the death of your husband and mother will come down as death by misadventure since none of the parties involved can be prosecuted. Nor will the Yard press charges against you for decamping."

"Thank you," she said fervently.

"The solicitors will have the papers for you by the end of the month, after a full accounting has been rendered, including the monies in profit from the *House of Correction*. Morfit had separate books for that, and a separate account into which he shifted money for himself. Once we can prove by audit that the profits were diminished by those sums, they will be allocated to Lord Tisne's estate. And that will also include the premises at Fanhurst. I think that is all."

All? All? He has just made me an impossibly wealthy woman and he calls that all.

Or is it reparation?

Mother—are you laughing?

Because I think I'm going to cry . . .

But she had shed enough tears to last a lifetime. What she needed now was to go away. And maybe, when she returned, she would undertake the dismantling of Fanhurst stone by stone and brick by brick.

It was a lovely fantasy, one to dine out on all the days she spent at Torquay, walking the beaches and soaking in the genteel atmosphere. Such a change from London, with everything quiet and even and nothing evil rippling beneath the surface.

Here, so far away from London, everything seemed to take on the quality of a bad dream. Here, she was not fodder for the gossips or the tabloids, or a mother's foolish schemes.

Here, she was just another young widow seeking to ease her pain.

She stayed in Torquay a month, soaking in the healing sun and coming to know a little bit more about herself.

And she thought about everything that had happened, including her incredible sexual odyssey with Roak.

And she thought she didn't regret any of that even though now it was over.

And once she had confronted the inevitability of that, she got a lot stronger. And she made some decisions.

And finally she thought it was time to go home.

Green Street didn't look the same.

A month away had changed the shape of everything, even the shape of her life.

She was not going to stay on at Green Street; she was going to bury the memories here forever and find a new home.

That was to be taken care of in the succeeding month, as well as selling Fanhurst and the little house at Skirling Vail.

And then—and then . . . she would travel and when she was ready to settle down, she would reenter society as a sedate matron and not a skittery young bride or a vengeful flirt.

And then maybe someday, she would find a connection as powerful as the one she had had with Roak.

And she might even think of marrying again.

All of this she had decided during the month in Torquay, and she felt supremely hopeful and at peace as the carriage drew up to the house at Green Street.

Immediately the door popped open and Joseph appeared.

"My lady."

"Joseph, it is so good to see you."

She let him help her out of the carriage.

"I can assure my lady, all is well."

"I'm happy to hear it. And you've taken care of everything."

"Everything, my lady."

"Excellent." She felt like floating up the steps. Everything was different, *everything*. Everything was clear and clean and *right* . . . as if it were ordained that this would be a new beginning.

She waltzed through the door into the reception room—and there, waiting for her, was Roak.

"What are you doing here?" She couldn't believe how shaky she felt just at the sight of him.

A month, it had been more than a month; the thing was over, the nightmares were gone.

Everything had changed, and now she knew why . . . he had disappeared and she expected never to see him again.

And so, being Roak, here he was.

"Your servant, my lady; I believe I was hired on as your butler."

She snorted. "I couldn't give you a decent reference, Roak. You were never on the job."

What was he thinking? What was he feeling? She was shaking and she didn't know why; the last she had confronted him, she had made him her enemy.

And now it was as if none of that had ever happened.

. . . perhaps it never had . . .

"Nevertheless, my lady, I do need the job." His eyes met hers and she could not read anything behind the opaque blackness of them.

This is impossible—he knows it's impossible.

"Until the next needy client," she snapped, turning on her heel.

"I have had done with that," he said, and she whirled around to face him.

"Why? Why?"

"You know why."

"I know nothing."

He held her eyes. "The cost was too great."

"Nonsense—you are an island, Roak, a kingdom unto yourself. The mystical potentate upon whom nothing and no one has claims."

He ignored that. "I could not save you, but I was not your enemy."

She turned away again. "I think it will take a long time before I believe that."

"No," he said. "You believe it now."

Did she? Did she? Hadn't she been thinking of him, even in the month away at Torquay? Was not her wildest dream to have him reappear on her steps, penitent and begging for forgiveness?

But the Roaks of the world never begged.

And the Genelles of the world were consumed with forbidden desire and subjugated it to their anger.

And she was still angry—and forever grateful that he had rescued her from the House of Correction, and between the two extremes, what was there?

What was there for them?

"And so you want to be my butler," she said skeptically, "and yet before, every time I wanted you, I was told you were unavailable."

"That will never happen again, my lady," he said gravely.

"What kind of game are you playing, Roak? Are you on another case?"

"There is only one thing pending, my lady, and I can handle it from here."

The expression in his eyes riveted her. She could hardly bear to look away. There was too much there; it was too naked, even for him.

I don't know what to do—

But I don't want him to walk out the door . . . not yet—

"Oh, all right. I assume you've settled back in your room and it is *fait accompli*. How can I say no?" she added testily. "I am only the one paying the bills."

Roak, two floors below her—

How did that make her feel?

It was strange and terrifying and exhilarating . . .

It brought back memories—different memories—tremors and fevers.

It made her feel like she was awakening from a long and dreamless sleep.

It made her feel things she wasn't sure she wanted to feel for him.

She began the process of selling Fanhurst, and searching for another house. It was time consuming and fully engaged her attention so she had no time to think about extraneous matters. There were only floor plans and decorations and whether or not to sell her furniture and start with everything brand new.

It was luxurious to be rich.

It was luxurious to lie in bed and think of Roak, two floors below her, and remember all the sensual games they used to play.

Did she want . . . her butler?

And he was the perfect and deferential butler, always at the ready, always at hand. Impassive and never impertinent. Flawlessly executing whatever she would demand.

Two floors below her—

Her blood throbbed with the thought of it. Her body stretched opulently as she remembered the hot push of him entering her. Her imagination flooded with the memory of all they had done and things they had not.

She discarded her nightclothes.

She began looking for him everywhere.

She found reasons to touch him.

When he wasn't looking, she would stare.

He had come back for a reason . . . all she had to understand was she could never hold him. She could have him only for as long as he was willing to be had.

If she could live with that—

Was she really thinking of that?

If she could live with that . . .

. . . nothing else would matter—

She found a house in Kensington that was much to her liking, and she arranged the purchase, the cleaning, and the painting of it before the move.

When she came home that evening, Joseph met her with an envelope in his hand.

Her fingers trembled as she took it and opened it.

Jade—come . . .

Her body reacted; her fingers closed around the note and crushed it into her palm.

Slowly she walked up the stairs to her room and pushed open the door.

He was waiting for her there, but not as he had been before; he was fully dressed, and her heart plummeted.

"You're leaving me," she whispered in agony.

His eyes darkened, and the planes of his face seemed to harden.

"I need you. But nothing is the same. And we started wrong. And we left it badly. And then—I almost lost you."

"And now—?" she hardly dared breathe.

"I am your butler—and you are my lady."

"I see no class difference at all."

"The move—it's a good time for change," he said.

Again, that wrenching, heart-stopping feeling.

"What kind of change?"

"I will be working with the Yard."

Of course—hadn't she known she couldn't hold him . . . ?

"In consultation. With Stiles and others. No more private cases. No more revenge for the death of my family. We have never talked about my family—but you need to know, you did have it right: I started by wanting to use any means at my disposal to avenge them—even if he had died, even if it meant using you. I couldn't do it; I didn't do it.

"But because of it, I lost you.

"And I cannot be in the same house with you and not have you."

Yes, yes—the words she wanted to hear . . .

"You haven't lost me," she whispered. "I can hardly stand it, knowing you are in the same house and we are lying in separate bedrooms and not—and not . . ."

He shook his head; she could hardly believe it when she was absolutely throwing herself at him.

"It will come," he said quietly. "For now, we will start again."

It was horrible; she wanted him . . . and all he wanted to do was confess his sins—all of which she knew and had absolved him of weeks before.

She lay in bed tossing and turning after he left her.

Start again—start again . . . how did one start again after everything that had gone before?

She got up and paced the room restlessly.

She was a Jade—he had named her—and now she was so slick with arousal she hardly knew what to do.

She knew.

No—they were starting again—whatever that meant . . .

Maybe he would give her a new name; maybe they needed a new place. But he had said he could hardly stand being in the same house and not having her—and she had felt the same—

So . . . what was holding him back? Some kind of stupid male code she couldn't fathom?

He was two floors down, and presumably as restless and aching as she . . .

. . . I will be your lover . . .

That had been all she had ever wanted . . .

All she wanted now.

She was a Jade after all, and always open and ready for him.

She got up off of her bed and pulled out a robe and wound it around her naked body.

And then she swiftly went downstairs to the servants' hall, and paused just outside his room.

The door was slightly ajar and there was a faint light within.

Her heart started pounding violently as she pushed open the door, stepped inside, and shut it behind her.

He was lying naked on the bed, his eyes closed, his manhood a rock hard jut, almost as if it had been waiting for her.

She felt suffocated. She pulled the tie of her robe and let it fall off her shoulders to the floor, and she approached his bed, knelt at his side, and reached out her hand to stroke the shafting essence of him.

He opened his eyes slowly, lazily, and watched her as she paid homage to his root, rubbing it, caressing it, kissing it all over, all over.

"Jade—" he groaned, thrusting his fingers into her hair as she began the long laving slide of her tongue on the underside of his shaft and worked her magic all the way to the thick-ridged tip of him where she paused to suck until he was ready to burst.

He wrenched away from her greedy mouth, and pulled her body up onto the bed to align with his.

"Kiss me, Jade," he growled, and then he took her mouth with the same rapaciousness that she had possessed his erection. "God, I missed this; I missed you . . ."

"Don't talk . . . don't stop . . ."

He deepened the kiss, and nudged her legs apart.

"Tell me you want me now—"

"I *need* you now," she breathed, and moaned as he pushed, pushed, pushed slowly and erotically into her satin core.

"Do you remember . . . ?"

"I can't forget."

"I kept thinking—"

"I kept wanting—"

"You feel so good . . ."

"Are we starting over?"

"We are starting—again."

And then he began, the steady unhurried rhythmic drive to completion. Slow, slow, slow, savoring it, feeling it, loving it, taking his kisses, taking his skill, his need, his expertise . . .

Who else—ever?

He pushed her onto her back, and his thrusts took on a powerful urgency.

Her body responded . . . *so good—so good* . . .

He was so potent, so forceful, he was in a fury to pleasure her and she told him with every wild undulating movement how much she loved it, how much she wanted it—and wanted it only from him.

Only from him—love it from him . . . want him . . . forever—to love it . . . from . . . him—

It caught her as she gyrated upward against him—the breaking, crackling, bone-melting explosion of sensation—and it was good . . . *it was good and good and good and good* . . . and he caught the backwash of her climax and drove full bore into it and a long wet slide into heaven.

And then slowly, they came down together, sated, in each other's arms.

"Jade—" In a breath of a whisper.

"Yes . . ."

"I wanted you to come—"

"I had to come . . ."

"Give me your hand—"

"Why?"

"You'll see . . ."

She caught her breath. "The ring—"

"Claim me, Jade . . ."

"Are you sure?"

"I haven't forgotten anything. Claim me forever—"

She sat up next to him, and pulled apart the delicate rounded gold ring and deftly wound it around his already stiff and throbbing manhood.

"I claim you, Roak. You are mine, this is mine . . ."

"And you are *mine*," he whispered, pushing her down on her back so that he could take her, "forever—"